MOLT BROTHER

Books by Jacqueline Lichtenberg

SIME~GEN UNIVERSE
House of Zeor
Unto Zeor, Forever
First Channel by Jean Lorrah and Jacqueline Lichtenberg
Mahogany Trinrose
Channel's Destiny by Jean Lorrah and Jacqueline Lichtenberg
RenSime
Zelerod's Doom by Jacqueline Lichtenberg and Jean Lorrah
To Kiss Or To Kill by Jean Lorrah and Jacqueline Lichtenberg
The Farris Channel by Jacqueline Lichtenberg and Jean Lorra
Sime~Gen: The Unity Trilogy, by Jacqueline Lichtenberg and Jean Lorrah

KREN UNIVERSE (BOOK OF THE FIRST LIFEWAVE)
Molt Brother
City of a Million Legends

DUSHAU UNIVERSE
Dushau
Farfetch
Outreach

THE LUREN UNIVERSE
Those of my Blood
Dreamspy

MOLT BROTHER

JACQUELINE LICHTENBERG

WILDSIDE PRESS: MMIII

MOLT BROTHER

Published in the United States by **Wildside Press**
PO Box 301, Holicong, PA 18928-0301
www.wildsidepress.com

ISBN: 1-59224-126-3

To Bradford Butler, Sr.
To Cecil Brice
May they Rest in Peace
and to Beth Hallam
for showing me Stonehenge,
getting me there at just the moment
when I could meet MZB
between the circle and the heelstone.

MOLT BROTHER AND
CITY OF A MILLION LEGENDS:
The Lifewave Novels

Jacqueline Lichtenberg

Family is a wonderful, magical thing. I ought to know. I just became a grandmother for the first time. Rebecca Elizabeth Seemann is my newest family member and I dedicate the re-issue of these novels to her. And one day I want her to read this foreword.

There is the family we are born to—and nothing can replace that. But in addition, many of us are lucky enough to acquire family that we choose, and are chosen by.

And that's what Star Trek fandom became for me. I wrote a whole book, titled *Star Trek Lives!*, showcasing that incredible sense of fellowship with like-minded people—people you may have never seen in person, or whom you see only rarely.

That fan experience provided much of the core material in the Lifewave novels. The people who have gathered together through Star Trek and Sime~Gen (**http://www.simegen.com/writers/simegen/**) have formed a kind of chosen-family, becoming involved in each others' pursuits and supporting each other with their talents and skills.

For example, I met Jean Lorrah when she first wrote a review of *House of Zeor*, the first Sime~Gen novel. She was at that time author of the Star Trek fanzine stories, *Night of the Twin Moons*. At first she wrote a few Sime~Gen fan stories. Then we sold her Sime~Gen novel. Now she is half-owner of Sime~Gen Inc. And she's written several best selling Star Trek novels. She helped raise my children. Few sisters are as close.

Since *Molt Brother* and *City of a Million Legends,* collectively known as the Lifewave Universe novels, (**www.simegen.com/jl/kren/**)were first written, many people primarily interested in my other Universes and in Jean's work, have contributed to my efforts as if they were my family. Well, they are family, chosen family.

Ronnie Bob Whitaker, and Karen MacLeod have been particularly helpful.

Ronnie Bob Whitaker is a supreme wizard of the scanning/OCR/proofing process. It turned out to be much easier for him to scan the printed Lifewave novels than to update the electronic text from my very first Word Processor (WordStar) on which I had written *City of a Million Legends.*

And of course *Molt Brother* was my last done on an IBM correcting Selectric. So Ronnie Bob made the text available in a form a modern computer could cope with. Had it not been for Ronnie Bob, who has also scanned in the Sime~Gen novels for their current reprint, I doubt you would be reading this now.

Karen MacLeod, who has established herself in the e-book field as an editor, has prepared these manuscripts for re-publication by updating the punctuation and hunting for typos Ronnie Bob might have missed. (There weren't many and they were hard to find.) Any mistakes left are entirely mine.

Patric Michael, a professional artist who is head of our Art Department at simegen.com, has contributed a great deal of spirit and understanding to the Lifewave Universe. Just talking to him creates images in my mind—and then he draws them better than I could ever imagine.

Cheryl Ann Costa (**http://www.cherylcosta.com**) is one of the newest to join the group. Cheryl Ann and I met while doing a panel at the Darkover Grand Council Meeting one recent Thanksgiving. She provided the impetus to make these novels available now. She is a successful playwright who has optioned the Lifewave Universe to create a tight story-arc of original one-act plays based on the Lifewave Universe, but using original characters. Scripts will be available on the web for performance by companies around the world.

In August, 2002 a number of things happened simultaneously. Meisha Merlin Publishing Inc. began gearing up to start production of the new

Sime~Gen novels, by Jean Lorrah and me, talking cover artists, and details of the editions.

Kevin Anderson Yancy contacted me asking for short stories to be recorded by professional actors and backed by mood music and sound effects. I pointed him to three of my vampire stories which he liked, and introduced him to Cheryl Ann. Watch **www.simegen.com/jl/** for links to recordings.

I also introduced Kevin to Erin Gould who is working on a script that may become a Star Trek docudrama. So as you see, Star Trek is the tie that binds this chosen-family together. You'll find the story of The Star Trek Connection told in my review column at simegen.com and see how this one interest has become a chosen-family coat-of-arms.

I first got the job of SF/F Reviewer for *The Monthly Aspectarian* in 1993 because the editor, Guy Spiro, was a fan of the Lifewave novels. He wanted to bring the books back into print, but couldn't quite get the project going. Nevertheless his efforts kept me going. You will find those plans discussed in my review column, Rereadable Books posted at **www.simegen.com/reviews/rereadablebooks/**

And lastly, the most heartwarming source of inspiration are the many fans who've expressed admiration for these novels. Most notably I remember a fan letter from a woman who, as a high school student, chose her major as archeology because of the inspiration in these novels - and grew up to be happy and satisfied with that choice. Now, isn't that what family does—inspire?

To keep up with the Lifewave Universe news, you might want to subscribe to the monthly e-newsletter *Lifeforce-L* where Jean Lorrah and I provide updates on all our publications and appearances. **www.simegen.com/archives/** will take you to the subscription page.

You should be able to reach me through **sgwelcommittee@simegen.com**

Jacqueline Lichtenberg
Arizona, 2002

CHAPTER ONE

"But, Arshel, committing yourself to a *human?* They don't even molt!"

A great whistling roar shook the house as the noon space shuttle set down at the new spaceport the humans had built at the far end of the island. Arshel was grateful that conversation was impossible for several minutes. She had expected her parents to be hostile to her choice of a life companion but had not expected this total incomprehension. After all, it wasn't as if she were planning to *mate* with a human.

Abrupt silence made the faint lapping of the waves of the hatching pond loud. Outside, the boom of the sea formed a constant background. *How am I going to tell them the worst of it?*

Trying to make her voice calm, Arshel said, "Others have taken bhirhir among the humans. It's done all the time on the mainland, in the mountains . . . I mean no disrespect, Surmother, but I am of an age to make my choice, and I've done so."

As Arshel moved, the sun glanced off her skin, displaying the mature fineness of her scales and their new silvery coloring. Her breasts were budding at last, filling out the light yellow shirt she wore. Anyone could see that she'd experience her first adult molt soon.

Her surmother moved nervously into the shadows, as if unwilling to look at Arshel's new maturity. "So, you've taken a human molt sister. Arshel, I don't even know if the molt sister's oath is valid with a human. What if she turns on you—on us? To bring a human into our family—you have no idea what it's like to be adult and helpless in molt. How can you give a human such power over you? Just look what they've done to our island, our world!"

Another, clearer voice called from the archway of the family room, "What's all this?" Arshel's mother came into the room, going directly to the other woman and adding, "Don't agitate yourself so, my bhirhir. You'll raise venom for nothing."

For the first time, Arshel saw the strong resemblance between herself and her mother. *She's beautiful. Maybe I'll be, too.*

Her mother looked up from trying to comfort her molt sister. "What have you said to upset your surmother like this? Was it something you picked up from the humans at that hole in the ground?"

Arshel's part time job at the Cross-Species Archeological Society's dig had been a sore point in the family for almost a year. She took a deep breath, determined not to stir that up again. "I said I'd taken bhirhir among the humans."

"Bhirhir, *you*—" Her mother choked off the words, too shocked to do more than hold her molt sister tightly.

"I did not say," Arshel added, "that my bhirhir is female. I've taken a molt *brother*."

Her surmother stared at her in renewed shock. Her mother's mouth fell open, and her venom fangs unfolded from their sockets.

Arshel backed away until the water of the hatching pond lapped her sandals. After an initial surge of alarm at the sight of her mother's fangs, she felt strangely lightheaded.

"Kill this human," said her surmother, "and come back to us. We'll find you a male, if *that* is what you really want."

They'd really go that far? She felt confused. The freshwater spawn, people of the mainland, often took bhirhir from the opposite sex, but it was a practice shunned on the islands. *They love me in spite of everything.* Her venom glands ached. "I can't kill him. We've already sworn bhirhir."

"He's immune to your venom?" her mother asked.

"Yes," she lied, surprised at how easy it was. She had never yet raised true-venom, only the watery prevenom. But she had inoculated him with it often. "Yes, of course he's immune, or how could we have sworn bhirhir?"

"Then he is immune to the whole family," said her surmother. "Why didn't you bring him here to speak for himself?"

"I only thought it would be kinder to warn you!"

"Then you knew how we'd feel!" said her mother.

"How you feel isn't important. He's *my* molt brother! It's how I feel that's important." Panting, she was gripped by the most peculiar sensations. "Dennis has been my only friend for all this year, my only real friend ever. He's never made fun of me because I look too young. He's fought for me—and I for him. And the venom doesn't come when he's with me. He's the only one who does that for me. Isn't that what bhirhir is?"

She looked from mother to surmother as they stood together facing her. Although the atmosphere was charged, neither of them had raised venom, while her own venom sack was straining at the neck of her blouse. With a savage jerk, she pulled open the top button, tearing the fabric.

In unison, they backed away two more steps, acknowledging her volatile condition.

"You don't realize," said her mother, "the power you're granting this offworlder over you."

"Dennis is not an offworlder!" Nobody seemed to notice the trouble she was having pronouncing Dennis' name. The "s" sound was as difficult and alien to them as it was to Arshel. In sudden relief, she thought, *Is that all they're worried about?* "He is from the colony. His grandparents were on the first ship, and both his parents were born here. He's not an offworlder—he's only human."

Her mother looked slightly relieved, but her surmother said, "It makes no difference. I will not have this within my family."

"It's too late," Arshel insisted. "It's done." This lie was the hardest thing she'd ever said, but the saying of it made it true.

Her mother made a small gesture of resignation, and hope surged through Arshel. But then her mother stepped to the edge of the hatching pond and dipped the toe of her sandal into the warm water. Her venom sack quivered with the power of her emotions as she looked into the water from which Arshel had emerged. Then, softly chanting the hundred repetitions of Arshel's name in mourning, she turned and left the room, her back straight and her head held high.

Her molt sister looked after her until the sound of her voice had faded among the pressed-sand archways and vaulted chambers of the family home. Then she turned to Arshel.

"You have struck out for your adulthood, Arshel, and must now be counted as an adult, but not of Holtethor. If you can choose and be chosen, then be also welcome at the home of your molt brother, for he is not welcome here now or ever. Nor are you welcome. We mourn your loss in Holtethor, but death has taken our children before. We will go on."

Moving to the edge of the gently lapping water, she touched it with a toe. Chanting, she too turned and without another glance went to join her molt sister in mourning the loss of a child.

Arshel was left alone in the silent house, with the noon sun barely glancing in the window through which the pressed-sand domes of the city could be seen glittering hotly. In all that city, there was only one place for her, and that was among the drylanders.

She went to her knees in the shallow water of the hatching pond where she had struggled for and won the right to life. Never to be allowed to touch these waters again, never to see her spawn churn their way to life from the waters that had served her mother and mother's mother for more than ten generations . . .Her venom sack stretched painfully as emotion raged uncontrolled through her. She had never been happy in this house. They had never understood her. Why should leaving hurt so much?

As she made her way across the island, back to the dig for the afternoon's work, it was as if she were seeing the city for the first time: the domes, the lofty spires, the sweeping arches blending together like the waves of a stormy ocean frozen in midrage and suspended forever, forbidden to strike. And the people, dressed in their floating veils, drifting from place to place among their buildings, seemed suddenly alien.

Closer to the dig, buildings gave way to open hillside crisscrossed with footpaths. She encountered other young people dressed as she, in shorts and shirt of the human style, moving in pairs back to work on the excavation. They were coming in to check the bulletin board for the afternoon shift assignments. Then they'd march out into the pit, toolboxes in hand, to begin the delicate work of dusting away layers of sand and soil, charting, recording, and mapping.

They were uncovering an ancient city, perhaps built by long-dead aliens from another galaxy. Here, on Vrashin Island, they might find the key to translating documents pertaining to the City of a Million Legends.

Known by many names on every planet of the Hundred Planets, it was called by Dennis "Shangri-la," "Atlantis," or "Camelot." It was the long-ago place where people had once achieved perfection. There, people knew how to avoid war, social crime, and poverty. But the City of a Million Legends, Arshel felt, had been a real place during the First Lifewave occupation of the galaxy. If only half the legends were true and they could bring all that alive again today—oh, how *good* life would be.

Standing in the shade of the open shed, she squinted against the glare to watch Dorsan, the human who was the dig's official computer Interface, sitting cross-legged on a huge stone cube they had uncovered a few days before. He was sorting through a large tray of minute items, turning each in his hands to examine it and then staring off into space with that glassy-eyed, frozen stare that meant he was using the circuitry implanted in his brain to enter data into the computer or to correlate data. She always found it disconcerting when he did that, and today she found it frightening when his wooden stare chanced to light on her.

She looked around anxiously for Dennis, knowing that he'd be reporting for shift now. When they'd parted, he had said that there'd be no trouble telling his parents about the bhirhir. At home on the mainland, he had said, lots of his friends had taken bhirhir. But what if his family too, rejected them? Where would they go? She felt her venom sack tighten until the skin of her throat felt as if it would split.

To distract herself, she picked up a toolbox and looked around for a spot nobody was working. There was a wall at one edge of the pit that would have to be dismantled, but the stones had to be peeled away microlayer by microlayer.

Arshel took down a medium weight molecular sifter, caressing the worn handle familiarly. What they were looking for was behind that wall. She had convinced Dennis of it, but he had not been able to convince his parents, who ran the dig. Yet it could do no harm for her to begin the long task today. She was good for little else at the moment.

She looked around again for Dennis, but he was still nowhere in sight. He had to help her express her venom before the tightness drove her to strike someone. She couldn't ask her surmother to do it for her anymore.

She climbed to the top of a huge, rectangular block that made a nice working platform near the top of the wall and then sat down on the rock, folding her legs under her. She began to peel the wall away, recording after each pass of the sifter and watching carefully for any sign of an emerging artifact. At intervals, she took specimens of the rock and put them in the recorder for analysis. She dug out a large chip to save for display and had the recorder label it.

The work was boring and repetitive but soothing. Arshel let her mind drift out of focus, dreaming of what it would be like to make a big find and have everyone come running over to congratulate her. Would they like her any better then, she wondered? Probably not, but it would be fun, anyway.

"Arshel?" called a deep human voice.

Startled, she dropped the molecular sifter as a spasm gripped her throat; her jaw dropped as her fangs swung out.

At the edge of her vision, his bare arm moved, and she struck. Her fangs sank deep into the human flesh, venom pumping through them in quick, satisfying spurts. He snatched his arm away, clutching at the elbow to cut off the flow of blood. Thick yellow venom dripped from her fangs.

"Arshel, you've raised true-venom!"

Pride and delight lit Dennis' eyes as his own blood mingled with her venom in the dust. But she couldn't control the voiding spasms. Weak, she sank to her knees, terrified that she had killed her bhirhir.

Shaking, his hand sought her venom sack to express her as a bhirhir should, just as they'd practiced when she raised prevenom.

At last her sack was empty. He hadn't spared a drop of her first venom from which to make a serum. Stunned, she watched her molt brother scuffing at the dusty rock to wipe out all sign of the venom stain there so that her first venom would be joined forever to the earth itself. In the distance, she heard the warble of the humans' emergency hopper. But all she could think was that her molt brother was giving his life for a custom that held no meaning for him. This was the man her surmother had urged her to kill—and she had killed him.

Panting, he noticed the still operating sifter and scrambled to turn it off, knocking the recorder over but ignoring it. It was pointed at the hole the sifter had made.

The sifter fell from his grasp, and as his knees buckled he laughed. "Look at that! My father will think you're a better Lakely than I am!"

As his eyes closed, her paralysis broke, and she caught him and eased him to the ground. Without looking, she rummaged in her toolbox and picked the first signal gun that came to hand, firing it into the air.

A great puff of white smoke blossomed over her head—the find signal. All work stopped in the pit as everyone converged on her. But the hopper arrived first, its ground effect dissipating the smoke as it touched down beside them. Two humans and a kren jumped out of the ambulance, going right to Dennis' side. Another human appeared and then climbed over the rim of the building block they were on: Dorsan, the Interface. Of *course*, she thought. *He'd seen and called the ambulance via computer hookup.*

Arshel spared him only a glance, anxiously watching the doctors work over Dennis as if there were still a chance that he might live. They snapped a portable respirator around his chest and injected a general antivenom into his heart. In moments they'd rigged a blood exchanger and strapped him onto a stretcher.

Meanwhile, the Interface was examining the venom stain on the rock. He picked up the recorder she'd dropped and pointed it at the hole in the rock with an absent look that meant that he was in touch with the computer that the recorder was feeding.

As they were lifting Dennis into the ambulance, the kren doctor stopped to say, "I saw what you let him do to you as we approached."

His tone was so carefully neutral she knew that he was revolted. She forced herself to meet his gaze straight on. "We had sworn bhirhir. It was my first venom. I couldn't help it."

He glanced at the hopper where they were securing the stretcher. "Come, ride with us. If he survives the afternoon, it will be only because of a specific made from your venom or that of your family."

My family wouldn't help him.

Below, people were gathering about the block. Nobody wanted to crowd the Interface while he was working. But now Dennis' mother climbed over the rim.

As the dust covered woman was taking in the sight of her son in the ambulance, the Interface said, "This is it, Madlain. It's a metal box, densely packed with leaves of something organic. Must be books. They'll have to be recorded without opening the box, though. It's older than our scales can estimate."

Those gathered below heard most of what he said, and a loud shouting went up from the humans: a cheer. It hurt Arshel's hearing as she climbed into the hopper beside the doctors.

Madlain gestured the Interface to silence and forced her way into the hopper, saying, "I'll he back to attend to it later. Meanwhile, Dorsan, let my husband know."

Heavily laden, the hopper barely cleared the far rim of the pit, landing with a bounce beside the humans' health station. Quickly, Dennis was taken to the venom treatment unit. It rarely happened that a human was attacked by a kren, but the humans feared it so greatly that they drilled their medical teams in antivenom routine.

As she waited in the sparely appointed alcove for news, Arshel was grateful for the humans' phobia. Soon, Madlain Lakely joined her, taking a chair across the tiny room from her. For a while, Arshel kept her head down, eyes lowered to her lap in the human signal that she did not wish to intrude or be intruded upon.

But finally, Madlain asked, "You're Arshel Holtethor of whom Dennis was telling me this morning?"

She spoke the Vrashin Island dialect with a mainland accent. Arshel summoned her courage to raise her head and meet the woman's eyes. There was the intelligence there that she had always respected, but she sensed no acceptance.

The human pinched up her face. "I don't blame you for the strike, Arshel. It happens in bhirhir."

The grief and tear clutched at Arshel and made her breath tremble in her throat. But no venom answered her emotions.

The human's eyes traveled to the closed door at the far end of the hallway. It was a hard, square hallway with sharp, square doors and dim yellow lighting. "Arshel, do you want to tell me how it happened? Was it before or after Dennis set off the find signal? Did the signal startle you?"

That stung. "I may be an islander, Ms. Lakely, but I'm not a primitive."

"I'm sorry, I didn't mean to imply anything like that. I just want to know what happened to my son. Arshel, he's my only child. And I haven't mourned him. I—my husband and I don't yet know how to welcome you. But we won't cast you both out."

Something melted inside Arshel. "I'm sorry. I'm being hostile. I can't speak now. I feel too threatened, too afraid." She had learned that she had to say things like that in words to make humans understand, had to treat them as if their wits were impaired. "I mean no discourtesy."

"It seems when kren is involved with human, most of the conversation consists either of apologies or attacks," said Madlain with a faint smile. "Dennis has been telling me for weeks that he wanted to have a go at that wall. His intuition has made the find even our expensive Interface couldn't. Now he's lying in there at the edge of death, and you and I can't even talk about it without hurting each other."

At last the human fell silent, and Arshel wrapped herself in the tension of her emotions. Years later she would look back on Madlain Lakely's words and realize that this was the moment when she had surrendered to fate. But at the time, all she knew was her personal agony: *Have I committed myself to bhirhir so deeply that I can't survive without him?*

Her thoughts were cut off by the hunger cramps that inevitably followed such a full voiding as Dennis had given her. She was doubled over and gasping by the time the door to Dennis' room opened and the two kren from the ambulance came out.

The doctor came to her saying, "We're ready for you now. Afterward, there will be a feeding."

Now, she thought, knowing that she had to raise venom and self-express it to save Dennis' life.

As they helped her to her feet, one on each side of her, the doctor added, "We could send an ambulance for your surmother—"

"No!" she said, gritting her teeth. "I'm old enough to do this myself."

Madlain rose. "We're not yet immune to her, but maybe I can help."

The kren doctor said, "It would be too dangerous for you."

"Just allow me a moment," Madlain pleaded, approaching Arshel cautiously. "Arshel, whether Dennis lives or dies, you're a Lakely now, and you always will be. You won't go nameless to your grave no matter what happens now."

They took her away then, stumbling because of the searing hunger cramps. When she was alone, she thought of Madlain Lakely standing in the square corridor, her brown hands smoothing back the white hair thinly plastered over her skull, and she knew what the human must be feeling.

She's given me the name to keep. I will live up to it. On that wave of emotion, venom came easily, but she had to force her hand to her own venom sack. Three times she failed. But on the fourth try, at the first touch of her own fingers on the sensitive skin, the voiding reflex was triggered, sending the thick yellow fluid through her fangs in painful spurts, setting every gland to a dry aching such as she'd never known before. In the end, she was almost unable to stop it long enough to devour the large, tender chunks of meat they had provided for her hunger.

Arshel moved into the Lakely home the day they released Dennis from the hospital. The family had rented a lovely kren dwelling on a hilltop overlooking the ocean instead of building a human style house. She and Dennis took over the half of the house normally used by indwelling mates, and so they had their own sleeping rooms, studies, and a kitchen.

Life regained a smooth rhythm of school, work on the dig and long, lazy evenings spent with Dennis on the beach or at their private hatching pond.

Soon, though, Arshel found it harder and harder to move about.

One morning, without fanfare, she was in molt. Disappointingly, it was no different from any childhood molt with her surmother. Dennis spent the whole day by her side, alternately expressing her molt-venom and laving it carefully over her splitting skin.

His hands were attentive and gentle. His touch was so different from her surmother's experienced firmness, yet she felt none of the deep pleasure she had expected from a bhirhir. She felt secure enough during her moments of helpless squirming and twitching as her body reflexively shucked the old skin. The raw shock of air on her new skin was deftly eased by the coating of venom he applied, but there was no real pleasure in that, either.

As Arshel lay exhausted from the ordeal, she realized that she had indeed grown up. The illusions of childhood were gone forever. There was no reason to be disappointed, for this was reality. It was as good as anybody ever had.

Shortly after she recovered, the standings of the graduating class were posted. She walked home proudly beside her bhirhir, knowing that so many eyes now followed her and that so many now were thinking: *So, Arshel the baby is bhirhir to the number two student in the class.* Surely some of them had learned not to underestimate anyone ever again.

But even over dinner, in the privacy of their own apartment, Dennis refused to share her delight over his achievement. He picked at his food, and when the intercom ticked quietly for attention, he jerked to his feet as if stung and keyed the relay with a stiff finger. His voice squeaked as he said, "Yes?"

"Son, I'd like to speak to you in my office right away."

"Yes, sir."

Nunin Lakely rarely put in an appearance at home in the evening. He had not even visited his son in the hospital, nor had Dennis expected him to attend graduation. Arshel had been puzzled over this, unconsciously expecting a father to be like a surmother. But everyone else seemed to take Nunin's absorption in the dig's affairs as normal.

Dennis said, straightening his shirt, "You'd better wait here."

She caught at his arm. "I'm your bhirhir," she insisted.

He sighed. "Well, let's not keep him waiting."

They passed through the family area with its central hatching pond and on into the other half of the house. Meant for the dwelling of bhirhirn, their relatives, and children, this side of the house was larger than the visiting mate's apartment. Dennis led the way through the atrium with its gaily-splashing fountain, across the reception room where windows over-looked the sea, and down a narrow corridor to a sleeping room that had been converted into Nunin Lakely's office.

Several computer terminals lined one wall. His desk was banked with monitor screens and an interstellar communications tuner. As they entered, Lakely sat rocking back in his chair. The only window in the room was shuttered tightly.

Dennis stopped in the small space before the desk, his shoulders and back stiff. There were no other chairs in the small room. Arshel took her place at her bhirhir's side, facing more toward him than toward Lakely.

The man opened with, "You owe me an explanation."

"I honestly did my best, Dad. I was second by only three points, and there's no disgrace in being second to Omar Pichulo."

"You realize this may have lost you any chance at the Cuzco Scholarship to Camiat University?"

"There are other factors they judge besides school standing."

"Are you making excuses?"

"No, sir." If Dennis were kren, he'd be raising venom.

"Did you spend enough time on your studies?"

"Yes, sir. I let nothing interfere with that." He threw an anxious glance at Arshel. "Nothing at all, Dad. Omar's record was perfect. Somebody had to be second."

"Not a Lakely."

"Yes, sir."

"What do you plan to do about this?"

"I've almost finished a paper on the prehistory of Vrashin Island to submit to the Cuzco committee together with the essay on my choice of archeology as my profession. It's an original approach I'm sure Omar hasn't thought of."

Lakely nodded tentatively and then clicked his gaze away from his son to the array of monitors before him. "We'll see how it works out. Mean-while, I've some things to go over here. Dorsan has made a little progress analyzing the contents of that box at last."

Back in their own quarters, Dennis collapsed into a chair. She could smell his nervous perspiration, and she could see his whole body shaking in reaction. Almost gagging on the smell, she sat on the edge of the chair and put one hand carefully on his shoulder, frustrated that her mere presence wasn't soothing him as a bhirhir should do.

"Dennis, does your mother know he treats you like that?"

Staring straight ahead, he said, "She's probably in her room, crying miserably over my failure."

"I can't believe this is really happening."

"Oh, it's real. I'm a Lakely, Arshel, and now so are you."

His bleak tone triggered off something deep in Arshel. "And *we're* going to live up to it," she said firmly, while privately she wished that she could have brought Dennis to Holtethor and left that man behind them forever.

Bitterly, Dennis said, "I should've sabotaged Omar's grade that one time I had the chance."

Her pride of the afternoon returned. "But you *didn't* because you're very much a Lakely. Omar wouldn't stop at anything to sabotage you if he had the chance. That kind of person can't win, not against a true Lakely."

It took another hour and several cups of coffee, but she infected him with her vision and enthusiasm. He went to work on his paper with renewed vitality. Now that she understood what was at stake for him, she curtailed their evenings by the ocean and preserved the serious mood of school during dinner. She let him talk on and on about his paper, building his confidence. Then, in a whirl, the writing was over, and graduation came. Before they had recovered from the celebrations, they were called to Nunin Lakely's field office at the dig.

They reported there covered with white dust and dressed only in work clothes. The field office was a small shack set on the rim of the dig, with one oversized window giving a comprehensive view of the pit. There was barely room for the two of them to stand before Lakely's desk. Through a door behind him, Arshel could make out the orderly room where Madlain Lakely worked, but it was empty.

Behind the desk and to one side stood Dorsan, the human Interface, his deep tan coated with a thick film of the same white dust that covered them. He had a packet in his hand. "I've got the tapes, Mr. Lakely. There are a number of good clear images, and I've done my best to clarify the rest."

Lakely took the package and said to Arshel and Dennis, "Just a moment, I want to check these."

He slid one of the tapes into a recess on the desk. Excited, Arshel strained to see the tracings of alien writing, meaningless to everyone alive today.

Lakely muttered, "Yes, Dorsan, this is a definite improvement. Has any word come from the Ortenaus yet?"

The archeolinguists Barinn and Hetta Ortenau had been asked to translate the find because they were the best in the business. But they lived high in the mainland mountains, in the city of Firestrip, where the renowned Camiat University was situated.

The Interface went into his blank stare for a moment, checking the comnet, and then said in a normal tone, "They're entering their reply now. A moment, and I'll fetch it for you."

"Good—"

"Nunin!" The Interface held up one hand. "There's something going into your file, a grant." His voice took on the flatness Arshel associated with all Interfaces. "The Interstellar Cross-Species Archeological Society, through the sponsorship of the Lantern Enterprises Affiliated Species Alliance for Progress, posts a full funding grant of six million to Nunin and Madlain Lakely to develop the Sorges River site on Pallacin." He came back to himself and repeated, "Six million."

Lakely was beaming. "We only asked for two! This is wonderful. Wait until I tell Madlain."

Arshel felt her world being flipped out from under her. Pallacin was almost half a year's travel from Camiat. What about Dennis' plans to go to Camiat University?

Lakely glanced up at Dorsan. "With six million to spend we can afford an Interface. Would you like to go with us?"

"I've found the work with you interesting and pleasant, but I'll go where I'm sent. If you require an Interface on Pallacin, the Guild will provide one."

He spoke as if he had no personal opinion or existence. Arshel felt a deep chill and hoped that she'd never have to work with an Interface.

"Well," said Lakely, "all these details can be dealt with later. What about the Ortenaus?"

With barely a blink, the Interface said, "They accept the job of decoding the tapes, and the University accepts the offer of Lantern funds for the project. They've all signed the contracts."

Lakely said, "We're just about wrapped up on Vrashin Island, then." And when the Interface had left, he looked up at his son and then at Arshel. "I asked both of you here because I have news. Dennis, your find has won you the Cuzco Scholarship—not your lamentable grades, and not your passable paper on Vrashin, but your find! Your mother is so proud of you."

"But it wasn't my—"

Arshel interrupted, seeing at last something she could do for her bhirhir. "The Vrashin tapes will be a great credit to the Lakely name. Dennis has worked so hard for that."

Dennis looked down at her, his face displaying emotions she couldn't name. But his father said, "The Cuzco will pay all your expenses at the College of First Lifewave Studies at Camiat University. The timing is perfect. You can go back to Firestrip to school while we begin work. In a few years, you'll be fully certified, and you can join us!"

Arshel said, "But to Firestrip, all alone?"

The elder Lakely said gently, "Arshel, you'll go with Dennis, of course. I've arranged passage for both of you. And since we won't have to pay for Dennis' education, we can see to yours. Just pick your school."

With a flurry of determined activity, Lakely sent them to pack. Arshel had dreamed of leaving Vrashin some day, but the precipitate reality left her shaken.

Dennis stopped on the path overlooking the edge of the pit. It was one of her favorite spots, just at the edge of the tangled jungle foliage where she could feel the moist breath of the jungle and the dry heat of the sun at the same time. *There's nothing like this in the mainland mountains.*

"Arshel, who told them it was *my* find? I never did. I never mentioned it on the Cuzco application forms!"

"I don't know who told them. The couple of times it came up while you were in the hospital, it just didn't seem important. I assumed your father would take the credit as head of the dig."

"It must have been Dad." Dennis's mouth made a straight line under his nose. "Arshel, you don't mind!? Giving up the honors and everything? It was *your* find. You sensed it was there; that's a real talent, Arshel. This could have established you as one of the greats in the field."

"It's a Lakely find. Does it matter which Lakely?"

His smile transformed his face into something alien, but she knew that it meant that he was pleased. He'd have done the same for Holtethor. He understood family, even if his father didn't.

Chuckling, he added, "You're too good to be for real. But I'm going to see that you get as much out of this as I do. There's a school in Firestrip that

24

can make you into the best archeovisualizer that's ever lived. I'll bet you've heard of the Mautri school even way out here in the islands!"

Without waiting for her reply, he gripped her upper arms and swung her around, leaping into the air with explosive joy. "Maybe *we'll* be the ones who actually find the City of a Million Legends!"

Then he took off down the trail, talking in loud bursts. She let herself be pulled along while her mind could only produce her surmother's scathing remark about the Mautri: *Their ideal is to live without bhirhir. Home wreckers!*

CHAPTER TWO

Zref Ortenau felt a once-in-a-lifetime opportunity slipping from his grasp. He hadn't felt such a bleak panic since he'd been rejected by the Mautri school at the age of five.

For the thousandth time, he took the tantalizing letter out of his pocket. Mist from the fountain behind him dampened the heavy document, a formal scholarship to Founders University on Rhobank V, with all fees and expenses paid. *For one person.*

As he folded the thing away, his bhirhir said, "It's not just that you want to go; it's that you *have to* go, isn't it?"

"Sudeen, I—"

"You're human." It was a flat statement, but it opened an issue that had never really come up between them before. A human could survive the loss of a bhirhir; a kren usually didn't, unless he was a Mautri priest. "If we can't raise the money," said the kren, not looking at Zref, "you go ahead, and I'll go back to Mautri."

He's lying. He'd rather die than go back to Mautri. Zref knew the shuddering panic that overcame his bhirhir at the mere thought of the Mautri school. Sudeen had the psychic talent to be welcomed there, but at his first adult molt, he had fled the school, almost dying in molt before Zref had found him and renewed their old pledge of friendship on a deeper level by pledging bhirhir. Zref shook his head. "No matter what, I won't leave you behind, Sudeen."

His venom sack quivering, Sudeen said, "I shouldn't have said that. I know better." His words were swallowed by the roar of a space shuttle taking off.

Zref and Sudeen were sitting on the edge of the fountain in the center of the plaza at the Firestrip shuttleport, waiting for a customer. In addition to the intraworld traffic, today the field was receiving all the passengers from the vast sunhopper *Mormorant III.*

At intervals, the travelers would emerge from the port building's broad array of wide doors and swarm down the shallow steps into the plaza. The stream would divide around the fountain, giving the two freelance tourist guides a good look at potential customers.

There was a Jernal businessman whizzing along on its six spindly legs as if weightless, a Theaten tourist standing head and shoulders above the crowd and seeming like a stretched-out human with a sunburn and one of the blue-skinned humanoids from Sirwin trying politely to keep a hat on his head to hide his horns. But the majority of the crowd was kren, with a heavy sprinkling of humans: Firestrip natives returning from their holidays, not customers.

It was already midsummer, and they hadn't made enough money to put a down payment on passage to Rhobank for Sudeen.

As the noise abated, Sudeen leaned his elbows on his knees; letting his webbed hands dangle between them. "Zref, if I have to, I'll go beg the money from my surfather. He wouldn't approve, but in the end he'd do it."

"Not unless you said I was leaving without you." He looked his bhirhir in the eyes. "Could you lie like that?"

"No."

"Besides, your father said we had to earn the money. If we go beg it from your surfather, that would be setting bhirhir against bhirhir. I couldn't live with that on my conscience. Could you?"

"Are you trying to shame me by being more kren than I am, after I called you human?"

"No. Sudeen, family is family, kren or human." Zref looked around the nearly deserted plaza. "We've seen the last of *Mormorant's* passengers. We ought to quit for the day."

"It's too early to go home."

"You wouldn't have said that last week when Sdilia was living with you," said Zref.

For the last two seasons he had been living at Sudeen's family home while his bhirhir experienced the most intense mating Zref had yet seen him through; the mating had been childless and painful for the whole family. Now that it was over, Zref faced the prospect of having to confront his parents with their money making project. Unlicensed tour guiding wasn't illegal, but it wouldn't bring much credit to his family. It was even worse, Zref felt, now that they'd failed.

Sudeen said, "Zref, what you need is a customer to take your mind off things."

"I don't feel like doing the patter for the tour right now," Zref answered.

When Sudeen failed to protest, Zref followed his gaze to the doors of the arrivals building. A kren and a human had paused on the steps to survey the huge Mautri kyralizth, one of the stretched-pyramid structures that were found all over Camiat. The human male stood close to the kren female, one arm casually encircling her shoulders, as only a bhirhir would dare. The kren female tilted her head listening to the human. Her skin glinted with the dark tones of the saltwater spawned kren of the distant islands, and she wore only a casual twist of light cloth about her body.

As his eyes lit on her, Zref was overcome with a shuddering constriction that sent cold dread knifing through his heart, as if something of great meaning to him were about to be ripped away, leaving life not worth living. An image froze his heart: *Bloody kren arm outflung against his mother's carpet. Sudeen's arm—*

"What's the matter, Zref?" Sudeen touched his fingertips to the side of Zref's face. "A flash?"

Zref jerked away. "I don't have flashes. That's your department," he said more gruffly than he'd intended.

Sudeen let his hand fall away; his eyes traveled back to the couple on the steps. "What a saltwater beauty she is! I'll bet she's just molted."

"Quench it, Sudeen. She wouldn't have anything to do with you, fresh-water spawn!"

On the steps, the human male steered his bhirhir off toward the under-ground train entrance, moving easily through the new flood of arrivals while the island girl gazed from side to side. At one point, she seemed to single Sudeen out, and Zref felt his bhirhir responding as any healthy male kren would.

"Come on, Zref. Maybe they could use a guide." He half rose, but Zref restrained him with one hand.

"He looks like he knows where he's going."

Then Zref's eye lit on a lone figure coming from the port clearance doors, perhaps the last of the *Mormorant's* passengers. The clenched dread he had felt subsided to a mild tingle as he watched the cloaked figure descend the shallow steps toward the fountain where they sat.

"Here's our customer, Sudeen!" said Zref, tugging Sudeen after him to meet the figure. As they neared, he could see that the man wasn't human or kren. He wore a full-cut traveler's cloak and hood with environmental controls. Only his eight digited hands, covered with what seemed a natural horny substance, were exposed. At closer range, they could make out a snouted face covered with a fine, red-brown fur.

"A Brenilak," Sudeen said quietly. "His cloak would be set on cool today, but he'd like the normal climate here. I think it's a he. The females have a lighter coloring."

Zref made what he thought of as his comical native bow for all purposes and started his spiel: A guide to the city was necessary, surprisingly inexpensive, remarkably entertaining, and incredibly knowledgeable. An irresistible bargain all around.

The customer listened, head cocked to one side in amusement or maybe interest. Sudeen finally caught fire and took up the patter, interspersing Zref's sentences with comments. They were so busy, neither of them saw the security uniform until the guard spoke.

"I thought I told you kids to clear out of here!" It was the human security guard they had had a running battle with.

"We're sorry, sir," said Zref while Sudeen kept up the patter. "We're moving, now, see." He demonstrated by skipping sideways after the retreating customer.

"Sir," said the guard to the Brenilak,"are these youngsters bothering you?"

The Brenilak glanced at them and then at the guard. "I was considering their proposition."

"You won't be wanting *this* pair as city guides!"

"Are they dishonest?"

"Oh, they'll show you everything and return you safe to your hotel. But don't believe a word they tell you or you'll end up thinking Firestrip is the City of a Million Legends!"

The Brenilak looked searchingly at Zref and Sudeen. The guard's comments seemed to have kindled real interest in their customer. He said, "I thank you very much for your information, but I believe I will take a chance on these two."

The guard began to protest but stopped as the Brenilak produced a gleaming gold clip and set it on the outside of his cloak. When he removed his hand, they could all see that he was now wearing the medallion of the Interface Guild.

"I doubt I'll be in danger of becoming misinformed."

Frozen-faced, the guard let the crowd swallow him. Zref stared rudely at the Brenilak until Sudeen nudged him.

"My name is Zref MorZdersh'n. This is Sudeen MorZdersh'n."

"So you have the same last name? Isn't that unusual?"

Again the Brenilak's interest was kindled in a way that made Zref uncomfortable. Sudeen answered, "Zref is bhirhir to me, so he's entitled to my family name. If you like, Zref will explain the bhirhir relationship while I get the car."

Beyond the colonnade that rimmed the plaza, Zref halted the visitor while Sudeen dashed off to the parking stack. But the Brenilak said, "I'm acquainted with the sociodynamic of the kren." He gazed at the distant Mautri kyralizth. "What can you tell me about that landmark?"

Zref hastily shifted focus. "The tour starts here with this view of the Mautri temple and school buildings. Behind them, on the peak rising highest in these mountains, you can see the Mautri kyralizth and its traditional, freestanding, archway that straddles the path to it. This temple was founded long after that kyralizth was built by... uh, I suppose you know about the Mautri priests, fugitive from their lowland order, founding the temple when not a soul lived in these mountains?"

"I did look up the facts about the city and its five hills." He brought his eyes to the south, where two of the city's peaks shielded the view of the lake. "Rayah Lake would be off in that direction."

"It's a volcanic lake, surrounded by a ridge that used to be its cone."

"I'd like to go down to the lake."

"They don't permit tours down there. It's all privately owned. Spawning grounds and nurseries and hospitals take up most of the lakefront. The healthful fresh waters here are one of the reasons Firestrip has boomed into a major city."

"So I understand."

Zref remembered again that he was talking to an Interface, a man who had access to all the information ever stored anywhere. It was said that they paid a dire price for that power, but the man before him seemed perfectly normal. "Sir Brenilak," said Zref respectfully, "I simply can't imagine what you want a guide *for*."

"As an Interface, you mean?" He paused, and there was something indefinably sad in the almost expressionless, muzzled countenance. "You may call me Zaviv." He glanced again at the Mautri temple and added almost wistfully, "What does being a guide mean to you? Merely the recitation of information?"

"No. Sudeen and I like to make our history come alive."

"Are you then archeovisualizers?"

"No, but the First Lifewave sometimes seems more real to us than the present. We want to finish our schooling and join the search for the real City of a Million Legends." Zref didn't like the measuring look that the Brenilak gave him, but he didn't retract his statement.

Zaviv held his gaze steadily. "Let us say then I'm curious to see this city through your eyes, not the eyes of comnet statistics."

Zref had never heard an Interface use the word "curious" before. He'd heard that for them curiosity replaced all other emotions and motivations, including sex. Before he could phrase a question, Sudeen drove up to the curb and presented the car with a flourish. And so they were off on their well-rehearsed afternoon tour of the city.

They climbed the eastern end of one of the five hills nearest the shuttleport. At the lookout point called Hermit's Cave, Sudeen told the legend of the founder of the Mautri temple, disenchanted with his followers, coming to live alone here, out of sight of the kyralizth, which might have been built during the First Lifewave. "The kyralizth is a structure found only on Camiat. The older ones are always found near the remains of a stone circle such as the Wassly Crown here in Firestrip."

Zref told the wild story about the kren who disappeared into the caves and reappeared in the middle of the Mautri temple fountain to live out his years as a white priest. "They say he met the ghost of the Mautri founder down there, and it changed him."

Sudeen shot him a dark look, but the Brenilak encouraged them, and soon they were both telling fanciful tales that held for them an odd ring of truth. At Firestrip Park, Zref told the story of how the first human colony ship, the *Stellar Dust*, had crashed, leaving a long furrow scarring the valley floor and giving the city its current name. At that time, the only inhabitants of the area had been the Mautri priests and their students. The humans, stranded, knew that they shouldn't establish a colony on an inhabited world, but the priests welcomed them. By the time the colony regained contact with the Hundred Planets, a small city had grown around the lake, with a thriving university, tourist trade, and health resort. As Camiat joined the Hundred Planets, Firestrip became the official port of entry, and offworld corporations began building offices. Embassies and Hundred Planets offices followed, and now Firestrip was Camiat's largest city.

Next they climbed the second of the five hills. It was nearly sunset, and the temperature was dropping. Zref said, "Perhaps you'd like to walk up to the peak."

"To see the Wassly Crown? Certainly."

The alien set off up the well-marked trail. Zref followed, discarding his usual patter about how the concentric circles of giant standing stones were of some material not found anywhere on Camiat and how they were precisely placed for observing the stars as they were positioned one whole revolution of the galaxy ago, during the First Lifewave. They arrived at the sheared-off top of the mountain just as the sun reached the right slant to set the translucent green stones glowing.

The Interface stopped, spellbound. The five concentric circles of megaliths loomed higher than a house and leaped at one with a reality that made the rest of the mountain seem cut from pasteboard. Many of the capstones still bridged the upright stones, lending an enclosed feeling to the place.

After a time, Zaviv uttered something, and at Sudeen's interrogative, he translated: "These were the first computers, and the men who used them were the forerunners of what I have chosen to become."

Zref had never thought of that before, while he was considering it, the Interface walked up to and over the chain marker that kept people away. At that moment, they were alone on the mountaintop, but there was a tour bus just turning onto the road.

Zref shrugged, and Sudeen said, "Well, we have no guide's license to lose. Let him go."

The Brenilak approached the oblong slab of translucent green stone set in the center of the circle. He laid both his hands on it, and Zref gained an impression of an overwhelming sadness, followed, as the Brenilak turned to come back, by a growing resignation. Zref knew that he shouldn't be seeing any of this in an Interface. He remembered reading that sensitives couldn't become Interfaces because the surgery destroyed the psychic brain functions. Had Zaviv been a sensitive who became an Interface? Zref was as curious now about the Interface as Zaviv seemed to be about them.

As they walked back down the path, watching the tour bus disgorge its passengers onto the overlook, the Interface asked, "Well, young gentlebeings, what is your theory of the origin of the Wassly Crown?"

"Our theory," said Sudeen, "assumes that this crown dates from the First Lifewave, and it takes into account that all the crowns found around the galaxy are reported to be psychically active."

The Brenilak said distantly, "Sensitives are notoriously suggestible."

Now Zref could not be sure that he'd seen that flash of sadness in the man before. "Yes, we know how the sensitives all predicted the arrival of beings from another galaxy within the year, but only a popular vidrama on the subject appeared. The sensitives had read the mass consciousness accurately but mistook a mass fantasy for reality."

"Have you read the new Lantern novel, *Skanqwin and the Emperor of Crowns?*" asked Sudeen, and continued without waiting for the Interface's assent: "What if the archeovisualizers who write those novels have it right? What if the crowns are the First Lifewave's interstellar communications network, letting telepaths transmit error free messages instantaneously?"

"To prove it," said Zref, "we'd have to find two perfectly intact crowns, calculate their proper alignment, and then station a pair of perfectly compatible sensitives in them! Meanwhile, it's just a fascinating hypothesis!"

Sudeen pulled their car onto the downward road. This was the older section of town, where rents were cheap, and many Camiat University students lived on the hillside.

Two such students caught Zref's eye, and he was about to point them out to their client when he realized that it must be the pair from the shuttleport. The kren female now wore a coat, while her bhirhir had rolled up his shirtsleeves. As Zref watched, they approached one of the apartment buildings. He glanced at Sudeen, who was busy coaxing the car down the narrow street while the Interface gazed at the view of downtown.

Then they were down on the level main road that tunneled through the hills and shot right up to the Mautri temple/school complex.

They parked on the overlook among the tour buses and hurried up the footpath toward the kyralizth. Just as the sun was setting, they paused in the freestanding archway.

"The door," explained Sudeen, "to the room without walls." He passed through to join the crowd of tourists.

As the shadows gathered, lines of robed priests climbed the stairs set into the edges of the kyralizth. When the leaders reached the summit, each stair down each edge of the kite-shaped pyramid, was occupied by a colorfully garbed priest, forming a perfect spectrum.

They were so far away, their chanting could barely be heard; but when it stopped, a hush fell. Above, as if flung out by the hand of a giant, stars winked into being, and full night was upon them.

Abruptly, there was a blaze atop the kyralizth—the crowning firebasin erupting in its nightly flame. The uppermost priests lit torches from the basin, illuminating their white robes like immaculate silver columns. They turned and lit the torches held by the second rank of priests, all dressed in purple. One could barely make out the bulk of the kyralizth except where the tiny points of light crept down the edges.

The preternatural stillness of the crowd stretched until the bottom priest stepped down and extinguished his torch. Then the line of priests filed down, extinguishing their torches as they reached the bottom so that the lines of fire retreated evenly down all sides of the kyralizth, leaving the firebasin at the top to burn until dawn.

As the priests reentered the gate to their private school where none came without invitation, floodlights came on so that the crowd could move to the parking area.

Zref turned away, teeth clenched over the memory of his childhood hopes. *I have no talent worth training.* They had told him so. He had to believe it.

Sudeen took over, leading their client back to the car, covering for Zref as if he knew the pain that lurked beneath Zref's stiff façade. *And he does.*

When he'd been just a young child, Zref had come to the Mautri outer court with hundreds of others to sit for admission. Day after day he had sat, under the discipline of silence and stillness, the youngest in the courtyard. Day after day, others had been chosen or had left while he remained. But he could not give up while the glowing certainty in his heart told him that his real life lay there.

His parents, frantic, had searched until they found him. Eight days and nights he had kept his vigil, never showing disappointment. He was sure on the ninth day that he'd be admitted—not the first human so admitted, but one of the few.

His parents had picked him up bodily and removed him before he could be chosen. He had struggled against them, and a white priest had come out.

He could never forget the words of his doom: *"You are not to climb the kyralizth here, young Zref. Your path lies elsewhere."* He knew better than to attempt that courtyard again. But the yearning never ceased to eat at him, especially at sundown when, watching, he could feel the rough handle of the torch in his hand, and its real meaning seemed to bump at the edges of his mind.

"And that completes the tour," Sudeen concluded as he opened the car door for the Interface and completed the credit transaction. "I hope you found the experience worth your time."

Zref got in, and Sudeen moved the car into the line heading down the hill. They were sandwiched between two red and green striped tour buses.

Zref turned to the man in the back seat. "I hope we've satisfied your curiosity, Sir Brenilak," he said, "because you have satisfied mine, showing that an Interface can be curious about something other than his work."

The Brenilak gazed out the window, wistfully it seemed to Zref, though he didn't trust his perceptions of the nonhuman's moods. "My curiosity is about the human/kren bhirhir because my employers here have a family involvement with it."

Driving through the downtown night traffic, Sudeen asked, "Which hotel are you staying at?"

"I'll be staying with my employers, in the human colony." He gave them an address. "Would you happen to know where that is?"

They knew. It was the residence of Hetta and Barinn Ortenau, Zref's parents. Sudeen recovered first. He punched a new route into the controls and flipped on the traffic monitor. When he couldn't busy himself with that any more, he asked Zref, "You want to tell him, or shall I?"

"I'll do it," Zref answered, still half turned in his seat to talk to the passenger. "Not that you need to be told. You already know who we are, don't you?"

"I have a probability estimate."

Zref felt the tension drain out of him. "My parents would have found out what we've been doing afternoons sooner or later. Besides, I'm curious about what they've hired an Interface *for*." There was no point asking Zaviv to divulge a professional confidence.

The house was well lit when they came up the drive. It was one of the low, sprawling kren-style houses with two sides: one for the family and one containing apartments for visiting mates. His parents rented the apartments to students, who paid by doing chores. He saw one of the students looking out as the car halted, and he could imagine an excited "He's here!" echoing through the building.

As they came up the front steps, the door opened and light flared. Suddenly, Zref felt out of place with his bare, dirty knees and rumpled shirt. His parents, dressed formally for dinner, greeted their Interface and then turned to their sons.

"Zref, Sudeen, we didn't expect you. Well, come inside. We'll set two more places for dinner."

They went into the library, while one of the students went toward the kitchen. The library was a huge, tidy room with an untidy work table along one wall where three comnet terminals chittered softly.

Going toward the one with the lit screen, his mother said, "The Vrashin tapes the other Interface enhanced for us are very clear now."

The Brenilak appeared to study the screen; following his gaze Zref saw three columns of repetitive, disciplined script in no language he could recognize. The pattern blurred before his eyes, and he had a few seconds of bizarre déjà vu during which he seemed to remember writing those words, although their meaning remained tantalizingly beyond recall. He came out of it, his heart pounding in his throat. Echoes of the cold dread he had felt that afternoon upon first seeing the saltwater kren female filled his skull.

Sudeen slid one scaled hand over Zref's elbow as cautiously as if Zref were about to strike someone. "Zref, you're shaking. What's the matter?" he asked, urging Zref away from his parents, who were deep in consultation with the Brenilak.

Dropping onto a reading lounge, Zref gulped air and replied, "Nothing. I just—I suddenly felt that fragment is going to be very important."

"A reasonable intuition," said Sudeen, but he was gazing fixedly at the distant display screen, and he sounded shaken.

Finally, his father broke away and came toward them. Zref felt Sudeen gathering himself as if to meet an attack on his bhirhir. Rising, Zref motioned Sudeen to stay seated. "Let me handle this one."

He intercepted his father a few steps beyond Sudeen, aware for the first time in years that his parents weren't fully immune to Sudeen. "Dad, I've got something to show you," he said, producing the scholarship from Rhobank.

Barinn Ortenau scanned the worn document with a light growing in his eyes. "This is wonderful! Your mother will be so proud of you! But, Zref, all the way to Rhobank? Break up the family . . ."

"Dad, they're only offering funding for a single person."

Barinn's eyes flicked to Sudeen, who was perched tensely on the edge of his chair. "I see."

"It's even worse. Sudeen was second in the competition. If I decline, they'll offer it to him, and we'll still have the same problem!"

His father's eyes focused again on the form. "Tell me truthfully, Zref, do you want to go?"

"I'll tell you how badly I—we both want to go. All season we've been working as tour guides to raise the money."

Barinn glanced at the Brenilak as if he now understood how they had all arrived together.

"The license costs almost as much as a starhopper ticket," added Zref, "so we decided to freelance. We put on a good show for the tourists, and we never used the Ortenau name."

Very seriously, his father asked, "Were you good guides?"

"Yes."

"How much have you earned?"

"About half the passage money."

"Then you've done well by the Ortenau name. Now, why don't you two go and wash up for dinner. Meanwhile, I'll talk to your mother, and we'll see what can be done."

His parents' room was just as he remembered it, though smaller somehow. Beyond the beds, the door was ajar to the bathing pool. It looked so inviting after the long sweaty day, he expected to have to race Sudeen to the water.

But the kren had halted in the middle of the floor, staring through the patio doors into the garden's lush summer growth. Zref slipped by, stripping as he went, and dove into the pool. He surfaced and grabbed a cleansing mat, rubbing himself all over as he watched Sudeen thoughtfully.

"Sudeen?" It was as if the kren hadn't heard. Zref hoisted himself out of the pool and wrapped a bath cape around his shoulders, throwing its cowl over his streaming hair. "Sudeen, come on, I'll scrub your scaly hide for you." It was an offer the kren could never refuse.

But instead of diving, clothes and all, into the pool, Sudeen turned and looked at him. "Your parents are going to offer us money."

"Dad's heard your father hold forth on the subject of kids leaving home before they can earn their own way in a trade. He wouldn't want to cause trouble in MorZdersh'n any more than I would. But if he does offer money, we just won't accept it."

"Even if it means staying here?" Sudeen's venom sack stirred as he responded to Zref's desperation and his own.

Abruptly, Zref was face to face with the choice he had been ducking for weeks. Founders University on Rhobank V was the only school both he and Sudeen were qualified for that offered the degree of Communications Generalist. As Zref saw it, the greatest problems of the Hundred Planets stemmed from communications failures. If the HP was to occupy the entire galaxy, as the First Lifewave had, they'd have to learn the secrets of the First Lifewave. Who'd be more likely to succeed than a human/kren bhirhirn?

Zref replied in a steady voice. "Yes, Sudeen, even if it means staying here. We're a team." Immense relief flooded through him, but Sudeen was riveted by some new vision. *A flash?* The kren turned slowly toward Zref, stark horror fading from his eyes, though in the presence of his bhirhir he barely raised venom.

"What was it?" asked Zref. "A premonition?"

"I hope not," Sudeen answered. "I was never trained at Mautri to know a true premonition from ordinary fears, but I'm sure this was just fear."

Because of his occasional flashes of vision, Sudeen had been trained at Mautri from his earliest years to his first adult molt, when he had fled the school and Zref had found him, late one night, beaten and robbed in a dirty alleyway, delirious with blue-voiding, babbling out his most personal fears between the bouts of involuntary writhing. Out of lifelong friendship, Zref had not hesitated to offer bhirhir.

"Sudeen, if you can't tell me, who can you tell?"

"I had a vision of you, wearing the insignia of the Interface Guild, with that peculiar blank look on your face. And I knew you'd gone offworld without me." He shook himself and went to the bathing pool, stripping off his street costume.

"Sudeen, when we pledged bhirhir, I knew what I was doing. You've never given me cause to regret it."

"Not even when I was too frightened to go back to Mautri and try again, leaving you free to live as a human, the way we planned?"

38

"You know what I was frightened of this afternoon at the shuttleport? I was afraid of losing you—and you know why? Because since we pledged bhirhir, I haven't had any of those insane yearnings to get Mautri to take me in."

"They're not completely gone. I can see that every time we go up to the kyralizth."

"But I can control it because there's something else important I can do with my life."

There was a sound at the door as somebody stepped onto the entry mat outside. Zref opened it to find a stack of clothing behind which stood a girl. Long honey blond hair, dark eyebrows and sharp cheekbones, two slender hands cradling the pile—she looked gorgeous yet vaguely familiar. As Zref stood transfixed, she smiled.

"Zref, you and Sudeen should be able to find something to fit among these—"

"Tessore!! Tess Kobre!" Her voice triggered a thousand memories of a lumpy, awkward girl who could outdare any boy in their class and outdream even Zref. "Tess, I thought you'd gone to Pallacin to study music. *She's lost weight or something.*"

"I was on Pallacin for a year, then Sirwin for three. I couldn't wait to get back to Firestrip!"

"I'm glad you're back."

"Well, aren't you going to take these?"

"Uh, sure." He took the load from her arms and found her standing before him in a blue floor length gown that left her shoulders bare and clung magnificently.

"We can talk later," she said. "I'm living here now."

"Great."

He pulled his eyes from her gown and smiled. She turned and walked down the hallway. Closing the door, he set the pile on the bed and began sorting it. Some was his own that he'd left here. Other items belonged to some other human. But there was also a kren jacket and trousers.

"Come on, Sudeen, get washed. They're waiting with dinner."

The kren was sitting in a chair. "I'm not hungry."

"Well, neither am I, suddenly, but I'm not going to miss this dinner!"

Sudeen got up and came to where Zref was sorting clothing. "Tess? You are attracted?"

"You saw. She's grown *up!*"

Sudeen looked Zref up and down. "It is your turn to mate. Come, scrub my filthy hide for me, and we'll go see how she responds to you."

The dining room was decked out in silverware from Theate, bluish plants from Sirwin in hanging baskets over the table, and as a centerpiece providing all the light in the room, a glowing Ciitheen water globe. In ornate decanters set about the long table, emerald green liqueur sparkled invitingly, an import from Horth.

The Brenilak Interface was seated in the place of honor next to Zref's father at one end of the table. Zref was placed across from the Brenilak, and next to him sat Sudeen. Across from Sudeen was Tessore, next to her was the sandy haired male student Ley, whose clothes Zref was wearing, and across from him was an older man Zref didn't recognize, in the place of honor next to his mother.

Tess and Ley served the soup as his father introduced Zref and Sudeen, saying, "You know everyone here except Mr. Ovid who is from the University's Office of Grants and Allotments."

Zref tore his eyes from Tessore long enough to make a polite reply.

"Zaviv," said Ovid, seeming to take no notice of Zref and Sudeen, "I just want to . . ." The Interface put down his utensils and brought his full attention to Ovid's face. Zref could feel the older man squirm, and his offworld accent became suddenly thicker as he finished, "to welcome you to Camiat and say how very much glad we are to have an Interface on the Vrashin Island project;"

The Interface blinked once and then turned back to the yellowish gruel he had been served in place of the vegetable soup the humans were eating.

Ovid's words riveted Zref's attention. "You mean that inscription was found at the Vrashin dig?"

"That much," said Ovid, "could never be kept secret."

Zref's father added. "We're not sure of the dating, Zref, so don't get excited about it yet."

Zref looked to Sudeen, who was staring speculatively at Barinn Ortenau. "I'd give anything," said Zref, suddenly knowing that it was true, "to meet the person who made that find! I'll bet it's going to be the key to the whole First Lifewave civilization!" *Maybe to their communications tricks, too!*

"Actually," said his father, "you've already met him. You remember the Lakely boy, Dennis? You met him at the mountaineering clubs' competition the year you climbed Sunivsz."

That had been almost seven years ago. All Zref remembered was the image of a short, dumpy boy who always had to be lead climber on the rope. They had never become friends, but they were the only two human boys from university families in the club and thus had often been classed together. *And he's already made a real contribution to history.*

"That's enough, Professor Ortenau," said Ovid. "As representative of the University, I'm here to acquaint you with the security precautions surrounding this project. The box the Lakely boy found is so potentially valuable that it won't be opened until the Professors Ortenau have completed their translation. Both the Vrashin dig and this translation project are funded by Lantern Enterprises. All the information belongs to them. They have specified—and funded—the tightest security to protect their property."

Lantern Enterprises had started in the tourist industry; to generate mass interest in interplanetary travel, they had published novels highlighting the unique historical sites on certain worlds. Public interest mushroomed, and with its sudden wealth, Lantern had funded research and development of archeological sites, which generated more interest, until they currently were the major source of funds for research into the First Lifewave occupation of the galaxy. Serious scholars such as Zref's parents disapproved of the highly romanticized novels of life in the extinct civilizations of a turn of the galaxy ago, but Zref and Sudeen had virtually grown up on them, believing the disclaimer Lantern put in each novel saying that whereas much was sheer invention, never did the text contradict known facts. Part of the appeal of the novels was the air of realism created by the use of the very latest discoveries by prestigious scholars and archeovisualizers.

Zref said, "Mr. Ovid, I can understand how Lantern would consider this information worth billions if they could be the first to use it in a novel. But no one here would consider talking to the press prematurely."

"We understand that," Ovid replied. "However, the contract with the University specifies the tightest possible security. So far as the University is concerned, you've moved with no forwarding address. All your computer work will be done through the Interface under complete *lock.*"

"There's no one here," said Hetta Ortenau, "who can't be keyed to that lock. Tess is an expert in tonal languages and is one of our graduate students, as is Ley, whose bhirhir is a relative of Sudeen's, which makes him family. Zref and Sudeen are our sons—"

"I don't think you understand, Professor Ortenau," Ovid interrupted. "The Cranston Corporation has been put in charge of security here, at considerable expense, because the Law Enforcement Agency of the Hundred Planets has picked up rumors of a new organized industrial espionage ring." He turned to the Interface. "Tell them."

"There has been a 30 percent increase in the number of successful computer taps during the last two standard years. Evidence indicates that it is nearly all due to one organization, which has never been identified. The Guild is researching newer security measures."

"They'd better do more than research on this project," said Ovid. "Lantern expects to recoup losses from a dozen other digs with this one. They have not cut corners on security, either. They've provided for two Cranston security guards to be posted right here in your home, day and night."

"Oh, no!" said his mother, rising and dropping her napkin on the table. She turned to leave the room, saying, "I won't have strangers in my home! I quit. You can send the money back and tell them what to do with it!"

Before she got to the door, Zref's father caught up to her. "Wait, Hetta, wait."

Ovid said, "Security is one thing successful people must learn to live with."

"Lantern," said his father, "and all its books, tours, and billions of credits doesn't matter to us as much as our family does. Our idea of family may be a little too kren for you to understand, but you've been on Camiat long enough to realize that you can't force strangers into our home."

Ovid seemed surprised. Barinn pressed his advantage. "I have a counterproposal. I haven't had a chance to talk this over with my sons yet, but if Cranston hired them as our live in security guards, my wife and I wouldn't object."

Cranston security guards?! Zref met Sudeen's eyes in shock. He glanced again at his mother. She was watching Ovid with one of her narrowed gazes that Zref had learned to respect. *She's acting to convince Ovid!*

"No," she said thoughtfully. "I wouldn't object."

"But they're too young," Ovid protested.

For the first time, Tess spoke up. "Men their age are allowed to enlist in the LEAHP armed field officers school."

"They have no training," Ovid insisted.

"Cranston has a six week training program for security personnel," Ley explained. "Chances are, any men they assigned to us would have little more experience. But you can bet Zref and Sudeen will have their hearts in this job because we're family."

"They haven't said they'd do it," added Tess as Ovid began another objection. Her eyes met Zref's. "Will you? It would mean having to live here in the house, at least all winter or until the project is done."

Zref wanted to say yes, naturally he'd stay, but he tore his eyes from her and said to Sudeen, "It's up to you. This house has been converted for human use." The boarded-over hatching pond and removed walls made the house useless for mating, and the only full sized immersion pool was the one in his parents' room.

Sudeen said, "If we go to Rhobank, I'll get used to roughing it. And if you turn down the scholarship offer now, by the time they offer it to me and I have the grace period to consider it—we could get there, Zref!"

And, thought Zref, *we'll have a trade we could earn our living with, as your father wanted.* "All right, Dad, we'll do it." Zref thought that he should feel jubilant. They were going to Rhobank with all the money they could use, and in the meantime he'd have all winter with Tess. But he had to force a grin, unable to dismiss his premonitions and Sudeen's.

CHAPTER THREE

It was near noon when Arshel and Dennis arrived at the mountain city of Firestrip. She stood with her bhirhir on the steps of the shuttleport building, a chill wind whipping her thin Vrashin-style wrap as she eyed other travelers in thick cloaks. Before them, the five ragged mountains were shrouded in purple mist and decorated with a matte of glittering points where the harsh sun struck square buildings.

"Dennis, can't we go someplace warmer?"

Cheerfully, Dennis said, "See those two guys sitting on the fountain edge, the human and the kren? I'll bet they're complaining to each other of the heat." He laughed. "Now listen. I'll point out our major landmarks so you won't get lost." Rapidly, he listed them and pointed to the Mautri temple. "That's where you're going to school."

She gazed upward. "But it's so far from the University."

The temple and the campus are linked by a main street and an underground tunnel. It takes only a few minutes to cross the whole town, even in winter. We'll find a cheap apartment on South Wassly, halfway between the two schools. Arshel, you're going to *love* Firestrip."

He went on telling her about the wonderful town where he'd grown up, but her eyes strayed again to the two young men sitting on the fountain. The kren's eyes seemed to meet hers for a moment in obvious interest. *No. No freshwater spawn would ever want me.* Firestrip would be a lonely home.

At last, he guided her toward a dark doorway in a kiosk jutting up from the pavement in the plaza. Inside, they found steps. By the time they reached the bottom, she was panting in the thin mountain air, and a sharp pain lanced through her body.

"Dennis—"

He slowed, saying, "Yeah, I'm out of breath, too. Don't worry. In a couple of days you'll get over it."

They came to an underground platform. There were people waiting for the train, and some of them weren't human or kren. An odor hung in the air: mixed species in a closed space. Though it was warmer here, it was also stuffier.

All her life, she'd seen pictures and read stories about the mainland underground trains, but now that she was here, it didn't seem so glamourous. She had to keep reminding herself that the ground here didn't shake, that there wasn't an ocean above them trying to seep in and drown them.

Still when the train skidded into the station, she jumped and felt a hot flood of venom rush into her sack. Embarrassed, she thought that all eyes had noticed her sack quivering, and that produced another small surge of venom.

"Hey," said Dennis, putting an arm about her. "Relax."

His touch soothed her jangled nerves, and her fangs slid back into place. He studied the markings on the train and said, "We must have just missed one."

They stood in the stifling atmosphere as three more trains passed. But at last they mounted one of the sleek blue trains.

He thrust a small map into her hands, and as the train glided along, he tried to explain the system of markings and destinations. But she could only cling to the soothing sound of his voice, telling herself that if he wasn't frightened, she shouldn't be. But her surmother's voice whispered that humans had no emotions; how would he know when to be scared? *Kill this human and come back to us.*

She shook herself out of memory, aware of the human flesh next to hers in the crowded car. *He's really immune to me now. I couldn't kill him unless I actually hated him. Even then I couldn't kill him and survive it.*

The University was all pink stone buildings and huge parks. In one of the largest buildings, they stood in a line until Dennis could seat himself at a desk terminal—reassuringly familiar—and enroll in his courses.

When they left the campus, Dennis had an envelope stuffed with documents. He held one under her eyes. "See, our first stipend. Now we can open a bank account, find an apartment, and buy you a decent coat.

Then we'll have to go back to the port and pick up our luggage."

He went on listing the chores that had to be done that day and the next, but Arshel couldn't take it all in. At one point, they emerged from another underground terminal into a hillside street. Dennis paused to survey the neighborhood. The houses here were older, fighting off shabbiness with worn dignity. Well, she thought, *I always wanted to live in an exotic setting.*

"I'm afraid we're going to have to hike up a few levels to find our place, Arshel. Come on, we'll go slowly."

Arshel eyed the switchback street that climbed the side of Wassly Hill and pulled her new coat up around her head. They'd eaten a hot meal in the students' facility, but all that heat was gone. She tried to breathe deeply as Dennis paused to read the map, but her throat constricted against the cold.

As he started to move on, she caught sight of a huge, old limousine with a Brenilak face framed in the rear window, peering at the natives. She glimpsed the human and kren pair they'd seen at the port fountain. The human was watching her, she was sure.

With a shudder that was from more than the cold, she followed Dennis up a stairway cut between massive buildings. *It's the weather that forces them to build this way.*

"There must be a tunnelway up this hill from the station," said Dennis, panting as they emerged onto the street above. "We'll have to learn the route before the first deep snow."

The apartment Dennis had the key to was small but decent enough to boast a small fountain in one corner of the living room and two full immersion basins, though no hatching pond. There was a balcony off the central room that gave a view of the sparkling lights of downtown Firestrip, scintillating in the deep shadows while the sky still glowed with twilight.

As the stars came out, she saw in the far distance an outline of a kyralizth picked out in points of flame. It seemed to float above the sea of purple shadow, kyralizth, of heaven, not of earth. Curiously, it made her feel at home, and it struck her with such a thrill of awe that she couldn't move until the fire rippled downward and disappeared.

It was the Mautri ceremony, but it was virtually identical to the Vlen sundown ceremony she had been raised on. To the Vlen, it meant the pledge of the bhirhir to surparent the children of the other. But what might it mean to Mautri?

"Come on, Arshel," said Dennis, unaware of her thoughts. "Let's see if they left any bedding sand for you."

After Dennis had expressed her thoroughly and they'd had something hot to eat, she found it remarkably easy to drift into sleep, curled on the artificially warmed sand. In the morning, after a good hot soak, Firestrip didn't seem quite so inhospitable. She went for groceries while Dennis made the trip to get their luggage. He wasn't back when she returned, and so she busied herself cleaning the kitchen and sweeping the balcony, trying to ignore the pointed roofs.

She was on the balcony when he drove up below in a beat-up taxi with a hauler behind. He had not only their luggage but desks, lamps, bookcases, and a computer console of an old but very expensive model.

"Stopped by to get some of my things some friends were storing for me, and they loaned me a desk for you, too," he said breathlessly as he helped the human taxi driver cart things up the three flights of stairs.

As Dennis paid the driver, the man said, "Youngster, go slow until you get your lungs back. That sea air will rot you from the inside out." Then his eyes lit appraisingly on Arshel, and he mumbled an apology and left.

Again, Arshel felt herself in an alien world.

The rest of that day and the next went in getting settled. Then Dennis' classes began. But one morning he announced, "It's a lovely day for a picnic, and I've got something to show you. Dress warmly; it's windy up on top."

She found out that the hill they were living on had the Wassly Crown on its summit. Surrounded by the translucent green monoliths, sun slanting through them to bring them alive, she felt as if she were looking down into the depths of the ocean.

She wasn't aware of having moved at all, but her fingers touched the surface of one of the monoliths, and it was as if she melted into the green depths, swallowed by a profound peace, while on the edge of awareness there was something she had to know and couldn't quite remember.

Only the shifting sun, darkening the interior of the monolith, brought her back to reality. Dennis was watching her expectantly. "Did you see anything?"

"See?" This was an archeological site as old as the Vrashin site, but it was still alive. "No, it was just, well, almost as good as taking a long, deep swim in the ocean. But there is something here, Dennis. I just don't know how to get at it."

Beckoning, Dennis walked out of the stone circle, gathered up their things, and said, "The Mautri are going to teach you how to get at it. Come on, today is one of their receiving days. Let's go talk to them."

He was already on the path down when she caught up with him and pulled him to a halt. "Dennis, I'm not Mautri. I was raised Vlen. The Mautri here are freshwater spawn; they'll all hate me. And Dennis, they teach balbhirhir!"

He put one sheltering arm about her shoulders, his fingers just brushing her sensitive venom sack, sending waves of relaxation through her. "Is that all you've been worrying about? I'm not talking about enrolling you in the priesthood! I'm only talking about the Outer School. Lots of kren send their children there for a year or so. They aren't going to make you learn balbhirhir." He stopped and gripped her by both shoulders, searching her face, as unable, she realized, to read her expression as she was to read his. "Shel, you can't think that I want to get rid of you."

There it was in clear words, the fear she hadn't really admitted to herself. *How could anyone think he doesn't understand my emotions?*

He went on with a sort of quiet desperation. "I've been replanning my life around you. You said you'd train to become my archeovisualizer. I thought you meant it."

"I did, but—"

"The Mautri have the best training in the psychic fields, and you're a Lakely now. The best school is the only place you belong."

She couldn't find any answer to that, and his face became animated with wide-eyed excitement. "Shel, this is going to make you a true Lakely. When my father finds out what you and I can do together—you'll see! The City of a Million Legends *will* be a Lakely find!"

Her bafflement melted then, as she understood that it was the family achievement that was so important to him. But as they made their way across the city in silence, she thought, *What if the priests send me away?*

They waited much of the afternoon in the outside courtyard, watching the fountain and the creeping shadows. All around the walls, on stone benches, other applicants also sat, waiting. Some with their bhirhir, some alone, they all sat in stillness, as if applying for the priesthood itself.

Most of the applicants were children or, like her, on the very threshold of adulthood. As time passed, others arrived, met by the same priest who had met them. The newcomers were also told to wait.

By late afternoon, the benches were full and the courtyard lined all about with dusty feet in summer shoes. Dennis was the only human and Arshel the only one bundled up for winter.

Then the inner doors opened in a nicely arched doorway that revealed nothing of the dark interior. A line of seven blue-robed priests came out, circled the fountain, and turned outward to face every way around the courtyard. They moved toward the applicants, and each chose a candidate. Only seven were chosen from the fifty or more there.

Relief and alarm warred in Arshel while the priest who had greeted them all said that those who had not been chosen were invited to come again. The seven chosen ones stood facing their choosers while the courtyard emptied.

But as they reached the gateway, the priest who had greeted them said, "Arshel?"

Startled, she stopped, looking about for anyone she knew, but it could only have been the strange priest who had spoken.

"Arshel, there is one within who would speak with you. I cannot invite your bhirhir to attend within walls."

No! she thought, catching her impulse to yell.

The priest added, "You will be safe with us. And so will your bhirhir."

"How did you know my name?"

"I guessed."

"Arshel," said Dennis in a whisper, "go ahead. I don't mind waiting. This could be our lucky break. I told you they always recognize talent and never turn away anyone with a solid measure of it—like you have."

The priest said, "This offer will not be available to you tomorrow. The one who makes it is dying. You must decide quickly."

She looked at the rising tiers of walls of the inner courts, at the tall spires with tiny windows all about their enormous square stone girth. If she left now, she'd be curious about the inside of a Mautri temple all her life. Of course, she could always say no. She answered, "I'll come."

The priest turned, barring the gate behind the last of the failed applicants. The accepted ones were already out of sight. He led her to a small door and closed it behind them. They were in a small chamber between walls, and then another door opened to let them into a huge court with tiered fountains bigger than any she'd ever seen.

They went up twisting narrow stairs and down long, broad corridors. Occasionally, niches were carved into the walls, displaying ancient works of art, each seeming to radiate some silent message she couldn't quite read.

Doors and more doors, and at last they came to a chamber fit for a feudal king.

Within the high room, woven hangings were draped from the ceiling, depicting the night sky. Under the hangings, the air was close for even the heat of summer; compressed kelp burned in the fireplace, an odor of home for Arshel. Beyond, enclosed by a circle of hangings, in a chair by the fire, sat the oldest kren she'd ever seen. The saltwater hues of his ancient hide were almost obliterated by the years.

Behind her, the door closed with a solid thump, and she was alone with the elder priest. He beckoned her to the fire, moving with ease, though his skin seemed taut enough to put him on the verge of molt. "Arshel, at last. Come sit by the fire. You must be cold in these mountains. But I've waited all this time for you, to welcome you."

"Venerable, though I'm glad to be welcomed, I've no intention of becoming a Mautri priest."

"Oh, no, of course not!" The old kren laughed, a brittle hissing sound that startled her. But oddly, venom didn't come in response to that surge of alarm.

"Your future lies," continued the old one, "if you're brave enough for it, out among the stars, among all the varied species of mankinds. Let me tell you a story."

His ancient eyes drifted to the fire, and she thought for a moment that he'd fallen into a doze or perhaps even died.

"Years ago," he resumed, "when I was still Chief Priest here, a human came to the inner court to sit for admission to the priesthood. He was hardly old enough to have begun schooling, yet he was worthy in every way. Eight days and nights he sat, determined to be chosen, though we passed him over every day. His instinct was good. He would have become great among us, if his parents hadn't come for him.

"For several previous lifetimes, he had been a Mautri priest and had perfected all that he could among us so that this time he was born as a human for a special purpose. When he was dying previously, as a white priest, he had instructed us that if he should return, we were to pass him over, for his destiny lay with the Arshel who would seek our training here."

Arshel didn't believe it. The Vlen did not believe that people could live again, let alone as another species. And how could anyone know it beforehand?

"He told us we must train this Arshel who would come with a human male as her bhirhir. Many such women have come—none, however, named Arshel, and none from the islands. Until now. And so we offer you our inner court and the best of our training. Many times before, you have chosen not to essay this most difficult path. But once again you stand upon the threshold to choose. This time you do not stand alone."

He's talking about Dennis. And he did know my name.

"Venerable," she said, "I don't wish to study for your priesthood."

"For the sake of our brother, we're offering you our training without the vows and obligations of a priest."

Since childhood she'd looked with yearning and wonder upon the kyralizth, certain somehow that to know its real secrets would solve all her problems. She wanted to say yes quickly, before the old man died. She caught herself.

"I must discuss all this with my bhirhir."

"Of course. You will return."

Suddenly, she realized that she had come to the temple wanting nothing to do with people who exalted balbhirhir, afraid of them as if it were contagious. And this old man in a white robe had simply spoken a few words that couldn't possibly be true, making her eager to take a place among the student priests!

She had ripped herself out of the bosom of her family, taken a human male bhirhir, followed him halfway around the world to a mountain city made of icy winds and square corners—and now she was eager to abandon her ancestral teachings and turn Mautri, as this white-robed priest must have done once.

What is happening to me?

51

CHAPTER FOUR

Zref and Sudeen approached their training as security guards with trepidation. There was physical exercise as if they were training for an athletic contest. There was personal combat, acrobatics, and gymnastics, competing against humans and other species. Every night, when they returned home, they nursed aches and bruises and wondered how they would face the next day.

There were classroom studies on everything from interspecies first aid to securing a post against physical assault. They studied crowd control, criminal psychology, and espionage. The class that most fascinated Zref, focused on the vast interstellar criminal organizations. Even he could see that the graphs were definitely changing; a new element had entered the information theft business. It gave him nightmares.

But in the end they graduated with honors, and Zref felt that the two of them could handle anything that might happen. They were immediately given full responsibility for leakproofing the house from the inside.

Already, the Ortenaus had identified a message segment on the Vrashin tapes that seemed to be recorded in eighteen different languages and five different notation systems. But none of them bore any resemblance to a living language.

Daily, Zref and Sudeen checked the house for intruding spy equipment. At first they took the job seriously, but after a while they began to feel foolish and tried to do their checking when others weren't around. Yet they always did the prescribed checks.

They told the neighbors that their parents were offplanet and that they themselves were staying here with a few students. The windows had all been boxed in from the outside so that the house appeared deserted, while from the inside cameras showed every detail of passersby while computer tie-ins ran identity crosschecks.

The locks had been changed on all the doors, even the one in the basement that opened onto the public tunnel. They could not have been more secure. Life settled into a routine.

Much to Sudeen's delight, Zref began to spend more time with Tessore. In fact, Sudeen would often comment casually on her last known whereabouts and then disappear into the immersion pool in the room that Zref's parents had vacated for them. Gradually those stolen hours with Tess became the high point of Zref's day.

At first, he kept up with his parents' progress through her. She would display for him the segment of the tape they were working on, showing all the cryptic notations, and try to explain it to him. But the sight of that alien writing always gave him the same shuddering chill it had the first time he'd seen it. After he began dreaming that he had written the original inscription, he randomly changed the subject whenever she brought it up.

She listened avidly to whatever flight of imagination he was playing with at the moment, discussing the latest Lantern novel, *Skanqwin and the Emperor of Crowns*, with him as if it were a real world they could enter together; and when he left her, there was always an afterglow of enriched satisfaction that lasted all day, even though he never so much as laid a finger on her.

Then, one day, on one of Sudeen's tips, Zref found her in the entry hall by the fountain, just before dinner. It had been warm that day, and though the fans were running, the house was very stuffy. She sat on the lip of the fountain, letting the spray bead her hair like a mist of jewels. She looked up at him, smiling. "Want to go out for a walk?"

"Sudeen's asleep, so I'm on duty. Can't leave."

"Nothing's happening. Nothing's going to happen."

"I suppose not, but I'm getting paid to do a job." He took out his pocket scanner and checked the entryway. "Not a bleep. We're safe here, and the sun's setting. It'll cool down pretty quick now. In fact, it'll be winter soon."

"Yeah. Another year gone."

It was something he'd been feeling, too. It was taking so long just to get started on what they wanted to do with their lives. An impulse he'd been keeping at bay for too long came again, and this time he reached over and kissed her on the forehead. Startled, she turned to him. With more naturalness than he'd thought possible, his arm slid around her, and he was kissing her urgently.

When the wave finally abated, there was a numb moment during which they just looked at each other, confounded by what had happened. He'd never kissed a girl quite like that before. He was ready to kick Sudeen out of the bedroom and take her to bed right then. But as much as he wanted it, it wouldn't have satisfied him. This was different.

The moment was over. She pushed away from him, half turning. "No, Zref, no." But from the way she said it, he could tell that she wanted it, too. "Zref, I have friends who've fallen in love with bhirhirn, even tried marriage. It never works. I promised myself I'd never get involved with any guy committed to a bhirhir. And I won't."

But there were tears in her voice as she thrust herself to her feet and plunged away from him toward the back of the house. He caught up with her outside the kitchen. "Tess, give me a chance. Sudeen will understand."

She met his eyes steadily and said in a voice so quiet that Ley, who was in the kitchen preparing dinner, couldn't have heard, "You don't even see how much you've changed since you took him bhirhir. He's got a part of you that I can't reach anymore." She fled.

Dinner that night was a noteworthy occurrence. Both his parents and the Interface showed up. Tessore and Ley were at the table as well. Ley's bhirhir, Khelin, had come that afternoon, wrapped in his blue priest's robe, but he had gone back to the Mautri school. As always after one of those perfunctory visits, Ley was sorely withdrawn.

From time to time during the evening, Zref caught Ley staring at Sudeen with a strange swimming pain in his eyes. Tessore, noticing it, gave Zref a smugly raised eyebrow.

True, with his molt brother living almost balbhirhir. Ley was suffering. Was Tess thinking that even if Sudeen should go into Mautri, he'd take a part of Zref with him a part she could never have? The thought was too chilled with pain, and he dropped it.

"Zref? Zref! You haven't heard a word your father has been saying!" His mother was frustrated.

"I'm sorry. I was thinking of something else."

"I asked," repeated his father, "if you'd consider it a breach of security to discuss our latest breakthrough here."

"Oh, no, not at all. We're all secure," Zref answered.

"Then I think you're all entitled to know the good news. And Ley, you deserve a good piece of the credit. It was the summary you prepared that suggested it to me."

"But I got the idea for that from Tess," Ley protested, "when we were arguing about the First Lifewave using gadgets like the Wassly Crown for telepathic amplifiers."

"I was just giving you Zref's ideas," said Tess. "Every time I start talking about the ideographic portion of the tape, he starts talking about the First Lifewave Crown network, and I just made the association."

"Well, this afternoon," his father continued, "Zaviv ran us a correlation on that peculiar jagged ideograph, assuming its base meaning to be 'communication.' With that, the computers were able to assign meanings to some other terms, and I think we may have a phrase almost translated."

"Tell us what it says!" Sudeen burst in.

"We can't be sure yet. All we have is a match between one of the languages of the Vrashin find and the Persuader Fragment, the one found in that asteroid halfway across the galaxy from here, the one we translated for Lantern and they used in that silly book *Skanqwin and the Emperor of Crowns.*"

"Lantern made a planet's ransom on that book," said Ley.

"It's not so silly," Tess added, and Zref glowed.

"The book is not important," his father said, temporizing. "What is important is that—if we're right on this—our translation of that fragment may have been wrong. What we called the Capital City of the First Lifewave is in fact the City of a Million Legends and is the location of the master crown, the Emperor's Crown mentioned in the Persuader Fragment. And now we *may* have a clue to the location of the City of a Million Legends!"

"Barinn," said Zref's mother softly, "let's not get ahead of ourselves." But she was suppressing a grin.

Sudeen said, "I think it's time to tighten up security. Zaviv, you've got all this under lock?"

"In my personal file, yes."

"I guess," said Zref, "we don't have to worry about computer theft, then." If Zaviv died suddenly, it would take the Interface Guild years to gain access to his personal lock code, and there were parts of that file that would be wiped clean before the combined might of all the Interfaces could get at it. "But, Zaviv, what if something happens to you?"

Levelly, the Brenilak answered, "That's what you're here to prevent."

With that sobering thought echoing in both their minds, he and Sudeen double-checked everything. They called in the all clear to Yeol Tai, the Cranston man in charge of the outside guards.

Then he noticed that Sudeen's venom sack was more than half distended. "Look at us." He laughed. "We're taking ourselves so seriously!"

"Something's going to happen," said Sudeen, with a quiet foreboding. "Maybe not right this minute, but soon."

"Premonition?"

"I don't know. I think so."

That was the most positive claim his bhirhir ever made, and so Zref glanced around again. They were in the basement below ground level, where the walls were carved out of living rock. At one end of the wide space, the access door opened onto the main public tunnel, which led in one direction into the heart of the human quarter and in the other direction onto the Camiat University campus.

The old door had been replaced with one made of the alloy used in spaceship hulls. The new lock was so intricate Zref never even tried to open it manually but just asked Zaviv to signal it open through the comnet.

Zref took one last look around the bare cellar, the rack of cycles the family used in the tunnels, the coat closet, and boot rack, and said, "There's nothing here. Come on up and let me express you before you scare everyone in the house half to death."

Their room, too, had the window covered and rigged with a viewscreen. Zref nervously scanned the camera up and down the outside of the building, but the area was deserted. He turned to find Sudeen kneeling in his sand bed, arms folded, gently rocking back and forth.

"Zref, I'm frightened."

"I can see that," said Zref, pausing on his way across the room to pick up the tempered leather bottle in which he collected Sudeen's venom.

He knelt beside his bhirhir, but the kren flinched away. Now that his venom sack was fully distended, his jaw unhinged into strike position, fangs exposed. Zref knew better than to make an insistent move on a kren in that condition.

"Are you *seeing* something?"

"Tessore. It has something to do with Tessore—afraid."

Zref was silent with shock for a few moments. Then he gathered himself. "I can guess what it's about, then. But first, come on."

With his left hand, Zref proffered the bottle while he rose on his knees to position his right hand over the sensitive venom sack. Finally, the kren gave a little shudder of consent, and Zref deftly fit the bottle around the now extended fangs. With his other hand, he triggered the reflex that would express the venom.

When the kren finally unclamped his jaws, the strong leather of the lip of the bottle had a new dent in it. The bottle was quite a bit heavier than Zref had expected.

Still trying to catch his breath, Sudeen said, "What would have happened if I'd struck you?"

"Oh, I imagine my immunity would have held. It was only fear-venom, not hate-venom! But I might have been pretty sick for a while. Look, about Tessore, I know what you may have been picking up on. What would you say if I asked you to immunize her to your venom?"

"Why?"

Even now, Zref often forgot some of the major differences between kren and human. "Sudeen," he said hesitantly, "I don't think we've talked about what would happen if I ever wanted to marry."

"Marry? Mate permanently?"

Zref nodded. When they'd pledged bhirhir, he hadn't been able to conceive of feeling this way, and he had pledged his children to Sudeen. The women he'd had were always told that.

"With Tessore? But, Zref, doesn't that take many matings to decide?"

"Sometimes, but not always. She's brilliant at languages, Sudeen. She'd fit perfectly into our career in communications. And this afternoon I discovered I don't want just a mating."

Sudeen moved to sit cross-legged, facing him. "I've always accepted that there was a part of you I'll never have access to as a bhirhir should have. I've teased you about being human, and I've been afraid you'd desert me because you don't really need me. But this is the first time I've ever felt how truly alien you are."

Zref knew what he meant. The kren venom glands go dry during the height of mating. One vital function of the bhirhir is to stand by, able to raise his or her own venom to protect the couple if necessary during the days of mating. Zref's lack of venom had caused Sudeen moments of anxiety that had almost ruined his first mating. But even then, they hadn't been alien to one another as they were now.

"Funny," said Zref. "Tess said almost the same thing when she rejected me."

"Rejected you? Then you weren't serious—"

"Of course I'm serious, or I wouldn't have brought it up! Do you think I don't know what I'm asking you to do?"

"I once would have thought you did!" He shook his head in the purely human gesture of negation. "I can't do what you want. She's not family. And if she were, she couldn't be mate!"

Kren never immunized a mate to their venom, because it would make the mating sterile.

"It *is* a little hard to encompass, isn't it?" said Zref. "I've never felt like this before, either, Sudeen."

A trifle desperately, the kren said, "Maybe the feeling will pass with the mating." And Zref hadn't the heart to press him further.

Once or twice during the night, Zref woke thinking of the venom bottle and how very simple it would be to take some to inoculate her with. But the thought revolted him.

The next morning he told Sudeen his fantasies. "But that isn't what I want." he ended. "I want you to like her. She's grown up from the pesky little girl we used to know."

Sudeen answered, "I can only promise to think about it."

He hadn't known Sudeen nearly as well as he'd thought. One day, they were alone in their room, washing up for dinner, when Zref broke out: "I can understand your point of view. Why can't you understand mine?"

Sudeen knew immediately what Zref meant. "I think I can see your side of it. I just can't bring myself to regard Tess as—maybe with time, Zref. I am trying."

Zref ached with the effort his bhirhir was putting forth, and he set himself then and there never to ask again. He picked up the venom bottle from the dressing table. "You let me know when you're ready, then. Meanwhile, come here and let me take care of that for you."

It seemed that Sudeen was raising venom more easily lately. Examining his skin, Zref could see no signs of molt. *We're all under too much emotional pressure.*

The Brenilak Interface was not at the dinner table, and so Zref volunteered to take his meal out to him while Sudeen made the rounds.

The gardener's cottage that the Brenilak used as an office and residence was attached to the house on one side, via a short corridor off the kitchen pantry. With the new security renovations, the inside door was the only entrance to the cottage. The door opened, and Zref pushed it wide, calling, "Zaviv, I've brought your dinner."

"In here," came the answer, and Zref followed the voice into the main room, where the fountain had been shut off and drained, the heat vents half blocked, and the furniture piled at one end to clear space for an electronic bench and comnet equipment before which was a chair designed for the Brenilak. Zref put the tray down.

"That smells good. Thanks for bringing it along."

"Welcome. May I check the place out?" He waved his beeper.

"You won't find anything with that," the Interface said.

"My job—" Zref started, and then caught the odd inflection the Interface had used. "What exactly do you mean?"

The man spun his chair about and looked up at Zref. "Someone has been tapping the private files of the Guild. They got into mine today, and I think they have our tentative translation of that ideographic section, though not our translation key or any long segment of the tapes. They'll be back for those I'm sure."

This is the attempt Ovid warned us about. Despite their best efforts, security had been breached. "Zaviv, only an Interface *could* do such a thing."

"True, one who is not and never has been a member of the Guild. A pirate Interface."

A chill went through Zref very like the chill that always struck him on sight of the Vrashin texts, a chill that said: *This is the end of the world as I know it.*

CHAPTER FIVE

Arshel followed the yellow-robed priest back through the frigid halls of the Mautri temple. Her steps were automatic, her eyes fixed blankly on the back of the swaying robe. Half her mind visualized herself among these people, while the other half still dwelled in the warm sunshine and ocean spray of Vrashin Island. Yet something irresistible pulled her forward into this new life, something as compelling as the impulse that had brought her to ask Dennis to become her bhirhir.

And now she was about to rejoin him in the Mautri courtyard, to face him once again with a question that would determine both their futures. *This can't be any harder than pledging bhirhir.*

She remembered the day when she had asked him to join her life. She had trudged over the ridge of sand dividing her family's home from the beach; the rising sun was on the horizon. Already, people were leaving after their morning swim. They had the beach to themselves.

He was seated cross-legged beside a driftwood fire, reading a book in a pocket viewer. He held up one hand to her and went on scanning. She examined his profile against the little fire.

He looked almost like a kren from that angle. His human ears, stuck onto the outside of his skull, didn't show. His hair was fluffy enough to be kren when you couldn't see the yellowish color. He was thin even for a human, and his nose seemed to jut out from his face like a piece of cleaved granite, but even that didn't make him seem impossibly alien.

In the growing light, she could see that he was reading the Lantern novel she had lent him, *Skanqwin and the Emperor of Crowns,* and she dared to hope. *If he understands Skanqwin's feelings, he'll understand mine.*

At last Dennis slapped the viewer off, complaining, "There's hardly a word of truth in this thing!"

"Then why did you bother reading it?"

"Now, *there* is the question! Everybody reads Lantern novels! Billions of the gullible believe every word is real. Even I really felt what it was like for Skanqwin to be excluded from the Crown network because he was a Persuader. As if there ever could have been such a thing as a Persuader!"

"There was," said Arshel triumphantly. *He understands! I knew he would!* "Didn't you read the preface?" She took the viewer and ran it back to the beginning, where the Ortenau translation of a fragment found in a warehouse asteroid between the stars was printed.

AND IN THE DAYS OF THE CROWN EMPERORS THE PERSUADERS KEPT ORDER IN THE GALAXY. THEY HAD THE POWER TO MAKE ANYONE WANT TO OBEY THEM. THIS IS NOT JUST LEGEND BUT FACT. I HAVE FELT IT. IT COMES FROM DEEP INSIDE, AS IF THE MIND WERE SUDDENLY CLEARER, MORE IN-TELLIGENT THAN EVER. IN A FLASH, ONE IS CONVINCED OF THE RIGHTNESS OF THE PERSUADERS' ORDERS.

IT IS SAID THAT TO ACQUIRE THEIR POWERS, THEY HAD TO DIE. STORIES ARE TOLD OF THEIR ENTRY RITE, WHICH CAN BE VERIFIED, IF YOU BUT GO TO THE CAPITAL CITY. THERE, AT THE EMPEROR'S OWN CROWN, THE MAZE OF THE PERSUADERS BEGINS. THE CRIES OF DANGEROUS ANIMALS FROM EVERY KNOWN PLANET HAUNT THE AIR. THE RUSH OF GREAT MOVING WATERS MINGLES WITH THE SOUND OF SHARP BLADES SLICING THE AIR. THOSE WHO LIVE NEAR WILL TELL STORIES OF PEOPLE GOING IN BUT NEVER COMING OUT.

YET I THINK THEY COME OUT.

I KEPT VIGIL AT THE MOUTH OF THE MAZE AND COUNTED THOSE GOING IN. FOR EVERY LIVING PERSON WHO WENT IN BUT DID NOT COME OUT, THERE DID EMERGE A THING—A PILE OF SAND, A MASS OF STONE, A SLAGGED PUDDLE.

I ALSO SAW SUCCESSFUL CANDIDATES EMERGE. SUCH A ONE WAS OSSMINID, WHO LATER BROKE HIS VOWS TO . . .

Here the fragment ended. Dennis sighed. "It's probably just a piece out of a cheap fantasy novel, but, Arshel, if I could have lived in that time, I'd have risked anything to become a Persuader!"

"I think," Arshel answered with trepidation, "Skanqwin felt about becoming a Communicator the same way I feel about becoming an archeologist. They'd never accept my scholarship because I *see*, and I trust what I see more than what I think. But you're going to be an archeologist, and if I were your bhirhir, I could be your archeovisualizer."

With the words spoken, she could only hold her breath, cringing before the expected rejection. But as he shoved the viewer aside and turned around to look at her, his face underwent one of those peculiar melting transitions she never could quite believe.

"You don't have to make yourself into an archeovisualizer to gain my acceptance. I told you last winter that if nobody else came along, I'd gladly take you bhirhir. I meant that."

It had been settled that simply. But she'd had no idea what she was getting into. *I had no choice; I really didn't.*

The courtyard was deserted when they let her out. Dennis was sitting on a bench in the last slice of sunlight. "Shel!"

Tasting venom, she went to him. "You're safe." *I never gave that a thought the whole time I was in there.*

Impatiently, he asked, and she told him what had happened. He fell into a deep silence that lasted until they got back to their apartment. But as soon as the door was closed, he burst out, "They'll make you go balbhirhir, anyway!"

Arshel thought that if he were kren, he'd be raising venom She'd doubted the old priest's story, but now, watching her bhirhir pace in barely controlled fear of losing her, she could see how his feelings might stem from having been kren in a previous life. What else could explain such panic in a human?

"Dennis, even the Mautri can't *make* a person go balbhirhir."

He flung himself into one of the kitchen chairs, facing her across the table, his eyes strangely alive now. "Do you really think you can learn all their tricks and not be seduced into their ways?"

"They think I can. They said I don't have to take vows."

"I never dared *dream* we could get you into the Inner School. But Shel, this may be our big break, and it sure is about time! If they're willing to give it away, we can't turn it down!"

But he was uneasy with the decision. Over the next few weeks, his fear of losing her to the Mautri practices erupted into short, bitter quarrels. She struggled to be patient, waiting for the lack of change in their relationship to allay his anxiety so that he'd become again the person she'd known on Vrashin.

Her first day at the temple, she was given a red priest's robe in winter weight material to wear over her street clothes, and she was assigned a learning room snug in the heart of the building complex, the warmest room they had. But it was chilly, and she dreaded the onset of winter.

Her instructor came in, dressed in the light summer robe everyone else wore. His was pale blue, signifying that he was an advanced student, almost balbhirhir.

"I am called Khelin."

Heat was coming through the floor ducts now. The room had only a desk, two chairs, a floor mat, and a bookrack holding an array of tattered old volumes next to a comnet access screen. The small fountain in the corner of the room tinkled.

She drew her robe tight and shuddered with chill as she said politely, "Venerable Khelin."

"I'm not that old!" he said, amused. "But one of the things I'm here to teach you is how to adjust to the mountain cold."

"That would be a very practical teaching."

Over the course of the first weeks, she did learn ways to control her circulation and the amount of heat her body produced. But she was never comfortable. Khelin set her tasks and then disappeared for half a day or more. At first, she told Dennis about each event of her day as they met in the evenings. But when he had time to listen, Dennis would only reply, "What good is that?" or "When did you say they'd let you start learning visualization?"

She put that question to Khelin.

"Arshel, you can't begin on visualization until you're ready to make your beads, and you can't do that until you've learned basic control. It will do you little good to learn visualization if it only makes you sick."

She swallowed her impatience and learned to report less detail to Dennis. The day of the first snowfall, a day etched in her memory with the sharp, tactile edge of ice crystals falling from the sky onto her bare face, she stood outside her body for the first time and watched it sleep.

She was so frightened that she woke with a start in her pale stone learning room, venom gushing into her sack, her heart fluttering painfully. The fright-venom felt like molten lava.

"Dennis!" she gasped, sure that she'd never regain control without her bhirhir. But within moments, Khelin had coached her to calmness.

"I think that's enough for today," said Khelin. "I'll escort you home."

It was the first time he'd offered such a thing, but she knew why: Her venom sack was more than half full. In that condition, she had no business out in public without her bhirhir. She had to tell him that her bhirhir was human and male, a student at the university. "He won't be home for some time yet."

He wasn't surprised or hostile. "My bhirhir is also human, Arshel, and male, and a student at the university!"

His gentle humor relaxed her. It was the beginning of friendship, and she was able from then on to talk of her difficulties adjusting to Dennis' ways, her doubts and fears. And as they talked, Khelin was always able to bring the abstractions she studied to bear on her personal life. That was the day that marked the beginning of real personal change for her.

The first snowfall was, the locals said, just a light dusting. Soon the warmer autumn weather resumed, but the stores filled with winter clothing and strange devices for coping with the snow that would soon bury the city's first story windows. With time, Arshel found herself talking to Dennis less and less about what she was learning.

Some of the friction eased. Still, occasionally Dennis would burst out with, "Why don't you tell me about what they're teaching you anymore?" Arshel would reply, "You don't tell me much about what you're learning!" Then he'd explain that his work was too technical to discuss with her, and she'd repeat that right back at him until they both laughed.

One day, Dennis mentioned a human girl he'd been seeing a lot of, and the sense of relief she felt told her what the real problem had been. Of course, she should have known. They did have needs outside of each other.

Autumn continued toward winter. The natives kept saying how uncommonly warm it was, but Arshel was perpetually chilled, often coughing or fighting some disease. This brought her onto the Camiat University campus occasionally, as she was under Dennis' health care contract. Gradually, she learned her way around the city; the sharp edges of the scenery gently faded from awareness.

Once, for three days, she had to stay home with Dennis, who was running a high fever and vomiting ceaselessly. She had heard that humans fought off infection by elevated body temperature, but the reality of the process was frightening. Yet when it was over, she felt curiously satisfied, settled within herself and adult somehow.

Examining the feeling under Khelin's guidance, she told him, "It's as if now, at last, we're *really* bhirhirn. Does that make any sense?"

"To most people I don't think it would. But I do know that feeling. It's as if you'd brought your bhirhir through a difficult molt, isn't it?"

"Yes!" With unbelievable pain she said, "I wonder what it's like to express your bhirhir."

There was a long silence until Khelin said, "That's something you and I will never know."

The truth of that was like the searingly cold winds of the mountains.

Khelin, she noticed for the first time, had the light skin tones, full lips, and deep-set eyes of the freshwater spawn. His hair was a dark fluff about his head, making his features seem so intensely virile that she wondered why she hadn't noticed before. Was it just the way he was looking at her now?

She glanced aside, confused and upset. But in the days that followed, she found herself looking forward to Khelin's visits to her learning room. He had three other, more advanced students, and very often in the evenings he'd leave the temple after the sundown ceremony. She knew now that he went to his bhirhir, just as she did. Overall they had never spent much time together, and now it began to seem like all too little.

Khelin would inspire her to work even harder by promising that soon she could begin to make her first bead. She began to learn about the bead string she saw in use all about her. It consisted of five spherical chunks of mineral connected by a long, handspun string wound about the tips of the fingers, just clearing the finger webbing.

"It is a concentration aid," Khelin explained. "You felt the sense of panic when you first stepped out of your body. The beads provide a focal point to prevent that, and so it's much easier to journey backward in time to view whatever one is interested in, usually oneself in a previous life."

"If I survive death," she countered, "I don't believe it can be in the form of matter."

"That is the Vlen teaching, and we don't dispute it except to say that it takes more than one lifetime for most of us to achieve survival without the form of matter. You need not abandon your Vlen ideals, even after you've experienced what we have to show you. You're under no vows here."

As Arshel learned more about the inner hierarchy of the Mautri disciplines, she began to wonder about that. It would be many years before she could reach a stage where her bhirhir would be threatened by any vows. She only wore the red robe of the beginner, whereas the grade above her wore orange, and those beyond wore yellow. The intermediate grades wore shades of green and then blue. Only in the deepest blue shades did one begin seriously severing the bhirhir bond. And it was the purples who began the practice of self-expression.

At first she'd visualized this to be the kind of ghastly self torture she had endured for Dennis' sake: placing her own hand on the sensitive venom sack to trigger the expulsion of venom. Whenever she saw a priest wearing the purple, she would avert her eyes and shudder. Khelin; asked one day why she behaved so, and when she told him, he took her to see the purple priests gather just before the sundown ceremony.

They knelt in a circle around the low-lipped fountain in one of the central concourses. Priests of other grades, reds conspicuously absent, gathered about them at some distance. Placing their bead strings across their knees, they spread their hands wide, stretching the webbing out for all to see. Most of them had very sparse webbing, as she did.

After a prolonged, hushed stillness, they all leaned forward over the fountain waters, fangs coming forward into strike position. And then, without so much as a shiver of tension in the neck and shoulder strike muscles or the jaw—with expressions of total serenity so startling on their faces—they voided their venom into the waters, not in sharp spurts driven by contractions of the sack muscles but in a lax stream.

It was a sight she would never forget. Afterward, none of them was out of breath, and it left her in total awe of those who wore the purple. Very quickly, she came to respect the new deep indigo robes Khelin wore.

One day, she found the courage to ask, "Khelin, are you going to take the purple soon?"

He was quiet for a while, as seemed to be the Mautri way. She'd been taught that it was impolite not to answer when spoken to. Finally, she felt impelled to add, "Because I was wondering if the purple ever mate." And then she stood aghast at what she'd said.

But he only returned her gaze calmly. "The still silence which is so necessary to the purple has deserted me, Arshel. I am filled with every perception of you. But it would destroy the student-teacher relationship if we were to mate."

"Where, I mean how, you're . . ."

"The temple is our home. We have our spawning pond here, but it would be too cold for you."

Tactfully, he didn't say saltless, but she knew it.

It was both possible and impossible that she'd found her first mate. The matter filled her days until Dennis asked one evening as he finished expressing her, "You don't raise much venom anymore, do you? Are you going balbhirhir after all?"

It was only half jocular, and she had to return seriously, "Oh, no, Dennis, no! I think I'm going to be mating soon."

"Wonderful!" His teeth all showed when he grinned.

"I'm not sure—"

"What do you mean, you're not sure?" His face changed from bewildered to something Arshel didn't recognize. "If some guy has been toying with you, I'll—"

She cut him off, flushed with pleasure that he would defend her, and explained.

After thinking a moment, he said, "The apartment right below us is empty, and it has a spawning pond with a room for a mate on the other side of the pond room, just like a house. We can get an extra heater for the pond and some brine and make it just like home. I got some money from Mom and Dad the other day, and I was thinking of doing that for you."

Whether she mated or not, she'd ovulate, and the egg would have to be passed with or without the help of a male. She'd been dreading the experience in the cold, shallow pools in their apartment.

He knows how I feel. She leaned against her bhirhir, and an unexpected glow of pleasure sent a trickle of soothing pleasure-venom into her sack. His arm about her shoulders, warm with tough little hairs all over, no longer felt alien. He'd provide for her mating, just as any bhirhir would.

During the next lull in Dennis' studies, he moved them down to the larger apartment and fixed up the spawning pond. He even found a plastic model of a tropical shrub to set beside the arch that stood free in the middle of the room, the door to the room without walls.

They seasoned the pond with a little private ceremony, inviting each other into the water and pledging to guard the eggs spawned in it. She was tremendously gratified when he recited the pledge from memory, Vlen-style.

They shared dinner as a picnic by the pond. Happy beyond measure, she asked, "Dennis, you've provided for me so well, but what can I do for you? You don't molt or raise venom, and I can't raise your children. Why did you take a bhirhir instead of getting married?"

"Freedom. You said it yourself once. It doesn't make sense to expect to find a life partner in a mate. And it doesn't make sense to go through life without a life partner. Humans get lonely, too, you know. I was lonely until I met you, in spite of all the women I'd gone with."

"Are you going to bring a mate here, too?"

"Well, I'm going to try. But don't worry. She won't get in your way."

Arshel understood that he didn't want her help in mating, but it was bitter to be excluded so firmly. "You do everything for me, and there isn't anything I can do for you. It's so frustrating!"

"Do you really want to do something for me?" When she nodded, he went on, pulling out his textbook viewer and flipping it on. "The final exam in this course is just a few days off. Let's see if you can predict what will be on it!"

"I'm not a precog!"

"I know, but I think there's a way. This course has been using the same text for years, and from what I hear, the same final exam, too. You try looking at the text to see what has been used the most. Here," he said, twisting the light pen to write in green for contrast. "Highlight the passages that seem the most important to you. After the exam, I'll check back on the paragraphs you mark and see how you scored. Come on, Arshel, I want to see if you're learning as much at Mautri as I am at school."

The page blurred before her eyes, and when it cleared, some of the type seemed bolder than the rest in a blotchy pattern all down the page. It didn't take long to do the entire book that way, but when she'd finished, she was tired.

"Won't it be fun if you get them all right?"

She laughed. "It'd just be a freak of probabilities."

"Well, we'll try it again some other time, just to see."

But he was so happy for the rest of the evening she resolved to cooperate with his experiments. And she renewed her resolve to become the best archeovisualizer she possibly could.

But her studies came to a halt over the next few days. Khelin, it seemed, was avoiding her company, only assigning her reading. One morning, she had to admit that she had not even done the reading. She had not felt particularly well for days: her breasts were tender and swollen, her body aching, her appetite all but gone.

Khelin looked at her and did not ask for an excuse. "You're not sick, Arshel. You'll be ovulating soon. You'll feel better after that."

"I think that's what happened last night."

Again his gaze rested on her, a masculine caress. The aching malaise lifted. Abruptly, he pulled the dark blue hood of his robe up around his face and turned away. "I've been spending too much time with you. I didn't mean to cause you this much distress."

"It's not really unpleasant."

"I *know*." He circled his jaw, flexing his fangs, and went on with more composure. "I asked to have you assigned to a different teacher. But I was refused."

"Then they want us to. I have a place now. My bhirhir provided it. But it might be too warm for you."

"Then go there. Practice the controls I've taught you, and the egg will not grow. It will pass easily."

"I don't want that."

"Consider it a test of what you've learned here."

"I'm still not convinced people should impose such control on themselves."

They had argued afternoons away on this subject. It was one of the differences between Mautri and Vlen, and she had thought she'd made him understand where the Mautri were wrong in their asceticism.

He turned, moving away from her, and said in a noncommittal voice, "You're not bound to prove you've learned anything here. You've taken no vows."

"Khelin, perhaps it was a mistake for me ever to come here," she said, suddenly cold inside. "It's not right that I have without cost the training everyone else pays for with their lives. I'll go home to pass my egg, and I won't come back."

He turned toward her, shocked. "No!" He broke off, composing himself. When he came a little closer to where she was sitting in her desk chair, he was again the teacher. "The knowledge itself will exact its own price from you. There's no resentment against *you*. I'm sorry if I've given you that idea."

"Then why do you hate me so much that you won't even mate with me!" It was out before she could bite off the words. "I'm sorry! I know it isn't that, but what *is* wrong with you?"

"I, Arshel, I had a difficult night, myself. I failed to take the purple. I

69

haven't been making any progress since you came, and now I'm worried that what's been happening between us is interfering with your learning."

Now she remembered how tense he'd been over the last few days, carrying a visibly growing amount of venom. "You went three days without expression, didn't you? Isn't that an achievement by Mautri standards?"

"I've done that before. I was sure that this time—but then I couldn't express myself. Eventually, in the middle of the night, they had to call my bhirhir for me."

She shuddered, imagining what it must have been like for his bhirhir, for him. "Khelin, *why*? Why are you pursuing balbhirhir so frantically, as if you were afraid of your bhirhir? Is it because he's human?"

"Oh, Arshel, *no*. We had three years together before I came to Mautri, three of the happiest years either of us has ever known. Ley still wants it to be that way between us. He hasn't faced the fact that it never can be again, even if I left my training now."

"Why did he ever let you begin, then?"

"My untrained talent was coming between us. I'm not a telepath, Arshel, but I sense other people's motives clearly enough to manipulate their behavior. I'd begun to do that to Ley, even after swearing I wouldn't. Sometimes I wouldn't know I was doing it until afterward. I was desperate when I came here." He added ruefully, "When I was accepted, I raised such a flood of venom, I almost went into blue-voiding with everyone watching!"

"Then your training should have strengthened your bhirhir, if it removed a source of friction."

"I think it has, for Ley." He glanced at her in surprise, as if he'd never really thought of that before.

"Then you've achieved your original goal. Why do you persist in seeking balbhirhir?"

He paced a circle about her, at a distance, keeping his robe closed so that his body odor would not further their mating. But she responded to the smooth masculine power of his stride, to the way his hair stood up around his head, fluffing out the hood he was trying to keep over it. He had to be wanting her as much as she wanted him.

He leaned against the antique bookcase that filled one wall of her cubicle and asked with apparent irrelevancy, "Do you recall Skanqwin, from *Skanqwin and the Emperor of Crowns*?"

"Yes," she replied in a whisper, renewed tension washing through her. "He was my favorite character."

"One thing in that book is very real: what Skanqwin felt when his oath as a Persuader excluded him from even approaching any of the crowns. Do you remember that feeling, Arshel?"

"Yes," she whispered, her venom glands aching but unable now to produce the gush of venom her emotions demanded.

"What did it mean to you?"

Since she'd visited the Wassly Crown with Dennis, she had reread the book. Skanqwin had worked within the Crown network before he had been found to have the Persuader's talent. He had lived daily with the pure, free joy she had felt from the Wassly stones. He had spoken across the galaxy and beyond.

"He gave up everything that had meaning in his life in order to search for an even larger meaning."

"Very much as the price of the higher training of Mautri is the giving up of one's bhirhir?"

"Yes! Exactly!"

"And that's just a rule someone made heedless of the suffering it would cause?"

"Well, isn't it?"

"What would have happened if a Persuader entered any of the crowns and broadcast some plea of his own to the other Crown stations across the galaxy?"

The image of billions of people giving up their own opinions and life courses to follow one person's individual choices made her shudder. Suddenly, she felt a whole new interpretation of Skanqwin's feelings. "He had a power he *dared not* enter a crown with!"

"And through Mautri, we gain a power we *dare not* approach a bhirhir with. So as we become more accomplished, we can see more clearly that we must seek balbhirhir. You really haven't been adult long enough to have seen how, when two lives must be twined so tightly, one or the other must dominate. The Mautri teachings are dangerous to those who may come under domination or who may be tempted to dominate."

"Then it's not that you're rejecting your bhirhir; it's that you're trying to protect him. But Khelin, what would happen if your bhirhir were kren? You can't protect someone by turning him out to die."

"Another bhirhir would be found for him. It often happens that new bonds are formed between the bhirhirn of advancing priests. We have ways of smoothing the transition, but Ley has rejected them. He is human. It won't kill him, but he suffers as any bhirhir would."

"Is your advancement here worth that suffering? Would you be such a danger if you left Mautri now? I was told we could quit at any time."

"That is true," he said, gazing off into a rounded corner. "I asked you to pass your first egg unfertilized as a test of what you've learned here. I'd forgotten that I, too, am a student and that any meaningful test must involve both of us. Arshel, if you'll permit it, I'll attend you. I do have family here in the city. They can make a place for us."

"I'd rather—I mean, I told you my bhirhir has made a place for me that's warm and suitable for me. It's small, but there's a room for you."

He put aside his enveloping blue robe, and his scent overpowered her with a heady euphoria. Dressed in offworlder's all-purpose attire, blending with the students who lived on Wassly Hill, he accompanied her to the apartment.

CHAPTER SIX

Work came to a halt on the Vrashin tapes now that they couldn't trust even Zaviv's personal file to be inviolate. Almost daily, Zaviv reported on the Guild's progress, saying, "So they expect to have it solved today."

The news carried a feature story on Lantern Enterprises suing the Interface Guild for breach of the confidentiality clause in their contract. Reporters interviewed people whose livelihood depended on confidential computer records: business leaders, investors, inventors, and politicians.

Reporters came to the house, asking for the Ortenaus, even though the phones were on automatic, announcing that the professors were offplanet and only recorded messages could be taken. Zref had to repeat that he didn't know where his parents were or when they'd be back or what they were doing.

Some of the reporters seemed to know that he was lying, but if he held to his line of ignorance, there was nothing they could do but leave. Soon stories of the Ortenaus' disappearance began to come on to the news.

Meanwhile, his parents continued to work by hand, using the copy of the Vrashin tapes that was in the house. Notes piled up, too voluminous for the safe, and Zref as well as Cranston began to worry.

Right here in concrete form was the only copy of the best clues ever uncovered to the location of the City of a Million Legends, which they now knew to be the Capital of the First Lifewave, from which they had kept peace all across a galaxy. *If we can find that city, uncover their secrets, we can solve most of the problems of the Hundred Planets, except maybe computer theft.*

Zref and Sudeen doubled their patrol schedule and even armed Tess and Ley with security bug catchers. One night, after a long succession of nights when he couldn't sleep, Zref went out to the kitchen to find something to eat.

Zaviv was there, having reheated his dinner. Zref asked, "Any progress?"

"Nothing worth reporting, but everyone in the Guild is working on it."

"That why you missed dinner?" He found some milk in the refrigerator and some crackers to munch.

The Brenilak hadn't bothered to turn up the lights, and so there was only the red security nightlight.

"Yes, I was running some crosschecks. We must restore trust in our ability to hold information confidentially, or . . ."

Zref could imagine the scene in his parents' library repeated on a larger scale everywhere. News stories showed interstellar commerce grinding to a halt. With forced optimism, Zref said, "Yesterday, when Master Interface Roylanta called for all planetary governments to offer amnesty to anyone giving information on that pirate Interface, I laughed. But this morning, every last government had complied! Zaviv, people are really scared."

"I know. But we believe we can prevent it from happening again. Eventually, we will know how it was done."

The poised confidence of the Interface had Zref believing him. "You know, now that the Guild has brought all the governments of the Hundred Planets into accord, we may not need the Emperor's Crown to end war, poverty, disease, and crime. We've got the Guild!"

The Brenilak's friendly demeanor froze. "The Guild is not a political instrument. We exist to serve seekers of knowledge. That is all."

"I was just joking!" Zref protested. "I don't seriously believe that finding the City of a Million Legends would produce all those miracles." *Well, not instantly.*

"Too many people do believe it, thanks to the Lantern novels." The Brenilak sighed, returning to his dinner.

"If the people of the First Lifewave had all the answers," asked Zref, "where are they now?"

"That is a very good question. One that even an Interface can't answer."

"There aren't many of those. Zaviv, why did you become an Interface?"

"That's a personal question. I beg you not to take offense if I refuse to answer."

But Zref couldn't let it go. He had a sudden paralyzing need to know.

"Why does anyone become an Interface? What could make a person volunteer for such a life?"

"Oh, curiosity, I guess, is the uniting factor among us. People joke about that, but it's one of the primary traits of all intelligent lifeforms."

"Then why can't the kren ever become Interfaces?" asked Zref. That was one of the inequities festering at the heart of the Hundred Planets: the Guild being so powerful, holding the keys to all the information flowing in the veins of civilization, and unable—some said unwilling—to accept kren. Only kren. "Some of the most curious people I know are kren. And they aren't all telepaths."

"Some new work has been done and the Guild may soon accept a kren bhirhir pair for another experiment."

They'd be looking for two kren, nor a kren and a human, he thought, shocked at his own excitement. *Besides, with or without Tess we're going to Rhobank.* "The previous bhirhirn who tried it all died, didn't they?"

"Yes. But now the Guild has been researching the Mautri practices. Apparently, the reason the kren die is that the bhirhir bond functions through the unconscious, very much the way telepathy functions, though it's not the same thing. Kren and telepaths cannot endure the loss of that contact. But the Mautri balbhirhirn are able to transfer their unconscious bhirhir bond to an abstract idea rather than to a living person. Thus, through the Mautri disciplines, a kren may be able to allow the comnet to become his unconscious, as it is for the rest of us."

Zref thought of Khelin and Ley. Khelin was a blue priest already, one short step from becoming truly balbhirhir. Would they be attracted to the Guild's experiment? "It's a terrible loss of personal identity, isn't it?"

"In a way. The content of the unconscious is recorded in the personal file and becomes easily accessible to the Interface. It's the emotional overtones in that information that are lost."

"You don't seem unemotional to me."

"Thank you. We do still experience the seven primary emotions: fear, surprise, sadness, disgust, alarm, acceptance, and curiosity. It's the flowing mixtures of these that we lose. I never want to forget what they were like as so many of my colleagues have."

Gathering up his dishes, the Brenilak rose to leave, emphatically ending the conversation. The awkward moment was broken by Tessore coming in and asking brightly, "Are there any more crackers?" as she poured herself some milk.

"Yeah," Zref told her, "a whole boxful."

She came and sat where the Brenilak had been. "Zref, we hardly have a chance to talk anymore."

Zref immediately canceled plans to go back to bed and try to sleep.

She added, "I think we're going to translate that damn fragment soon, if our nerves hold out, that is."

"You seem calm enough."

"Can't sleep lately, and I think I'm imagining things."

"Like what?" Zref asked alertly. That was one of the key phrases Cranston had taught him to watch for.

"Promise you won't tell Sudeen I said this?"

"Well, he's on security here, too."

"This isn't a security matter. It's personal."

"In that case sure. I don't tell Sudeen everything."

"I keep catching him staring at me strangely. And I'm sure, three or four times now, he was raising venom just *looking* at me. I can't think of anything I've done to make him angry at me."

"Tess, maybe it wasn't anger. All kinds of different emotions raise venom, you know."

She crushed a cracker accidentally and scooped the crumbs together. "You didn't tell him about me, did you?"

It took courage, but he confessed. "And I asked him to immunize you."

"Oh, Zref! How could you do such a thing to your own bhirhir! You ought to be ashamed!"

Leaving her milk and the pile of crumbs, she whirled out of the kitchen without a backward glance. Stunned, Zref sat in the dim red light, trying to assimilate her reaction.

Over the next few days, as he paced restlessly about the house, he often encountered Sudeen talking to Tess, or just leaving as he approached, or apparently changing his mind about pausing to talk to her. Khelin, Ley's bhirhir came on his regular visits, and occasionally Zref saw Tessore talking to him. Once Ley was called to the Mautri temple late at night, which stirred up a furor among the external security detail. As soon as Ley returned, Zref saw Sudeen go into Ley's room and not come out for hours. A few days later, Zref interrupted a sharp exchange between Khelin and Sudeen, after which Sudeen refused to talk to anyone for the rest of the day.

Finally, he got Tess in a corner in the hallway and demanded, "What have you been up to?"

After several protestations of innocence, she admitted: "I had to apologize to Sudeen for your rudeness and assure him there was no question of you and I ever getting married. At least he knows now that I understand him, and all we have to do is get this romantic notion out of your head."

There was no way to argue with that, and so he kissed her. He was becoming very afraid that the only way he'd ever have her would be simply to take her. That she'd accept.

The next morning, Sudeen came in from the early check while Zref was bathing in the immersion pool. He sat down on the end of Zref's bed and watched through the door as Zref splashed about. "Zref, I've been thinking, about Tess. I still don't understand why you want to marry her, but I don't think I'd really mind having her around as family."

Unmindful of the water streaming off his body, Zref got up and walked right out into the bedroom to hug his bhirhir. "You really mean that? Sudeen—not just because I want it?"

"Mostly because you want it. I've noticed you haven't been sleeping. You've lost enough weight that if you were kren, it would force you into molt!"

Zref shook his head. "I'm not going to give you sleepless nights just—"

"She's not that bad," Sudeen interrupted. "She understands what bhirhir means. That's rare. If it's got to be someone, I'd rather her than anyone else."

This wasn't the way Zref wanted it, but it was progress.

"Zref, your mother is going to scream when she sees that water on her carpet!"

Laughing, Zref grabbed a towel. Now he had to persuade Tessore to take the immunization and come to Rhobank with them. With the Cranston salary, they had the money to cover it, and in a few years they might be on the first expedition to the City of a Million Legends. Or if it was found before then, they'd be among the first to study the finds.

But Tessore read Sudeen's motives right back at him with relentless precision. "He doesn't care how much he suffers as long as you're happy. The kren bhirhir of a human often feels he has nothing to give half so valuable as what he gets. I don't think Sudeen is an exception. You've even pledged your children to him, and he's just realized that's another sacrifice on your part! So, he'd try to give up, being surfather to our kids, and you know about how far he'd get trying to pit intellect against instinct and custom!"

Something in Zref recognized a hunger he hadn't known was there. He wanted to have lots of kids. But he also wanted to go offworld.

"There'll be time for all that later, Tess. But if I ever have a kid, I want you to be the mother. I think Sudeen and I can work it out."

She shook her head, exasperated. "In some ways, you are so naive, you remind me of Khelin!"

She stomped off, and he let her go, thinking that there would be time to finish the discussion. But she wasn't at dinner that evening, and that very night everything came to an end.

It was Zref's turn to do the predawn rounds, and so he hauled himself out of bed into the chill as Sudeen was coming in.

"Nothing to report," said the kren wearily. "About two hours ago I let Khelin in the front door. That made Yeol Tai jumpy, and he demanded I make an extra tour, which I did. Everyone's asleep."

Yeol Tai, the Cranston man in charge, knew that the fragments were nearly translated. He had argued against even letting Lantern know that the City of a Million Legends was described there, but he'd been over-ruled, and all security could think about now was that hundreds of Lantern employees knew a secret that certain thieves would spare no expense to get. *And if they'd put it into the comnet . . . Zref couldn't help remembering Sudeen's premonition that something was going to happen.*

On his way to make himself a hot drink, Zref noticed that the Interface's cottage door was open and the lights on. He stepped into the corridor leading out to the cottage, and called, "Excuse me, did I wake you?"

"Oh, no, not at all."

The light was so cheery that Zref moved into the room. "I've been think-ing about what you said the other night, about kren becoming Interfaces. I think I understand why becoming an Interface is such a personal decision. I wanted to apologize for ever asking."

"Apology accepted," said Zaviv, turning from where he'd been fiddling with the mechanical terminal.

Zref laughed. "Strange to see you working the terminal!"

"That pirate is active again."

"What's he doing?" Zref asked, fingering his scanner.

The Brenilak turned to another console. "I suspect I'm the target again, though I can't imagine what they want with me. All the translation work is on paper."

Zref knew that. Deliveries of stationery supplies had become an almost daily trial for security. "Yeol was asking whether you've been doing any data retrieval for the project lately. He was wondering if the pirates might trace the questions you've been asking."

"That could be what they're trying to do now," Zaviv answered. "And it might be good because I have a new theory about how to trace that pirate." He broke off, eyes wide, breath catching in his throat. Slowly, glassy eyed, he toppled to the floor with a thud.

Zref stared for a moment, and then something from Brenilak first aid clicked in his mind. He checked for a pulse and then licked the inside of his wrist and held it before the snout. He felt no stirring of air. Quickly, he cleared the air passages and began to pump the Brenilak's lungs. It took most of his weight to move the huge rib cage. He interrupted his rhythm only to reach up on the console and punch in an emergency call to Yeol. There were already sounds in the house as if people knew that something was happening. He put it all out of his mind and concentrated hoping that he'd remembered the Brenilak rhythm correctly. The man's snout was re-turning to a normal color.

The movement in the house got no nearer, and he was about to call out when it struck him that the air currents had changed, as if the cellar corridor access were open. But he was *sure* that it had been locked a few moments before.

Suddenly, there was a quiet hiss of a small sidearm and then the crack of a beamer hitting something. Someone screamed, an ululating shriek stained with terror.

There was a pounding of running feet on the other side of the kitchen. Zref jerked toward the door but checked his motion as the Brenilak stopped breathing. A lot of the Vrashin project's information was still locked in his private file. He might already be dead, but Zref couldn't know that.

Down the corridor, Sudeen yelled urgently for help, beamers cracked, and Zref heard his parents' voices raised in alarm. There was a mighty crash as the front door went down; feet pounded through the entry hall and past the kitchen door. Above the house, the heavy beat of a flier shook the roof—rescue! Everything was all right. *Thank you, Yeol Tai!*

Zref realized that he'd been pumping Zaviv's chest too fast, and so he slowed down. Orders were shouted up and down the halls of the house. There was a thunderous roar and crash that sounded as if the whole side of the building had been blown out and more shouts as the flier came lower.

Sudeen's voice cut through the noise in a panicked scream that warbled in and out: "*Zreffff!*"

Every muscle in Zref's body twitched in response, but he couldn't leave Zaviv.

The flier sound faded into the distance, and beamers sounded through the house in a volley. Then a sudden silence swept through, punctuated only by kren or human shouts of all clear. The entire action had taken no more than four minutes. At last a uniformed kren spotted Zref, and in seconds an ambulance crew was on the scene, taking charge of the Brenilak, asking Zref questions that he answered crisply while inside he turned numb.

As they were carrying Zaviv out—it took four kren to manage the stretcher with the huge offworlder on it—a tall, skinny human woman wearing the medallion of the Interface Guild watched them pass and then fastened her deep blue eyes on Zref. Her white hair framed her paper-white face, making her seem unreal. "You saved Zaviv's life. You're the Ortenau, Zref?"

"Yes."

"Good." She turned and followed the stretcher out.

He went out after her. The kitchen seemed normal, but out in the hall he had to pick his way over toppled furniture and the rubble of one of the interior walls felled by a beamer. In a distracted reflex effort to clean up the mess, he picked up a fine chain with a picture of the Wassly Crown holographed into a medallion—a cheap trinket. But he didn't ask himself who in the house might have owned such a thing; he merely pocketed it.

People were rushing everywhere, the sounds of their voices drowned out momentarily by the ambulance taking off. Lights streamed through the gaping front door. In a daze, he entered the room his parents had been sleeping in. Coughing on dust, he realized that the exterior wall had been torn away.

The only ones in the room that he recognized were Ley and Khelin, dressed in his blue priest's robes. There was a singing fear that he couldn't let himself feel yet.

"There he is," said someone, and Zref was quickly surrounded. Questions: Where were you? What were you doing? Where's the Brenilak now?

Finally he demanded, "Where's Sudeen? Where are my parents? Ley, where's Tess?"

One of the uniformed humans said, "Their library and office was ransacked, and the thieves seem to have come here to attempt to kidnap the professors. But they resisted, and both of them were killed when the wall fell. They took three of the raiders with them."

Zref lost track of the voice. *He means Mom and Dad, both. Dead.* "Sudeen, I have to tell Sudeen. He'll raise venom. I have to go—"

"Zref, take it easy now," said Ley, close to him on one side and, Zref realized, preventing him from approaching the heap of rubble that filled half the room. Khelin came up on his other side, one hand tightening on Zref's elbow as Ley said to the uniformed humans, "You'd better let us do this."

The tone of it all suddenly struck through the black shock like lightning. "Sudeen! *Ley!*"

Zref bolted down that long rubble strewn hall to the closed door of his own room. A guard stood waiting for the police Interface to record the scene before they moved anything.

He drew up before that solidly closed door, the image searing an indelible scar into his brain. Khelin and Ley pounded to a halt beside him, but he hardly heard them argue with the guard.

The hysteria didn't break until he saw the bodies. Sudeen sprawled with his arms outstretched in front of the twisted remains of Tessore Kobre as if he'd been protecting her from the blaster fire with the thin protoplasm of his own body. Human and kren blood and flesh mingled everywhere on his mother's carpet.

Realization came in wave after wave of acid tipped needles that swept through every cell of his body, until he was again dead inside.

The last words he remembered hearing were Khelin's soft priest's voice: "They were bhirhirn. If you want him to survive this, let me take him home to his family. MorZdersh'n isn't far from here."

CHAPTER SEVEN

When Arshel and Khelin arrived at the apartment, Dennis had hot food ready. "Will your bhirhir be along for supper? I'll set a place."

"Not today."

Dennis peered sidewise at Khelin, apparently noting the blue medallion he wore, and nodded. Then Arshel noticed that the extra place was set already. Dennis said, "Trice is here, Arshel. I don't think you two have ever met."

His new mate. "No, we haven't. Is she staying?"

"She'll be sleeping in my room. There's plenty of space in this apartment."

With somewhat mixed emotions, Arshel went into the bedroom to meet Trice. *Why did he choose to begin a mating when I'm beginning my first, and without telling me?*

Behind her, Khelin was saying softly to Dennis, "I rarely now require the presence of my bhirhir. I hope you and Trice won't be uncomfortable if I don't bring him here at all?"

I wonder, thought Arshel, *if that's the test he's chosen.*

Cheerfully, Dennis said, "It may take some getting used to, but we'll manage. Trice is a native of Firestrip, too."

They went on talking as she turned into the bedroom and found the girl unpacking a box of cassettes and stowing them on the corner shelf beside Dennis' desk. She was slender, with flat black hair streaming straight down her back, longer hair than Arshel had ever seen. When she turned, Arshel was startled by her rounded face, and strange eyes until she realized that the girl must be of a human race she'd never met before.

"I came to welcome you, Trice. Would you like to come and meet my new mate?"

Trice rose, unfolding a long, straight-lined body with scarcely any bust. "Dennis didn't mention that."

"He didn't know until just now, and neither did I."

"It's been a day for surprises," she replied in an oddly hostile tone that Arshel didn't like.

Dinner was awkward. Arshel had little appetite, and the two humans guarded their curiosity about Khelin to avoid offending in the absence of his bhirhir. At last, Trice suggested that they look at the day's news, and so Dennis switched on the screen and keyed for the subjects of interest to them.

They got no further than the lead story. Lantern Tours, the largest conglomerate of service industries, was suing the Interface Guild for breach of guarantees, specifically the confidentiality of their private files. It had something to do with the Vrashin tapes.

"What!" exclaimed Dennis, charging toward the screen and then stopping as the announcer read the story under scenes of Vrashin Island, the Guild Headquarters building on Hengrave, the Lantern Industries headquarters, which was the entire largest moon of Raynat, and the quadrant capital where the litigation had been filed.

They reran the story, listening more intently. Following it were reports of sagging economic indicators, panic in industrial research, and sudden failure of several interstellar treaty negotiations, all of which painted a grim picture. It would all affect the funding of the university communities, too.

Over the next few days, the pirate Interface was dubbed a Wild Interface, and the main topic everywhere was how they could possibly trace him. Daily, the Guild issued reports that they expected a solution within the day.

As each day passed, Arshel's egg grew under the stimulus of Khelin's presence. They spent hours in her spawning pond, his caresses opening whole new worlds of sensation to her. As the egg stretched the pleated skin of her abdomen, her venom sack became dry and itched ferociously. Minor miseries mounted; the only relief came in the water with Khelin, when an upwelling sense of impending triumph wiped all else aside.

As the moment of mating approached, there were peaks of such vibrant tension that she would shrink from Khelin, feeling that he was about to force her egg from her before it was ready. She would look to her bhirhir at such moments, seeking protection, but Dennis' lack of venom set off a shriek of alarm, knotting her abdomen and pulling her dry fangs down into strike position. At such moments, she'd be certain that she was about to pass her egg, but she couldn't stand to be touched.

At Khelin's suggestion, Dennis anointed Arshel's skin with her own venom. At first, she thought it ridiculous, but then her nerves settled down enough for her to trust Khelin again. He was, after all, a blue priest and very gentle; not at all what her parents had led her to expect from a male.

As the time grew near, she lay on her warm sand bed, lulled into a fog by the rhythmic lapping of the pond and the quiet conversation of her mate and her bhirhir. Dennis had not stolen a moment from her for his mate. *If he can get me through this, I'll never let him down, never.*

She swam up out of the fog, hearing Khelin and Dennis talking softly. "The difference between the purple and the white is the ability to go through molt itself without the aid of bhirhir."

"That must be dangerous."

"I didn't mean without *any* aid; but to accept the aid of a stranger and to be content to let him remain a stranger afterward, or offer such aid when necessary and make no further demands—to live easily among those not immune to one's venom—that is the white community."

That sounds against kren nature. How do they do it?"

"The Mautri practices dispel the fear of dying. Then one finds very little that can raise venom. One learns to walk the world with an empty sack and not feel helpless."

"Hmmmm, but you said Arshel's trouble was that when she went dry, she began to panic from helplessness."

"She has hardly taken the red. The power raised in mating is the very power which runs the universe; it's terrifying to surrender oneself to it. This is her very first egg. It's not even my first time without my bhirhir, though it is the most intense mating I've ever had. Sometimes I almost don't recognize myself in the urges that come over me."

"Is that why you went to your bhirhir last night?"

"No. He worries about me, Dennis. He's human, as you are, but he worries as any kren would."

"I understand."

He does. She wanted to tell Dennis that she appreciated him, but she gasped reflexively as hot pain pierced her body. "Arshel?" asked Dennis.

But it was Khelin's hands that came to her abdomen, gentle and trembling. "Dennis, take her down. Now."

Leaning on her bhirhir, she made it down the soft slope into the water. Immediate relief spread through her. Khelin turned the surge pump on, giving the water the feel of the sea.

Dennis called out the ritual of welcome to Khelin MorZdersh'n from du'Arshel Lakely. Her name sounded so strange, she only half heard Dennis repeating his pledge to guard the eggs spawned here. This was not the spawning pond where she had emerged. None of her other children would emerge here. In frantic regret that she had not gone to MorZdersh'n, which at least had some tradition, she struggled to speak.

But the water rocked as Khelin leaped in beside her. Seized again with pain, she saw her mate push Dennis roughly aside. Khelin's arms came around her from behind, adding his strength to her muscles that sought to expel the egg.

"You be gentle with her, Khelin, or I'll break you in two."

Khelin breathed softly into her ear. "Ventilate well. With the next contraction, we go down until it's over."

His hands spread over her abdomen his webbing caressing her ovipositor. Behind, his genitals hardened as they often had when he caressed away her miseries, but now the elongated member entered the channel above the egg to bathe it in sperm.

She relaxed into his grasp, and together their ragged breathing deepened to true ventilation. Hearing this, Dennis backed away to give them room for the coming struggle.

And then, with firm, sure movements, Khelin took her down, timing perfectly with the contraction. His stroking opened her ovipositor sphincters just before the egg reached them. His strength squeezed the egg from her, leaving relaxation behind. The struggle lasted only moments, and the egg slid smoothly to the bottom of the pond.

He turned her to face him, suddenly every touch as delicate as if she were made of glass. She'd have bruises where he had held her.

Not even breathless, they burst free of the water, glorying in their accomplishment.

"It was a huge egg, Arshel! I was so afraid you were going to fight it. But you were magnificent! No blue priest could have done better."

Arshel felt suppressed venom flowing in a warm, joyful trickle into her sack. "How could anyone fight you?"

He scooped her up and carried her out of the pond.

She slept an entire day away, with Khelin and Dennis taking turns sitting with her and gazing into the pond at the egg. The next day, she felt fine again and could tolerate the cooler portion of the house, and so she had them turn the heat down to readjust to the outside world. With that, Khelin retreated to his room for an entire day.

Just after midnight, she came out into the main room of the apartment. Trice and Dennis had taken up the yelling part of their mating ritual the previous night and were at it again now. However many times he insisted that he didn't need her at those moments, she still had to squelch a desire to rush to his side. She would never understand human biology.

"I see you've recovered nicely."

It was Khelin's voice behind her. "Yes, I feel fine. But I have a question. I don't know why it didn't occur to me before."

"I can't be your teacher anymore, Arshel."

"No, it's about us. Is it possible—I mean, the egg—you're from fresh water, and I—"

"Arshel, you know the survival rate for such crosses isn't high. And this is your first, Arshel. It's a large egg, but even so, you shouldn't really expect emergence."

"I know," she answered. "But it just now occurred to me that it *might*. My girls are pledged to Dennis, but—"

"In that case, you can reach me at MorZdersh'n. I've come to a decision, Arshel. I'm leaving the temple. I'm not going to attempt the purple again. You were right. I've learned enough now to protect Ley. This experience with you has taught me that I've failed to take the purple because I don't *want* to break my life from Ley's. And so I dare not go on at Mautri."

"I, I'm sorry." *What have I done?*

"No, feel joy for me. You've taught me to see clearly again, even as I've taught you to begin."

And then it hit her: *You can reach me at MorZdersh'n.* "You're ending? So soon?"

"If I stay any longer, I'll have you ovulating again. It was beautiful, Arshel, but you've had enough for a first time, and I could gladly spend the rest of the winter with you. But that would be hiding from the task of rebuilding my life. I'm going now to tell Ley."

Through the empty shock of disappointment after he left, she became aware of the shouting again. She curled her legs under her in the chair and leaned her head back, supposing that she would nap between shouting rituals. But all she could think about was Khelin. Without intention, she had ripped him from his devotion and lost him as her teacher and mate.

In any relationship, one or the other must dominate. It was a Mautri idea that still felt wrong to her. The ideal was equality. *Is it possible to dominate from a passive role?*

She sat there until just before dawn, dozing fitfully after the shouting died down. When Trice came out into the kitchen, dressed for school, she switched on the news, as seemed to be her custom at every meal.

Shuffling pots on the stove, Trice called to her, "Is Khelin coming to eat this time?"

Dennis came out of the bedroom then, crisply dressed, his jacket flung carelessly over his shoulder, his hands full of study cassettes. She told them both, "Khelin moved out last night. He had other things to do."

Dennis dropped his things onto the couch and came to her. "That's too bad, Shel. Do you want me to extend my emergency leave and help you watch the egg?"

"No," she said, unaware that she'd come to a decision during the night. "I won't go back to Mautri until it's hatched. I'll be here. I can tend it if you'll help evenings."

He smiled, showing all his white teeth. "Sure, if that's what you want."

He went to the kitchen, setting the table while Trice cooked and muttered about primitive living conditions. But at one point, Arshel heard her say quietly to Dennis, "I'm glad that creep is gone!"

Just then the volume on the news channel increased as the scanner picked up something on their interest list. The announcer, a reddish-skinned Theaten with a sharp Sirwini accent, said, "And now we have a live remote from Firestrip on Camiat."

Over background noise of shouting and the roar of heavy construction equipment, she continued, "The home of the famous Professors Ortenau was raided this morning, and the professors are feared dead."

By the time Arshel got to where she could see, there was a steady shot of a bedroom where one outside wall had collapsed. The focus was on a bloody human hand protruding from the wreckage, clutching a human ankle just above a bare foot.

"It is assumed that the Ortenaus fought their kidnappers until this wall collapsed upon them all."

"They were there all the time!" shouted Dennis, and explained that he'd been told they were offplanet,

There was a scene of a corridor littered with bodies. Three figures passed before the camera, two supporting the third between them. Her eyes went to the figure farthest from the camera: Khelin! He was wearing his dark blue robe as he had when he left a few hours before.

She recognized Ley from a picture she'd seen, and the human between them was identified by the announcer as a Cranston guard from MorZdersh'n whose bhirhir had been killed in the action. She thought he looked familiar. She couldn't take her eyes off him, but she couldn't place him, either. Yet she felt compelled to memorize every line of his body.

With a promise to come back to the scene as soon as the rubble had been cleared, the announcer switched them to the Interface Guild Headquarters on Hengrave. The story unfolded gradually. The Cranston security locks on the underground door had been opened by the Wild Interface, who had attacked the resident Interface through his own private file. The resident Interface had survived only through the action of one of the MorZdersh'n Cranston guards. If the resident Interface recovered, he'd put the Wild Interface out of business forever. The Guild promised to be back in full operation hours after that.

"This isn't going to stop here," said Trice in a low, threatening tone that drew venom in Arshel. "This isn't just industrial espionage. It's *war*, with archeology caught in the middle. Drop out of archeology, Dennis. There's no percentage in getting killed."

"What about my parents! They're sitting on one of the biggest grants ever and expecting Arshel and me to come and help them as soon as I get my degree."

"And what am I supposed to do when you actually find something? Act like a brave widow at the funeral?"

"Now don't get hysterical again. As I said last night, every profession has a certain risk—"

"Not like this! The Interface Guild has broken the Guarantees. Some-body's willing to kill for First Lifewave secrets, and *you* discovered one such secret!"

"And Arshel and I are going to discover a lot more!"

"Arshel this and Arshel that! Ever since I moved in here, that's all I've heard out of you. Have you gone so native that you don't even care how I feel?"

"Trice, archeology is my career. My family is already at the top of the field. Imagine where we'll be twenty years from now! With Arshel's talent, I—"

"Arshel's kren! But you said you loved me. You said you want to marry me. And, and—" Clear venom—no, *tears*—spilled from her eyes. Arshel had never seen that up close before, and it held her transfixed.

"Trice, I do love you."

"And I love you! But you're already married to your career and to your kren! There's no room in your life for me! So I'm leaving! I'll send for my things."

Grabbing her bag from the table near the door, she was gone before she had touched a bite of breakfast.

Dennis stopped half out of his chair, his arm reaching toward Trice. Then, slowly, he folded himself back into the chair and put his face into his hands, his elbows on the table.

Arshel wasn't sure what to do. "Dennis, were you seriously considering life-mating with her?"

He looked up, his expression shifting with a fluidity no kren could match. "Oh, Shel, I just told her that… it's only what girls expect. But—" He chewed a lip. "What are we going to do about the rent?"

"The rent?"

"Trice was going to be paying nearly half of it."

Dizzy with the change of subject, she looked at him as if for the first time and saw a stranger.

He reached across to cover her shaking hands with his own. "Don't worry, Shel. They'll let us keep the place until your egg is hatched, and meanwhile I can ask my parents for some help. Things will work out somehow."

Then she understood. Her bhirhir had been willing to take a mate to provide her with a spawning pond. He was more concerned with her egg, as a proper surfather should be, than with any other consideration.

The day of the expected hatching, Dennis arranged to stay home with her. The egg was still alive, and that was miracle enough for her to call the MorZdersh'n number Khelin had sent her. As the day wore toward evening, the first real blizzard of the season howled outside. Khelin soon arrived, still wearing his dark blue robe.

With him was his human bhirhir, Ley. After introductions were made, Arshel said, "I saw you on the news the night of the Ortenau tragedy."

He glanced at his bhirhir before answering. "It was a terrible shock. We still haven't gotten over it."

There was an awkward silence until Khelin said, "May I see the egg?"

"Oh, yes."

She turned and led the way to the door of the pond room. When she paused, Dennis took over smoothly, inviting Ley and Khelin to enter.

They had only left the room to answer the door, yet already there had been a sudden change. A visible crack traced itself across the upper surface.

Looking down through the surging water, Ley said, "Is the pond rigged with underlighting?"

"No," answered Dennis. "We have this, though." He turned on the lamp they'd recently lowered into the water. "It's supposed to be about like sunlight at noon."

It was bright enough now to see the egg rolling about as its crack widened. Khelin said softly, "It's vigorous."

"We don't really expect it to emerge," said Dennis.

Her eyes were drawn to her bhirhir. *If it's a girl and does emerge, will he be as happy as he said he'd be?*

She glanced to where Khelin and Ley were gathered by the lip of the pond. The human was clutching his bhirhir's arm and smiling. "It's got a good chance, Khelin." *He wants it.*

They waited then as the hatchling struggled, rested, and struggled again. The crack finally etched its way all around the egg, and a piece of it fell out.

The tightly folded body began its struggle to emerge from the water before it had to breathe air or die. Arshel watched it move, lighting free of the confining shell, resting and then groping up the sanded slope of the pond.

Tiny hands with thick, visible webbing between the fingers unfolded. Then the legs and a wobbly little head completed the form of a living kren—a person.

The adults around the pond were all barely breathing now. A kren had to fight for its right to survive. The humans understood that.

Now that they could see where the hatchling was headed, Arshel moved to the point at the edge of the water where she could meet it. Khelin and Ley squeezed aside to let her kneel in the sand to wait. The hatchling was at the steepest part of the slope now, its webbed hands spread and scooping at the sand, creating a cloud in the water.

As its time ran out, it no longer stopped to rest but struggled ferociously. Arshel was so proud; she felt venom seeping into her sack. Dennis had remained where he was, but Khelin knelt beside her. Ley was on his other side, straining forward as if struggling to emerge, himself.

The hatchling reached the shallows, part of its rump now poking into the air, but its head was still shoving along on the sand under water. Its efforts were becoming weaker, but still it moved. Bit by bit, closer to the very edge of the pond, it moved until one last scoop of the tiny hands shoved the head out of the waves.

On contact with air, the hatchling lapsed into stillness, and Arshel thought that it would die, for the next wave covered its head again. Two more waves, and she had given up, when the tiny arms scooped and scooped again, shoving the head up above the reach of the waves, where it again collapsed.

"A future lives!" she cried, and swept the infant to her. It came to life in her arms, emitting a small cry as its air passage cleared. She could see now that it was a male, and a joy lit in her as she turned to Khelin, handing the infant over to him. "Your future lives!"

With awed reverence, he took the infant to himself and then glanced back at her. "Is it custom among your people to nurse your male children?"

It hadn't occurred to her that his family might not be able to provide nursing. "No, but if you have no one . . ."

"MorZdersh'n has several women who will be delighted to have him," said Khelin. Gazing at the child in his arms, quiet now from exhaustion, he seemed happier than she had ever known him to be.

Dennis came and put his arm about her shoulders then, saying nothing, but she had the impression that he would not have been as pleased as Khelin was now.

Khelin turned to Ley and offered the infant. "Our future and many futures."

Awkwardly, the human took the infant kren to his breast. The expression on his face was one she had so hoped to see on Dennis'. She had been sure that a human could show such feeling.

Then Ley met her eyes, grinning, and asked, "Well, what's his name?"

She looked to Khelin. "Isn't it your custom to name your child?"

"In MorZdersh'n, the child will be named if he survives the year, but at least one name should be of your selection. You have a future here, too."

In the time she'd spent in Firestrip, Arshel had become accustomed to oddities like this. She thought quickly and said, "Then call him Skanqwin, and perhaps like the character he'll make many friends and find fulfillment."

Khelin and Dennis looked at her strangely, but Ley said, "I think that's a splendid idea. And I'll name him Adsim after the kren who first discovered the Rayah Lake, and perhaps he'll become an explorer."

Khelin said, "Skanqwin Adsim MorZdersh'n. Lovely."

Ley stroked the infant's hide and said, "I'd better get him wrapped up for the trip home. It's warm in the tunnels but not *that* warm! Can you give me a hand, Dennis? I've never done this before!"

Khelin followed Ley's movements, pleasure written in every line of his face and body. Then he turned to her. "I didn't expect an emergence today, but I brought this along just in case." He took out an elaborately carved gold bracelet with an inlaid glyph made from the letters of MorZdersh'n and slid it onto her wrist.

"This is yours for having given MorZdersh'n a child. Should you ever meet, he will recognize it and know you for his mother. Should you ever be in need, any branch of the family will give you shelter. I hope you'll wear it always, Arshel. You're one of the most beautiful things that's ever happened to me."

Deeply moved, she accepted the bizarre custom.

Returning to Mautri without Khelin was difficult, but soon the work claimed her interest and the succession of teachers became a blur.

The winter deepened. News stories of the Guild's imminent triumph over the Wild Interface punctuated by accounts of the interstellar trade paralysis came almost daily. Student life droned on, though, and the Firestrip natives were talking of spring when Arshel first realized the magnitude of what was happening.

She was at the temple, studying some ancient documents on her own comlink screen. Without transition, she found herself looking at a male human face. The high forehead was accentuated by a silly headdress of jingling gold links and striped folds of cloth. A fringe of blond beard emphasized the large nose. The neck and shoulders were likewise draped in a collar of wrought gold links. The face spoke:

"I am the reincarnation of Ossminid, Emperor of Crowns, Persuader Exemplar of the First Lifewave. I have made an Interface who answers only to me, and thus all the secrets of this modern civilization are mine. I have taken possession of what is rightfully mine—the secrets of the First Lifewave—as my own Interface has finished the Ortenau translation of the Vrashin texts. Soon I will repossess the mazeheart object described therein, that which made me a Persuader. I will rebuild the Persuaders Maze and the Crown network. There will be peace and plenty throughout the Second Lifewave. The Hundred Planets will become the Thousand and occupy this entire galaxy! Our former glory will rise again!

"Join me, and partake of my abundance. Oppose me, and learn what millions have found, that I cannot be stopped!"

The screen faded back to the former display as if it had been an apparition. But Arshel learned later that every screen on the comnet had carried that unforgettable chiseled face and its coldly passionate speech.

The Guild announced that it had been a fabricated simulation done by the Wild Interface: Ossminid's Interface.

Chaos reigned for days. School was suspended. But gradually things returned to normal. Shortly after that, the Guild announced that they had raided Ossminid's headquarters and destroyed the Wild Interface.

Business returned to normal throughout the Hundred Planets.

With a sigh of relief, Arshel sank back into a total absorption in her studies. She completed her bead string, polishing each carefully chosen bit of mineral herself, weaving her own strings until her teachers were satisfied. And she learned to work with the bead string until she could summon visions at will.

She learned to read the faintest impression left on an object. She learned to read ancient impressions left millennia ago. And she sharpened her ability to locate things.

During those years, both she and Dennis took many mates, but always without issue. She clung to her bracelet more with each failure. She wanted children, but it would be impossible to go to Pallacin if they had young children now.

Just after Khelin left, she took the orange, and the next year she progressed to the yellow. The big step of commitment came when she took the green by gaining a measure of control over her venom glands. She became much harder to startle into a strike; remembering how she had almost killed Dennis, she thought that that was a good thing. But it was only a side effect of the training of her visualization talent.

All during this time, Dennis took a close interest in her progress, testing her in the peculiar manner he'd devised. She'd failed the first test, having chosen passages from his text that did not pertain to the questions on the final exam.

But the following year, when he tested her again, she got most of the passages right. By the third year, she was scoring 100 percent. After that, she quickly became bored with his game. Close to Dennis' graduation, he asked, "Just this once more, Arshel, to see if you've really got it."

She argued, but in the end she marked out the passages she thought were most important. There weren't many, compared to the whole book.

Dennis smiled broadly. "Next year, there will be lots of money, and the Lakely reputation, riding on your advice. I've got to build up my confidence in your ability. Here, do this book, too."

So she did, and she thought no more about it. She had more vital issues on her mind, for now she had been offered the final green grade and the chance to take the blue.

"You've the ability, Arshel, if you've the will."

It frightened her. She discussed it with Dennis, but he was so distracted studying, he responded only when she explained that if she took the dark green, she'd be put to work teaching in the Outer School at a small stipend.

"If they'll pay you for it, why not? I've been tutoring for a year to pay the rent. It's fun, and you learn a lot. We could use the money."

She accepted the dark green robe and a new set of responsibilities. Her new venom control was convenient because she saw even less of Dennis now.

Then came the wild flurry of graduation. She had to hand over her responsibilities at Mautri in order to attend the festivities with him. She enjoyed seeing him happy with his friends, seeing him triumphant at last. He had taken the number one spot in the graduating class. She knew what that would mean when he saw his father again.

They were clearing out of the apartment, heaping trash in the middle of the floor and packing cases for storage, when, dusting off the luggage his parents had bought her when she was sent to Firestrip, she knocked some things off Dennis' desk. While picking them up, she accidentally turned on the textbook viewer, and it flipped to a workbook where long sections were blank.

Flipping pages, she found that only some of the questions had been worked or filled in. She fumbled around and found the text that went with the workbook and then keyed up her own markings. Sitting in the middle of the floor, she matched the marked sections to the workbook sections that were filled. Dennis' marginal notes were thick beside the sections she had marked and almost nonexistent elsewhere. She took her time, checking and crosschecking until she was sure.

He studied only what I indicated would be on the exam.

"Arshel!" called Dennis from the living room, where he was bagging trash. "Do we want the brown dishes?" He came toward the bedroom door. "I said, do we—" When he saw her, he stopped. "What are you doing?"

"Dennis, you cheated on your finals!"

"I did not. Arshel, what have you got there!"

"You only studied what I said would be on the exam."

He sat down beside her. "Oh, Shel, I thought I explained that back when I asked you to mark them for me one last time. I have to be able to stake the Lakely reputation on your ability. I had to test my confidence in you. We're a team, Arshel. *We* passed those exams. Didn't I say that to anyone who'd listen all during the festivities?"

Her eyes rested heavily on the workbook page before her. "It's not the same. A degree means you know everything in these books, not just the items on an exam."

"Well, I do. At least I know where to find what I need."

What am I going to do? Turn him in to the dean?

She thought that she might even be able to do that. He was a stranger again. But before long he was helping her pack her clothes and babbling out his plans for Pallacin and beyond, unaware of her misgivings. And soon she was caught up in his vision anew.

All during the long trip outplanet, she remembered Khelin's idea that with a bhirhir one will become dominant. *He used my talent, but he's my bhirhir. It's as much his as mine.*

CHAPTER EIGHT

Zref knew that it was spring. The shutters were open, and the bright snow still choked the city up to the second story in places

The winter had been brief and fierce, much like his grief. MorZdersh'n was the same yet not the same without Sudeen.

Khelin and Ley had moved upstairs into a deserted wing of the old building, and they had a kren infant fostering at the heart of the household, as he and Sudeen might have had. The infant had come from some difficult experience of Khelin's that somehow had led to his abandoning the temple and returning to Ley.

Zref and Khelin had become very close over the winter. Ley had even allowed Zref to help with their child's care, trying to convince him that it represented Sudeen's futures because Khelin was a relative.

This morning Zref was at an upper hall window that had just melted clear of snow. He had picked up the Wassly Crown trinket again that morning, fingering it abstractedly and obsessively, remembering that the first thing he'd become aware of after leaving the house was the abominable ache in his fingers as he woke, still clutching it. It had not belonged to anyone living in the house. It must have been brought in by one of the raiders. But millions of the things were sold to tourists every season. It wasn't evidence; it wasn't a clue they could trace. He simply couldn't let go of it.

Down on the snowfield, runabouts were scooting along over the ice crust, carrying people in holiday caps, who were singing and spraying snow on one another. He and Sudeen had always loved Moontide Festival.

"I thought I'd find you here."

Zref turned to find Khelin wearing the short native tunic and tall boots instead of the long blue robe he had worn all winter. Pinned to one shoulder was a copper disc medallion covered with blue enamel, the only badge of his achievement at Mautri that he would take into life with him.

"I was just thinking," said Zref, "that it's past time to start putting my life together again." He listened with astonishment to his own words.

"Were you thinking of picking up on that scholarship you won and completing your education?"

"No. I'm not going back to Communications. I can't, without Sudeen. What are you two doing?"

Khelin sat on the stair beside Zref and spread his webbed hands over his knobby knees. He had thick, ropy muscles in his arms and calves that Zref knew made him an attractive male, and he had the long-boned fingers that kren women called sexy. "It appears my training is in high demand offworld. And with Ley's knowledge of languages and cultures, Lantern is willing to pay us nicely to become crisis consultants for stranded travelers."

"I think I'd be bored stiff with something like that. It gets repetitive and limiting. And I don't think I'd want to get involved with Lantern again. They're still dedicated to rediscovering all sorts of First Lifewave technology. I'm not sure anymore that's what we should be doing."

"I see. Well, I came looking for you because you have a visitor."

"I don't think I'm up to seeing anyone yet."

"I thought you might be interested in talking to Zaviv."

"Zaviv!" Suddenly eager, Zref got to his feet, babbling questions while Khelin put him off with, "Come ask him yourself."

When they arrived at the room where the family received outside visitors, Ley was sitting with the Interface across a small table on which cool drinks stood. The tall windows were still blocked with snow; the only illumination in the room came from the underwater lights of the fountain.

The Brenilak's face was a study in colored shadows; it was hopeless for a human to try to read any expression there. As they entered through the archway, the red-brown snout swept toward them. "Zref Ortenau MorZdersh'n."

"I've dropped the Ortenau," answered Zref "It's gotten too much publicity." *Besides, the family is dead.*

"It has been a difficult time for all of us. But I am personally glad you are well."

Zref knew that that was all the acknowledgment he'd get from the Brenilak for saving his life. The Guild had sent him a handsome reward that effectively ended his financial problems for several years, but somehow he'd have valued a simple "Thank you" more.

The Interface glanced at Khelin and Ley. "If Zref is agreeable, you may stay to hear what news I have brought."

Zref momentarily laid an arm around each of his brothers. "I wouldn't have it any other way."

They gathered about the small table. "I presume you've been following the news this winter," the Interface started. "But much detail of what has been happening has never reached the media. The Guild is planning to release most of the story today. I'll gladly give you a little more background, but I must have your solemn pledge not to reveal any of it that you do not see in the news."

Zref looked at Khelin and Ley and then said to the Brenilak, "You know we all have the security clearance. We won't talk, especially not to the media."

The other two agreed, and Zaviv said, "You may not be aware of it, but we feel about the Guild just about the way kren feel about family. And so we reacted as a unit and went to war against the Wild Interface and 'Ossminid.'

"After 'Ossminid''s announcement, we traced the Wild Interface to a planetoid in the Arcalnida Cluster and sent armed mercenaries along with a large detail of the Guild's best. It was a long and bloody battle. We lost fourteen Interfaces. The Wild Interface is dead.

"Later today, with suitable ceremony it will be announced that the Guild has restored full protective confidentiality to our private and locked files, and all malfunctions and traces of tampering with the comnet have been eliminated."

"That's wonderful!" said Ley.

"Congratulations," said Khelin. "Was it your contribution that did it?"

Zref remembered that the Guild had cited him, in the award certificate they sent him, for his quick wit and wisdom in realizing that the Wild Interface was attacking Zaviv because Zaviv held the clue to finding him. He had thought no such thing at the time, but there was no arguing with fame.

"Khelin," said the Brenilak heavily, "because of my contribution, some of my closest associates are dead."

"You were at the battle?" Zref asked.

"Yes. The laboratory they'd set up to turn out their own Interfaces was well defended. When the battle was over, there was little left of that planetoid but dust."

"You mean," said Khelin, "no bodies were recovered and identified?"

"No bodies," the Brenilak assured him, but Zref noted an omission. Before he could ask point blank whether anyone could have gotten away, the Interface continued. "But during the battle, six of us combined to strip their memory core. We know how they made their Interface."

Diverted, Zref asked, "How?"

"Their leader—who took the code name 'Ossminid' from that Persuader Fragment your parents once translated—found some bit of First Lifewave technology that gave his scientists the clue to develop an entirely different and much more dangerous system than the one we use. They tried it on hundreds of their own people, but only one survived to function in our comnet."

Zref interrupted. *"First Lifewave technology?* It was the discovery of something from the First Lifewave that almost destroyed us?"

"Yes. The Guild has decided this little bit of First Lifewave technology will remain one of our secrets."

"Will the Guild withhold any other First Lifewave discoveries?" asked Zref, worried and trembling with shock. He and Sudeen had planned so eagerly to become heroes of the Hundred Planets, using First Lifewave knowledge to solve current problems. *We were wrong. It was this kind of thing that destroyed the First Lifewave.*

"This, too, is very confidential," said the Brenilak, looking at the three of them. "The Guild is adopting a new policy. We will honor all existing contracts, but we will accept no new contracts on First Lifewave research."

"You mean you're against progress?" asked Ley incredulously.

"Not really. Most of the archeological work of an Interface can be done by a number of people hand programming the information into the data banks and then writing their own correlation programs. It will merely take them longer. If this information is brought to light in small bits over a long time, our civilization will be better able to adapt to it."

"It's a dangerous path," said Khelin, agreeing. "I wonder if the alternative is more dangerous."

"I think it might be," said Zref, his opinion beginning to crystallize. "I'm with the Guild."

"I'm glad to hear that," said Zaviv, "because I've brought you a proposition. The Guild is in grave danger. Fourteen Master Interfaces have been lost in this battle. Over the last few years, we've barely been able to maintain our numbers from volunteers. To replace the lost and maintain our strength is going to take a massive effort. If we can't do it, we won't be able to fulfill our contracts."

"You mean in a year or two, we could be in danger of this same kind of collapse again?" Zref asked.

"There is hope," countered Zaviv. "What we learned about the Wild Interface seems to be applicable to the research I once told you about involving kren volunteers and the Mautri practices."

"Khelin and I have a job," said Ley, too loudly.

The Interface's eyes flicked aside for an instant, masking the blankness of his gaze as he checked the data banks. Zref watched that gesture with avidity. The Brenilak had added another bit of social finesse to his manner.

"I see," said Zaviv, "with Lantern as crisis consultants." He focused on Zref. "The new research program is asking for human volunteers, people who are or have been in a bhirhir relationship, but they need not have any connection to the Mautri. With this new data, we should be able to bring such a human through surgery successfully, where we have failed consistently in the past."

Khelin and Ley seemed to be shrinking from the Brenilak, but Zref said, "I'm interested."

"Zref, no!" said Ley.

"You don't have to do this," said Khelin.

Zref had never seen the kren so upset. The blue priest was actually raising venom.

Ley shoved his chair closer to Khelin's and said, "Zref, we'll help you find something you really want to do."

Zaviv said, "I'm not here to persuade you to volunteer. The danger is no secret. For every two thousand who apply to the Guild, only one and a half are selected, and not all of those survive the alterations to the brain. Some survive but fail to master the Interface; they spend the rest of their lives in our hospitals. Where bhirhir is involved, there have been *no* successes."

"Well then, it's about time there were," said Zref.

He remembered Sudeen's vision of him wearing the Interface medallion. The Guild had destroyed the outlaws who had killed his parents, Sudeen, and Tess, and they'd almost destroyed themselves in the process. He fingered the Wassly trinket, and the certainty grew in him that despite the air of final triumph pervading the issue, they had not heard the last of 'Ossminid.'

Zref took a few days to think it all through. Meanwhile, the news carried the story of the Guild's battle. The confidentiality of the files was guaranteed again, and Interfaces went back to work. Items began to appear on the hardships caused by the sudden dearth of Interfaces, and two or three times Zref caught stories regarding various archeological projects held up for lack of an Interface. Then he saw a huge ad from Lantern Enterprises offering fantastic salaries to programmers who knew archeology.

Three government-Guild contracts came up for renewal and the Guild provided complete service to the two planets that did not have official First Lifewave projects and ignored the one that did. Through all the bitterness and cries of favoritism, the Guild remained silent.

Lantern hired another translation team to complete the work his parents had started, and they disappeared behind a security screen a parsec deep. Zref concluded that Lantern was as unconvinced of 'Ossminid''s demise as he was. Somewhere there was a criminal with the power to create Wild Interfaces, with most of the translation of a clue to the location of the City of a Million Legends, where they once created Persuaders.

Zref told himself that he was just fantasizing. There was no evidence that any of those criminals had survived. But the thought nagged at him. He had rubbed the Wassly trinket almost to a thin wafer on the many sleepless nights when he could not close his eyes without his mind replaying the nightmarish events of the attack on his home. He would find himself sitting bolt upright in bed, with Sudeen's scream echoing in his mind, not in the dark room. And he would get up to sit by the window, his heart thundering, knowing that he had to do something to prevent a second 'Ossminid.'

If ever there's a breakthrough on finding the City, or the mazeheart object, or another Wild Interface, it would be known to the Guild first. *If I were an Interface, I'd always know the very latest news. I could help keep the lid on before anyone else decides to take over the Hundred Planets.*

He left the family a note on the housecomp, to be delivered in the evening if he didn't return. Then he went to see Zaviv.

The Guild had the top several stories in the tallest building in Firestrip.

The waiting room was all windows, and Zref feasted on the dazzling view of snow drowned Firestrip, perhaps for the last time.

The offices of the Guild were decorated in neutral shades of white and shadow with gentle contours designed not to offend the sensibilities of any species. As a result, it was a depressingly bland place. He waited for nearly an hour and then was ushered to a mechanical terminal, where he punched in his application to become an Interface. He waited again, was interviewed briefly and told to wait, and was then interviewed again.

The third interview was with a human woman. "Call me Penner," she said in a quiet, low pitched voice. "And tell me why you're here."

Exasperated, Zref said, "I'm here because the Interface Zaviv invited me to volunteer for a dangerous experimental program. I want to see him."

She consulted a desk terminal and replied, "He's gone to Horth on a job. If you wish to wait, I can patch through a contact via the comnet."

Deflated, Zref said, "Don't bother. He'll find out soon enough." And then he realized what she had offered to do. "Are you an Interface?" She didn't have any of the mannerisms and seemed perfectly normal.

"No. I'm one of the failures," said Penner. "I'm here to tell you about what you stand to lose if you're accepted." She clasped her perfectly manicured hands and leaned her well-proportioned bosom over the desk. "I'm one of the lucky ones. I can work at a productive job and even decide what I'm going to have for dinner tonight. But I can't remember who I was before the first operation. I have no sexual desires and no interest in any of the pleasures that mean so much to people. I don't count myself as human anymore. But I'm not an Interface, either."

He didn't doubt that she was speaking the truth, but suddenly he caught on to something. *It's a test, to see if you can be discouraged.* "You don't seem to regret your decision."

"I don't even remember making that decision, though I've seen my own consent recording made just before surgery. The pain is not in the loss of something remembered but in the tangible presence of that something in everyone else."

"Including successful Interfaces. They don't lose their memories of who they were."

"For a while, between the surgeries, they do. What they get back isn't the same."

"Yes, I know," said Zref. "I'm volunteering for this, you see." He was aching to mention the new technology the Guild had picked up, but he'd promised Zaviv that he wouldn't. "I understand the risks, Penner, but I also understand that if the surgeons fail with me, they'll have learned something. If they succeed with me, they'll take the next step with the kren."

"Why are the kren so important to you that you're willing to give up your *self* for them?"

"Not for them, for the Guild. Because I think the Guild is the most important thing in this galaxy right now. And, because the only thing I want to do with my life is join the Guild."

She nodded. "Right now, yes. But what if you change your mind?"

"I've never been fickle in my dedications. You can ask—" He almost said, *You can ask my bhirhir.* "You can ask my family."

"We might do that."

They wouldn't lie about me to keep me from doing this. Khelin and Ley had opposed the idea adamantly when he had discussed it with them, and so he'd stopped discussing it. *But they wouldn't lie.*

"If you'll wait in the outer office, the Interface will see you. Please feel free to leave if you change your mind."

As simply as that, the interview was over and he was ushered out. But this time he waited calmly, fingering the Wassly trinket. He'd caught on to their game of nerves, and now he was sure that he was winning. It was almost dinnertime, and he was hungry when he finally was shown into the last office.

The Interface was a Jernal. Zref had never met one before. The Jernal looked like a huge puffball teetering in the middle of the desk on six long, multijointed legs. But it wore the Interface medallion and spoke clearly. "We have one more question for you, Zref MorZdersh'n."

"I'll do my best to answer."

"In your opinion, what is the purpose of the Interface Guild?"

A trick question. He had no prepared answer, and so he temporized. "To serve those who seek knowledge, or rather to serve the Interfaces who serve the seekers of knowledge. The Guild alters people to work as Interfaces and supervises where they are hired to work."

"Those are the things the Guild does, but what is its purpose?"

"I, I suppose you could say the Guild exists to protect the integrity of the comnet itself, to enforce the Guarantees so that the Hundred Planets can continue to thrive. Look at all the damage that Wild Interface did. You could even say the Guild exists to police the Interfaces."

"If you were running the Guild, to what lengths would you go to prevent any Interface from breaking the Guarantees?"

"I really don't know. Apparently, what has been done in the past has worked. I'd probably continue doing that."

"Are you willing to subject yourself to this process? Without knowing what it is?"

He thought of Zaviv and the other Interfaces he'd met. They lived with it; he could, too. But the tone of the proposition—submit yourself without knowing to what—made him pause a long time before he said, "I'll do it."

He couldn't tell whether the man was actually looking at him. The eyes were not visible on the round, floating body. But the voice came, reedy but understandable. "That concludes the testing we are able to do here. You will now be sent to Hengrave for further evaluation." He plucked up a disc and proffered it with one long, jointed appendage. "Your ticket for sunhopper *Mormorant III.* There is a car waiting to take you to the port. If you hurry, you can make it aboard just in time for supper."

"My family, they don't know. I can't leave without saying goodbye. And I didn't pack to—"

"An Interface needs few possessions. All will be provided aboard *Mormorant.* If there is anyone you can't leave thusly, you had best not go at all."

There was a rush of urgency to seize this priceless opportunity, but a lifetime of training blocked him from simply disappearing without a word. "Is there time for a quick call, just to let them *know?*"

From the drawer of the desk the Interface took a small hand viewer. "We took the liberty of informing your family you wouldn't be coming back. Here is their reaction." As he passed it over, the screen lit with the stricken face of Ley; behind him were Khelin and three others.

"You must go now or miss your appointment. There will not be a second one made for you."

Zref was never sure when he'd begun to move. He never remembered making the decision to leave. The next point at which things began making sense was in his cabin aboard *Mormorant.* An announcer was rhythmically repeating instructions in the ten official languages of the Hundred Planets.

He was off on the very adventure he and Sudeen had dreamed of, to travel the Hundred Planets and maybe find the City of a Million Legends.

But without Sudeen.

CHAPTER NINE

When Arshel saw the Sorges River, she knew that it wouldn't be so bad after all.

During the long trip from Camiat to Pallacin, she'd felt a growing dread of their first expedition. But if she could adjust to Firestrip, she could adjust to anything, she told herself. Pallacin was the single planet of a yellow sun much like Camiat. The continent where the Lakely expedition was encamped had been abandoned by the natives as unlivable. High plateau desert formed the interior, and it was cut across by the long, meandering gash of the Sorges River Valley.

The river was so wide; you couldn't see the other side. The valley was gently sloped, fertile, and dense with myriad life forms, bounded in the far distance by a sheer rise to the plateau surface. There was desert up there, but here the air was warm and carried a touch of moisture that made it seem almost like home.

"Come on, Shel, let's see if we can find Mom and Dad!" As soon as their flier touched down, Dennis was out and running, his face alight with anticipation.

They caught up with his parents at the cluster of silvery tubular living modules that had been dropped into a rough circle in a clearing near the river's edge. She thought at first that he'd fling himself at his parents as she'd seen young humans do, but he stopped just short of that. She was too far behind to hear what was said, but then his father grabbed him for a rough squeeze.

"And Arshel!" Madlain Lakely held her hands neatly folded at her slim waist. "Nunin, will you just look at the young people! Firestrip seems to have agreed with you, Arshel!"

Dennis' father turned to her. "I believe you must have grown, Arshel."

"Not much," she replied. "But I've gained some weight." *Three unseasonal molts worth!*

"In all the right places," said Dennis, "to judge by the reactions around town these last few years!"

"Oh," said Madlain. "I'm afraid you won't find any kren males here. They did tell you that, Arshel?"

"Yes. I think I can handle it."

"Didn't I write you?" asked Dennis. "She's taken the green and was even invited to take the blue before we left!"

"No. Congratulations, Arshel." Nunin Lakely was impressed. "I guess you *can* handle things here!" He said to Dennis, "You're lucky you didn't lose her to the Mautri, then."

"Yes," replied Dennis. "You'll never know how lucky!"

"Let's not stand here in the sun!" said Madlain. "Come in, children. Let's get reacquainted."

That evening, there was a party held in the center of the ring of living modules, with Dennis and Arshel as the guests of honor. Arshel found some familiar faces from the Vrashin dig. Dorsan the Interface was still with them, along with three or four of the engineers and overseers. The ones who hadn't been at the Vrashin dig had a tendency to stare nervously at her. They knew of kren strike reflexes but obviously had never met a kren.

Over the first few days, as she learned her way around the new site, Arshel tried to make friends with some of the workers. As at Vrashin, the bulk of the unskilled labor was done by natives of the planet. But here the crew was all adult males. They were short, wiry men with a blaze of golden fur down their spines. In this hot climate they wore very little, and their exposed skin was dark lavender. They were housed well apart from the humans and spoke their native language among themselves.

It took her several days to realize that they had no interest in the work they were doing but only in the next pay posting.

At that point, she ceased trying to convince them that kren don't strike indiscriminately and concentrated on the dig. The site was much larger than the excavation on Vrashin Island. The Lakelys had been led there originally by paleontological evidence of wildly disparate evolutionary chains coexisting in time. Such evidence had led to First Lifewave sites before.

The Lakelys had chosen a straight stretch of riverbank. A vast pit had been opened, running north and south as far as she could see. It revealed a few bluish stones, indicating that this had been a cluster of buildings. But nothing identifiable had been left from that occupation.

"Our best estimate of the age," said Dorsan, "is plus or minus twenty thousand years. It could have been any time from the end of the First Lifewave onward as much as forty thousand years."

She had been at the conference in Nunin's office because Dennis was there. She'd been most puzzled when Madlain had replied to the Interface's guess peevishly: "You've not been very much help lately!"

The Interface had said smoothly, "I'm simply reporting the machine correlations."

Arshel had never liked Interfaces, and something about Dorsan's remoteness made her shrink from him now.

Nunin said in measured tones, "If all we wanted was machine correlation, we could use hand programmers. We're paying for an Interface; we expect an Interface's services."

The human Interface did not answer. Nunin made a strangled sound and dismissed them all with a gesture.

Arshel spent the next few days surveying the monolith that stood in the middle of the remains of the village. It was several times her height and seemed to be made of a single, huge quartz crystal.

Somehow, Dennis got Dorsan to show them around. At one point she asked, after gazing up at the white, sharp edged monolith, "How could such a thing have survived from the First Lifewave?"

"If it were really quartz crystal," answered the Interface, "it would have been ground to powder when this continent was folded and submerged. But it's not crystal in any usual sense. We're not sure what it is."

A voice drifted down to them from the edge of the pit. "Hold that pose, please!"

Dorsan froze obediently, though his eyes were fixed on Dennis as he said, "Ever since we uncovered this object, Lantern has had that documentary crew crawling all over."

"It was this monolith," said Dennis, "that led you to the Crystal Crown, wasn't it?"

"Yes. We got some odd instrument readings from this one and sent crews up in fliers to search for other such anomalies. It isn't exactly like the other crowns."

The voice drifted back: "Thank you!"

"Let's go see the Crystal Crown," said Dennis. "I've only seen it from the river. I want to get down onto the site."

"This way," replied the Interface, and led them off at right angles from the approaching documentary crew.

They slopped through the muck that covered the bottom of the pit—it was below river level and had to be pumped constantly—and then climbed a metal stair at the edge of the pit. At the shore, they climbed into a red painted cable car strung out over the river on big orange pylons. The documentary crew had to take the next car.

In the river, a force field cylinder—all but invisible, but making a faint buzzing sound—had been thrust into the river bed, and the water inside it pumped out, making a hole in the river to expose the bed, which now steamed foul odors at them in the sunlight. The otherwise placid waters rushed by this obstruction with an angry roar. At the bottom of the cylinder, where layers of rock and sandstone had been removed carefully, a circle of standing stones like the crystal monolith now stood exposed to the air.

She could see where the stone that stood in the ruined village had been removed from the top of the arch that formed the entryway. But otherwise, not a capstone was missing, not a monolith had fallen.

They spent the afternoon sliding through the mud, examining every aspect of the Crystal Crown. Over dinner that night, Arshel, Dennis, and his parents discussed the find.

"There's a lot of excitement now: best stone circle ever found, that sort of thing," said Nunin. "But Dennis, if we can't get some sort of information out of this thing, it's going to be the biggest embarrassment in the whole field. With those cameras looking over our shoulders all the time—"

"Worse," Madlain interrupted. "Our article on the dating of the crown was rejected today for insufficient documentation! And Dorsan says he can't help!"

"Can't or won't," added his father. "The Guild won't give us a renewal or an extension on his contract. I even offered them a 50 percent increase in fee, but they just say there aren't enough Interfaces to go around!"

"The Wild Interface battle was over four years ago," said Madlain. "Surely by now—"

"It takes about five years to make an Interface," said Dennis. "But I don't think that's it. Mom, I used to know Dorsan pretty well. He's not the same. Oh, he's helpful enough, but he's not *interested* the way he was on Vrashin."

"Interfaces can't be interested in anything," Nunin said, correcting him. "They can only be curious, and I always thought that was spontaneous curiosity about anything you stuck in front of them. Now it's as if the Guild had adopted a policy against us."

"There's no point in becoming paranoid," said Madlain.

"I'm not. I took this whole thing to Selig this morning." Selig Ernske was the Lantern representative who'd brought in the documentary crews and now acted as if he owned everything. He said none of Lantern's archeology contracts with the Guild were being renewed. But he told me not to worry. When our contract is out, they'll send in twenty programmers and a construction crew to put up a building and install terminals."

She sat back, her shock evident even to Arshel. "Nunin, our funds will run out before we can crack this thing unless—"

"You're beginning to see!" Nunin turned to his son. "What we need is another miracle like you pulled off at Vrashin. We've got to justify the money we've spent here to get more."

"I've been thinking about that. Dad, where is the lab report on the specimen from the stray monolith as compared to the liths of the circle?"

"We don't have a lab report because we couldn't chip off a specimen. We tried everything short of destroying the lith. That's the documentation we needed for our paper."

"That's probably why it's survived all these millennia. I wonder—Mom, why not send the whole thing to the lab and let them worry about analyzing it? Maybe do diffraction studies on the entire thing?"

"Do you know what that would cost? The nearest decent lab is halfway around the planet on top of a mountain!"

"I'll bet Lantern would go for it," said Dennis.

"I don't know," Madlain replied. "Their credit isn't as spotless as it used to be. We've had to pay for several orders with cash in advance rather than use Lantern's credit."

"I can't see why," said Dennis. "Their books are selling!"

"I read about some bookkeeping problem they've been having."

"Then maybe it's only temporary," said Dennis. "If they're having trouble getting Interfaces, that could be why they're having accounting problems. Let me talk to Selig about my idea."

Dennis spent days closeted with his father and Selig Ernske. Evenings, he wandered about the site with Arshel matching the actual places with the catalogue numbers of minor finds.

Dennis regained the deep skin color he'd had on Vrashin. Arshel's scales thickened and stiffened to protect her from the ultraviolet and the heat—and the predatory insects that plagued the soft skinned humans and natives. As she learned to distinguish the friendly flora and fauna from the rest, she began to feel more at home than she had in years.

Dennis buried himself in his references and computer studies while she took to swimming in the river in the early morning before the large predators came out. Meanwhile, the ordinary work of the site continued: Fliers were sent up every day scanning the countryside, sounder crews were graphing underground echoes, detector crews were searching for anomalies underground.

One evening, as Dennis was about to express her before dinner, she tried to tell him how isolated she felt.

"It's just your imagination. Everybody's busy. Don't you realize there isn't much time before the Guild contract runs out? An uncooperative Dorsan is better than no Dorsan! You knew you'd be the only kren here. I told them a green priest could handle it. Don't let me down."

His hand on her venom sack shook as he expressed her. *He's afraid.* When she could speak again, she had to say, "I'll do my part. I'm your bhirhir, remember?"

All the next day, it seemed to Arshel that she'd been selfish. She wandered about the site, handling some of the artifacts in the laboratory shed and searching for some trace of life in them. But there was nothing except the distrustful stares of the humans and careful avoidance by the natives. *I'm too nervous. No wonder I'm not getting anything.*

She sat down near the river and began a systematic relaxation technique she had learned at Mautri. It took a while, but alone by the water, she stilled her mind until she could ask questions and expect to hear answers. She wanted to know why the people here had perished.

But instead of the panorama of the site as it had been in its last days, she saw Dennis' face. She felt his hand on her sack, expressing her. She remembered how, at first, expression had been the high point of her day. Now his touch was perfunctory, as if it were just another chore, like brushing his teeth.

The sad pain threatened to raise venom, and she had to concentrate on her breath control, holding the Mautri pattern of calmness. Again she asked. But she only recalled her first molt, her bhirhir's touch seeming to say that he understood her suffering and wanted to help. Her latest molt, on the way to Pallacin, had only annoyed him because it had kept him from the game room for three days. His hands had been gentle but disinterested. *A bhirhir's hands can turn molt into a pleasure,* went one of her surmother's favorite sayings.

A shiver of mental pain threatened her calm, and again she resorted to concentration to dispel the unwanted thought. And again, when she addressed the ruins, she received Dennis' voice: *I told Mom and Dad a green priest could handle it.*

It had been a long time since he'd objected to her Mautri practices because they had relieved him of the duty of attending her. *Perhaps I should have tried for the blue and for balbhirhir.*

She recalled the previous night and relived it with new eyes, remembering what Khelin had said. *In any bhirhir, one will dominate the other.* She stroked the bracelet he'd given her. It had become the symbol of everything he'd taught her. Now she knew that she couldn't read the site because it was Dennis who wanted to know, not herself. If she were to be his archeovisualizer, ironically enough, she'd have to gain some independence from him so that it would be by her own will that she sought answers.

She resolved to consider herself in training for the blue. The idea didn't terrify her as it once had. The blue was only a small step from where she was now. It wouldn't make her balbhirhir.

That evening she was comfortably ensconced in the sands of her bed, reading, when Dennis came in, jubilant. "I did it! They're going to start tomorrow!"

"What?" she asked blankly.

"Moving the monolith to the Cairnhigh Labs, of course! What have I been working on all this time? Now, Shel, what have you found?"

"Not a lot," she admitted. "The site is much older than they're guessing. It seems totally dead to me."

His voice rose in sudden anger. "Is this what I sent you to Mautri for? Is this how you repay me for all those years of sacrificing to keep that bigger apartment for you? Is this how you repay me for *this?*" He thrust out the arm bearing the two white scars where she'd struck him when she'd raised first venom. "So that now, when I really *need you,* you don't even try!"

The twin marks on his arm were stark white against his tan. He'd never mentioned them before. Clinging to the inner calm left from the afternoon's meditation, she thought: *Ley would never say such things to Khelin. This is not my human bhirhir, this is my Dennis bhirhir. Perhaps I chose the wrong human for bhirhir, but I did choose, and I did promise to become his archeovisualizer.*

"Well, why don't you answer me?"

Something in his tone sounded familiar, almost like the yelling ritual he performed with his mates. *Is that all that's wrong?* Suddenly sympathetic, she schooled her breathing and said, "Dennis, I've been trying to read the site, but I can't quite imagine what I'm looking *for.*"

He subsided. "I'm sorry. I guess I've been pushing too hard or something. Shel, what Lantern wants out of this is another clue to the location of the City of a Million Legends, the Emperor's Crown, the Persuader's Maze. You remember *Skanqwin and the Emperor of Crowns.* Remember how Skanqwin impressed you as being so real? What we need to find here is the reality behind the fiction."

That would add a certain symmetry to her life, she thought. The next morning, she woke early with a question: What part had the Persuader's Maze played in the demise of the First Lifewave civilization?

Before sunup, she took her bead string and swam out to the Crystal Crown, leaving all the cable cars on the bank side. No one would know that she was there. With work starting in the village to move the stray monolith, they might not send a crew there at all.

She sat down between the pillars that had supported the capstone that was now in the village. The erect monoliths loomed over her in an open structure, a building that was not a building. *The door to the room without walls.* Yes, it was like that: a building without key or door or walls, a building to house memories and dreams.

She thought of the Persuader's Maze. Why couldn't it have saved them? *What happened?*

Far above her, the river pearled around the force wall. The rushing sound, together with the quiet hum of the slush pumps, the buzz of the force wall, and ever-present bird calls, was a white noise background. She draped the bead string between the tips of her fingers, letting it twist around the smallest finger and fall gently over the backs of her hands. One gem was caught on the back of each hand, one swung on the loop between her hands, and one weighed down each free end, tracing ellipses.

The key to the door of the room without walls, the Mautri called it. *The door that could never be closed or locked.*

She imagined the last capstone back in place over her head, the whole white crystal circle ablaze with a life of its own. Back in time, past the transit of this continent under the seas, back past the upheaval of the continental plate, back to when the world and the galaxy were new and life had just started—back to the building of the Crystal Crown.

Surrounded by a toroid of minute flying craft, each of the tall crystals arrowed down out of the sky. She sensed the cold of absolute zero turning to the throbbing heat of reentry friction as they dropped to the ground like missiles. Their pointed ends buried themselves deep into the ground, precisely on target.

How long ago? The gem dangling from her left hand swung once, twice, three times, and the right one swung five times before coming to rest. Three hundred and fifty million years. No, it was impossible. She did it again and got the same answer. A star could be born and die in that time.

While her attention had been partially diverted, the scene before her mind's eye had assembled itself, and now there were people—humanoids, though with a red and yellow plumage that may have been natural feathering or some kind of clothing. The crystals of the circle formed flashes of white as they stationed themselves under each archway, facing inward.

She saw huge beaked faces and large flat eyes. She was seated just behind the central standing figure, whose outstretched arms were joined to his body by a cascade of feathers. A wink of sunlight broke through a chink between two monoliths and focused directly on the red and yellow plumed figure before her. There was a stillness that lasted until the sun passed.

And then, with a crisp purpose, they all moved together, turning to leave. She was aware of a warmth in the gems that lay on the backs of her hands. There seemed to be a rippling of the gravity under her, as if she were on a sunhopper again, breaking orbit.

The crystal circle lay about her, worn and ancient now as in her own time. People came, people like the natives of this world, short and wiry with lavender hides and ridges of fur—or feathers?—down their spines.

They tore at the capstone with ropes, hauling on it in teams, chanting as they worked.

Her point of view shifted dizzyingly. The Crystal Crown stood on the edge of a vast cliff. Seven teams of men heaved on their ropes within the circle.

Atop the capstone under which she'd been sitting, she could see a gold sphere shining in the light of three moons. Her attention was riveted on the sphere as it began to rock to the rhythm of the tugging on its supports. She never knew how many times it rocked hypnotically back and forth, but as the three moons separated and kissed the archways of the stones, each in its own proper place, the golden sphere broke loose and came arcing toward her as if it had power jets of its own.

She felt the air under her feet ripple as it fell past her into the canyon below. She got one good look at it. It was made of some darker gold with dots of a lighter gold painted systematically over its surface. The dots were points where spheres of the lighter gold, embedded in the darker, touched the surface. It seemed totally familiar.

Her mind's eye followed the sphere as it disappeared into the river below, gleaming so brightly in the moonlight that it hurt to look at it, so brightly that it bored twin tunnels into her brain—so brightly that it was the sun.

"Arshel? Arshel!" It was Dennis' voice calling from the high rim of water about her as he climbed out of the cable car.

Behind him came three of the documentary crew, recorders unlimbered, shouting directions. But Dennis wouldn't stop to pose. He scrambled down the stairs and sloshed across the muck to where she was sitting. "Arshel, what's the matter?"

She couldn't respond.

"Hold it like that!" yelled one of the photographers.

Dennis shouted back, "Are you crazy or something? Put that recorder down and get the medic!"

The man shifted the device on his shoulder and reached into a pocket, handing Dennis a flat object. "Here, call her."

Dennis swore and groped in his pocket for his pager.

Arshel laughed, her fangs vibrating against the roof of her mouth with dry clicks that hardly sounded like laughter. She'd been breathing with her mouth open. How long? Hours? She looked up at her bhirhir. "I'm all right. Don't worry."

Her limbs were stiff, but she managed to roll up her bead string and tuck it away. He helped her to her feet. Her swimming outfit was caked with dried mud. Her scales itched.

Dennis fussed over her all the way back to the force wall, where he said, "You folks take the first car. Arshel and I will take the second." As they rode back across the water, he asked, "What did you get?"

She told him.

"Three hundred fifty million, that's incredible. Could you locate that sphere now?"

"Maybe, but not soon. I can't do that too often."

"Then for now, let's just keep quiet about this."

The car docked, and he helped her into their living module, scrubbing her hide down and rubbing her carefully with venom, his hands the most attentive she'd felt in several molts. "You take care of yourself now," he kept saying. "I don't want any infections putting you out of action."

Later, she overheard his father scolding him for missing out on having his picture taken with the monolith as it soared on its way to Cairnhigh for analysis. To search for her, he'd given up the spotlight he so desperately craved. That, too, was her Dennis bhirhir.

Over the next few days, he didn't pressure her about the sphere. He spent the time closeted with Selig Ernske. The security teams guarding the site were increased by another group of humans. Some of them were women. She regretted that she'd never caught the knack of finding mates for Dennis.

But these new guards turned out to be all business. They curtailed her swimming in the river, and when the Lakelys interceded on her behalf, they posted a double guard on the bank every morning and lofted a flier to keep watch for kidnappers.

Dorsan told her, "Don't take them too seriously. The only person at Cairnhigh Lab who knows where the crystal came from is the Interface, and our private files are secure now. We're in no danger here."

After that, Arshel relaxed, and it was only then that she realized that she had to get away from the guards. She chose a time just past midnight on a night when Dennis had at last found company among the new women. She didn't know much about the night predators of the river, except that there weren't any really large ones, and so she took a small boat from the dock and paddled out toward the spot just downriver from the circle, where she thought the gold sphere might be. Anchored, she took out her bead string and wound it through her fingers.

They were much nearer the center of the galaxy than Camiat was. The sky seemed to her one breathtaking blaze of rainbow hued points. The starshine infused her gemstones with life attuned to this world.

Four more nights, lonely and cold, she fished with her imagination downriver, eventually going so far that she had trouble rowing back by dawn. And then she found it. Both her gemstone pendulum bobs swung in frantic circles to mark the exact spot. The elation made all the years of effort at Mautri worthwhile.

When she told Dennis, he shared her joy, dancing about their living room, emitting whoops of delight. She went with him to the Lakelys' office, where Dennis asked, "Don't we have a metal detector?"

"We had a couple," answered his father, "but this mud gets into everything. It's corrosive, too."

"Well, we've got to get another one."

"Why?"

"Arshel has a great talent as an archeovisualizer."

The two Lakelys turned toward her, and Arshel felt a sudden panic that Dennis was going to tell them that the Vrashin find had been hers, not his.

"Dennis," said his mother, "we've used archeovisualizers and wasted a lot of money doing it, too. The few spectacular finds don't really pay for all the failures."

Dennis fumed, and Arshel was again sure that he was going to say something about Vrashin. She said, "I've retrieved impressions that were checked out by my tutors at Mautri. It's just that before this, two hundred million years was the oldest thing I'd handled."

"And what was that?" asked Madlain, interested.

"The Wassly Crown," she answered. "I never got any real visuals with that, though."

"So how old is the Crystal Crown by your reckoning?"

"Three hundred fifty million," she answered, recalling that the official archeologists' estimate of the Wassly Crown was barely one hundred million. "The crowns seem to have been built at the very beginning of the First Lifewave and to have been used long after its demise."

"I don't see how our dating could be off by that much," said Nunin.

"Perhaps the trip through space and reentry heat account for the error," she suggested, and then had to tell them of her vision of how the crown had been built.

"So you're suggesting the crystals come from another planet?"

"Or," said Dennis, "they might have been fabricated in space. It's hard to see how they could be natural."

Nunin sighed. "That could become the basis of one of Lantern's wildest novels yet."

Arshel said, "Hasn't it been only recently that archeovisualizers have become a really bad risk?"

"Well, we had all our big successes with them at the very beginning of—"

"Yes," Arshel interrupted, carried away. "Wouldn't you say the failures began about the time the Lantern novels became so popular?"

"Just about," said Nunin.

"I see!" cried Dennis. "When a site gets a lot of publicity—people imagining things strongly about it—the visualizer can pick up on those fantasies instead of on what really happened. And with the Lantern novels so popular, why, I think everyone on this dig has read them all! Who knows what they're dreaming about this site every night!"

"Were you trained at Mautri to filter out that kind of noise?" Nunin asked.

"Not completely," she answered, and told them the rest of what she'd seen.

"But," asked Nunin, "you did *see* this gold ball?"

"Yes," she answered, not adding that she'd also recognized it.

"Can you take Dorsan out to where it is now?"

"Yes, I think so."

"How far did you say it was?"

"I think about a kilometer."

"Was there any inscription on this thing?' Madlain asked.

"I don't think so. Just the embedded light gold spheres."

"Embedded," Nunin repeated. "How could you know that?"

"I don't know," she admitted fretfully.

Dennis said, "We ought to dig it up. It'd certainly be another curiosity to add to the mystery of this place."

Nunin muttered to himself, punching queries into his desk console and watching the screens. "The detector equipment is going to *cost*, unless I can pull in some long owed favors."

It took weeks to make arrangements. Meanwhile, Dennis relaxed, going with Arshel on her morning swims, taking time to play on the shore as they had on the Vrashin beaches. She felt for a time that she had the old Dennis back, and they were friends again.

The mood was heightened by the news from Cairnhigh that, using her assumption of reentry heating, the magneto-dating had worked out to 339 million years, confirming her figure closely enough for them to trust her.

One morning, as they were toweling after their swim, Dorsan came to the riverbank, squinted at the dawnlit sky, and said, "The *Stealthy Susan* is up there now. Watch for a tiny spark just west of the small moon."

The *Stealthy Susan* was the Terran registered sensor ship detached for this job from the Hundred Planets Explorer Corps. Arshel supposed it had come to repay the favor Nunin had mentioned.

"They're scanning the river now," said Dorsan. "Wait—"

The Interface went into his computer mode, eyes glassy, the constant expansion-contraction of the pupils gone as if he'd died. She shuddered. *I'll be glad when he leaves.* Then she rebuked herself. Dorsan had saved her bhirhir's life at the Vrashin dig. What would things have been like if he hadn't?

She forced her eyes back to the human. He stood, hands on hips, face tilted to the dawn, sandy blond hair rippling in the slight breeze. She started to say something, but Dennis hushed her with a gesture.

"Dad said he has to work the scan through their computers without leaving a trace. Security is really getting tight now."

It seemed a long time before Dorsan blinked life back into his dead eyes and turned to them, with all his teeth showing. "Arshel, it's right where you said it'd be."

Dennis picked her up and swung her around, yelling, "I told you so! I told you!" And then he was running toward the offices, his feet showering sand over her.

She looked at the Interface. "And the ship is going to leave without any record of why it was here?"

"Its computer registered a delivery of supplies, but it didn't indicate that the supply was information. Security is tight here."

A few days later, they sank a shaft just large enough to bring up the ball of gold. It took four days and a truckload of broken equipment before they got it up. As soon as the mud washed off, faint lines were discerned engraved on the surface, which Dorsan identified as writing the same as that on the Persuader fragment, but she was sure that it hadn't been there when she'd *seen* the ball. Using the Ortenau lexicon, Dorsan identified some of the words, the most repeated one being "Ossminid."

This was an inscription on a public monument. Possibly, the Persuader fragment was not fiction after all, and this was indeed the clue to the location and demise of the City of a Million Legends that she'd set out to find.

But by the time Arshel was able to take the sphere aside to examine it, many people had handled it. The camp was filled with fantasies about it, she knew. Yet the moment she laid her own hands on it, the wildest fantasy of all sprang into her mind. *I made this thing!* The recognition went bone deep and proved impossible to shake.

Exasperated, she got permission to work on the sphere in the office late at night while everyone but the guards slept. She spent several nights poring over the object and picking up shreds of its history.

It was all nebulous, save for one thing, which she reported with confidence. "The inscription is not nearly as old as the ball itself. The ball was made for one purpose; the inscription was added to negate that purpose."

"We're going to send it to Cairnhigh for molecular scan," said Madlain. The inscription had been rubbed away in places. It would take fine scanning to discern some of the words that remained. "The whole inscription may tell us *where* to look next."

A few days later, Dorsan left them, his Guild contract up. Lantern announced a delay installing their programmers, and Nunin sent his native workers home. At first the rest of the personnel relaxed, but it wasn't long before inactivity began to pall and tempers frayed.

Dennis had been mating with one of the new security guards in her own place, and now he took to spending most of his time there. Arshel was glad because when he was with her, he only pressured her to find out more about the gold ball. But she couldn't.

She felt fretful for a couple of days, which sparked a meaningless quarrel when Dennis came home one evening to express her, and she wouldn't let him touch her. That should have been an obvious tip-off, but in the heat of the quarrel, neither of them saw it.

He stalked out the door, saying over his shoulder, "If you're going to go all green priest on me, you can just wait until the day after tomorrow for me to express you again! We're going camping, and we won't be back until then!"

When the door shut behind him, she said to the blank walls, "Well, I asked for it. I suppose it's about time, too." The discipline would do her good, and the vacation might do him good, especially with his mate along. She settled down to spend two days alone in her module.

But later that night, she ovulated. That explained why she had been so wretched. Feeling silly, she called the security bunker where Dennis was staying, only to be told that he'd left with his lieutenant. Then panic set in. *I need my bhirhir!*

It took her sternest discipline to quell the wrenching terror. But since she hadn't even seen a male since her molt, the egg remained in its tiniest form and traveled rapidly. She'd have had to live in total seclusion in order to achieve such ideal conditions for her first balbhirhir passage of an egg.

It was one of the things she'd have had to do to take the blue. When she saw that she'd pass it during the afternoon of the second day, before Dennis was due back, she told herself that there was no reason she couldn't do it without his help.

There was no pond in their module. She'd have to use the river. By that hour, the predators would have all fed well. She spent the waiting time doing deep relaxation routines. The trick, she knew, was to keep the ovipositor from spasm by controlling hormone levels. That was related to the venom control her recent practice had improved for her. She still had it under control by the time her ovipositor was extended so far that she couldn't stand contact with sand anymore.

She threw on her beach robe and made her way across the quiet camp to her favorite swimming beach. Apparently, everyone, including the guards, was taking an afternoon nap. The water was a soothing relief to her exposed tissues, and she sank into her meditation as if she'd never moved from her bed. She concentrated now on controlling the key muscles and sphincters as the egg passed. Shadows crept over her, but her concentration never wavered. The tiny egg had reached the final sphincter, when a shrill cry shocked her to outer awareness.

"Shel! Shel!"

The gentle rocking of the river eddy turned to a choppy splash as Dennis waded toward her. She couldn't suppress a shriek of pain as the egg was pushed through the last sphincter by a sudden harsh contraction.

In a panic, he grabbed her out of the water where she'd been floating face down, and he was halfway back to the beach before he realized that she wasn't dying. He sank to his knees under her weight, relief sapping his strength, as she explained, "I had to pass the egg!"

"Is that what this was all about? Why didn't you *tell* me?" Then he launched into a tirade of foul language such as she'd never heard him use. She answered back, and he accused her of going wholly balbhirhir on him.

She pointed out that he was encouraging her to do so, and he turned bitter, and then pleading, and then sulky. In the end, she had a full venom sack, but when he offered to express her, she wasn't sure that she wanted his touch. But he persisted, and when it was over, she felt much better.

She went to sleep that night wrapped in the cold feeling that she didn't know this man anymore. But he was her bhirhir. If she left him, she'd die.

Not for the first time, she wished fervently that she could talk to Khelin. But late in the night, she dreamed.

Dressed in her finest feathers, she was presenting the golden model sphere to the Emperor of Crowns, surrounded by all the symbols and ceremony of the Capital. She was hailed as a great artist and master craftsman, and a special white crystal crown was commissioned to display the model.

She woke with a start, her heart pounding. All the signs she'd been taught to look for were there. *It wasn't a dream. It's a memory.* She wrestled with it the rest of the night and by morning had made her peace with it. *I've lived before; therefore, others have probably lived before. Even as different species.* And at breakfast, she looked at Dennis with new eyes, remembering what the dying white priest had said about her human.

"Dennis, I think I know now what the gold sphere represents. It's a symbol of the heart of the First Lifewave civilization. It represents a zone of space somewhere in the middle of the galaxy here. Each of the smaller gold spheres is a sun located on the surface of the sphere. Each yellow sun has a single planet. And each of those planets governed a portion of the galaxy! Dennis, the suns are identical, and so are the planets, except for their inhabitants. Those suns and planets are *artificial!*"

"Ridiculous! Arshel, I'm sorry I was so hard on you yesterday. It must have given you nightmares."

"No, no, listen. Aren't we on a single planet of a yellow sun? This is one of them, Dennis. It has to be. We should be able to locate the whole sphere."

"Something like that couldn't have been overlooked all these centuries!"

"It's an artifact of the First Lifewave too big to find! But the City of a Million Legends is on one of these planets!"

CHAPTER TEN

Zref struggled to consciousness against the weight of the anesthetic. His eyes came to focus: gleaming blue walls, bulging instruments swinging on jointed arms over his bed, his left arm tied down.

Two doctors, both human, watched as someone slid a needle out of his immobilized arm, sprayed on a bandage, and released the restraints. It was coming back to him now. He'd lost count of how many times he'd gone through this procedure, how many times he'd come to, mouth dry, eyes gummy, stomach rebelling.

Five years. How many operations might have fit into five years?

"How do you feel?" the doctor asked. She was short and stocky, with a dark complexion and quick, sure movements, but she was definitely human and an Interface. She had access to the moment-by-moment computer profile on him. Her question was just a formality. But he had to answer, just to prove that he could.

"Terrible," he said. "Just as I always do at this point."

The attendant held a bent straw to his lips, and he sipped some cold water. It helped. His head was immobilized.

"You're doing fine, Zref," said the other doctor, a man whose accent branded him as a Terran colonial. "All the implants are done, and we've reconstructed your skull and scalp so the hair will grow back naturally. The healing lamp has almost finished. Soon you'll be ready to go to work."

At one time Zref would have whooped for joy over those words. He was an Interface now. Despite all the setbacks, most of which he'd known nothing about until he came to consciousness to be told he'd almost died, despite it all, he was glad. *Sudeen was right. I survived!*

"Does this mean the kren will survive, too?" A couple of years after he started, they'd taken a pair of kren into the experiment, using what they'd learned from him.

The two doctors glanced at each other, and then the woman said, "It's too soon to say. But we're all grateful for your contribution. Now, you're to sleep. You mustn't open the interface until your instructor shows you how. Understand?"

As Zref mumbled assent, she reached above his head and flipped on the somnosonic. His last thought was that he was so tired, she really needn't have bothered.

They moved him while he slept. When he woke, the sun of Hengrave was just up, a very distant red ball in a purplish sky Two new Brenilak doctors were in the room. He caught them muttering about salvaging anything from a mess and wondered whether they meant him. But he felt fine, considering.

"Ah, you wake! And you're feeling this morning?"

"Yeah, I'm feeling."

By now he was used to the constant switching of doctors. Each stage of the process had its own specialists. The tall Brenilak loomed over him, peering at the blipping meters over the bed. He reached up and flicked off one of the rays, and the coloring changed in the room. The healing ray was off.

"Now," said the doctor, "we remove the head restraint."

The other Brenilak approached as Zref's head was freed. He seemed vaguely familiar. "You don't remember me, Zref?"

The voice, the accent: "Zaviv?"

"The same. I see your memory has survived."

The doctor's eight digited hands were gently placing Zref's head on a hard pillow, cradled to surround his neck. Zaviv pulled a tall stool up to the bed as if intending to stay for breakfast, while the doctor finished and, with a gesture to Zaviv, left them alone.

"There's a part of you that's gone now, Zref, a part you never knew was there. Most of the time you won't miss it. But when the situation calls for a deep, almost instinctive reaction in common with your species and that reaction doesn't come, you'll feel fear."

"They already warned me about that," said Zref, exploring his inner workings as he might search for a sore tooth. He did feel different.

"But you never need act awkwardly in a social context."

"Fake it, yeah."

"For the reputation of the Guild, if not your own."

"Is that what you do?"

"Occasionally."

Zref didn't even feel betrayed. Did he have any emotions left at all? Or was he still drugged? He wasn't sure that he wanted to know. Then the dietitian brought in two trays, one with a bland, light diet for him, and a crunchy vegetable breakfast for the Brenilak. Zref didn't bother to uncover his tray. He always gagged on the thin gruel.

"Eat, Zaviv. I'm not hungry."

"Zref, I'm here to teach you to open the interface. But if I'm going to do that, you've got to show that you're well enough to take the strain." He swept the cover off Zref's tray. "I can understand your being through with hospital food, but I think you'll find it a new experience today. Try it."

Zref remembered learning something about the effect on appetite. Suddenly he was intensely curious, a sensation that lit up his whole body. He sniffed at the ghastly gray stuff in his bowl. It smelled like gruel. He picked up a bit with the end of a spoon. It tasted like gruel and had the same wretched texture, but it went down his throat without making him gag. Wondering why, he tried a whole spoonful. After all, if he vomited, he wouldn't have to clean it up.

A thread of thought surfaced, like a recording: *Peristaltic action of the digestive tract resumes.*

"Zref! Don't!"

The Brenilak was shaking his shoulder, slopping the gruel off his spoon and onto the tray. He lost the voice in the midst of startlement. "Hey, what—Zaviv!"

But the Brenilak had resumed his seat unperturbed. "You're not supposed to open interface until I show you how to do it without knocking yourself and half the comnet to pieces."

"Did I open?" The warm thrill had subsided.

"Yes. Note, Zref, that your chemosensors are working as well as they ever do after anesthesia. Your food preferences are the same as ever. What is missing is the deeper, apparently sourceless objection your body has to this food. Cravings from that level will also have disappeared. Such cravings can function to correct nutritional deficiencies; such objections can keep you from poisoning yourself. From now on, you must pay conscious attention to your nutritional needs. I'll show you how to program a watchdog function into your personal file."

The screen beside Zref's bed lit up and pinged for attention. Zaviv flipped the switch.

"Zaviv," said the tinny voice, "I told you to be careful!"

"I caught his opening in time. It won't happen again."

"See that it doesn't."

When the screen darkened, Zaviv turned and said, "Let's put breakfast aside and get down to business before you have another accident." He shoved the tray table away and began.

Zref listened remembering that he'd learned it all before. But this time it seemed more real and more important. Curiosity was the key. Formulate a question, and the comnet will answer: as a tiny voice, visual images, or simply an intuitive knowing welling up from nowhere. The important thing was the process of questioning.

Zaviv said, "Remember, upon opening, your blood pressure will go up. You won't live very long if you don't learn to control that, but there's another side effect. If you open—as you just did—with peak curiosity, you disrupt the comnet functions for many nets around you. Every machine will drop everything to answer you. Put enough into it, and you might bring down the whole system, all Hundred Planets! Presumably, that would kill you, and maybe any other Interface open at the time."

"How can you not feel curious about something you want to know about?"

"You just did it. You asked me a question and didn't open for the answer. Obviously, you know how; you just don't know that you know."

"How do I find out?" But he realized as he said it that Zaviv was leading him to ask questions so that he could find out. *It is standard procedure.*

"There, you see? You controlled the opening that time and got only what you were after."

"I did?"

"The clue that I'm here to give you is just this: To gain fine control over opening, you must simply control your blood pressure as you were taught."

"What if I forget and a question occurs to me out of the blue?"

"Anything that comes to you with that out-of-the-blue feeling comes from the comnet."

A chill went through Zref again. *But that's my self!* No mere theory could prepare anyone for this.

Zaviv allowed him no time to think about it. "Haven't you wondered what exactly happened to me that night your parents died? I don't think the news reports ever made it clear."

"I wasn't watching the news at that point," said Zref. But it had been almost six years ago, and he was curious again.

Zaviv's rough hand clamped his biceps. "Lower!"

The interface opened. Zref saw the vastness of interstellar space sweeping off in every direction. Dizzy, he clung to the edge of himself and peered into the gulf inside his mind. An eyeblink, and he was back in the gardener's cottage as Zaviv had rearranged it. Zaviv was before him, only this time he could also hear the constant traffic to the computer. Even when the interface was technically closed, there was a rhythmic leakage. *Zaviv's private file.*

Shunt. And he could hear Zaviv's watchdog program inserting reminders to control blood pressure and to mind the house locks and take care not to leave traces for the Wild Interface to pirate. And then there was another presence, the subliminal chatter of another private file, another watchdog. But this one was oddly distorted. The Wild Interface.

Two, three times the Wild Interface queried Zaviv's private file, getting the same *shunt* away from it that Zref had experienced. He began to see how the thing functioned. There was a searing whiteness. A moment later, it was gone, and the constant background chatter of Zaviv's private file was gone, too; the watchdog was dead. But before it had died, it had sent a command shrieking along Zaviv's nerves: *Die!*

He heard Sudeen's voice, the last sound he'd ever heard from him. "Zreffff!"

He was back in the hospital room, red sunlight streaming in the window. His hands were glued to his face. He forced them down and tried to meet Zaviv's eyes without horror. He himself had chosen not to answer Sudeen's cry. It wasn't Zaviv's fault that he was alive and Sudeen was dead.

The Brenilak touched the button to flatten the bed out. "There's just one more thing we have to do before you sleep."

"I'll never sleep now."

"Zref, there's no longer any reason to be frightened. The Wild Interface and his creator, the self-styled Ossminid, are gone. The private files are redesigned so there's no way the watchdog can be turned against us now.

Before I can allow you to rest, you must program in your reminder to keep your blood pressure down."

"To do that, I'd have to open again."

"No. Your access to your private file is always slightly open. You'll find everything that's happened since you woke stored there, and so is everything that's ever happened to you. You remember me, which proved that your access is functioning."

"Everything is stored there?" *Even Sudeen's scream.*

"Everything," the Brenilak answered reassuringly. "Now, all you do to program your watchdog is lower your blood pressure and body temperature as you were taught. Then formulate your intention to keep the readings just so, constantly. Allow for them to lower during sleep and rise at waking but never higher than now. All right, now tell me about it aloud."

Zref repeated the instructions he'd formulated.

"Again," prompted the Brenilak. "And a third time." As Zref finished, he asked, "Do you hear it now?"

The soft chatter took up a rhythm in the background of his thoughts just as he'd heard Zaviv's watchdog. But this was *his*, and it felt good.

"All right it's safe now. You can go to sleep and wake when you choose and not be afraid that you'll damage the comnet with a stray thought."

Zref realized that he'd been afraid of just that. The fear had been with him since the human doctor had warned him not to open until he was taught how. It meant that his Guarantee was working. Nothing could make him turn against the Guild or the comnet now. Nothing could make him a Wild Interface.

* * *

As soon as Zref was well enough to sit up for more than an hour, they gave him back his personal effects, including the well worn trinket of the Wassly Crown. Intensive training began again. With practice, he learned to think, using the comnet as he would have used his mind. The high point of his days came when he began to communicate with other Interfaces, using the private files as a message drop. It was almost better than telepathy would have been and much more reliable.

The day came when he knew by name, by sight, or by private file code every Interface alive. There were only 734, counting himself. Yet he made no friends.

There were no cliques among the Interfaces keeping him out of the social order; there simply was no social order. He was comfortable with the situation but not content. He spent time searching the comnet for all the latest developments related to the City and the mazeheart object, feeling that his life should have some purpose. But more often than not, contemplating the search for the City only led him to glancing around for Sudeen and to the fresh realization of his loss.

Such feelings should have disappeared with his final surgical scars. But when asked by his psych examiners how he was doing, he simply said, "Fine!" without reference to the episodes of melancholy, grief, or piercing bereavement. They only came after he experienced that indelible scream of Sudeen's, which had somehow etched itself through the deepest recesses of his private file. And that only happened when he stayed open for a long time, which he rarely needed to do, not even to follow the quest for the City.

Lantern Books had a new novel out: *Ossminid, Emperor of the First Lifewave*. Ossminid, a Persuader, had used his powers to seize the Throne of Crowns in a bloody interstellar war. The first half of the book was such a nonsensical description of the war that Zref almost set the book aside. But in the last half, Ossminid used his throne to restore order, scrupulously refraining from entering any crown himself as per his Persuader's Oath. His reign was depicted as a time of peace and prosperity, and in the end he was hailed for his greatness.

In five years, the Guild had not seemed to slow the progress of the Lantern books or the research behind them. They were more realistic than ever. It was then that Zref found Lantern's persistent requests for Interfaces turned down. Reading that file, he discovered Lantern's accounting difficulties and cash losses. There he ran up against privacy locks to which he had no keys, but he couldn't dismiss his curiosity.

If, Zref reasoned, 'Ossminid' had gotten away during the raid on his headquarters and had started immediately to make another Wild Interface; the earliest he could have one would be now. But 'Ossminid' would also have needed money. And where would be the best place to get it? From the enemy, the other seekers of First Lifewave secrets. From Lantern, which was mysteriously losing money trusted to comnet accounting.

Zref *knew* with a vast intuitive certainty that Lantern either had a Wild Interface or was the victim of one. But there was no proof to be found anywhere in the comnet. He added frustration to the list of emotions an Interface could feel.

One day Zref was sitting by the window of his room, looking down at the bustling capital city of Hengrave, brooding over the Wassly trinket. The Guild was still stubbornly turning down Lantern's requests for an Interface, while there he sat.

He caught a new plea being entered by Lantern, this time by a live envoy. The building tie computer flashed half a dozen summonses to various Interfaces, but Zref was not called. And as he read the messages in the open files, they were preparing to turn Lantern down again.

On impulse, he dropped a note to Rodeen, Master Interface and chief dispatcher for the Guild. *I'm volunteering to do the Lantern audit. Zref.*

She opened, riffled through his file, and dropped back, *You haven't been discharged from Medical. I've no jurisdiction. Rodeen.*

Zref dropped duplicate notes to Lyria, the human woman in charge of his surgery, and Nesfil, the Brenilak who was the chief trainer. *See attached notes to and from Rodeen. I request medical discharge so I may cover the Lantern audit. Zref.*

It took a moment while Lyria and Nesfil consulted each other and then Rodeen, who was in conference with the Lantern visitor. The return, when it came, was just what Zref had expected: *Request denied. Medical.*

Zref returned the note, tagged it Lyria and Nesfil, and added: *On what grounds? Zref.*

By this time Nesfil had arrived at Zref's door. Zref admitted the aged Brenilak, very much aware that he was stirring up trouble. At the same time, he dropped to Rodeen: *Please don't dismiss the Lantern representative until it has been determined if a new Interface is available. Zref.*

Zref knew that Rodeen had dropped a private message to Nesfil when the trainer said, "Zref, if you haven't learned Guild policy on archeology yet, how can you be ready to go out?"

"I know the policy," Zref countered. "I want to know why I haven't been certified yet. I've passed all the tests."

"We're not totally satisfied we haven't missed something. And now *this*. It does make one suspicious!"

Zref explained his reasoning regarding Lantern. "So one of us must go into the Lantern books. You can't keep turning them down for lack of personnel now that so many of us are becoming functional. And you've got to field test me soon."

The Brenilak scrutinized him so long that Zref thought the man must be reading files. Then he said ponderously, "Your recent interest in Lantern has caused the Medical Department much concern. Even a Brenilak can see you've cause to seek revenge against Lantern. But an Interface should have no such motives. If you do—"

"No!" said Zref, his voice loud in his ears. But his blood pressure and respiration were coolly normal. "It's just that I can't shake the conviction that there is another Wild Interface. 'Ossminid' is not done for. He's still after the mazeheart object. Maybe it's slightly paranoid, but maybe it's a genuine Interface's intuition. Isn't it worth risking an Interface—well, just a journeyman—on it?"

A note dropped into Zref's private file. *I've asked the Lantern representative to stay over, as you requested. Rodeen.*

Zref caught Nesfil retrieving a dropped note himself, and he figured that Rodeen had duplicated the message. "You see," said Zref, "even Rodeen is willing to consider reason."

"I'll discuss it with Lyria and the others."

As the Brenilak turned to go, Zref went to pack.

* * *

Lantern's headquarters was one sprawling city occupying the large moon of the giant quasi-planet Raynat. As he came into orbit, Zref's attention was captured by the awesome sight of the night glittering from horizon to horizon with lights. Hanging just beyond the moon, the bulbous face of Raynat itself, a ruddy orange and brown fraught with reds as befitted a planet that wasn't quite a star. Then the local comnet node, which was the center of the vast Lantern holdings, intruded on his awareness, chattering away madly in dozens of languages, shooting orders in every direction, recording, correlating, and moving data faster than he could comprehend, and at the same time casually jockeying their lander down to the surface.

"You don't talk much, do you, Master Interface?" asked Hattan Rowlett from the seat next to Zref.

Zref tore his eyes from the port. It was true. He'd kept to his cabin all during the trip to Raynat. He'd made the mistake of boarding the ship wearing his Guild medallion in plain sight. After that, he found that he couldn't take the stares that followed him everywhere, the almost overheard whispers, the people trying to make friends in order to get him to work the comnet for them without Guild charges. Thus he had stayed away from his fellow passengers.

Now he made an effort to talk to Lantern's envoy. "I was trying to decide which is more awe inspiring, Lantern's own comnet or *that*—" He gestured to the port.

"You can interface the computers from here?"

"There isn't anyplace in the Hundred Planets where I can't hear some part of the comnet, Mr. Rowlett. But between the two, I think the view wins. Nothing people build will ever rival what nature has provided."

The minute he said it, Zref knew that it described how he had felt once. But he didn't *feel* that way now.

"It's gratifying to hear you say that," the envoy replied.

But Zref heard the unstated finish: *You're not just a flesh-and-blood machine. You're still human.*

They were met by a nondescript Jernal, who drove them to a sprawling office building, where they were escorted to a conference room decorated with genuine Theaten antiques. Although Zref had never studied the period, every detail he noted evoked a subliminal commentary from the comnet, which he ignored. The chairs around the long, oval table seemed too fragile to hold his weight, and they were much too high. But they were equipped with a little step on which he could rest his feet.

He sat gingerly, accepted a hot drink, and listened to the cross talk of the computers all around them. The building went ten floors straight down and housed the main accounting data units for Lantern. Somewhere in there, he thought, were the pay records for Khelin and Ley, and somewhere else there were records for himself and Sudeen. One day he'd look them up just for fun.

"So you're the Interface!"

The booming voice didn't startle him, but it should have. *Another change?* Turning, he said smoothly, "I'm called Zref."

"And I'm called Mark Maross, chief accountant of Lantern Enterprises." He was a portly human in the grip of middle age, and he had the thumb missing from his left hand. Zref wondered why he hadn't had it regenerated and then quelled his curiosity. It was none of his business.

Maross rested his portfolio on the table, tapping it as he spoke. "I'm going to lay it right out for you, Zref. We haven't been able to get an Interface here since we had to sue the Guild for breach of security in the

Vrashin matter. Now, if you folks have been holding a grudge against us for that, I want you to realize that Lantern acted entirely without malice in the affair, and—"

"Mr. Maross, I was sent here to trace your lost funds." Surprised at his own calm, Zref wondered at Maross' anger.

"Well, you've been assigned quarters on Staff Floor B. You'll have to arrange office space with the government auditors; they've taken over the gymnasium." He mopped his forehead with a handkerchief, and Zref realized the man's problem. After two years of watching his department foundering, he had official auditors combing his books, and only now would the Guild spare him one Interface. With visible suffering, the man said, "Rowlett is outside. He'll show you to your rooms and escort you to the reception tonight."

Finding his luggage already in his rooms, Zref would have been content to unpack and start playing with the accounting computer they'd given him the keys to. But Rowlett said, "The reception is in your honor. All the resident visitors and the Lantern officers will be there."

It seemed that Lantern wanted to demonstrate to the Guild that they no longer held Vrashin against the Interfaces. But Lantern wasn't being boycotted because of the lawsuits. It was the new Guild policy to slow First Lifewave research. Zref dropped a note to Roylanta for permission to avoid the party. She responded: *You must go. Allow them to believe as they will. Do not mention the First Lifewave research policy without consulting me. Can we trust you in this, Journeyman Interface? Roylanta.*

You can trust me. Zref. But he wanted to know when they intended to announce the policy.

The reception was held in the Lantern museum. It was a cylindrical area with tier after tier of balconies overlooking a spacious floor dotted with display cases and scale models of things Lantern's research had uncovered.

Scattered among the display cases were tables set with all manner of food and drink, a riot of color against bright gold tablecloths set off against rich brown carpets and drapes. It was so appetizing; Zref checked his watchdog file to be sure that it was instructed not to let him overeat.

Accompanied by Rowlett, he entered on the first balcony level, where a uniformed attendant took his coat. Another attendant, a tall Theaten male, announced him over a speaker system. The glittering crowd turned as one body to gaze up at him. They were all dressed in elaborate formal wear.

Zref would have expected to feel out of place in the severe black uniform of the Guild, but he stood forth to be examined without a qualm. *There are advantages to being an Interface.*

With Rowlett at his side, he descended the ramp to the crowd and was immediately besieged. "I've never met an Interface before." "Is it true humans make the best Interfaces?" "You look awfully young to be an Interface." "Would you mind signing my napkin for my nephew on Sirwin?"

And when that group had faded away, Rowlett brought him a plate of choice tidbits and a drink. He installed Zref at one of the scattered tables before announcing, "I'll be right back."

Before long, people invited themselves to sit with him. "How long do you suppose it will take to untangle the books?" "It's been so long since we had an Interface here. Would you say the shortage of Interfaces is over?" Or "I work for the Tours Department, and I was wondering if when you're finished at Accounting, you might give us a few moments of your time. We're trying to set up a branch on Pallacin, and . . ." "If you want my opinion, the whole problem with Accounting is that overstuffed Maross character." "I'm a little embarrassed to admit it, but I work for the Legal Department, and we were wondering if you might find a moment or two to consult on the Eiltherm question."

By the time Rowlett appeared with his own meal, Zref had finished eating, and he took the opportunity to escape. "I think I'd like to look around. The displays are spectacular."

The Jernal who held the unflattering opinion on Maross floated to Zref's side. "Allow me to guide you through the museum, then."

"I don't think I'm going to need a guide," said Zref, remembering the time he and Sudeen had sold themselves to Zaviv without knowing that he was an Interface. He stroked his medallion as meaningfully as he could, and the Jernal took the hint and faded into the crowd.

Zref sighed and turned to the displays. He knew that the Vrashin find was there someplace. Opening, he checked the catalogue and then followed the signs upstairs to a display alcove. But it was sealed by a heavy opaque door and two armed guards.

"Is this display ever open?" Zref asked.

"Only by special permission," answered the Brenilak guard. His partner, a female Sirwini, was silent but alert. "You'd have little trouble getting permission. But security prefers not to open the display when there are so many people in here. A small scale war was fought over a mere copy of this thing, destroying a house and killing more than ten people."

"Yes," said Zref, remembering vividly. But the memory held only the haunting echo of pain. "Thank you," he said, turning away without any intention of asking special permission.

About halfway around the balcony, he found the display of the Sphere of Ossminid, as they now called the gold sphere found on the Sorges River site. He'd heard that it represented an actual sphere of stars so big that galactic mappers had missed it. Beneath the sphere, which was on a slender pedestal, a case displayed an enhanced print of the inscription.

Three people were discussing the inscription. Zref intended to withdraw without disturbing them, but his eye was caught by the worn and scratched sphere. He could make out the regularity in the scratches. In a sudden fit of curiosity, he opened and scanned all the work that had been done on the translation, storing it in his reference file.

His parents had laid the groundwork with their translation of the Persuader Fragment and part of the Vrashin find. The others Lantern had hired had completed the Vrashin work, drawing a picture of the capital city of the First Lifewave, the City of a Million Legends. There the Emperor's Crown lay beside the Persuader's Maze, which contained the mazeheart object that had created Persuaders. But 'Ossminid' had not yet found the City. *There's still time*, thought Zref. *If he's still alive, I'll get him before he gets the City!*

"He's the one. I've never read an Interface before, but I know he's the one."

It was the Theaten man beside the display case. The human woman beside him tried to gesture him to silence, and the Jernal who was with them floated forward on its six spindly legs and said, "Let me apologize for my colleague's rudeness."

The human woman stepped forward, saying, "My name is Neini Mori, and this Theaten with no manners is Iebe Arai Then. Our associate over here is Waysjoff. We write some of those infamous Lantern novels, under various names."

"Are you some of the people who have not been paid?"

"Maybe," answered the Jernal. "Who can be sure when records of book sales may not be accurate? But that's not what Arai is interested in."

"You see," Mori added, "Arai is our archeovisualizer."

The Jernal said, "He used to work for real archeologists. But now he's turned to reading people's past lives for us."

Mori picked that up. "We found it lends authenticity to our stories when Arai can find someone who had an incarnation in the period we're writing about."

Waysjoff was a pink hued Jernal, and now it puffed itself up, showing its excitement. "And apparently, you're just the one we've been looking for!"

All this time, Arai had been leaning his toothpick slim body against the display case, his dark eyes fixed somewhere beyond Zref's shoulders. He had the dark, reddish-brown skin that predominated among Theatens.

Glancing aside, Zref flicked open and checked the Lantern files, discovering that these three were in fact the creators of his favorite character, Skanqwin.

"I've often wondered," said Zref, "whether Lantern writers know how terribly powerful their fiction is. The power of a dream shared by many species is awesome."

"It works," replied the woman, "because we create the vision out of the dreams of many species. Waysjoff studied on Camiat, I went to school on Ciitheen, and Arai learned archeovisualization on Sirwin. We try to give people who've never met someone of another species a feeling for what it's like to be, oh, say, kren."

Zref nodded. "You do succeed. But—"

"A vast compliment coming from one who knows," Arai cut in.

Zref raised an eyebrow. "Who knows what?"

"Over many lifetimes, you've worn the flesh of many species and be-friended those of other species. You're at home among strangers."

In the Mautri view, almost everyone had lived such sequences of lives. "Any Interface is at home among strangers."

"The kren. You've some strong connections there that go back—surely, you recall all the lives you spent—*no*. It is sealed. And now you'll never re-cover them. An Interface can't."

Mori stepped to his side with a quick gesture to Arai. "If he can't read them himself, can you read them for him?"

The Theaten was still in his unfocused abstraction, and the Jernal was fumbling a recorder out of the depths of its fluff with an air of someone about to get down to serious work.

"Now, wait a minute," said Zref. "I'm not sure I want to provide material for your next book."

The Theaten rolled his head sideways in a gesture that Zref found odd. "You're familiar with the theory that everything that happens is recorded for all time in the very substance of the universe? Now that I know who you are and what your connection is with this sphere, I can follow the threads of your lives into the tapestry of reality. If you don't wish to know what I find there, I won't say. But from what I see now, much of your lives is of historic record and public knowledge. That we may use, but we'll never mention your current identity."

Zref glanced aside and checked on Iebe Arai Then's personnel file. It was a thorough file with a high security clearance, and it included his years at the Glenwarnan School on Sirwin, years among the archeologists, and years of unemployment, which technically were still going on. As far as Zref could tell, the man had been living strictly according to the Glenwarnan code. Therefore, he should not be a fraud.

"On several occasions," said Zref, "I've asked Mautri priests for life-readings and been turned down. I've never had a qualified person offer me a life reading. So I'm interested, but I know better than to believe any of it."

The Jernal moved with its recorder to where it could get a good level on Arai's voice. The Theaten gazed up at the gold sphere for several moments, and then, somewhere beyond Zref's left shoulder.

"Long before your work at Mautri fitted you to become a human Interface, you knew the artisan who made this sphere. You revered her for her talent and wisdom. You both wore feathers then, but you adhered to different codes of life.

"The Emperor of Crowns had commissioned the Crystal Crown, and you built it to house her sphere. You used the fame the Crystal Crown brought you. I don't understand this, but it is important."

He paused, gazing at the sphere. "I see clearly the monoliths of crystal arrowing down from space, heated to glowing in atmosphere." He paced to the balcony railing and then whirled and said in a whisper, "You built the Persuader's Maze! You used the fame she had brought you to get the Emperor of Crowns to sanction the Persuaders and make them an official arm of government. She opposed you. It was a lifelong battle of fury, and in the end you swore with an oath that rang to the ends of time that you would publicly prove—I don't understand—but that you'd prove her wrong."

Zref smiled faintly. "I was taught to beware life readings that make one famous."

"Oh, you've had lives in which you were less well known. I've been getting flashes of some of them, but I didn't understand any of it until now. Since that oath, you've lived a long sequence of lives to fulfill it: a magician on Earth in the twentieth century, you died of a failure of your magic. Before that you were a petty king on Ciitheen, and sometime before that you aided in genocide on some planet I don't recognize. Somewhere, you were involved in genetic engineering and died when one of your plagues got loose. You've been executed any number of times. I should imagine you had your share of nightmares, unless your lives at Mautri expunged that. Lately, though, your failures have been less disastrous."

Failures. "Did I fail at Mautri, too?"

"Oh, no," replied the Theaten. "You spent several lives there, more than one as their Chief Priest. You left voluntarily."

I don't believe that. Zref asked, "What of all this can you use in your book?"

"I have many visual detail impressions of the time of the Crystal Crown now. And I understand the man who built it."

"We're writing the story of the building of the Crystal Crown," said Mori. "And we were completely bogged down for plot. Now you've given us material that even involves the Emperor and the Persuaders." She turned to Arai. "Do you have any visual impressions of the mazeheart object?"

"I, he, it's—" The Theaten broke off, eyes going suddenly wide. Then his long slender hands covered his face, and a strangled gasp escaped as he sank to his knees.

The Jernal whisked to his side, but almost immediately Arai looked at Zref, their eyes almost level now that the Threaten was kneeling. *You died in the maze you built. I can't see the inside of it. I don't think I want to.*"

Back in his rooms Zref had to admit that he was shaken. but at the same time he felt curiously detached disbelief. *If it were my own lives he* was reading, *I should have had some sense of recognition.* But then he recalled that the Theaten had said that Interfaces could no longer recover past lives.

The next morning, he reported to the gymnasium. The ordinary work on the Lantern books was normally carried out by the responsible employees from their own dwellings. Rarely if ever was it necessary to concentrate this many people in close proximity. But the Hundred Planets auditing teams had their own procedures.

The gymnasium had been divided into small compartments by portable walls and force fields that dampened sound. Shielded cables were strung above or ran along the floor, giving each cubicle a comnet and interstellar communications.

"You must be Mr. Zref," said Alfara, the man in charge of logistics for the Hundred Planets team. "This is your office, then." He showed Zref into a fully equipped cubicle just like all the others. Then he turned. Ah! I guess you won't need a terminal, will you?" He gave a nervous laugh.

Actually, Mr. Alfara, it would be convenient if I could use the equipment. I'll want to watch how the system responds to various types of input."

Sitting at his new desk, Zref could smell the fetid mingling of the scents of a dozen species, a smell very reminiscent of Firestrip. But the nostalgia was only a memory.

He spent the next few days browsing at random through the accounting system, sampling the points at which credits and debits were entered from outside computers, and monitoring the ceaseless chatter.

One evening, the news carried a flashbreak. The Silmaran planetary law enforcement offices had received a threatening note demanding that they wipe their cash flow monitor files. It was signed 'Ossminid.' They naturally refused, and the next morning the entire Silmaran Law Enforcement Comnode was wiped clean. The Guild was calling in all Interfaces who had ever worked on Silmara to try to reconstruct the information. Zref was afraid that his best clue had just been lost.

Yet the wipe *could* have been done by hand rather than by an Interface. Nevertheless, Zref was sure that the original 'Ossminid' had returned.

That made him think of Khelin and Ley, and before he knew it, their pay records ran through his mind. They were stationed on Boex, helping tourists stranded by the Hundred Planets trade embargo of Katstin. He'd wanted to be a communications generalist and prevent such embargoes. Now he had all the communications in the galaxy at his command, and there was nothing he could do about their situation.

He redoubled his search of the Lantern computers. Toward noon, when all the other auditors had deserted the gym for the cafeteria he fetched himself some hot black tea. On his way back he came upon a very frustrated accountant sitting at a desk in the rose pink cubicle next to Zref's gray one. The man jabbed his index finger at the console too hard. In obvious pain, the human muttered curses in three languages, glaring at his machine.

"Excuse me," said Zref. "Perhaps I can help."

"Who're you?" the man asked without looking up. "From the company that made this thing?"

"I'm Zref. Interface Guild."

"Oh!" he said, spinning around, his face lighting with respect. "Would you talk this thing into giving me the records on *Ossminid, Emperor of the First Lifewave?*"

Zref glanced aside and opened, calling up the records for that title and then shunting the display to the console before him. "Is that what you were looking for?"

"That was quick! You folks sure are worth your pay!"

The screen was lit with a multicelled pattern of numbers. Peering closely at the display, the accountant noted the code reference for the whole display and then threw away most of what was on the screen, focusing on the section he wanted. Even as Zref watched, the numbers in the array were changing steadily: books sold, books ordered, books printed out, both temporary and permanent.

The accountant became lost in the numbers before him, and Zref withdrew quietly. The man's problem had given him an idea. Suppose Lantern were being paid for temporary copies of their novels but actually delivering the more expensive permanent copies, at least in a percentage of cases. That'd be felt as an untraceable loss.

He could determine whether this was the case more easily than the accountants, who would have to get court orders to check the records of other companies involved, whereas the Guild had contract access to most of them.

Back in his own cubicle, he felt the tingle at the verge of opening to satisfy a rising curiosity. It had been several days since he'd felt that, and he gratified it shamelessly.

Is there any change in the ratio of the amount of material manufactured for permanent book cassettes to the amount manufactured for temporary book cassettes at the time Lantern Enterprises began to register a drain? He ran a similar check simultaneously on the aggregate finances, set up the scans he wanted, and sat back to watch the comnet gathering and correlating the data he'd asked for. The figures began to come in, forming in his mind a graph with many colored lines snaking up and down. It was like thinking with a blinding intelligence. He became totally engrossed.

The shriek lanced through Zref with a rebounding shock wave that ripped apart his link with the comnet.

When the room solidified around him, he was in his cubicle, half standing over the desk with both hands flat, as if he were about to vault over it. With a shudder, he forced himself back into his chair, knowing that Sudeen's cry was not echoing off the high ceiling of the gymnasium. It was just a memory.

He wiped at the sheen of sweat on his upper lip and noted that his hand was shaking. An Interface was not supposed to have this sort of emotional reaction to anything, least of all a memory. But it happened only when he lost touch with where he was. Thus, he had quickly learned to make his openings short and his questions precise. It had won him some praise from his instructors because he didn't play with the comnet and get into mischief as the other apprentices had.

"Is something wrong?" Standing in the doorway was the accountant he had met just a while ago.

"Oh, no, not at all. Come in. What can I do for you?"

"I really shouldn't need help with this, but you see, I was trained on Silmara. I just can't seem to master this system."

"Silmara? You didn't mention your name."

"I thought you folks knew everything about everybody."

"Oh, I could look you up, but why clutter the circuits with noise when I can simply ask?" At that point, the idea of opening sent a cold shudder through Zref.

"The name is Ruy Armendariz. I don't think I thanked you for helping me out before."

"My pleasure," answered Zref, thinking that it had been a pleasure. "It seemed there was enough material in that file to keep you busy for several days."

"There was, but I lost the display. When I punched up the reference I'd copied off the screen, nothing happened. I must have done something wrong."

"Well, sit down and let me see if I can find it for you," said Zref, a faint curiosity beginning to overcome his reluctance. "You might have a defective terminal over there."

But as he cracked open the interface timidly, half expecting that howl of anguish to hit him again, he found the reason why the simple punch-up of the code for the book had drawn a blank. There was a security-blind monitor set up in the circuit, automatically shunted out for Interface queries.

"There it is," he said, displaying the file on his own screen and swiveling it around for the man on the other side of the desk. "Next time you want it, run in five 1's before punching the code."

"You mean it wasn't my fault?"

"Nope."

"Ha! Maybe I'll whip this system yet!"

That was the start of a loose friendship. Every few days, Armendariz came to Zref for some sort of assistance. Before long they were making a habit of taking the evening meal together. Armendariz couldn't quite grasp that Zref was not a lifelong devotee of computers, that what he had now was an instinctive grasp, not true expertise. The man's discussions of accounting practices around the Hundred Planets supplied Zref with ideas that seemed good but proved to be blanks. He was spending enough time open to be sure that he'd have detected another Interface, wild or otherwise, also working in the Lantern computers. But there had been nothing.

One day over lunch in the employees' cafeteria, Armendariz said glumly, "Maybe I'm getting paranoid, but I keep thinking this new 'Ossminid'—you know, the one who's always sending letters to the newsnets claiming to have created the Wild Interface, and panicked the Interstellar Currency Exchange, and wiped the Silmaran law enforcement computers, and so forth—this character, if he's that powerful, wouldn't be announcing all his real projects to the Hundred Planets."

Suddenly alert, Zref asked, "What are you getting at?"

The man looked around as if tangible spy devices might be trained on him. "I'm still working on that book file, *Ossminid, Emperor of the First Lifewave,* and not making any progress. It's spooky thinking this modern day 'Ossminid' might be trying to block me. But then, maybe I'm just in the wrong profession."

Zref didn't think so. "If it's proving that difficult, maybe you've found what I've been looking for. Why don't you tell me about it?"

The question unloosed a spate of technical jargon that Zref could barely follow. One problem was that the number of copies distributed was posted immediately when the copy was made for a customer, but the payment to Lantern had to go through several intermediaries before it was entered on Lantern's books, and each handler deducted a percentage before passing the money on.

"But, Zref, even with the time lag figured, I can't make the numbers come out right. Lantern is making more copies of *Ossminid* than they're being paid for. When I talked to Maross about it, he just waved a hand and said that *Ossminid* has been selling better than any title they've published before, thanks to the free publicity the modern one is giving them, so who cares if it takes longer for the computers to catch up with the transfers of funds."

"Sounds reasonable."

"On the surface. So I checked with some of the other auditors. The book-keepers are rapid enough on all other titles, even hand programming without Guild help, so why not on this?"

"Let me see if I can help trace those monies," said Zref.

He began then, with Ruy's help, to comb through every figure on the *Ossminid* display. The accountant would explain to him exactly how the number had been generated, and he'd trace it back through the comnet until he came to the world of origin.

Before long, word got around that they'd found something irregular, and late in the day Mark Maross showed up.

Maross strode into the cubicle and said, "Well, what is it you think you've found?"

Armendariz replied, "We haven't determined that yet. We've only been working on it since noon."

"Since noon?" Maross turned to Zref, who was seated at the console display screen while Armendariz was pacing about. "Surely an Interface could audit one book's sales in a whole afternoon's work!"

Zref had been holding himself to limited open periods to avoid the nerve-shattering scream. "Armendariz here has been explaining the entries to me as I search them."

"That shouldn't be necessary with an Interface." There was a sudden calm suspicion in Maross now. "We sued the Guild and won. Now you're stealing the money back by pulling a slowdown on the job! Stop playing around with single column entries and audit the *Ossminid* account for us, or explain why an Interface I'm paying full price for can't do a simple Interface's job!"

I can do it. He'd been able to stay open a few seconds longer each day. And now the test was upon him, with the Guild's reputation at stake.

He turned to the console on the desk before him so that the blankness of his eyes and slackness of his face wouldn't disturb them. He opened the *Ossminid* file, letting an uprush of curiosity take over. Where *was* that money going? Surrendering at last to that curiosity was a tremendous relief.

Instantly, the interconnected computers of dozens of worlds lit up in answer to him, and he had the giddy sensation that he actually understood the ebb and flow of currency in interstellar publishing. He could feel a vague tingle every time a book was ordered. He followed each one with an avidity that dismayed him. It was as if he'd been starving himself by staying out of deep contact with the comnet.

And then, as he watched, a book was ordered but not paid for. Had it been printed? Yes. Lantern had been debited for the job. But the sale had not been credited. Had the customer paid? That proved harder to trace.

Frustration swelled as he was torn between an urgent, personal need to know and some barrier that grew in strength as he assaulted it. He had never heard of a security barrier that behaved like that. The more determined he became to overcome it, the more it resisted. And the more it resisted, the more strident became his Interface's curiosity, impelling him to cling stubbornly and beyond all reason to that barrier.

Flypaper for Interfaces! He'd remain stuck until he died.

With the cold shock of that raining through him, he perceived a ghost image within the comnet beside him. A message dropped into his personal file and came to him as loud laughter. The ghost began to recede, an echo of his own presence.

Wild Interface! It was certainly no one whom he recognized. In that flash of realization, the deeply personal need to gratify curiosity became unimportant. Instantly, the barrier released him. He sped after the ghost image, tracing it from link to link. They were like two spiders racing across a web that filled the galaxy.

He found himself in his parents' home, men and women rushing by firing weapons, yelling—again, the SCREAMMMMMMM—

The next thing Zref knew, he was lying in a bed with soft, smooth sheets against his skin. The ceiling was white, the walls hospital blue. A human doctor standing over him was saying, " . . . don't know, with them the whole autonomic system is involved. I wouldn't dare try to—ah, you're awake."

"Yes. What happened?"

"You were working," said a familiar voice. It was Maross, standing at the foot of the bed. "Then you suddenly keeled over in a dead faint. I just barely moved fast enough to break your fall."

The scream. He remembered now, though the interface allowed only the barest trickle from his personal file.

"Thank you," said Zref to Maross.

The doctor was examining the instrument beside the bed. "I can't find anything grossly wrong. But I'm keeping you here tonight. I've already called the Guild consultant, and someone should be here in the morning. Meanwhile, I wouldn't advise you doing whatever it was you were doing when this happened."

"If you insist," Zref conceded, while privately the idea of opening filled him with a shrieking horror.

The doctor left. Maross seemed to want to say something. Then he glanced at the monitor box chuckling to itself and politely took his leave. "You'd better get some rest."

As he left, Armendariz slid quietly into the room. His manner more than anything else told Zref how concerned they all were. "Ruy, I don't feel ill. Don't tiptoe."

"Your heart almost stopped, and you don't feel ill?"

"Was it that bad?" Zref felt sore and weak, but he'd become so used to that and worse in hospital beds that he discounted it, especially the headache.

"I was scared to death!" said Armendariz. "I thought that some new Wild Interface was attacking you!"

A sudden rush of curiosity took Zref unaware, and before his watchdog damped his blood pressure, he opened a crack and was flooded with memory. He had to suppress an urge to tell it all. "I encountered some new kind of security barrier. I think it caused me to hallucinate and I don't know what else. I'm going to leave a good briefing for my replacement, but I want you to know where the barrier is." Zref described the comnet location of the barrier.

"But," Armendariz objected, "I've checked those files myself! There wasn't any barrier."

"Manually, you probably got doctored figures which they couldn't pass off on an Interface."

"That's very fancy computer work. Are you sure there wasn't a Wild Interface involved?"

"There was nothing resembling the Wild Interface of five years ago," Zref insisted. It was true. This one had seemed only a ghost, a hallucination.

Interfaces can't hallucinate, whispered his reference file.

He couldn't tell Armendariz or anyone else about the ghost Interface, because it could start a panic that would bring the Hundred Planets' economy to its knees again. And he couldn't report it to the Guild, because they'd certainly class him as nonfunctional and close his interface, relegating him to the failure ward.

CHAPTER ELEVEN

"Shel!" called Dennis. "Come take a look at this!"

Arshel pulled herself away from the window of the Lakelys' rented house in Firestrip. She had been watching the sunset, just barely able to make out the top of the kyralizth beckoning to her from beyond the intervening hill.

"What is it, Dennis?" she asked, coming into the central room of their suite, where the news monitor was on.

Immediately, Dennis rolled the news display back for her. A Jernal reporter was interviewing the youngest member of the Hundred Planets Assembly, who happened to be chairman of the commitee of research grants.

"And is it true that your committee has received over a billion individual citizens' pleas supporting the Search Bill which funds an all-out drive to locate and secure the City of a Million Legends for the Hundred Planets alliance?"

The man, a human, was obviously embarrassed by the question. What public official wouldn't be? Half the voters still believed, despite the tremendous pressure of the Lantern novels and tour publicity, that the City of a Million Legends was just a fantasy dreamed up by Lantern to sell novels.

"We have actually heard from less than ten percent of our constituency," the politician answered.

"Which would be about a billion souls," the Jernal prompted.

"That's about the right order of magnitude."

The human High Rep was seated in a rounded chair, while the Jernal perched its puffball body on what Arshel realized would have been a coffee table in the Lakely home. "And tell us, High Representative Fendmor, what is the previous highest percentage of your constituency that has expressed itself on issues of popular concern?"

"The ten percent figure has never been exceeded during my term of office. However—"

"Yes, of course." The puffball rotated, apparently to face the camera, although Arshel couldn't see any difference. "And so we have confirmation of the rumor. For the causes of this, here now is Rowan Wilther at the Hundred Planets Justice Department."

Rowan Wilther was a human with a bush of black hair and heavy black eyebrows that gave Arshel a shudder. The Theaten next to him was seated and still towered over the squat human. So slender that it looked fragile, the Theaten turned sidewise to the camera for a moment, and Arshel thought that it must be male.

"This is Demshoc Jun, Chief Justifier of the Law Enforcement Agency of Hundred Planets, LEAHPs," announced Wilther. "Chief Jun, the government is under extreme pressure at the moment to mount an all-out search for the mazeheart object at public expense before 'Ossminid' or some other criminal finds it. How close are you to apprehending 'Ossminid'?"

"Every time he strikes, he leaves a trace. In the end, they'll add up to enough to convict him."

"Do you think you can do this before he finds the actual City of a Million Legends and possibly makes himself into a Persuader none of us can resist?"

The Theaten's expression didn't change. "You did say you had some serious questions for me."

Wilther frowned. "Private industry has offered a reward for information leading to 'Ossminid''s capture," he announced to the audience. "Apparently, the leading financial planners of the galaxy put some weight to the urgency of stopping 'Ossminid' from finding the actual City of a Million Legends. Chief Justifier, at last count, what did that reward amount to?"

"Lantern Enterprises is offering a full share of their pension fund. Lorday Holland Industries is offering a fully equipped and stocked home on the resort planet Valdeez. A number of others are offering small sums of money, which together add up to quite a fortune. I wouldn't advise private citizens to attempt to apprehend this criminal, though. He could be very dangerous. If you come across any information, notify your local LEAHPs office. Or for complete confidentiality, the Guild of Interfaces has offered their services. Just mention the information to any Interface, and if it leads to a capture, the Guild will see you get your reward."

"Which brings us to a related subject. In the new Lantern Enterprises affair, the *Ossminid, Emperor of the First Lifewave* theft, has the theft been traced to our modern 'Ossminid'? Was there a Wild Interface involved?"

"The Guild has found where the programming had been amended. The leak has been stopped, and new safeguards have been devised to prevent a similar tap being put on any other corporation's accounts. The Guild reports that the amendment that had been inserted was inserted by manual programming. There is not and has not been a Wild Interface for over six standard years."

Wilther turned to the camera. "We put the same question to the Guild representative on Hengrave."

The scene shifted to the imposing edifice of Guild Headquarters, stretching almost as far as the camera could see in either direction along the main thoroughfare of the Hengrave capital city. This was, Arshel knew, the place where all the Interfaces were made. The scene dissolved to a roof garden setting, where two humans sat at a small table, shaded by an umbrella.

The woman was the oldest human Arshel had ever seen. Thin and wrinkled beyond belief, with a wisp of white hair artfully fluffed to cover her scalp, she sat straight and composed before the reporter. A sign came on the screen, labeling the old lady as the Guild's Senior Master Interface, Roylanta. Her voice was firm and clearly modulated.

The reporter asked, "Does the Guild believe that 'Ossminid' has a Wild Interface under his command now?"

"No."

"Is the Guild working on any current leads in this case?"

"Yes."

"Would you like to tell us a little about them?"

"No."

"Complete silence on the Guild's part could lead to many exaggerated rumors."

"It could."

"Does the Guild welcome such rumors?"

"No."

"Well, then, won't you tell us a little more about your current efforts?"

"When the Justifiers have caught and convicted this criminal, the entire file on the events will be made public, and the public may judge our efficiency and efficacy. For the moment, people should remember simply that once there was a Wild Interface. There will never be another one."

The scene shifted. A Brenilak female reporter said, "There you have the Guild's statement on the—"

Dennis snapped off the monitor. "Did you hear what kind of reward they're offering for information leading to the capture of 'Ossminid'? Why, you could make a name for yourself overnight! People would sit up and take notice then!"

It was something about him that she had to grapple with. He'd been born into a famous family, had carried a famous and wealthy name through life, yet there was still a deep inner need to increase that fame. *How could this be a man who spent lifetimes as a white priest?*

"I wouldn't have the least notion how to locate a living criminal, Dennis."

"Shel, he's after the same thing we are—the City. Somewhere in our profession there must be a clue to his operation!"

She set to helping him with his project. It was beginning to be summer in Firestrip. They walked onto the University campus surface daily, sifted through the specialty journals accessible through the departmental library.

Before long, Arshel molted her thickened hide, ridding herself of the last memories of the Sorges River. Time passed, and Dennis' brief spasm of optimism became a dogged determination. At some point, though, she began to feel her bhirhir's dedication. One morning, she woke up and the project had become her own.

During this period, the documentary on the Sorges River was released. Dennis, his mother and father, and Arshel gathered over dinner trays in the main room of the house to watch it. Dennis was spotlighted as the hero of the dig, and the weary drudgery was passed over in favor of the exciting moments of discovery.

When it was over, Nunin turned off the screen and said sarcastically, "Very poetic!"

Madlain sighed. "It would be nice if it really were that glamourous, wouldn't it?"

"One day," said Dennis, "we'll write our autobiography. It will be a best seller, and it will set the record straight."

"Well," said his father, "I think it's time you considered your next employment. Now, on the strength of your work at Sorges, I think I can get you a job as a teaching assistant. A few more courses, and you'd qualify as a lecturer."

"Ah, Dad, I'm a field man, not a teacher. I like to get my hands dirty!"

"I thought you'd say that," said his mother, leaning back with her cup and eyeing him over the rim. "But you must realize that if you don't work, money doesn't come in. The more on campus credit you have the easier it is to get funding."

It was true that they were using up the money they'd earned at Sorges, thought Arshel. "I was thinking I could get a job at the temple, teaching in the Outer School."

Dennis said, "I think we'd rather not stay in Firestrip over the winter."

Madlain nodded. "Have you checked the news briefs lately?"

"Did we miss something?' Dennis asked, sliding to the edge of his chair and darting a glance at his father.

Madlain continued: "The Search Bill passed, and now the *government* is offering research grants."

His father added: "I have our proposals drawn up and in the computer. It will be submitted, with University approval, as soon as the channels open for business. Now, do you want to tell me about your secret project?"

"Oh," said Dennis, his face ruddy under his fading tan, "I don't have a proposal ready to go yet, but I will have! And it will be a winner! Come on, Arshel, we've got to work!"

The rented house was of kren design, with enough room on the family side for both his parents, and Arshel and Dennis to have private suites. At the moment, the spawning pond was closed, but Arshel had the keys. Special heating equipment had been installed for her in case she wanted it. The Lakelys never skimped on her comfort.

Arshel followed Dennis to the main room between their two bedrooms, which had been turned into a study. Along one wall they had placed a long workbench on which sat a star globe model with the single-planet star systems scattered over its surface. As the mappers discovered new ones, Dennis added them to their model.

He rolled back the news brief recording to the item about the passing of the Search Bill and jotted down the details of how to submit proposals.

Now that they'd discovered the globe of stars that must house the City, and the Explorer Corps was mapping it, finding the City was only a matter of time.

"Now, Arshel, *we* will go right to the City while everyone else is still patiently sifting for it. Which one of those planets do you pick?"

"Aren't we going to look for 'Ossminid' anymore?"

"Of course. He's bound to turn up on the planet we pick, if it's the right one, and we'll get both the reward and the fame!"

She sat up all night with her bead string dangling between her fingers, pondering the model of the sphere. If it were up to her, she'd stop the search for the mazeheart object. But now there was a race on between the HP government and 'Ossminid,' who, like the first 'Ossminid,' intended to become dictator of the galaxy under pretense of reviving the glory of the First Lifewave. If he succeeded, it would be partly her fault, because *she* had revealed the globe of stars. She'd rather have the HP government in possession of the object than either 'Ossminid' or any single planet or corporation. And that was what Dennis planned to work for.

She stood over the rough model, letting the bead string dangle off the sides of her hands as she moved it over the globe. As if it were magnetized, the beads of both ends of the string pulled straight toward one star; every time she made the pass, that one star system grabbed both beads and held strong. Never before had the beads given her such a definitive response, but never before had she wanted so much to support Dennis' efforts, the efforts of her white priest.

When Dennis woke, she showed him the planet. It was near the equator of the sphere, on a line where other stars were located, with absolutely nothing to distinguish it.

"This can't be right," Dennis complained.

"Maybe the City isn't actually there. Maybe there's just a clue to lead us to the City. But it is the right track. I've never been so sure of anything before."

"But it's on the other side of the sphere from the edge of HP space. You realize what an expedition way over there is going to cost?"

After many assertions that it was impossible, he got down to work on it. The days they'd spent at the library began to pay off now as he worked up a presentation for the government grant, his first independent application. Arshel had to listen to many monologues on that subject. He was desperate to demonstrate his mastery of archeology to his father.

One morning, before students began streaming onto campus, he left before Arshel woke. When he returned, she was making the family some breakfast.

"Well, it's done!" He flung his jacket aside and came to the kitchen bar, where she'd set four places. "For better or worse, Shel, it's done."

"It'll be for the better," she replied calmly. She was relieved that the long working stints were over. Her bhirhir had deep sunken eyes and a pallor she recognized now as unhealthy in a human. He'd lost enough weight to throw a kren into molt, too. "Have something to eat. The parents will be up soon."

He said, after pouring juice and laving spread on a roll, "We ought to do something to celebrate."

"You ought to sleep."

"Tonight or tomorrow. Right now, let's go up to the Wassly Crown for a picnic! And then this evening, we can go over and watch the sundown ceremony at the kyralizth."

"We haven't done that together in years. It'd be nice."

They spent a pleasant and relaxing afternoon in their favorite picnic spot, just off the edge of Wassly's top. Arshel wandered through the crown while Dennis napped. Later, as they neared the temple, climbing up the public path, she felt her spirits lift.

They made their way among the throngs of tourists and residents who had come on this fine evening to view the famous sundown ceremony. As she paced along at Dennis' side, through the huge arch that framed the kyralizth, she could feel eyes following them and could occasionally hear a whispered "bhirhir."

"Arshel, do you have your badge? Maybe we could get into the students' area for a better view."

"Yes."

She reached down inside her tunic and pulled out the green enameled copper disc she wore on a gold chain. Making their way across the crowds now, past the mobile souvenir stands that were doing a brisk business, and up to the rail that divided the students from the tourists, Arshel felt the attention of the crowd lifting from her. There was someone nearby attracting more attention than she was. And with her medallion displayed, that was indeed strange.

At the gate in the fence, she identified herself and Dennis and passed into the student area, where already the Outer School students, mostly kren too young to have bhirhir, were assembled for the evening ceremony.

On the other side of the barricade, tourists mingled with people from the city. One lone kren she saw crushed against the barricade looked to be the thinnest kren she'd ever seen. She heard him exclaim in protest, and then the crowd melted away from him. He was the one attracting more attention than she and Dennis.

She looked for his bhirhir but saw no one taking that role. *This could become an ugly incident.* But even as she glanced back at the ultrathin kren, she noted that his venom sack was flat.

And then the ceremony began. She was swept into it.

The priests in their flapping summer robes climbed the steps set into each edge of the kyralizth, their pace well timed so that the sun was just kissing the horizon as the presiding white priest reached the apex of the kyralizth. He was so far away, she couldn't see him hand out bundles of torches to be passed down the rows of priests standing one to a step all down the edges of the kyralizth.

She had begun participating in the ceremony herself just after she'd taken the dark green. She wasn't sure whether the others had been instructed in the full significance of the ceremony, but she hadn't been. Yet even so, she had experienced something that would stay with her for a lifetime.

Now that feeling returned as the unlit torches reached the last priests on the steps. In the dense twilight, she could see the white flame of the white priest's torch at the apex of the kyralizth, and she imagined Dennis in that role, lifetimes ago, as well as now, bringing the light of discovery to the modern world, fighting the darkness of Ossminid.

She found herself holding her breath as he turned to each of the priests around him, one on each of the four approaches to the apex, and lit their torches. Then, at an even pace, the flame flowed down, reaching the last priest on each row at the same time. As the fire traveled down the kyralizth, she had felt a growing inner warmth, which now burst outward in a flush that was almost like raising venom.

A ripple of darkness engulfed the kyralizth as the sun itself ceased to give light, and she began to understand something about the sundown ceremony.

Life consists of both light and darkness: the kindling of questions in another, and the facing of one's own dark lack of answers. Even the white priests face that darkness. But they know that the alternation of these states is what brings progress and happiness to life.

Exhilarated with her insight, she turned to Dennis, putting her arm around his waist and leaning against his softness. No single factor in her life had led her to greater questions, or greater confrontations with darkness, than Dennis. Even if it hurt sometimes, still he was doing her good. She wanted it also to do him good. He had given up taking bhirhir lifetimes ago and had taken her for her sake and the sake of his mission in this life, not for his own needs. If she became less dependent on him, if she took the blue, perhaps . . .

The crowd began to disperse, engulfed in hushed mutters that grew as they chattered their way toward the bus parking area. She looked around at the Outer School students, and beyond to the watching priests, who were now filing away. The only one she might have wanted to meet was Khelin, and she wasn't sure that she was ready for that.

"Let's go, Arshel," urged Dennis, one hand on her elbow.

As they emerged from the railed area, the crowd was thinning. Already the summer moon was lighting the night from the edge of the world. The archway at the entrance to the viewing area was blazing with artificial lights, some trained onto the parking area, others onto the paths to the underways where people could catch trains for the city.

The emaciated kren she'd noted earlier was standing just inside the arch, looking up at the carving. Something about the way he turned his head to follow the frieze bespoke a concentrated curiosity. She paused, holding Dennis back. He followed her gaze, took her arm again, and moved along through the arch, hissing between his teeth.

"He's an Interface! A kren Interface! I saw his medallion!"

The man was indeed wearing the Guild blazon. At first glance, he'd seemed ancient and withered. But now, as they paused to view him from a different angle, she could see that he was quite young. The shadow concealed the top of his head, but his fluff seemed too short. Had it been shorn for surgery? His hands caught her attention as they graced the lower carvings. The fingers were long enough to be fascinating to her, and the webbing was full and pronounced.

Dennis followed her gaze, poised on the balls of his feet, and then stepped quickly up to the kren. "Benign venom," he said politely. "Perhaps my bhirhir could help you. She's a green priest of this temple."

Even in startlement, the kren Interface raised no venom. She began to wonder whether that was part of the affliction of an Interface, a reason krens never survived it. Despite her fascination with the man's hands, she wanted to run away down the hill when the kren's eyes lit on her. He approached, his gaze fixing momentarily on the green medallion she wore.

"I'm curious of your customs here. I'm from North Calrory," he explained unnecessarily, as his accent told his origin, "and I was raised in the Vlen way. I've never seen sundown treated with such significance."

"I know," Arshel answered, amazed at how steady her voice was. "I come from the islands where the Vlen predominates."

"Perhaps you are the ideal person to explain this to me, then." He gestured to the frieze surrounding them, which depicted the same sundown ceremony they'd just seen.

"I've never been instructed in the intended meaning of the ceremony," said Arshel. "The Mautri expect you to find your own meaning in things."

He scanned the carvings. "Do the Mautri make no ceremony to mark the four points of the sun?"

She knew that he'd have checked the comnet information on the Mautri and found it barren of any other ceremony. "There's no other ceremony I know of. The Mautri teaching is to know consciously all that is known to you, thus to gain mastery of all reflexes."

"Strange discipline. Hardly like a religion at all."

"It's not, any more than Vlen teaching is. The priests here hold all kinds of ideas about deity. But they're all totally dedicated to the concept of the ideal kren made real. Have you ever met a white priest?"

"No, I haven't. They live in seclusion."

Dennis said, "I should imagine someone in your position could get in to see anyone he chose."

The kren froze as if Dennis had struck him, but his venom sack remained still and empty at his throat. She heard no strain in his voice as he said, "Thank you for your assistance."

He turned to go. Arshel darted around him. "Apologies for my bhirhir. He didn't mean to imply you'd use the power of the Guild to invade anyone's privacy. He knows that the whites will receive any genuine seeker."

The kren stopped, glanced at Dennis, and said to Arshel, "I shouldn't have taken offense."

Dennis, Arshel noted, was tremendously relieved, and it pleased her that she'd been able to function as a true bhirhir to him. He rejoined them, saying, "May I offer my own apologies. We'd be glad to ride back to town with you."

"It appears unavoidable since there's only one more train," the kren commented.

"Let's hurry," said Dennis as a distant rumble signaled a train pulling out.

They all crossed the parking area to the underway entrance. As they arrived, the automatic lights went out on the archway. The last train pulled in as they came down the steps. There were only a scattered few waiting.

They took a nearly deserted car at the rear of the train, and as it jerked slightly and then glided down the track, Dennis asked, "Are you in Firestrip on business?"

"I'll be working at the University."

"Then let me introduce us."

As Dennis spoke their names, she saw the interfacing slackness settle over the kren. She had to brace herself against an inward shudder, and by a conscious act she forgave the man both for his unpleasant vacuity and for the reflexive curiosity that was part of being an Interface. In his place, she'd have wanted to know all about two such acquaintances.

The kren fastened his gaze on her now, a living gaze that caused a faint stirring within her. "My name is Uslin, Guild of Interfaces. So far, I'm the only kren to survive to work as an Interface. This is my second assignment."

She sensed his calm tones masking some fathomless tension that should have registered in venom. She caught him gauging her venom responses with quick, darting glances.

Oblivious, Dennis asked, "What department of the University are you going to be involved in?"

"Registrar's office, transferrals mostly. There've been some complaints against Camiat for excluding students with certain credentials. Decisions have to be made on the basis of individual credential reviews."

"Have you found a place to stay yet?"

"I'm at a hotel down near the Rayah."

"That's quite a trip out to the campus from there, but I doubt if you'd find any vacancies closer in now."

"There haven't been any listed."

"You could stay at our house. It's half empty."

Arshel felt a rush of venom as a thousand horrified objections rose in her. The Interface noted her reaction and smoothly replied, "The Lakely generosity will become known through me. However, I don't think I could."

Dennis, too, had noticed her reaction, and he placed his hand on her arm. As always, his touch arrested the venom flow.

She said, "What Dennis forgot to mention is that the vacant half of the house is the visitors' half. Dennis and I and his parents are living on the family side."

"I see it would be inappropriate, then. I assure you I had no intention—"

"Actually," Dennis interrupted, "there are two whole suites on the visitors' side, each with its own entrance and plenty of room for two. In fact, if Arshel invited somebody to come for a while, there'd still be enough room."

His grip tightened. Her bhirhir wanted the Interface to stay in the Lakely home for some reason, and so she offered what support she could. "Uslin, it would be a pity to let good living space go to waste. You'd be welcome, as long as you understood that that's all that's being offered." She met his eyes then and was surprised to detect a hint of disappointment. She'd always understood that Interfaces didn't mate.

Dennis' parents greeted the new guest enthusiastically. Dinner was half over before Arshel realized that the Lakelys had assumed that Uslin was her guest. Uslin didn't seem to catch the humans' attitude, though, and conversation flowed freely. By the time she and Dennis were alone that night, she'd been putting off getting angry at him for hours.

"Dennis Lakely, *what* are you doing?" The emotions held in abeyance surged to produce venom until she could hardly talk. "Now, what am I going to say to your parents? To Uslin! What are you up to?"

"Shel, I'm tired. It's been a long day, several days! Let me express you again, and we can both get some sleep." He took her venom bottle down from the bookshelf and said, "In the morning—"

"*Now!* Or I'm going to march right over there and tell Uslin what you let your parents think!" Despite her hard won control of her strike reflex, her fangs swung forward and down, her jaw opening as hot venom rushed up behind her nasal cavities.

Moving with exaggerated slowness, speaking in a low whisper, he said, "All right, we'll talk about it now. But first let me... come on, it'll feel so much better."

She succumbed to his touch. As the venom pumped from her, she felt the tension draining away, too.

When it was over, she curled up in the warm sands of her bed, and he sat on the floor beside her.

"In the morning," he said, "I've got to go on campus and do some research on Uslin. Shel, if we can get him obligated to us somehow—say, by mating with you—we might be able to get some free interfacing done!"

"What makes you think Uslin would be interested in me?"

"I saw the way he looked at you. And don't deny you were looking back! I've never seen an Interface play that game before. Maybe the Guild's new process doesn't take away the ability to mate but just cancels the ability to pair-bond. Maybe Uslin himself doesn't know whether he can mate, and you could be the one to give him that gift, Arshel. He'd owe us for that! Never mind the usual mating obligation!"

A mating obligation was for the care of children and alliances of lineage. She twirled the bracelet Khelin had given her and looked at Dennis. How could a soul trained at Mautri to the white ever generate such twisted ideas?

"Shel, I saw the way you looked at his hands. You couldn't keep your eyes off them all evening. Mom and Dad saw it, too. Don't think Uslin missed it! It's not as if I'm asking you to do something you don't want to do."

With an Interface? She shuddered again, and she hardly slept during the night. The next morning she found Dennis and the Interface in the main kitchen, just finishing breakfast. As she came in, Dennis excused himself and left for the campus.

To make conversation, she said, "There's plenty of room over there for your bhirhir, Uslin. I don't think you mentioned when he was due."

She was utterly unprepared for his reaction. His face went stiff and distant, an imitation of many Interfaces she'd met. "I live balbhirhir like the Mautri."

"Oh." Stunned, she added, "I'm sorry I asked."

"A natural question. I'm not very used to answering it, though. Everyone else seems to have heard all about me on the news."

For all the emotions stirred up by the subject, though, the kren didn't raise even a trickle of venom. *So he doesn't need a bhirhir to express him, but how does he manage in molt? Or during mating?* She wanted to ask him but was too embarrassed. Her own venom was seeping hotly into her sack.

At that point, Madlain came into the main kitchen and began urging the gaunt kren to eat more as she made up the grocery list with items to tempt him. She reminded Arshel of her own surmother in that moment, and it seemed that she also reminded Uslin of his parents, for he took it all in good humor, joking about being driven to an extra molt before he'd even mated. She thought that he was beginning to feel more at home, but she also detected a faint strain when he mentioned molt.

Later, she asked, "I suspect you haven't lived around humans much if you're not from Firestrip."

"There were a few in my community, and I came to know several on Hengrave. But, no, I've never had a human friend before."

Arshel sympathized. "It is often hard to see what a human is after. Dennis, for example." She hadn't planned this, but she had to say it. "I'm not exactly sure when he had this idea. Maybe it was after I mentioned that the spare rooms are on the visitors' side of the house. But, well, we are planning to go offworld again soon, and there won't be another chance for me to mate for a long time. He's always been so protective, and now he apparently has the idea that you and I ought to..."

There was an awkward moment, and then he said, "A bhirhir frequently is the best judge in such matters. And after all, he has to live with the results. I'd say he knows what he's doing."

"Oh, he knows! It's just that every time I start to trust him, I end up getting a shock to remind me he's not kren. This time, I think he's going to ask you to use the comnet for us as a mating obligation. I'm not sure that would be proper."

He looked at her a long time, although his eyes never went vacant. It had been so long since a male had looked at her like that, it felt like the first time, new and mysterious and lovely. The smell of their mutual desire became thick between them. He'd be the first male she'd had who would feel at home in her saltwater pond.

"If," he said slowly, "it's what you want, it could be arranged." Then he glanced pointedly at her bracelet. "But you must understand, I am sterile. It was the price I had to pay."

His manner was of a grief long since burned away, and as always, there wasn't the faintest stirring of venom.

"Uslin, Dennis and I do plan to go offplanet. There's no place in our lives for children right now. But that doesn't mean we must live without pleasure or meaning."

For the first time, she really wanted to give him a good mating. Somebody should care about what he was doing for all kren.

That night, she found that the spawning pond had been opened and filled: the pumps were working softly. Madlain came in as she was standing in the hallway, listening and smelling the brine.

"Oh, I'm glad to see they got around to it!" said the human woman. "Nunin insisted I get that tended to immediately. If it's not just right, leave a note in the clip on the door for the maintenance people."

She had a briefcase dangling from one hand and a package of groceries in the other arm. Arshel took the package from her and said, "I'll put these away. Is there more outside?"

"No, this was just a little idea I had to tempt your half starved mate into eating something. Poor thing, I wonder what they did to him on Hengrave. Dorsan never lacked for appetite! Do you suppose it could have something to do with his not raising venom?"

"It might," said Arshel, putting the package on the kitchen table. It turned out to be some tender cuts of ground fowl from the lowlands where Uslin had grown up. The birds there grew taller than a man and twice as heavy, with deadly venom. "Mom, you really shouldn't go to such—"

"And why not? We're on vacation now. Why not a little luxury?"

Arshel and Dennis had become accustomed to a tight budget. But she couldn't argue with her bhirhir parent.

Over the next few days, Arshel spent as much time with Uslin as she could. He worked during the day on campus but seldom had much to do at night. She spent time in the visitors' kitchen, creating tempting dishes for him, and she gradually came to regard the Interface as a broken man desperately in need of mending and the Guild as the force that had shattered his personality.

Dennis all but disappeared from her life, working feverishly to formulate a question to pose to Uslin for the comnet.

Uslin, meanwhile, seemed to grow more tense and distant with each day. The time they spent in mutual pleasure was satisfying to her but not to him. Something vital was missing, but she couldn't pin it down.

There came a day when Uslin said, "The Registrar's job is done. Now all my time is for you."

"Isn't the Guild going to snatch you away? They're so shorthanded."

She'd ovulated some days before, and the egg was growing visibly each day. He spread one gentle hand on her bulging abdomen and said, "I convinced them to let me stay, to finish."

Relieved, she told Dennis that night, and he said, "When do you suppose would be the best chance to talk to him?"

"He's asked me to take him into the temple to meet a white priest tonight after the sundown." They'd made a regular practice of going up to witness the ceremony, and to her it seemed that each night was more beautiful than the last. "Perhaps when we get back; he may be in a mood to listen."

He nodded. "Shel, this is going to be the luckiest break we've ever had. You go ahead now. Keep him happy."

She was all too glad to do that. She hadn't enjoyed herself so much since Khelin. Thinking back, she realized that she had had only two such times as this, both excruciatingly brief: the moment when she knew that Dennis was going to survive her venom, and the glorious feeling she'd had when her first and only child had fought his way out of the spawning pond. Both of those moments had been tarnished. This one was lasting longer and shining brighter.

The sundown ceremony reinforced her mood, and as she led Uslin into the temple courts, she was feeling exceptionally good. She had sent word in to a white priest, Jylyd, who had worn the purple when she had been a student. She had known him slightly after Khelin had left.

"Many futures from the experience," Jylyd greeted them as they came down the inner corridor to his room.

Her condition by this time was obvious, and she was enjoying the attention it drew. They returned Jylyd's greeting and entered the room.

There was a sand bed along one wall, a low desk and cushion after the manner of his homeland, and a tall closet for his few personal possessions. He lived mostly in the world of ideas, of practices and disciplines, of teaching and learning. In a rush, her life among the Mautri came back to her, and it now seemed a sweet interlude.

"Jylyd Venerable, I have Uslin of the Interface Guild, who would seek with you for a time."

"Arshel, you've known me since I took the violet. How can you give me Venerable? I welcome any you might bring. Come, we'll seek together for the lives that have led the two of you here."

"Uslin is of the Vlen, as I was. He hasn't come for a life-reading." She cast a searching glance at the impassive face next to her. "That is, I don't think he has."

"Ah, but *you* have."

Forgetting Uslin for the moment, Arshel asked, "Will you read my lives for me, then?"

"Arshel, I must not give you what you may win by your own effort. You have the immense talent you were born with and the skills you learned here. Use them."

"My skills don't suffice," she said, thinking of Dennis and remembering her new resolve. "Jylyd, I've thought to return to take the blue, as you once urged me to do."

He looked at her with half closed eyes, his expression distant but not vacant. "I regret that invitation can't be honored now. You have reentered the world and must find your answers there before returning to us."

She stood before the white priest, feeling as if a welcoming door had just slammed in her face. It was almost like the time she'd left Holtethor.

Jylyd shifted his gaze to the Interface. "You seek?"

"I had hoped," said Uslin, "I'd be able to speak with you alone, Venerable."

Jylyd regarded him for a few moments with that stillness she had almost forgotten. Then he said quietly, "It's been several years since I took the white." He went to his closet and sorted around inside it before continuing: "Sometimes the more advanced students such as myself find that by living in isolation, we develop difficulty communicating with the outside world."

He turned, holding in his hands a shoulder drape and cord of the green priest. The garment was frayed from use but clean and mended. He brought it to Arshel. As he continued talking, he draped the smooth material about her shoulders and wound the cord expertly about her torso.

"To overcome this difficulty, we often ask the newer students to attend our conferences as interpreters. Very often, this work falls to those such as Arshel, who have taken an advanced training and live now in the world."

By this point, Arshel, long schooled to stillness, could not restrain a questioning gesture.

Jylyd said, "Patience was never your chief feature, Arshel. This garment is the gift I had meant to give you upon your leave taking. It was given to me by the white priest who first greeted you within our walls. It is for you to carry forth into the world."

She was overwhelmed. To be rejected so firmly and then welcomed again should have raised half a sack of venom, but because of her condition, only the barest trickle responded to her emotion.

Jylyd sat on one of the cushions and gestured them to take places before him. "Sit with us, Arshel, and aid me as you have been taught."

Uslin reluctantly took a place and sat.

Jylyd said, "If Arshel seems unsuitable to this seeking, I'll call another. But Arshel will be with you for a while to answer any questions that occur to you later."

Uslin glanced at her apprehensively. And she said, "What is spoken at a seeking is not respoken elsewhere."

The Interface turned to Jylyd. "Venerable, the question even the comnet cannot answer for me: How is it that the white priests of Mautri survive sane through molt without bhirhir?"

This would, of course, be the central issue in the Interface's life. And yet his voice only held a shadow of grief, not the urgent torment she'd heard from the violet priests facing the white as a challenge or the wistful query she had felt when Dennis was being difficult.

After one of the longest pauses Arshel had endured from a white, Jylyd said, "I negate the title of Venerable in your presence and offer it to you instead. Uslin Venerable, you have shown the greatest wisdom that has come through our gates in a decade. So many of the worlds seem to worship the comnet as if it were all-knowing. But you've learned it can't search out some of the most important answers."

"I didn't come here to be praised. I came to seek."

"Arshel, in what way is this question inappropriate?"

"He has asked what method the whites use when it could have no benefit to him to know, for he has not even taken the red." And then she realized that she'd been critical of an Interface's question formulation. "I meant no disrespect, Uslin. This is only the drill which I learned here."

"I meant to demonstrate," said Jylyd, "that Arshel knows our ways well and can be of service to you. I derive a question for further seeking. Why are you attempting to live balbhirhir?"

"I have no choice."

"And what choices have you used up to come to this?"

"I chose to become an Interface. Now I must learn to survive it. I thought your method might provide me a clue. If it's too secret a method, I'll leave now."

He seemed about to rise, but Jylyd waved him back. "The Guild has long been studying our methods, and we have held from them no secrets. Yet a few years ago they ceased to inquire, having found some new approach they said. For our methods require a total life dedication to apply, as does becoming an Interface. Venerable Uslin, why did you choose to become an Interface?"

"I asked of your methods, and you probe my motives for needing the information. If you can't tell me, I'll leave."

"I want to hear the story of your choices and your reasons for them. Somewhere lies an unasked question which is the key to *your* answer to your question. Not my answer, *yours.*"

"I see." He glanced at Arshel. "It's an ugly story."

"Tell us," said Jylyd softly. "We don't judge; we seek with you for your answer."

Uslin began his tale. Jylyd listened with half closed eyes. Arshel knew that the white priest was listening to a tale of many lifetimes; a more complex weaving than Uslin was willing to admit existed. But she could not divine those lives so easily, and she listened only to the words.

"When I came of age to take bhirhir, my surfather arranged for me to take the son of a family in a neighboring town. Ghernt was almost a stranger to me, even a year later when we swore our lives to each other. We thought at first we could make a fair life of it.

"Ghernt was never a bad sort. But as we grew older, found mates, finished school, and sought work away from our families, we became different people. For a while, we took turns giving in to the other's desires. But to give in like that is to give oneself to misery in life. He was my bhirhir. I couldn't stand to make him miserable; he couldn't stand to do the same to me.

"I came to hate him. And I think he came to hate me. We fought with bared fang. I was raising hate-venom. I could have killed Ghernt with one strike. Somehow, in the confusion of our struggle, I struck our only child. And he died.

"For a time, that brought us together, and together we made the only decision we both stuck to. We applied for the Guild's new kren experiment, and we were chosen to go first after the human who was a bereaved bhirhir. And now Ghernt is dead, and I survived. For all kren, can't you help me?"

Arshel knew that if she'd had to retell such a life story, pregnant or no, her venom sack would be stretched to bursting. Uslin was still dry. He only remembered what it meant to grieve. The prime teaching drilled into her as a red priest came back: *You must feel your emotions fully in order to grow. If the venom rises, let it.*

Jylyd said, "You can't raise venom now?"

"No."

"Then how do you survive molt at all? Even if the Guild had taught you all they learned from us, they could not have learned such a thing."

"The Guild has developed a salve for the skin, but the strangers who tend me—Venerable, I can't endure like this. I know now why there are no other kren in the Guild. And there may never be."

In the long silence, Arshel thought: *Perhaps only a white priest could endure it, but no white priest would want to.*

Uslin sat with his eyes down, his face tilted so that it was grotesque with shadow. Arshel saw a man utterly destroyed by the power to do his own will. It made her shudder with a cold foreboding.

"Uslin Venerable," said Jylyd, "to surrender to *anyone* during molt goes against primal kren nature. We struggle alone to emerge from our hatching pond. But we, as a species, learned to take bhirhir; we learned to accept one person into our moments of helplessness. We had to learn in order to build a civilization. Now, as individuals, some of us are trying to learn to accept the hands of strangers during molt. No two people find the same method, but all the methods come from the same place: the unconscious side of the mind."

Uslin rose to his feet and turned to the door without a word of parting. From the side, she could see his jaw bunching as muscles tightened, but no venom flowed for him, however much he needed it then. In an instant, he was out the door, striding away down the corridor.

She rose, turning to Jylyd helplessly, and began an apology that should have been Uslin's bhirhir's place to offer.

Jylyd waved her to silence. "Go after him. He'll probably get lost looking for the gate. And Arshel, if he asks, answer him truthfully, for you're not bound by our vows. I believe he's a man doomed, and he just found it out—from me."

She had to run to catch up to the wiry Interface, and he had indeed lost his way. When she found him, he'd opened the interface to check a map. Then he glanced around and saw her.

"This way," she said, and led him out to the gate.

They had taken the Lakelys' car, leaving it parked in the lot in anticipation of missing the last train. As she drove home, her awareness of the man beside her shifted to a stark etching. The growing egg sat heavily within her body, reminding her: *He struck and killed his own child, and the Guild took away his ability to feel true remorse about it.*

She drove the car with an abstract precision as she concentrated on controlling the flood of venom threatening to overwhelm her. Peripherally, she was still aware of the green draping, the cord winding around her breasts and over her shoulders. She could not disgrace that in public.

The ride across town became a fight against the traffic control computer, a flight to reach the safety of Dennis' hands. About halfway home, she felt the car rolling to a stop at an underway intersection designed to let cross traffic flow, and a whispered exclamation escaped her.

Uslin reached to flip out the route program cartridge. Holding it in one hand, he opened the interface. Immediately, their line of traffic began to move. Other cars were squeezed aside to let them through, as if theirs were an emergency vehicle. Very quickly, they were rolling into the underground garage of the Lakely house, where Dennis was waiting.

Uslin poked the cartridge back into its slot but didn't move to get out of the car. She got out on her side and went to her bhirhir, but Dennis didn't seem to note her tenseness.

He fingered the green sash. "What's this?" he asked. "You aren't going back to them, are you?" He yanked the drape from her shoulders.

She snatched it from him, hearing threads pop. "I did ask Jylyd to let me try for the blue!"

"Shel, no! We've got to be ready to leave the planet."

"Dennis, this is something I *want* as much as you want to go after the City and 'Ossminid'."

"I thought we were a team!"

"We are, as long as we're doing what you want to do!"

"But this is *important!* We could change the course of civilization in our own lifetime! Doesn't that mean anything to you?"

"Yes, but—" She broke off, desperate to make him understand. "Dennis, don't you remember how you felt when you sat for entry into Mautri and they turned you down? Why do you want to make me feel like that?" Jylyd, she knew, could be talked into readmitting her if Dennis was willing. But as long as he insisted on going offworld, Jylyd would insist that her destiny lay there, too.

Dennis had withdrawn a step, regarding her with a deep frown. "What are you talking about? I *never* sat for Mautri!"

"But—" Certainties she had built her life on shattered. Either the white priest had admitted the wrong Arshel to the temple school, or... *maybe I've taken the wrong human bhirhir.*

Uslin had gotten out of the car on his side. Dennis gave her a shake. "Pull yourself together. I've got work to do." He went toward the Interface. "Uslin, I did want to talk to you. In a day or two, there won't be much time for talk."

The Interface paused, one hand on the door. "I think you'd better tend your bhirhir." He turned then and disappeared into the house.

Astonished, Dennis finally looked at her. By now her venom sack was more than half full and throbbing with the venom production that defied her mated condition. "You do pick the damnedest times to need expression!" He put his arm about her shoulders and scooped her into the house, going right to their rooms.

By the time Arshel had curled up in the fine sand of her bed, her venom sack was filled with the whole flooding reaction she had been fighting all the way home.

As Dennis brought her venom bottle over to her, his manner was abrupt. "Come on, let's get this over with. Maybe I can still catch Uslin before the night is out."

She accepted his touch because the venom would not stop flowing. He held the bottle steady for her, working hard against the full power of her strike muscles. But there was nothing of the deep satisfaction she usually felt when being expressed.

When it was finally over and she was catching her breath, he raised the full bottle and sniffed it before drawing it away. "What in the world could have scared you so at the temple?"

"I'm not frightened," she protested.

He pushed the bottle under her nose. "Really?"

The warm venom did have the sharp reek of fear to it.

"I don't know. I don't feel frightened. Just, I don't know. I've never felt like this before."

"Maybe it's just your condition. Why don't you see the doctor in the morning."

And that's where they left it. In the morning, she did see the physician who had handled all her previous matings. But all tested out normal.

Uslin was waiting for her in the spawning pond when she arrived home. When she saw him relaxing in the surging water, she wanted to turn and bolt out the door. But her feet hurt, her back hurt, and her skin cried out for the oceanlike water. In this warm room, she had to shed coat and jacket and even her normal housewear. Ordinarily, they used the pond naked. But today, she left on the elasticized undergarment that supported her tender breasts and abdomen.

She sat on the edge of the pond on the deep side, dangling her feet in the water. "I'm sorry you had to witness all that unpleasantness last night. It must be worse for you than for almost anyone else."

"I thought by now you'd understand. I remember what happened to me as if it had happened to someone else. As if it were a past life memory!"

"Past life memories usually have terrific emotional impact or they couldn't get through from the unconscious."

He swam over to her and raised his arms. "Come on."

She steeled herself and slid down into his arms. Instead of the pleasure they'd enjoyed in each other, his touch now grated against her skin. The chemistry wasn't there any more.

She pulled away and swam to the center of the pond, floating. "Uslin, Jylyd asked me to help you, but if you won't even ask me questions . . . "

Floating, he stretched out, bringing his head near hers. "My question was answered fully, as I'd feared it would be. My only hope, Arshel, is that they're wrong that the only helpful answers come from the unconscious."

He was so grim, she had to ask, "Why?"

"Because I no longer have access to that part of my mind. No Interface does. The comnet becomes our unconscious. The rest—along with any past life memories, is gone forever."

She understood then why he'd run from Jylyd, from a death sentence. Part of her thrummed in sympathy, yet at the same time, she recoiled from what the Interface really was: a tremendous power without the governor of conscience.

"They've got to be wrong, Arshel. And I've got to prove it. But even if I'm going to die in molt, can't I live now? Come here."

Her mind was paralyzed, and she could only lie in the surging water and let him touch her. His hand against her body, which had brought such pleasure, now grated unendurably. She stood it as long as she could, and then, in a burst of motion, she bolted from the pond and ran through the freestanding arch and out the door into the family side of the house, where he couldn't follow.

As she began to move, the horror of what she had left behind grew until she was streaking down the corridor, screaming, "Dennis! Dennis!"

From the back of the house, where his parents had their offices, Dennis came running toward her. Breathless, she flung herself on him, holding on as if he were her only salvation. "Keep him away from me! Dennis. Don't let him come near me again. I can't stand it." Her venom sack was swelling, choking off her words, and she felt a deep urge to strike at the kren who had been her mate. The thought brought her to a horrified, cold soberness.

Behind Dennis, his parents came slowly into the room, and from their glance she knew that Uslin had followed her. She could hear, in the sudden thundering silence, the drip of water and the slap of bare feet as he came across the tiles.

"Dennis, send him away! Please, Dennis, *please!*" If the Interface came one step closer, she thought she'd strike at him to kill. The Guild had left him without venom, defenseless. She could kill him as easily as he'd killed his own child.

I won't become like him. I won't! "Dennis! Help me!" For a moment, she thought he wasn't going to answer her plea, and blinding white terror flashed through her mind.

She tore loose of Dennis' grip and dashed for her own room, slapping the door of the suite shut behind her and then closing her room door, too. All she heard was a distant, faint sound of voices, mercifully brief.

She grabbed the venom bottle from the bookshelf and thrust her fangs into it. Without anticipating what she was doing, she put her other hand to her venom sack and forced her fingers onto the reflex trigger. The jangle of insulted nerves ripped through her, washing out the last traces of the feel of his hand against her body. It had been years since she'd expressed herself, and it was worse than she remembered. In the end, the voiding turned to retching. She didn't hear the door open behind her.

She barely heard Dennis's words. "Arshel, it's all right. I sent him away. He won't come back."

My bhirhir! But she couldn't speak. Her throat constricted around each expelled breath until it came out a sob. More venom poured from her glands, the irritated reflexes surging anew, and she was blue-voiding uncontrollably.

"Dennis, I've never seen a kren like that. Be careful!"

"I can handle her, Mom. Leave us alone."

A deep-pitched mutter came. "Dennis, maybe you shouldn't tell her about your research application being rejected just now. Save it for later.

After all, you two are still welcome on our project. We need you."

"Skip it, Dad. We'll settle it all later. Mom, call the doctor for Arshel. She's got to pass that egg."

As he stepped into the room behind her, the door closing softly, Arshel thought, *My bhirhir will take care of me.* Then, in a bubble of mental clarity, she remembered that he wasn't her white priest at all, and everything that had ever happened between them was turned inside out with new meaning.

Yes, he'll take care of me, but only so long as I'm doing what he wants me to do.

CHAPTER TWELVE

Guild Master Interface Uslin was dead.

They let Zref out of bed to attend the funeral, a full-dress, formal affair with every news service in attendance. Counting Zref, an even four hundred Interfaces were there, and for the duration of the ceremonies, all the other Interfaces scattered about the Hundred Planets ceased work. It was a formal day of mourning on Camiat.

Uslin had returned from his second assignment and, facing molt, had committed suicide by slashing the main artery to the venom gland at the base of his neck. He had code-locked the doors to his rooms, delaying rescue until he'd bled to death.

Zref stood with the other Interfaces as the kren's body was carried across the roof garden atop the Guild Headquarters building to the small crematorium where, according to Vlen custom, he'd be reduced to ash.

Will I be next?

He banished the thought hastily but couldn't close the door on memory. After being shipped home from the Lantern audit, he'd recovered slowly until he could hold the interface open a little longer each day. The labs were working on the strange flypaper barrier effect, but he hadn't dared to report the ghost Interface. Nobody else had encountered anything similar.

They'd sent him out on a succession of small jobs, which only left him frustrated, until one day he'd stayed open too long, chasing a glitch that might have been the ghost Interface. He'd been brought home by hospital ship again. This time he recovered less of his ability to stay open, but he begged for one more chance, driven by the idea that 'Ossminid' was going

171

to beat everyone to the mazeheart object and gain a power that would destroy civilization again. He argued them into letting him go to Sirwin to help a LEAHPs task force trace some Ossminid activity.

In deep rapport with the Sirwin planetary comnet node, he'd experienced an intuitive flash identifying Eiltherm, capital world of the Hundred Planets, as the seat of operations of 'Ossminid.' And the question finally came up: "What species is 'Ossminid'?"

Zref had undertaken the correlation. It had been routine: no flypaper barrier, no ghost Interface, just his own up-welling curiosity drawing forth from the comnet the full flood of data on 'Ossminid,' gratifying his instincts. Until suddenly he'd found himself back in the gardener's cottage, astraddle Zaviv, pumping life into the Brenilak as in the distance his own bhirhir died screaming.

In that instant, he thought he was dying, too, and had struggled to leave the message: "'Ossminid' is human!" But as he'd been told later, every display screen on Sirwin had lit up with the word "HUMAN" flashing on it like a scream. His first thought after they told him was that now he'd broken the Guarantees. The Guild would close him permanently, for surely there was something terribly wrong with him.

But they had not. They'd once again carefully nursed him back to health. As he stood watching the slow procession of ten senior Interfaces carrying the draped remains of Uslin, the first successful kren Interface, out into the glaring lights of the news services recorders that lit up the midnight dark, he couldn't help but ask himself: *Why did Uslin give up? Did he face the plea of his bhirhir, too?*

The interface within him trembled on the verge of opening for the first time since the scream had hit him on Sirwin. Only he knew that the comnet couldn't answer this question, and so he negated the query and let the interface go dormant. Secretly, he was elated. *I'll be all right again soon.*

The procession passed by Zref's position near the end of the line and then turned to approach the crematorium. The small, square door to the cubical structure was open, and the body slid to rest half inside.

Roylanta, the Chief Interface, took her place in front of the body. Her wispy white hair blew about in the stiff night wind, and her environment cloak shrouded her form. But he knew that she was a frail old human, although he'd seldom seen her. He was mildly startled to feel her drop him a message, until he realized that this was the final tribute to Uslin.

Open now and record in Guild permanent record what you would have remem-

bered about Uslin. Roylanta.

The Guild's permanent records were not normally accessible to individual Interfaces, but Roylanta opened them at funerals. Each of them had received the same message from her, and in response a flood of personal recollections poured into the permanent records. Zref could only add: *I regret I never knew him. Zref.*

Zref, you're back! Lyria.

But Zref's interface flinched closed, sending shooting pain through his head. He caught Lyria's eye across the ranks of the Guild and gave her an apologetic shrug.

Roylanta moved then, shoving the draped body, pallet and all, into the chamber. Two others closed the doors, and a third uncovered the controls and armed them. Then, together, all the Interfaces opened and signaled the computer to flash Uslin's body out of existence. There was a shrill hoot of danger, signaling the use of the crematorium, and then all was still.

Roylanta was the first to make her way back to the roof entry door. Interfaces clustered around her, preventing the reporters from shoving microphones into her face. The other Interfaces broke ranks. Lyria was trying to come toward Zref through the crush, but a reporter made it to him first.

"Master Interface, I understand that you were once bhirhir to a kren yourself. Can you give our viewers a definitive statement on the Guild's treatment of the kren? Will there ever be another kren Interface?"

Zref's mind was whirling, and he felt weak from his long stay in bed. But, his curiosity aroused, he opened just a millisecond and said, "There are no kren applicants to the Guild at this time. I can't predict what individual kren will do in the future, nor can I predict Guild policy, which may be based on new medical breakthroughs."

Zref had kept moving toward the roof door. Those around him paused, aware of Zref's shaky health and ready to divert the reporter. As Zref gave his answer, he received several brief drops of congratulations on his recovery.

And then Lyria was at his side with Nesfil, the Brenilak trainer. "I understand you wished to interview someone who knew Uslin. I was his trainer, so perhaps I can find the information you need."

As the reporter's attention was diverted, Lyria took Zref's elbow. "I'll want to get some measurements on you now."

It turned out that he could maintain himself open for barely fifteen seconds, much less than on previous recoveries, but it was a start.

The next day, the question came up in his session with Nesfil. "We don't understand what is happening with you, Zref. And the phenomenon is getting worse, not better. It took you longer to recover this time, and your recovery is less complete than last time."

Fingering the trinket that had once held a holograph of the Wassly Crown, Zref said, "I know what I did, and I won't do it again.

"Nesfil, I was working fine for a long time. I'd learned how to skirt the edges of the scream, pull out before it hit full blast. And day by day as I worked, I found I could stay open just a bit longer. I was getting *better*, but then—" He couldn't say that he was tempted beyond his limits by the importance of what he was doing. How could he explain his obsession with 'Ossminid' and the City of a Million Legends without it seeming like another aberration? "Maybe, if whatever job you send me on next, you let them know I have a limited open-time capacity . . ."

"Half an Interface at half price? What do you think the news services would make of it? 'The Guild is so desperate for manpower, they're using their cripples to do our work. Can we still trust the Guild? What if one of these defectives becomes a Wild Interface?' That's what they'd be saying within a day of our sending you out under those terms."

Zref couldn't meet the Brenilak's eyes. The teeth protruding from the man's muzzle were just too ferocious. "Are you going to ask them to disconnect me, then?"

"Zref, none of us enjoys sending an untrainable for disconnect. We've all faced it, and you don't need access to your unconscious to oppose that end, vigorously."

"You're saying yes."

"I'm saying maybe. Now that you're regaining your capacity again, I'm going to try to work with you to build up your open time to its former level. But if we fail, Zref . . ."

And so the long period of rehabilitation began again. Zref moved from the hospital up to the residence floor. He had appointed times for exercise and for therapy sessions in which they probed his feelings for Sudeen and the way he'd overcome his losses.

Eventually, they began allowing him to fill time in the query booths in the Guild Headquarters lobby. The quick queries people brought there never needed more time than he could remain open, and he soon regained his skills and self-confidence. His thoughts began to turn insistently to 'Ossminid,' and he followed the spectacular machinations attributed to him in the news.

As Zref saw it, it was war between LEAHPs and 'Ossminid.' Five of the best LEAHPs officers had been killed while on the trail of 'Ossminid.' And if only a fraction of what the news services were reporting was true, 'Ossminid' already had an organization that spanned the Hundred Planets. Zref spent all his spare time holding microcorrelations, keeping well within his time limits. The labs had decided that the strange flypaper barrier he'd encountered at Lantern was another spinoff of First Lifewave technology, like the Wild Interface, and now they were hot on the trail of duplicating the effect. But nothing was said to the public. The Guild's hope was that out of each new development of technology might come both new weapons *and* their defenses; this time at least, it seemed to be working.

Many other Interfaces were also interested in 'Ossminid''s doings and were correlating their own data. Zref was able now to drop messages to them, comparing results with Interfaces of many other species and viewpoints. Since he had the most free time for this hobby, it rapidly became known as his project, on which the others were just helping.

The day came when he'd regained 90 percent of the open-time capacity he'd had before the Sirwin assignment. It appeared that he'd make no further progress. He was in the roof garden, sitting in the rain, watching birds nesting on top of the crematorium and pondering Uslin's suicide, when Lyria dropped him a note: *Nesfil and I will meet you in Roylanta's office, now. Lyria.*

He knew that this was it. He'd either be put to work or be disconnected and retired to a full-care ward, spending the rest of his life as a near vegetable. They'd made him visit that ward before he signed the first surgery authorization. He fingered the trinket again, his resolve hardening within him.

Roylanta's office was a corner of the building, with a window that opened on both sides of the corner. It was open now to the sound of the rain and the street far below. Along one wall stretched a purple divan with movable pillows to allow various species to find comfort. Around the divan were spread leaning racks and stools considered comfortable by others. At the moment, only Roylanta sat on the divan. Jim Diebold, his therapist, Lyria, and Nesfil sat in chairs around her. A place was left for Zref beside Roylanta.

He sat carefully, not wanting to jar the old lady. "I came as quickly as I could."

"We've come to a tentative decision," said Nesfil, "which we don't think will displease you too much."

"If I were he," said Roylanta in a clear voice with traces of the resonance it must once have had, "I wouldn't be pleased by it."

"Tell me," said Zref, "or I'll get too curious and look it up!"

"It seemed best to us," replied Roylanta, "to allow you to continue as you have been these last months. You can be of use working the query booths and possibly in the training programs. And there may be other chores that will come to you in time. But we can't see allowing you to go out and represent the Guild again as an Interface."

"No!" he blurted out, and then be apologized. "I suspect," he added slowly and with emphasis, "that if I must spend the rest of my life within these walls, it will be as short a life as Uslin's was." His hand was clamped over the trinket.

Jim Diebold slid to the edge of his chair, reaching toward Zref. "You've never mentioned contemplating suicide!"

"I haven't, yet. I'm human, not kren, you know." He looked around at them. "Because I'm human, put me in a box and I'll have to break out or die trying."

Nesfil looked to the therapist. "Jim Diebold, is this wholly normal for a human? We've just saved him from disconnection, yet he sees limitation, not liberation."

"It's within bounds for a human of Camiat, and he's a young man. Actually," he said, turning toward Zref, "if you keep fighting, you just might lick this thing."

Zref took a firmer grip on the trinket and said, "I have a counterproposal. Since you think I'm all right enough to leave me connected but not all right enough to work as an Interface, is there any reason why I have to stay here at Guild Headquarters and do nothing?"

"Where would you want to go?" asked Nesfil.

"Eiltherm, to search for 'Ossminid'."

They all began talking at once. Zref got their attention again and added, "Look what we have so far. My intuition that 'Ossminid' is on Eiltherm came out of the work I did on Sirwin. My correlation that 'Ossminid' is probably human. And the extensive work of all these Interfaces." He gestured to the screen behind them and displayed his hobby file for them. "Tracing supplies and equipment to Eiltherm way in excess of averages, equipment that can be used in exploration or archeology!"

He displayed the curved estimates that showed a better than 60 percent chance that 'Ossminid' planned an expedition to search for the mazeheart object within the year. "With the passage of the Search Bill and all that grant money pouring out, it's a race between 'Ossminid,' the HP government, Lantern, and who knows who else. The Guild fought 'Ossminid' once before. We can't afford that again. LEAHPs will put the man out of action if we can only identify him."

"That will not stop the race for First Lifewave technology," said Diebold. "The Search Bill is a fact."

"It might not stop the race, but it will slow it down," Roylanta said. "Right now, the main impetus behind public support of the Search Bill is the idea that a criminal who has once nearly crippled the HP commercial sector is bent on setting himself up as Emperor of the Second Lifewave and is going to beat everyone to the mazeheart object. Funding would be much harder to get without 'Ossminid'."

"True," Lyria added thoughtfully. "People may not really believe that the City of a Million Legends is a treasure trove of First Lifewave technology, but they're not willing to risk anyone else getting there first, just in case it is real."

"It's going to take an Interface to stop 'Ossminid'," said Zref. "Where are you going to find an expendable Interface if not me? No." He gestured to Diebold. "Not suicide but a calculated risk. I was once trained as a security officer of the Cranston Corporation. I can take care of myself. And as you well know, an Interface is most effective when personally immersed in a situation. *People* ask questions, and they ask them most easily of a flesh-and-blood Interface rather than a console. In this case, they won't even know I'm an Interface. I'll just be there to hear and overhear what people are asking."

"There's no doubt that personal involvement brings best results," said Lyria. "But with your stability—"

"Unless I wear the medallion, there's nothing to mark me off as an Interface. Nobody's going to demand a long opening."

"If you open in public," said Lyria, "they'll know."

"One thing I've learned is how not to open so casually. Believe me, I think twice now before each opening. Jim has taught me how to use the watchdog to prevent myself from overstaying an opening. I *can* do this job!"

Nesfil said, "In a Brenilak, such an attitude might be interpreted as 'wscil,' or revenge."

Jim Diebold said, "He has, as you all know, more than enough motive for wanting revenge on 'Ossminid,' if, indeed, this character is the same one responsible for the Wild Interface."

"Revenge," said Roylanta uncertainly. "An Interface should not be capable of such a motivation."

Diebold said, "I've never found a trace of it in him."

Roylanta asked, "What is your motivation, then?"

Forcing his hand away from the trinket, Zref looked at them squarely. "I want to serve the Guild and all seekers of knowledge."

Roylanta considered and then said, "I'll put your proposal to the Guild, Zref, and we'll see."

The discussion went on both at the Guild Headquarters and by general access message drop among all the Guild members. It took several days, but in the end they voted to let him try his scheme.

The Eiltherm shuttleport thronged with a never ending stream of travelers, even though it was late night when Zref arrived. Eiltherm was a planetwide city that never slept.

His personal Guild medallion had been welded into a larger steel casing artfully decorated as a piece of jewelry. He shepherded his baggage through customs and arrived at the security station, where his identity and purpose for being on the planet would be verified.

"Name," said the Jernal clerk, digits poised over a keyboard.

Zref put his hand on the identifier plate and said, "Zref MorZdersh'n."

"Planet of origin."

"Camiat."

"Purpose on Eiltherm."

"Looking for employment."

"As?"

"Security guard."

The Jernal rotated its spherical body, bringing its full attention to bear on Zref. "You don't look very strong."

"I've been trained by the Cranston Corporation."

The Jernal's digits again danced over the keys of the computer tie-in. "That was some time ago. What have you been doing in the meantime?"

"I worked for Lantern Enterprises. Then I did a stint with LEAHPs."

This was absolutely true, and the Jernal's screen verified it by flashing a security seal over the details. It was appallingly easy to fool a screening if you could address the comnet permanent records directly. 'Ossminid' might not have another Wild Interface yet, but Zref wondered whether his very accomplished hand programmers couldn't pull off the same stunt and walk on and off any planet of the hundred without a single challenge.

The Jernal had finished his scan and was working up an identity chip for Zref. "You shouldn't have much trouble finding work. Keep this with you at all times, and if it sounds, slip it into any phone. It could be an offer of work. Next."

The first thing Zref did was take a tour of the planet to bring his inner knowledge of maps and facts up to conscious knowledge of places and relationships. He understood now why Zaviv had hired him and Sudeen for the grand tour. When it was over, he chose a residence hotel for his stay.

It was clean and neat, run by two expatriates of Firestrip City, a human and a kren, who were bhirhirn. It had an elegant restaurant frequented by officials and their staffs and families, yet it wasn't so expensive that it would seem strange for an out of work security guard to stay there.

His room had a lounging pond, a sand bed behind a decorated screen, and a bed set within reach of the computer controls. There was even a quickchef to provide light meals.

Once he had an address, he went roaming through the neighborhood. In a city of offices and corporate headquarters, this was an oasis of purely residential buildings and their ancillary supply centers. The next day, he took an underway to the section where the government dealt with people who came to Eiltherm to regularize their businesses or to appeal some decree or another. He wanted to see for himself what security measures were taken there in order to compare it with the area where he was residing. He was especially interested in one thing he couldn't get from the comnet: How did people react to these measures, and how easily could they be circumvented? Would anyone turn in a trespasser?

Could 'Ossminid' be living on Eiltherm without any official record of his presence existing in the comnet? Or would he have another identity here?

In an afternoon's walk, he saw four angry encounters with door guards, one physical attack on a comnet station that brought local guards down to restrain the violent Sirwini, and twelve instances in which people walked past guard stations while the guards were not looking and other pedestrians ignored them. In six such instances, automatic scanners deeper into the building reported the unauthorized presences to the comnet, and presumably the individuals were stopped and authorized. The other six incidents went without notice.

Later that night he opened, trying to calculate how long a person might exist on Eiltherm in anonymity, but he didn't have enough data. He was concentrating now on a type of work he'd done with Sudeen. Grimly, he kept his open time to half his limit, knowing that that might cause symptoms resembling lack of REM sleep but also aware he must not succumb to the scream while alone. Medics, not knowing that he was an Interface, might do him real damage.

The next day, he stayed in his room, scanning the city's local computer services manually and mentally. The five Interfaces currently on Eiltherm dropped him notes of welcome, and one of the humans wished him good luck.

In short, intermittent openings, he made contact with all the volunteers he'd developed throughout the Guild and apprised them of his lack of progress. He picked up two interesting suggestions, the best coming from an accountant who had later become an Interface.

Trace the flows of funds in and out of local pockets and then check by eyeball the standard of living of those receiving public monies. You'll find many discrepancies, but the greatest one will be your man. 'Ossminid' is nothing if not vain. Cheurlin.

The second suggestion was only a reprise of his own thoughts. *Check anything under the subject heading of archeology and related fields. Dislik.*

He had the data amassed that evening, realizing that the people receiving public money would be the Representatives and Assembly members themselves. But he had no way of getting to know them. They lived in the remote houses behind the secure perimeters that rimmed the residential area.

With the vague idea of applying for security guard work at the residence of his prime suspect, he turned down several invitations to interviews and spent the next few days in the galleries, watching the Representatives debate. One day, he watched three heated debates among the three Representative bodies considering the Search Bill extension that would provide even more funding for the search for the City of a Million Legends. It was defeated resoundingly all three times, and he chafed at being unable to open to find out which Rep had voted which way while he could see their faces. One human in particular, the Low Rep of the Explorer

Corps, captured his attention, sitting ramrod straight, stroking his red beard, and watching his colleagues with a smug satisfaction that repelled Zref. By the time it was over, he was shaking with the need to open and satisfy his curiosity.

The Representative building was star shaped, with the assembly hall in the middle and wings jutting in every direction, catering to the needs of various species. There was only one place Zref could count on for real privacy, and so he went down the Camiat wing, searching for the expression rooms.

He found them in an alcove just off the Representatives' own entrance to the hall, and he ducked quickly into the foyer from which opened a dozen private rooms. He took one that stood with its door ajar, showing just a hint of purple and gold decor. With the door locked behind him, he allowed himself to open.

The voting records flooded into his mind, and quickly evaluations formed, correlating with the things he'd noticed as the Reps voted. He had to close the data channels by an act of will when his watchdog called time and then wait a while to reopen and finish the job. It stood to reason that 'Ossminid' would want that bill defeated to choke off the heavy government funding to the competition, and so the Explorer Corps Low Rep with the smug expression—Balachandran—couldn't be 'Ossminid.' He had voted for the bill. Yet it would have been suspicious if an Explorer Corps Rep had voted against exploration. Was he smug because he knew that he could safely vote for a bill he had to have defeated? Zref needed more data.

Hungry and tired, Zref forged his way out into the busy corridor just as the Representatives were pouring from the main hall. People were waiting for a word with them. Others were milling about at the bottom of the gallery stairs, and some bhirhir pairs headed purposefully toward the expression rooms behind Zref. He set his course for the exit.

"Zref?" It was a kren voice, somewhat familiar.

And again, "It *is* Zref!" from a human.

He turned. Making their way toward him were Khelin and Ley. Startled, he opened. They were now working for the Diplomatic Services Administration, helping government employees adjust to life on Eiltherm.

Khelin said, "They told me at the hotel there was another MorZdersh'n registered, but I couldn't imagine who it could be. You've got to tell us the whole story. What are you doing here? What's to using the family name?

How long are you going to stay? Can we have dinner, perhaps?"

"Have you been home lately?" Ley asked. "And how come you never send so much as a holiday greeting?"

"Not here," said Zref. The crowd was thinning and moving swiftly. "And I have a few questions of my own."

"The hotel restaurant," Ley suggested. "They have privacy screens on the pool terrace, and the weather should be good."

"We have our flier right here," said Khelin, "and since we're all staying in the same hotel—"

"That's something of a coincidence," Zref interrupted.

"Not really," answered Ley as they walked. "You're MorZdersh'n, too."

Zref smiled. He and Ley, even as outsiders, had picked up a mark of the family's style. *Never skimp and never waste.* He'd chosen the hotel that best fit the family style.

"I'm glad to see you can still smile," said Khelin.

Zref covered his teeth. "Sorry."

"I meant only, after the operations and—"

"Not here," Zref snapped.

They were entering the parking structure. On their level, a line was forming for a bus. Khelin led the way to an orange coded bounce tube. Zref was last up and found that Ley had already gotten the flier started. They took off from the rail, right into the sunset, with the front windshield darkening against the glare.

Zref had the rear passenger seat; Khelin and Ley were in the front pilot positions. When they'd programmed their route, Khelin swiveled his chair about to face Zref.

"Something is wrong. No, don't argue with me. It's my business, and my talent, to know. You're not wearing your medallion."

Guild security or no, Zref would have to tell them a little or they'd have it all over the planet that their relative the Interface was in town. Averting his gaze a moment, he used the comnet to check the security of the flier.

"All right, I'll tell you here, but don't let it go any farther, not even to the rest of the family."

"What is it, Zref?" Ley asked. "The Guild hasn't found another Wild Interface?"

Things were really bad if that was the thought uppermost in Ley's prosaic mind. "No. But listen, I came through Eiltherm customs as Zref MorZdersh'n, a Cranston trained freelancer. So far, no one has suspected

I'm an Interface."

Ley examined him critically. "No scars showing. There really isn't anything they could tell by. But I never knew the Guild did things like that."

"They never have before. I talked them into it." He explained that he was on Eiltherm to pick up 'Ossminid"s trail. As they parked at the hotel, Ley flashed him a clear smile.

"With all the fancy surgery, you're still our Zref!"

Dinner was spent catching up on family news. Later, in Zref's room, Khelin shed his clothing and relaxed in the water while Ley sat on the side of the pond, dangling his feet in it. The room, too, was secure. Nobody had any reason to target them for surveillance yet.

"Khelin," said Ley, catching at his bhirhir, "surface a moment. I want to talk to you."

"Hmmm?" said the kren, letting his face rise out of the water. "I doubt if much talking is necessary. I say we should."

"Good. You tell him."

The kren raised himself to a sitting position and said, "Zref, do we really have to volunteer formally? Or aren't you just assuming we're going to help you any way we can?"

With the closed lip grin that came back to him so naturally, Zref answered, "MorZdersh'n, right? I asked for it."

"Then it's settled. We'll start tomorrow." Khelin settled back into the water. "Awfully shallow pool, Zref."

"A single, unemployed security guard can't afford deeper." Zref was beginning to understand why the Guild insisted on separating recruits so completely from their families. The emotion wasn't there anymore, but the implicit family loyalty was still a part of the fabric of his personality. Yet an Interface dared have no loyalty except to the Guild, cutting across all lines of species or politics.

Khelin was submerged again. Ley, still wearing street clothes, bent over and yanked at his bhirhir's head fluff, forcing the kren to surface again. "What do you mean, tomorrow? We have the Horthane reception!"

"Well, get on the phone and order up an invitation for Zref."

Ley just looked at him.

"You don't expect me to do it, do you?" Khelin stood up, naked and dripping. "What do you suppose Ireda Maytom, for example, would make of a call from *this?*" He gestured to his long, perfect, but distinctively kren male body.

Ley threw a handful of water at him and got to his feet. He still looked perfectly groomed from the waist up; only his bare feet and damp, rolled up pants legs spoiled the effect.

He said, "Zref, this is a rum tasting party sponsored by the Horthane embassy. They want to cut off the illegal rum smuggling by making all their exports legal. Ireda Maytom is one of the statisticians working on the new law because she used to work for the LEAHPs department that goes after smugglers. She's *always* in need of an escort."

That was the beginning of Zref's acquaintance with Eiltherm society. He met people who were interested in both Lantern and LEAHPs operations, and he learned quickly that 'Ossminid' was not a name that could be mentioned in social contexts without causing a nervous change of the subject.

He began to realize just how much real pressure the government was under from the public and how irrational some of that pressure was. He gained invitations to other functions on his own after that, and from time to time when something exclusive and interesting came up, Khelin and Ley would get him an invitation.

Some time after he'd met his brothers, he found himself at a huge Nipshelanti holiday celebration. It was held at the Nipshelanti's main residence complex built out under the sea on a continental shelf. Sparse sunlight filtered down, augmented by lights that radiated across the spectrum of the various guest species.

Undersea gardens had been built much on the order of those Zref was used to on land: something from everywhere, and as much mixing as environments allowed. Guests who were of aquatic species had access to the colorful gardens where an exterior party area had been set up. Semiaquatic guests such as the Ciitheen and the kren mingled within the dome with the air breathers.

Some humans, Brenilak, and even Sirwini donned aqualungs and took short swims. The water here was warm, and Zref and Ley had a good time swimming with Khelin. But it was so deep that it was soon exhausting. They dressed and reentered the party dome, where latecomers had gathered, talking, playing scobit, or eating from the lavish buffet.

After their swim, they were hungry, and so Ley led them up to a balcony where he had found a table laden with some of their favorite delicacies. Zref glanced about, wondering who among this crowd would be worth meeting. From the comnet entries his interface network had discovered,

Zref was sure that the expedition he had been tracing was being marshaled on the Explorer Corps Reserve. Too much gear suitable for archeological research had been disappearing through those gates. The activity had started, it seemed, when the Search Bill extension had been voted down.

Now Zref saw the Low Rep of the Explorer Corps, Balachandran, standing near the stairs that wound down to the main floor. With him was a human, not much older than Zref, and a kren woman, saltwater spawn. Her skin tones were enhanced by the underwater lighting, and Zref could see that she was quite attractive in her exotic way, the sort Sudeen would have gone for. *Ah, Sudeen!*

The day he'd first met Zaviv, there'd been just such a pair standing on the shuttleport steps, and Sudeen had been attracted. Zref had been sharply disturbed by her, but now there was nothing. An Interface never had flashes. *I had no gift worth training.*

"Long before your work at Mautri fitted you to become a human Interface, you knew the artisan who made this sphere." Iebe Arai Then's words came back to him unbidden. For the first time, he wondered whether he'd been rejected at Mautri because he had no gift worth training or because it had already been thoroughly trained. *If Arai was correct, I may have lost a great deal in becoming an Interface.*

"Zref? Zref! What are you doing?" Ley's voice sounded choked with concern.

Zref shook himself out of the train of thought. "I was just wondering who those bhirhirn are." He gestured vaguely.

"Don't wonder too hard in public." Khelin said, glancing at them. "That woman is Arshel Lakely. You may have heard of her. She hates Interfaces."

Ley added, "Saltwater spawn. I wouldn't risk her venom."

"Watch them carefully," said Khelin. "That's Dennis Lakely. I'm sure your parents knew his parents. But this boy is not of the same cloth."

Zref watched, as the three seemed to be having an argument. The female gestured at the swimmer's lock, while her bhirhir stood stiffly beside her, and Balachandran seemed to oppose her suggestion. She started off on her own, but it was the Rep who put his hand on her arm to restrain her, taking the part of the bhirhir while her own bhirhir stood mute. Then the tension among them broke as Dennis Lakely cut between the two and directed their attention toward some new arrivals.

Khelin said, "I wouldn't bet Ley's life on Dennis' ability to control her. But it wasn't always that way between them."

"You've known them before?"

"Remember the baby Ley and I had in the nursery when you were convalescing that winter? Skanqwin. She gave him to us."

Now Zref could make out the MorZdersh'n bracelet on the kren's arm. "Oh." *And she hates Interfaces.* Yet those two were the hottest thing going in archeological research, which supported his theory about the clandestine expedition and pointed toward Balachandran's being involved with 'Ossminid' somehow. "Well," said Zref, "she *is* a green priest. I'm going over there and see if Balachandran has any openings for a security guard."

But before he could cover the distance, the three had been surrounded by a group of Sirwini, and Zref never got another chance to approach Balachandran during that party.

The next day he applied in person at Explorer Corps headquarters for a security position and was told he'd have to join the corps, which of course he couldn't do. He learned nothing of interest in the outer offices.

Several weeks passed in one party after another. Zref used every resource he had developed among the interested Interfaces and through Khelin's contacts to be on hand when Balachandran was there. He wanted to get him alone, but always the few times he appeared, the Lakelys were with him.

Meanwhile, he applied to the Guild dispatcher, Rodeen, to be assigned as an Explorer Corps Interface if they should request one. This opened the whole argument of his fitness again. He could point to the weeks he'd played his part on Eiltherm and the progress he'd made. Probability studies showed a better than even chance that 'Ossminid''s expedition was being prepared on the Explorer Corps Reserve.

During this time, Lantern published a new novel, *Maze Builder.* Zref bought a copy and realized that it was based on his own life-readings. It was receiving rave reviews and outselling the *Ossminid* title. Yet try as he would, he could not get beyond the opening.

Stories reached him about Balachandran, outrageous things he'd done at various parties and a trick he'd played on some kren and the Ciitheen at a shore party before Zref had arrived. The man had a colossal ego and was in a perfectly camouflaged position. He could easily *be* 'Ossminid.' Zref set his Interface team to work on Balachandran's background and recent doings, and circumstantial evidence began to mount. There was absolutely nothing to turn over to LEAHPs, but Zref became convinced that he'd found his man.

While he considered, watched, and probed, the expedition mounted behind Explorer Corps fences finally took off, leaving Balachandran behind.

At that point, Zref was suddenly certain that he'd been wasting his time. If Balachandran was 'Ossminid,' he'd have gone with the expedition. His previous disappearances all coincided with 'Ossminid' activity, and this expedition obviously was expected to get final results. Vast amounts of capital had been diverted into it from corps funds. When the annual reckoning of accounts came around, Zref's Interfaces assured him, there'd be a hard time explaining that diversion.

Rodeen reported that the expedition had never even requested an Interface. *Because they knew they'd be turned down or because they have one of their own? Zref.*

There is no Wild Interface, asserted Zaviv by general drop, *but I m going to spend some time tracing that expedition's comnet activity. Zaviv.*

Time passed while Zref chased from party to party where Balachandran was expected and failed to lay eyes on the man. He didn't show up in the Low Rep chambers anymore, either. He was definitely in town, for Zref spoke with people who had seen him recently. But the comnet listed him as being on vacation.

Once Zref called while the comnet listed him as in his office and was told that Balachandran was indisposed. Comnet revealed no records of medical treatment. An Interface wasn't supposed to feel frustration with quite so much edge to it, Zref reminded himself during those weeks.

And then, without warning, he was called by Roylanta to open for funeral proceedings.

The Brenilak Master Interface, Zaviv, was dead.

Catching his breath from shock, Zref hastened back to his room at the hotel, where he could open unguardedly. He dropped to Lyria: *What happened? Zref.*

She cut her answer into bits he could take in short openings. Zaviv was receiving burial with supreme honors, for in the course of his investigation, he'd encountered a vague trace of a nonregistered Interface. It wasn't at all like the Wild Interface who'd attacked him years ago, but he pursued the trace determinedly. Several other Interfaces had witnessed the final moments of the struggle. Zaviv died of breaking the Guarantees, but he took the new Wild Interface with him, preventing any real damage to the comnet.

The Guild's public stand is that the disruption was mechanical and killed

Zaviv. But Zaviv made it seem to 'Ossminid''s investigators that this Wild Interface died of faulty surgery, giving way in a brain hemorrhage. Roylanta has ordered everyone to spend all spare time searching for any trace of other Wilds. Lyria.

Zref digested the information grimly. His ghost Interface had killed one he had called friend. When it came time to enter something in the permanent records about Zaviv, he dropped: *He taught me how much people appreciate it if we just turn our eyes aside when opening instead of blatantly opening while staring at someone. Zref.*

When the formalities were over on Hengrave, he dropped to Rodeen: *I'm sure Balachandran will ask the Guild for an Interface, possibly using a government contract to the Explorer Corps as a cover. I want that job. Zref.*

A few days later, he was visiting Khelin and Ley—Khelin had flatly refused to spend another evening in Zref's shallow pond—when a flagged drop came into his private file.

Ley was in the water, scrubbing Khelin's hide. The kren, uncomfortable with an approaching molt, was submerged, luxuriating. But both of them sat up to watch Zref as he closed.

Khelin said worriedly, "I've never seen you go so blank for so long before."

"I can open for longer than that," said Zref. He had finally explained to them the whole of his problem. "It was a message from the Guild dispatcher. They're sending me on the Explorer Corps expedition I wanted. I'm to report to Lumar Balachandran at his office, ready to travel. Now."

My last chance. Rodeen said. She meant it.

CHAPTER THIRTEEN

Eiltherm greeted Arshel and Dennis with a burst of dry heat as their shuttle's hatch opened. Arshel followed Dennis without any of it registering in her mind. On the trip to Eiltherm, they'd heard that Uslin had committed suicide.

Cut off from the roots of his being, Uslin couldn't contact his own emotions to work out his problems. Her revulsion for all Interfaces grew to the point where she wouldn't enter the dining hall on the ship when any of the Interface passengers was there.

She knew that her emotions whenever she saw an Interface indicated a deep subconscious problem of her own and that this might well constitute the reason why Jylyd had refused her reentry to Mautri. She followed Dennis, hoping that he would help her solve her problem and free her to return to Mautri.

Arshel's only lasting impression of their arrival on Eiltherm was of emerging from the port building, luggage in hand, to confront the Arch of Planets.

It was a colossal door to the room without walls. Somehow it made real to her the immensity of that room in a way all her years at Mautri never could.

The arch had been built freestanding in a sprawling park, which it almost dwarfed. The structure was covered with the hundred planetary emblems made from the jewels native to each planet. At the top was the emblem of the combined Hundred Planets. The distant, dark red sun raised umber and fire glints from the massive array of precious stones, and it seemed to her that each glint held a separate drama woven skillfully into a whole greater than its parts. It was very much like the Crystal Crown and its gold sphere, and it shook her to the core.

"Arshel!" Dennis' hand on her arm distracted her. "What are you going to do, raise venom right here? Can't you wait until we find a place to live first?"

"I'm sorry."

She followed him as they searched the public rolls for suitable housing. At last, tired and hungry, they found themselves in an amphibian neighborhood. The apartment Dennis led her to was a single large room with facilities tucked away behind screen partitions. But fully half the floor was water, a pond large enough to swim in. And it was warm.

"Suit you, Shel?"

"Yes, but can we afford it?"

"It's not nearly as expensive as that bhirhirn-run hotel. I don't think we'll find anything cheaper."

He left her to unpack while he made the rental arrangements. They were very low on cash. After their grant application was rejected, Dennis had waited until she'd recovered from passing the egg and then asked her whether she was still certain about the planet she'd picked. She had worked the beads repeatedly, getting the same definite answer each time.

"All right," Dennis had said grimly. "Let's go to Eiltherm and fight for that grant."

They'd taken all their cash and bought tickets, leaving them only enough to live on for a short while. Early on their first morning, they picked their way through the city to their first point of attack, the Budget Mandate, Appeals Division. It took both of them to fill out the forms, and then they compared notes.

"I wonder," said Dennis, "if we should put down archeovisualizer as the source of some of the information. We didn't on the first application, and it was rejected. What do you think?"

"I'd rather not be known for my talent. But I'll do whatever you say." Mentally she braced herself against the two knots of emotional turmoil. There was something about this whole business that she was resisting the way she resisted Interfaces and further knowledge of her past lives. But she knew that Dennis would force her to face it, and he did.

"Look, this is our last shot. Let's play our high card." And he wiped the relevant items, keying in her identification as an archeovisualizer. He punched the application through with a flourish and then said, "Let's go out to lunch."

They were in a section of the planetwide city open to the air and the cheerless red sun. There were wide parks set formally with plants from a dozen worlds. Above them, buildings reached for the sky, and balconies and tiered ledges spilled over with a thousand shades of green, ocher, red, and blue leaves.

They sat beside a fountain in an area of Camiat foliage to eat the food they'd brought with them. To one side, among the trees and bushes, was a little building labeled "Expression Rooms." Momentarily, Arshel felt at home, and it was such an astonishing relief, it told her what a strain she was under.

Looking around at the other kren passing through or pausing in this small oasis of home, she saw the relaxation come over them as it had over her, despite the purple sky above turning slowly mauve-silver. She wondered how the plants of Camiat could grow under such a sky, and then she noted batteries of lights aimed down at the garden from every angle.

Dennis strolled to the fountain, breaking off bits of the fruit bar he'd been eating and tossing them to the birds. Arshel got up and drifted around the huge, round fountain. She had long since finished the meat cake that had been her meal.

Overhead, a distant rumble accompanied a shuttle taking off. The air was hot and breathless over the city. It would be so refreshing just to dip her feet in the water. She held one hand under the spray and glanced around at the other kren in the area. And then she saw him.

"Dennis! Look! Isn't that—" As the distant kren turned profile on to her, she was sure. "Khelin! Khelin!"

He had been coming out of the Expression Rooms, and as he paused to search for the source of his name, he was joined by a human she identified as Ley. He was sandy haired, and his fair skin was blotched in a way that seemed worse under this lighting than it had on Camiat. *Freckles,* she reminded herself. *It's not a disease, and he's not in molt.*

The two came toward Arshel and Dennis, with Khelin rapidly taking the lead. "Arshel! Dennis. The room without walls may not be so huge after all! What brings you to Eiltherm? Planning to excavate the Hundred Planets Assembly building?"

"No." Dennis laughed. "Forms to fill out and officials to see, that's all. What about you? You're the last couple I expected to find here!"

Ley looked at the livid sky and said, "We can't stand around here talking. It's going to be hailing in a minute or two. We were just on our way to lunch. Join us?"

"We've eaten," said Dennis.

"We do have time until our next appointment," said Arshel. "Dennis, would you mind if we went along for the company?"

He glanced from Khelin and Ley back to her. "Why not?"

"Hurry, then," said Khelin as slashing ice rain began to pelt them.

Here and there a large hailstone bounced, and a cold wind rose around them. Khelin led the way through winding paths behind the Expression Rooms to another small kiosk shrouded in vines. Beneath the park, they found broad avenues set with flowering shrubs and glittering signs. Khelin led them straight to a bounce tube down another level and out into a side alley from which three heavy sets of doors led to a quiet restaurant that looked expensive.

Dennis glanced at her, and she could read the words in the set of his lips: *Now look what you've gotten us into.* She buried a flash of annoyance.

Khelin was speaking to someone stationed at a computer terminal. He was kren, old and so dignified that she felt she had to flip her green medallion out of her shoulder pocket in order to be accepted.

Presently, Khelin came back. "We'll have a table up on the third level."

The dining area, as she glimpsed it off the long hallway before her, was filled with dozens of species, though there were many kren among them. "Is this a kren restaurant?"

"After a fashion. They cater to those who want to sample Camiat's cuisine without inconveniencing themselves. However, the management welcomes bhirhirn as well."

A waiter came to escort them up two flights of stairs to their table. They had a corner overlooking the main floor and a balcony beneath them. On this level, most of the diners were kren, some even without their bhirhirn. It was a level where offworlders wouldn't want to be seated.

As they took places about the round table, taking their street shoes off and easing their feet in the fine, warm sand, menu cards lit up in the table surface.

Khelin took the light pen and marked off a solid lunch for himself and Ley; then he said, "If you won't be eating, at least let me order you something to drink. Spansu?" To Dennis he said, "They have an interworld sangria here I think you'd like."

Reluctantly, Dennis nodded. Then he sat in a stony silence that made Arshel almost regret accepting the invitation. But looking about at the place, she realized that she wouldn't have seen the real Eiltherm if not for Khelin. Here, officials from high up in the HP government came to discuss matters of galactic scope.

In an effort to make conversation, Arshel said, "You never did get around to telling us what you're doing here. You certainly seem very prosperous at it."

"Oh," said Ley, "by a long chain of circumstances we've ended up working for the HP, helping government employees just moving to Eiltherm. We go everywhere—even to parties!—escorting officials, trying to make sure they don't accidentally insult one another."

Khelin added, "A few days ago we worked for one of the more popular hostesses onworld, to keep her party from becoming unpleasant. We did so well, she threw in a bonus, credit at this restaurant! So don't feel you're imposing. This isn't actually costing us anything."

Dennis looked around and then down onto the main floor of the restaurant. "Dare I ask who this hostess was?"

"The Brenilak known as Jiltam. She's in the Planetary Certification Department; she heads one of the divisions. She asked us to freelance her party. It's completely legal. So's accepting the bonus!"

Thoughtfully, Dennis said, "I haven't heard of her."

Ley nodded. "It's a very exclusive circle of Eiltherm society she moves in."

Arshel noted that Khelin was wearing his blue medallion. "I somehow find it difficult to see you in such a job. I wonder what Jylyd would think of this!" She added that Jylyd was a white now.

Ley moved forward on the sand where he was sitting, his jutting knees colliding with the low table. "When Eiltherm functions smoothly, all the Hundred Planets benefit."

Arshel was suddenly conscious of the way Ley answered for Khelin as the subject verged on the personal. Their bhirhir had almost been sundered by Khelin's attempts to take the violet, and yet there they were, human and kren bhirhirn, and functioning in that *mutual* way she yearned for with Dennis.

She said, "Ley, don't you find it difficult—bhirhir to a blue, and offworld at that?" It was a deliberately personal, almost offensive query.

"Living on Eiltherm," Khelin replied, "is not exactly like living offworld. You have places like this," he said, gesturing to the Camiat decor, "and there is a community of kren spread all around this planet. Surely you've found them. Where *have* you been staying?"

While Dennis answered, Arshel considered the way Khelin had diverted the conversation. *Almost as if Ley could raise venom.* It was something she herself had found herself doing automatically for Dennis until he'd made it clear that he didn't appreciate it.

As their order came, Khelin said, "I'm still very puzzled about why you're here on Eiltherm."

Dennis explained that they hoped to win a piece of the Search Bill grant money.

"I heard about that program," said Ley when he'd finished. "There weren't many grants to begin with, but there has been some talk of a Search Bill extension."

"We can't wait. We've got the right place, and before long 'Ossminid' will find it, too!"

As they talked, she watched Khelin and Ley avidly, hardly touching her drink, compelled to analyze what they had that she and Dennis lacked. The next she heard, Dennis was asking, "Would Arshel be considered qualified to do the kind of work you're doing?"

Before Arshel could swallow her shock and say something, Khelin replied, "I suppose so, with a little training."

"If we get stuck here on Eiltherm for very long, do you suppose you'd be willing to help her get started?"

"I'd be glad to look into it for you."

"Well, not just yet," replied Dennis. "We might hit it lucky even today!"

"Dennis," said Arshel. "Look at the time. We'll be late!"

As they got up hastily, Khelin scrambled to his feet and said, "Don't rush off. I don't want to lose you." He was inspecting her intently, his gaze almost tactile. "You didn't say where you were staying."

Dennis answered, "I doubt we're going to remain there very long. Why don't you give us your number?"

Khelin gave him an embossed chip. "You can reach us with this, but—"

"We'll be in touch, definitely," Dennis interrupted, and before she knew it, they were out in the corridor, following signs to their appointment.

"Dennis, you didn't have to be so rude. We could have told him where we're staying. I wonder if they have access to such a large pool as we have."

In the bounce tube, where they were alone for a moment, he said, "Are you interested in mating with him?"

They stepped out and headed down another corridor. Arshel had not been able to look at a male as a potential mate since Uslin. She'd felt herself recoil from Khelin's gaze when it became intensified that way. "It may be a long time before I want anyone again. But I'd like to see Khelin."

"That's good, because we don't really have time for a mating right now. But Khelin and Ley are in a position to know everyone of consequence. If our direct bid fails, they can help us find another avenue. Things like meeting Khelin here don't just happen by coincidence. Isn't that what they teach at Mautri?"

"True." Their meeting Khelin with a free meal ticket when they were so low on funds could mean that they were doing the right thing.

"Come help me fight round one, then."

She did hold up her half of the interview, but her mind was on Khelin. She wanted to ask about Skanqwin. She didn't even know whether he still lived.

After the preliminary interview, they were told that grants could not be pulled from people who already had them, even for a more worthy project. The interviewer was a human woman who seemed terribly cold and distant to Arshel. They were told to wait, and then much later they were shown to the office of a kren whose title Arshel didn't catch.

"Your appeal is very well presented; I do wonder why your original proposal omitted mention of your bhirhir's talent as an archeovisualizer."

"I didn't want to be known," said Arshel. "But we decided that this is too important for personal considerations."

"Understood," said the kren, noting her green medallion. "How much of this," he asked, indicating the proposal summary in his viewer, "is fact, and how much is visualization?"

"It's all fact," Dennis told him. "Her methods have verified everything in there as well."

"We have had several dozen equally meritorious proposals come to us on appeal since the grants were announced," the kren explained. His bhirhir came into the room, carrying a rack of tapes. The official stood and came around his desk to speak to them as equals. "To be honest with you, Camiat has already gleaned one of the largest grants, and I don't believe any elected official would dare give us another while other planets have none."

She felt Dennis wilt. Yet they had half expected it.

"I thought," she said, "the object was to find the City of a Million Legends. If you don't give grants to the best proposals, you're wasting public funds."

The pair of kren hid their amusement well. The official said, "Perhaps if you stay on Eiltherm a few seasons, you'll begin to see the multiplex factors that have to be considered with each high level decision."

His bhirhir said, "Translated, that means the object of the Search Bill's program is to demonstrate that the authority structure responds with alacrity to public demands in such a way that no large sector of the economy is threatened."

The official added, "Our job is to evaluate your proposal and judge its merit. Others will decide what to do with the merit."

"I see." said Dennis, and Arshel didn't like the way he said it. But her mind was fully occupied by the two kren before them—bhirhirn. If she hadn't seen just the same fine-tuned cooperation between Khelin and Ley, she would have been asking herself whether a human ever could be a true bhirhir. *You can't go balbhirhir before you've been bhirhir.*

They left the building well after sundown. The sky was ablaze with crystal stars and strangely huge bubbles of planets. As they walked in silence toward their apartment, Arshel could not help glancing at Dennis and wondering: *If he's not my ex-white priest, then who is?*

The next morning, Dennis said, "I'm going to call Khelin and pick up that lunch invitation for today. And this morning, if we have to, we'll haunt every waiting room from here to Sithorn Deeps!"

The lunch conversation this time centered on Ley's remark about a second grant program being discussed.

"And just which Representatives are the ones behind the Search Bill extension?" Dennis asked after Khelin and Ley had taken turns explaining the workings of the hierarchy.

Arshel had been concentrating on the succulent chunk of meat in front of her. The restaurant held secrets of the utmost luxury. When she and Dennis had visited the Expression Rooms, the attendant had presented her with a wriggling young gheeling, its venom sack distended in readiness to strike. A sign read, "Today's special: gheeling of your own kill." Several more of the animals were in a tank in the lounge entry hall, and their squealing had her venom pouring within seconds. When Dennis took the struggling thing from the attendant's hands and held it for her, she couldn't resist. She hadn't had her own venom-killed gheeling since she and Dennis used to hunt the reefs on Vrashin.

The carcass had arrived at their table thoroughly dressed, fluids pressure-exchanged for a tangy sauce and the surface lightly cauterized just the way she liked it. Dennis had refused a portion. Now, the few bones left were nicely cleaned, and her stomach glowed with pure satisfaction while the others talked business.

"Frdorn," said Khelin, "the Mid-Rep from Theate, started the extension idea, but actually it's the High Rep from Sirwin who's made it go over so big. Only I don't know him personally."

Dennis scanned the room below them. "Is be here?"

"No. He wouldn't be seen in a kren establishment. He's been voting consistently against Camiat's mixed society for nearly fifty standard years. Wants to force all the human colonists to leave Camiat!" Khelin glanced at Ley. "Imagine how MorZdersh'n would react to that!"

"How can we get around someone like that?"

"I wouldn't know," said Khelin. "But Frdorn has a lot in common with you. She firmly believes these grants and contracts should be awarded strictly on merit. That's her down there. Like to meet her?"

They went down the stairwell, passing from an area redolent with homey smells to the lower floor, where air scrubbers kept the atmosphere clean. Khelin spoke to the hostess, and as they gathered around Frdorn's table to be introduced, chairs appeared for them.

Arshel acknowledged the Theaten's greeting to her. "I've never really known any Theatens before."

"I'm not familiar with the societies of Camiat, either," the woman answered. "I came here today to learn a little more. Forgive me if this is rude. I've only known Khelin for a short while, but it seems you're of a different race."

Under the Quintana Code, practiced in such mixed societies as Eiltherm, any matter could be inquired about. There were polite ways of declining to answer, but Arshel simply explained.

"I see. I've heard the term 'saltwater spawn' used in derision. As distressing as that is, it actually makes me feel more at home among you. Theate is also a world divided by superficial barriers that run deep." The Theaten glanced at Dennis. "And yet, on Camiat, something tremendous is happening. You're bhirhir to her, are you not?"

Khelin had left that obvious fact out of the introductions, yet in mixed company nothing could be taken for granted. Dennis answered readily, "Yes, many years now."

Frdorn glanced toward Khelin and Ley, now seated to her left. "It's interesting how I was just sitting here pondering the anomaly that is Camiat's Firestrip City, and here you come with a perfect example of it. Is that a talent of a blue priest?"

"It's a talent of mine. My employers have found it a very useful talent. Arshel here was one of my students. She's only one grade behind me now. She wears the green."

"Another?" Frdorn asked. "Is it then only the Mautri priests who take a human bhirhir?"

"No," Arshel answered, seeing that Dennis was not going to do it for her. "When Dennis won a scholarship to Camiat University in archeology, I spent the time training as an archeovisualizer at Mautri, so now we can work together searching for the City and the mazeheart object."

Frdorn glanced from Dennis to Arshel and back. "Dennis Lakely, of the famous Lakely family? Why aren't you off on their new site?"

"My parents are working along a different line." He began to explain the details of their proposal.

Frdorn listened for some time and then interrupted. "I'm deeply interested in all of this, more than you might guess. But there's no time for it just now. May I invite you both—all four of you—to the Kistrin gathering tonight? There are people I'd like to have meet you."

"Khelin and I will be there, working for Jiltam and some of her guests," Ley answered.

Arshel had been about to decline, sensing that she'd feel wholly out of place among such people. But Dennis said, "We'd be delighted to come. We'll cancel everything else we'd planned for this evening."

They'd had no other plans. On their budget, they couldn't afford entertainment.

The Theaten woman stood, towering high over the humans and kren. "This evening, then." Then she walked away.

"Dennis, do you really—"

"Just a minute, Shel. Ley, you'll have to tell us where we've been invited to and what to wear."

Ley laughed, showing all his teeth. Then, apologizing, he said, "Kistrin is one of Jiltam's friends. He carefully schedules his 'gatherings' between her parties. But I think he wins more points on the social scale by keeping the gatherings so small."

"The drinks are worth the night's work all by themselves," Khelin added. "It will be work, too, Dennis. I think Frdorn is planning to present the Sirwini I was telling you about, Agranad, with you two and see which way he jumps in public!"

The High Rep from Sirwin, thought Arshel, *the one who wouldn't even come to this restaurant.*

The rest of the afternoon was taken up with shopping for clothing and tending to their grooming. Arshel never got her moment alone with Khelin to ask about Skanqwin. But she was aware of how Dennis had engineered lunch to get the party invitation he wanted. Meanwhile, Dennis was jubilant.

"Arshel, you'll charm the eyelids off those people tonight! Archeovisualizers may be out of fashion in archeology right now, but thanks to Lantern's novels, they're a meal ticket in Eiltherm society! And you're gorgeous, too!"

He dressed himself meticulously in his new light green and burgundy suit with shiny dark green shoes, belt, and shoulder flashes. His head was concealed under a stretch turban. He looked conservative and dignified.

She was still floating in the pool, wondering how she could wear the gold and green drape and brown sandals chosen for her. "Shel! They'll be here any minute!"

"So let them in," she replied. Khelin and Ley had volunteered to pick them up for the party since they had the use of an aircar. "After all, there isn't much Khelin doesn't know about me, including what I look like wet."

The door chimed, and the screen lighted with the image of Khelin and Ley, dressed much as Dennis was. At her insistence, Dennis opened the door.

"You're right on time," he greeted them. "But Arshel isn't ready yet."

Khelin came in. His eye went immediately to the pool where Arshel still floated. Reactions flashed across his features: surprise and then a kindling of excited hope followed by the sharp realization that if she'd intended to invite him into her pond, she'd have chosen a better time.

Noting his bhirhir's disturbance, Ley moved into the room to station himself beside Khelin, facing at right angles to him.

Arshel said, "If you'd like to wait in the kitchen, I'll be ready to go in a few minutes." She hauled herself out as Khelin watched, and she could see his sad but gentle disappointment as her manner spoke clearly: *No.*

When Dennis finally enticed them into the kitchen to serve them drinks, she was perversely proud of herself. It was the first time since Uslin that she'd been able to handle even a vaguely suggestive encounter without needing to retch. *I'm healing. I'm going to be all right.*

They had only half finished their drinks when she joined them. By this time, it was pelting hail outside. At the front door of their building, Ley left them and ran to get the car.

While they waited, Dennis said, "I forgot to set the newsprinter! I'll be right back."

Khelin broke the awkward silence. "Something's happened to you, Arshel."

"I had a very bad experience with a mate. I may never take another. But since I first saw you here, I've wanted to know about Skanqwin. Is he alive?"

In the dark of the night and the storm, she could just make out the fleeting concern that passed over his features, raising not a drop of venom. Like Uslin. She shuddered and moved a step away from him.

"Is it that bad, Arshel?"

"Won't you just answer me, please, Khelin." He surely knew how much it cost her to make such an inquiry.

"He's your only child?"

"He's still alive then?"

"Thriving. We're all proud of him. He gets along well with the other children his age in the family, but outside he's a half-breed, and it's difficult. But I think he's destined to become the youngest white priest ever!" And then, to change the subject, he asked, "What happened, Arshel? Didn't Dennis protect you?"

"Of course he did!" she said more loudly than she'd intended. She lowered her voice. The hiss of the falling hail covered the roughness in her tone as venom seeped from her glands. "I wasn't attacked, Khelin. I simply—*couldn't*. He, he was an Interface, Uslin. I didn't realize what it meant to *be* an Interface and kren."

"Few people would," he said, looking out into the storm and being every inch the blue priest. Khelin had been the best she'd ever had. "Arshel, if ever you decide to tackle that trauma, well, MorZdersh'n would be glad to have another of yours to raise. Or I'd be delighted to give you a girl."

She remembered how gentle he'd been and how she had not wanted him to go away so soon. "I'll remember that, Khelin. I think I'd like it to be that way." But at the idea of giving a helpless girl baby into Dennis' hands, she shuddered. *There was a time I wanted that, more than anything.* Bleakly, she thought: *Khelin's right. Things have changed. But why?*

The party was on the top floor of the third tallest building of the Academic Affairs sector. By the time they got there, the hail had stopped and a fresh breeze was stirring. Lights glanced off wet and ice coated surfaces, turning the night to sparks of colored fire.

Khelin and Ley took leave of them at the door, where blue-uniformed Sirwinis took their cloaks and announced them by flashing their names on an overhead screen.

They stood on a platform above the crowd and were showcased against a screen that created a dazzling backdrop tuned to their clothing and coloring. All over the sprawling, multichambered room, discreetly placed monitors showed them to the crowd.

Arshel marveled at the arena. The roof was a single molded piece of clear material. As they were introduced, she watched the walls folding themselves into thin storage poles so that the area was entirely open to the warming night breezes. Outside the walls, roof gardens spread in every direction so that she couldn't see the edge of the building. She'd read about such fabulous parties but never thought she'd see one.

As they moved out onto the floor, a Jernal teetered by, all six legs dancing adroitly to avoid stepping on guests. He was wearing a blue fringe twined in his fluff, the Jernal version of the Sirwini's uniform, and on top of his round ball of a body a tray was neatly balanced. He paused beside them and rotated to present the section of the tray containing tall green glasses of Horthane rum. "Of what I have, this would be compatible for you."

"Thank you," replied Dennis, taking two glasses and handing one to Arshel.

A Brenilak wearing an environmental cloak of the uniformed service's blue paused beside them. "Perhaps I may escort you to the kren area or the human?"

"Make it the human area," Dennis answered. "Unless you happen to have seen the Mid-Rep from Theate, Frdorn?"

"Frdorn? Yes, of course, right this way, please." The Brenilak glided off, cloak swaying only slightly with his smooth steps. They followed.

The room was contoured by dips in the ceiling, curving semiwalls, and artfully placed planters into a large number of discrete areas each with its own air circulation, buffet, and drink service. Yet every area swarmed with a number of species.

They were led to an area of plush chairs, racks, and platforms around a game board. Arshel didn't recognize the game, which seemed to be played with live insects the size of her hand sealed into a maze under the glass surface of the board.

The players around the table included the Theaten, Frdorn, a Brenilak female swathed in a gold environment cloak, and a Sirwini with sharp horns and a grayish pallor that she thought might mean age. Beside the Theaten, and sitting almost as tall as she, was a human male sporting a thick, bronze-colored beard, his head hair hidden by a dazzling white turban.

Frdorn rose and ordered their escort to provide them with suitable furniture. The others about the table also stood. "We were just enjoying a game of scobit," Frdorn announced. "Would you like to play?"

Arshel said, "I don't know the game."

"It's a little new. Exported from Horthane, as is your rum."

Arshel had barely touched her drink. She set it down on a round area that seemed meant to hold glasses. Just in time, she realized that nobody else was seating himself, and she remained standing with the chair placed behind her.

Frdorn then made the introductions around the table, telling them, "This is the son of the famous Professors Lakely who discovered the Vrashin Island time capsule *and* the Globe of Ossminid! And this is his bhirhir, Arshel, who does archeovisualization for him."

There was a silence until Frdorn gestured them to be seated with a hesitant movement that said: *You've missed a cue.* As the play settled into routine once more, Khelin and Ley emerged from the crowd behind Frdorn and took up places beside the Brenilak woman, who had to be Jiltam.

The Sirwini pointedly moved his chair away from Khelin, which put him a little closer to Dennis. "Frdorn," he said plaintively, "you arranged this on purpose, didn't you?"

"Agranad," said Frdorn firmly, "these Lakelys have a new approach I wanted you to hear. Tell them your idea. Dennis."

"Venerable Representatives," he began, and then he nervously swallowed several gulps of his drink. "I won't bore you with the mathematical details; we've filed the proposal. It should be available for your inspection now. Briefly, the theory is that the heart of the First Lifewave was located on the other side of the galaxy, and so in tracing the City of a Million Legends, we should look to the other side of the Globe of Ossminid. For technical reasons, we have chosen to explore a particular world on the globe."

The Sirwini turned to the other human. "Balachandran, do you, as Explorer Corps Low Rep, have any data to support this?"

The human toyed with an amber colored drink in a tall glass. "We've sent one ship on a brief excursion to map the Globe of Ossminid. But we've no data yet on the planets."

The scobit game continued as the discussion became more technical. It seemed to Arshel that the Explorer Corps Low Rep was very unenthusiastic, almost serving to block the entire consideration of their proposal. The Sirwini never spoke to her or to Khelin directly, even when Khelin had the boldness to address him by name.

The game finally broke up. Arshel watched as they took out pocket credit meters and adjusted balances. The magnitude of the adjustments exceeded the amount she and Dennis had earned on the Sorges dig. She felt very much out of place.

As the others left, Frdorn came around the table with Jiltam, Khelin, and Ley. "Thank you for a very informative session, Dennis," said Frdorn. "They'll all be talking about you for days. I do hope you get your grant." Then she was gone into the crowd, the Explorer Corps Low Rep at her side.

Jiltam watched the two weave through the crowd. "An unlikely alliance, are they not?" asked the Brenilak woman.

"I'd have expected," said Dennis, "the Explorer Corps to be more enthusiastic about exploring, especially where our maps are still so blank."

"Perhaps that's why he's remained only a Low Rep all these years," said Jiltam. "But then, one would also expect a High Rep, especially from Sirwin, to be more accepting."

"Agranad," Arshel added, "seems to me to be afraid of kren. He may have good reason for the way he feels."

"I expect Arshel's right," said Khelin. "His attempts to provoke me earlier tonight bespeak deep, and perhaps, hidden feelings."

"He wields too much power to be allowed such personal quirks," said Jiltam. Arshel felt that the woman was testing them.

"At least," said Arshel, "Agranad is open about his feelings."

Jiltam grinned at Arshel, a fearsome enough sight as her snouted face split to expose blue teeth. Arshel held steady. After all, Jiltam had no venom.

The Brenilak eyed Arshel's venom sack. Through the entire discussion, she'd hardly raised venom, though she knew that when she relaxed at home, it would come.

Jiltam asked, "Are you two planning to stay on Eiltherm?"

"Our plans," answered Dennis, "are flexible."

"In six days, I'm planning a large party at the Gilthamon Beach Club. Where shall I send your invitations?"

Khelin said, "We'd be glad to pick up their invitations for them. We see each other often."

"That would be convenient," said Dennis. "We weren't planning to stay long at our current address."

Apparently, thought Arshel, they'd passed the test.

Jiltam detailed Khelin and Ley to escort them around the party and then took her leave. In the course of the evening, they ate more exotic food than they really wanted and met more people than they could remember all with important titles. They were invited to gatherings dinners, lunches, and even one swim sponsored by the High Rep from Ciitheen, the aquatic world known for its hospitality to tourists who could swim well.

"We'll bring in some popayunze for you to kill under water," the Rep said, "provided you'll kill me one. I haven't eaten a good venom-killed popayunze in years."

That sounded strange to Arshel. After all, there were many kren on Eiltherm. But Dennis accepted for them both before she could find a way to ask tactfully.

As they were leaving, she saw the tall human with the beard talking with the Ciitheen. On the way home, she told Khelin about the odd invitation.

"And you accepted?" asked Ley.

"They didn't know," Khelin said.

"Know what?" Dennis asked as Arshel held her breath.

"Ahncil, he's a kren-venom addict. It's a well known weakness of the Ciitheen."

"I'd forgotten!" said Arshel.

Ley said, "When we first came, we were invited to one of Ahncil's swims. It was a lovely afternoon until Ahncil presented Khelin with this huge, fat popayunze. It was a mouth watering sight, too. But Khelin saw the signs of Ahncil's addiction and put that together with the odd way people had been treating us at the party."

"I simply decided not to kill for him or anybody there. They were mostly Ciitheen, anyway; most of them wouldn't have eaten from a venom kill, but—"

Ley took it up. "Hardly anyone knew he was a blue priest, and when he simply picked a harpoon off the floating dock and handed it to Jiltam, asking her to do the honors so everyone could partake of the delicacy—and then he held the popayunze by the tail while she speared it—I don't think anyone there believed his eyes."

"Kren have a reputation for lack of self control," said Khelin. "People tend to be overimpressed."

"Jiltam was impressed all right. She hired us that day, and life just hasn't been the same since."

"It certainly is different from Firestrip City," said Dennis. "But how is Arshel going to get out of Ahncil's trap?"

Khelin said, "We have a few days. Let me see if Ley and I are invited to this swim. Maybe we can arrange a diversion."

Ley said, "Meanwhile, let me check with some importer friends we have. It could be that suddenly there are no popayunze or gheeling or any substitute!"

"The other Ciitheen," said Khelin, "try to protect Ahncil from himself. When he's sober, he's a very good Rep."

Alone in their apartment, they carefully put their clothes away. Arshel said, "Why did you have to accept all those invitations? Dennis, we're so out of place here!"

"I don't know about that. We're doing all right. If we have to spend a little money on clothes, think of all the free meals! At these functions we're going to be able to make the contacts to get that grant, one way or another!"

She didn't like the way he slammed one fist into the palm of his other hand, baring his teeth in a snarl. For days afterward, that image of him remained. Contrasting him with Ley, she found that many of the traits she'd classed as human and had therefore endured were actually traits of Dennis, and she began to compare the Dennis of now with the Dennis she'd taken bhirhir.

The Ciitheen swim was held at a saltwater lake, not quite as salty as the ocean but very pleasant to her skin. Arshel, for the first time in many days, didn't have to worry about what to wear. She had never before paid great attention to her clothing, and the sudden relief was so vast that for the first time on Eiltherm, she felt as if she were really at a party.

She dived and swam, testing her strength against the minor waves. The dim red sun was hot this day and the sky a milk violet that she was told promised good weather.

Their hosts had provided aqualung equipment for the guests who could use it, and so she and Dennis had a real underwater race for the first time since leaving Vrashin. She won easily, and they burst from the water panting.

"Arshel!" It was Khelin, standing waist deep in the water to one side. "Race you to the boat dock!"

She looked at Dennis, who was sagging under the burden of the aqualung. "Go on if you want to," he said. "I couldn't move another step."

As Khelin drew nearer, Ley came down from the shore to join them. "Tired?" the blue priest asked.

"No," she answered. "I don't know why."

"There's a lot of oxygen in this water," said Ley. "You're probably getting more through your skin than you'd normally expect."

"I think he's right," said Khelin. "At least, I'm good for another lap before Jiltam arrives and we have to go to work. Coming?"

"Wait," said Dennis. "Khelin, what about Ahncil?"

Khelin glanced around to see that they were out of earshot of the other guests, who were spread up and down the curving red sand beach. The distant noises from the rafts placed out on the lake reached them as a pleasant babble.

Ley said, "I don't think Ahncil was able to get any popayunze or gheeling. But don't bet on it."

Dennis frowned. "Do you think they ought to go off alone?"

"I can't keep up with Khelin in the water, and I don't intend to try." He glanced up the beach to where the blue-uniformed catering service was setting up tables and roasting pits.

Arshel saw his gaze linger on two human guests, females of the size and coloring Dennis preferred. "Khelin," she said, "let's swim."

Dennis, too, followed Ley's glance and then added abstractedly, "I hope you realize I wouldn't let Arshel go off alone with just anybody."

Serious, Khelin answered, "I do realize that, Dennis."

When they were stroking along on the surface, Arshel asked, "Do you ever have trouble understanding Ley?"

Khelin had been looking for a clear lane to set up their race. He stopped swimming and held his position. She matched him, and then he said, "Because he's human? It doesn't make so very much difference. Surely you knew they were both thinking of those women over there. Look, there they go!"

The two humans in the distance were centered on the human women they were approaching. Arshel said, "Most kren would laugh if I said this, but sometimes Dennis seems so ferocious, it scares me. I used to think it was just his human masculinity, but it's really his personality. Isn't it?"

Some people were swimming by beneath them, and they moved out farther from shore. Stroking lazily, Khelin said, "Arshel, I've often wondered how you ever came to take him bhirhir."

She rolled onto her back and sunned herself. "Khelin, you never met the man I took bhirhir."

He stopped beside her. "What?"

"We used to hunt gheeling in the surf off the Vrashin reef. When I was first raising prevenom, I'd strike the young ones we caught, and we'd have a feast. After a while, he wanted to try eating from my kill, but of course it made him sick. He had no immunity to the saltwater clans, being from Firestrip. That was when we started immunizing him to my venom. Khelin it was perfect. We both wanted the same things out of life. But I don't know this man anymore. He's changed. He's been *using* me, my talent, and my Mautri training, to impress people and get their attention and then manipulate them, the way he tries to manipulate me. I don't like it, and if I say anything, he only growls or snaps at me."

She ran out of breath, shocked at her own vehemence.

Treading water, he asked, "What do you suppose has caused him to change like this?"

She matched his movements, her mind clicking over in high gear. "Me!" Slowly, incident by incident, she reviewed the years in Firestrip, the time on Pallacin, and the recent affair with Uslin. "As my talent became more dependable, he staked more on it. Every time he achieves a goal through me, he seeks a bigger goal and expects me to deliver that, too. Khelin, where will it lead?"

"Wherever you want it to."

She stared at her mentor in shock, her mind churning up his words of so many years ago: *The Mautri teachings are dangerous to those who may come under domination or who may be tempted to dominate.*

"When we returned to Firestrip," she said, "I sat in on a seeking-with of Jylyd's. I asked him to admit me to the blue trials. He refused. Why would he do that if I must go balbhirhir to protect Dennis from even the little power I've gained?"

"I'm not a life-reader. But I don't see how you can find your way out of the situation until you've found out how you got into it in the first place. That's nearly impossible to do from the Vlen standpoint."

Very softly, she confessed, "I think I've abandoned that standpoint. On Pallacin, when I was reading the Crystal Crown and the Sphere of Ossminid, I contacted a past life memory. But there's no way it could pertain to this situation, except that now I really believe the old prophecy that got me into Mautri. But it doesn't pertain to me." And she told him how she'd discovered that Dennis could not possibly have been a white priest in a prior life. By the end of her tale, she was raising venom.

"I never thought he was, either. But I think you are heading for a point in the time currents where you will provide the destiny of our brother who was our chief. Apparently, this rendezvous has been attempted before and failed for lack of courage to make the necessary choices. I think Jylyd was telling you that if you are to make it this time, you must confront the problems Dennis presents. To return to Mautri now would be to run away and miss your white priest."

Miserable, she said, "I still don't know what to *do.*"

"Study Dennis and draw your own conclusions. See if you can figure out how you got involved with him in past lives. There's a clear lane. Let's race!"

She was tense enough that the prospect of physical exercise was inviting. They agreed on a finish line and submerged. The hard swimming stretched her muscles, and the competition held her mind in a single, pointed focus. It brought back the years at Mautri, when she'd learned to focus herself, and in the purity of the exertion she began to feel that she might succeed in the task Khelin had just set her.

By the time she neared the finish line, she'd altered her consciousness far from the norm, and her speed through the water was a record for her.

A shadowy human figure loomed as if materializing. It held a wriggling popayunze by the tail. She saw not a real flesh-and-blood person but a translucent apparition surrounded by dark swirling blotches of black ichor. With a shudder of revulsion, she altered course. The apparition dodged to intercept her, holding the popayunze out to her. It, too, seemed unreal and had no power to raise her venom.

Then reality superimposed itself, and from her exertion she felt sharp hunger juicing her venom glands. *No, not here. There are too many Ciitheen. And Ahncil!*

The rhythmic gush of bubbles emitted from the human's aqualung seemed the most evil sound she'd ever heard. Her fangs came down, and potent fear-venom rushed hotly into her venom sack. She wanted to escape, but hunger pinned her into place. Yet she held her strike, refusing the temptation.

A silver streak descended from the surface in a cloud of bubbles, snatching the succulent animal from the human's grasp. It was Khelin, silhouetted against the surface. He wrenched the animal's head off and thrust the bleeding carcass away from himself. In a piercing instant of self-knowledge she realized that she would have struck if Khelin had simply let the animal swim free. *He doesn't trust me,* she thought, deeply shamed. *And neither do I.*

Flashing around the clumsy human, he took Arshel around the waist and urged her to the surface beside the raft. His strong arms lifted her onto the platform, and then he came up beside her, eyeing her venom sack. Behind them the human broke surface in a sloppy splash and clambered onto the raft: it was Balachandran, the Explorer Corps Low Rep. They hadn't been so near him since Kistrin's party.

The human shoved his faceplate back onto the top of his head. He was no apparition now. Yet the eerie feeling of wrongness about him persisted as Arshel watched him confronting Khelin, who was standing to face him.

"I wouldn't have given it to Ahncil." the human protested. *The popayunze.* But into Arshel's mind flashed the picture she had noted while leaving Kistrin's: Balachandran and Ahncil laughing together. *He's lying.*

The others on the raft, a human pair and two Theatens, were far enough away that they probably couldn't make out words, but they were all looking in her direction. Khelin met Arshel's eyes, and she knew that he didn't believe the lie any more than she did. "That animal," he said, "doesn't belong at any party of both Ciitheen and kren. And what you did to Arshel was worse than impolite."

"I do imagine it was something of a surprise to both of you. But I was testing you to see if the lady here was also as good as you are. Apparently, she is. So I owe you both more than an apology, and I intend to pay up."

"You owe me nothing," Khelin said flatly. He had not raised venom at all. "But you're going to have to settle with her bhirhir over this."

The human turned to Arshel, coming toward her as if he did not perceive the slight bulge of her venom sack. "I think the lady can speak for herself. And I'd like a chance to explain in a more relaxed atmosphere."

When he'd reached arm's length from Arshel with no sign of stopping there, Khelin clamped a restraining hand on his arm. "That's close enough. Her bhirhir is way over there on shore. I'm taking her back to him now."

She wanted nothing more than to get away from the suddenly oppressive human. She was no longer producing fear-venom, but her glands ached, and she knew that it would be easy to strike at him. *I'm not going to disgrace the green.*

She swam beside Khelin on the surface all the way back. On the beach, Khelin kept his distance carefully as they searched for Dennis, Ley, and the two women. They found them near the caterer's tables, sitting at the water's edge, trying to build sculptures with the red sand.

The moment he saw them coming, Ley got up and came to Khelin. "Something wrong?"

"Under control," Khelin answered.

But Dennis was wholly occupied cleaning sand from between the dark skinned woman's toes, while she resisted, laughing.

"Dennis?" said Arshel.

He turned and saw the three of them standing together. With a quick apology, he got up and came to them, brushing sand from where it stuck to his skin. "What happened, Shel? I thought you two were off for at least the rest of the afternoon."

In low tones, Arshel told him.

Ley said. "You must have really impressed Balachandran!"

"I don't think he's worth impressing," said Arshel.

"I could argue that," Dennis said. To the two women, he said, as he picked up his jacket, "Ley and I will be gone just a few minutes. Don't you two go away, now."

Throwing the jacket over one shoulder, he said, "This way," and led them up the beach. Arshel noted that his fair skin was turning pink, a sign of impending agonies.

When they'd gone a few steps and the women couldn't hear them, Ley said, "Dennis! What are you thinking?"

The two humans were walking now between the two kren. Dennis took

Ley's arm and said, "Arshel and Khelin were set up. Don't you suppose we were set up, too? Doesn't it seem strange to you that the girls would have made such a point of telling us we could use the privacy rooms up here as expression rooms if we wanted to? They even pointed out that these were the closest!"

"We're being watched?" Ley asked.

"And listened to, I'll bet. Those rooms will be bugged. So will you two play along and let them think you're as much in need of expression as Arshel is?"

Ley said, "They'll be led to overestimate Arshel's control. That could get her in a lot of trouble."

"No, it won't. They don't know much about the difference between a green and a blue. So it will lead them to underestimate the blue, and that could keep Khelin out of a lot of trouble."

"Ley," said Khelin, "I don't think it will do any real harm to let them underestimate the blue. It might even damp down my reputation so we can live with it!"

When they finished and rejoined the two women, the bearded Explorer Corps Low Rep was with them, gay and animated.

Dennis remained standing as Khelin, Arshel, and Ley sat in the sands across from the three humans. Balachandran looked Dennis in the eye and said, "Khelin suggests that I owe you an apology, and I do apologize. But I want you to know I did that for a purpose."

"Which is?"

"A job interview."

"With the Explorer Corps?"

"Why not?"

"We're archeologists."

"Right," said Balachandran. "You find things. We look for things. Why don't you come up to my office tomorrow and talk it over? I've taken the liberty of leaving my directions on your home monitor. You shouldn't have trouble finding me."

He stood up, unfolding his giant frame until he towered over Dennis almost like his father did. She wasn't seeing through Balachandran now, but she still felt a repulsion.

Dennis stood and watched the human ambling away from them, sand stuck to the backs of his legs. Dennis' expression was thoughtful, and that filled her with foreboding.

The next morning, as they were getting ready to leave the apartment for the day, she asked, "You don't intend to see that man, do you?"

"Balachandran? We have to, Shel. Do you know how low our account is? This may be our lucky break. After all, it did come through you, and everything you've ever done has turned out lucky."

"Dennis," she said slowly, "if you want to, go ahead, but I don't ever want to see him again."

"Hey, look, you've got to go with me. It was you he was interested in, remember?"

"I think that man would have gladly given the popayunze, venom-killed, to Ahncil!"

"If Ahncil had known he had one, it would have been Ahncil's very quickly. Ahncil didn't get it, so Balanchandran isn't the villain Khelin would make him out to be!"

"I don't like him any better than Khelin does."

"You'd follow Khelin in anything he wants to do, but you won't do a single thing for me!"

It was an expression of pain that pulled forth from her every instinct of a bhirhir. But she checked the impulse. Sudden insight brought her awareness of how he was truly afraid, but only of losing his power to coerce her.

Continue to study Dennis. Go where he takes you. Khelin's advice was going to be harder to follow than she'd thought with all her courage, she said, "All right, Dennis. I'll go with you."

Balachandran's office was in the building adjacent to the Lower Assembly Building. They took a skybus to the nearby roof terminal and then walked down the hill along routes and past landmarks she'd seen many times on the news. She saw the Horthane ambassador talking to the Brenil ambassador, surrounded by a crowd of people who had attended some of the parties she'd been at.

The people working here knew that they were doing things that would affect billions of lives, and they took it seriously. She and Dennis were now a part of that. *Is that why I'm tied to him? To force me to a responsibility I'd never have sought alone?*

The office, when they found it, was a suite extending around a corner of a lower floor of the building. They were passed from waiting room to waiting room and finally shown into a cluttered office, where Balachandran was talking to two screen images and shuffling through a stack of cartridges.

He said, "My next appointment has just arrived, so I'll have to get back to you tomorrow." He blanked the screen, punched up a secretary, and issued instructions. "Now," he said, turning to them. "I don't really have much time to discuss this, but I want to devote every moment I can to it."

"We aren't sure that we should be here at all as archeologists. But you did capture our curiosity yesterday. What could the Explorer Corps have to offer us?"

"Bluntly—I see I can be blunt with you, Mr. Lakely—the Explorer Corps has nothing to offer you." He picked up a cassette. "This is strictly confidential between you two and me and the man I work for."

"Mr. Balachandran," said Dennis, "we'd really prefer not to become involved in any unofficial transactions."

Arshel felt exactly the same way and was preparing to leave, when the bearded human palmed the cassette into a slot on his desk; the screen behind him lit up with the report on Dennis' proposal. Diagonally across the text, in purple, was stamped "Not Recommended."

"Your project has come to a complete halt through official transactions. But of course, if you're not interested in unofficial ones, we have nothing further to discuss."

Dennis' frozen stare finally shifted from the cassette to the man's face. "And if we are interested in unofficial ones?"

"In that case, you might still find out what is on the planet that interests you. But the details of how this is arranged would have to remain confidential."

"Only the government could fund something this big," said Dennis. "And it would require an Interface."

"All that could be arranged. In fact, I could have let you think your proposal had been approved and your backing was official. But as head of the project, you and your bhirhir would be in a position to suspect otherwise. So your pledge of silence is required before we say any more. Now, I know I can trust the word of a green priest of Mautri. But you, Dennis Lakely, are human, and I know exactly what not to expect from you."

Arshel said, "You surely can trust the word of a green priest *once given*, Mr. Balachandran. But I don't know that I would care to give my word." Her venom glands ached.

"I have something here that might change your mind." He selected another cassette and slid it into the display machine.

It was a Camiat University Course Credit form. The display split into two, one half of the screen showing a form labeled "actual" and the second half showing "recorded." Dennis' recorded course standings differed from the actual ones just enough to edge him from second to first place in his graduating class. Only in the final semester did the two halves of the screen match; she recalled the method of cheating he'd used then.

Stunned to coldness, she listened as Balachandran said, "Do I have to tell you what will become of the Lakely family reputation if this is ever made public, Mr. Dennis Lakely? The complete ruin of your career is at my fingertips now. And I've no idea what a full investigation might turn up about your parents' backgrounds."

"What do you want?" Dennis' voice was a husky whisper. Arshel was numb with conflicting reactions.

"Just your pledge of silence about our sources and methods in setting you up as head of Expedition Ossminid."

"Let me get this straight," said Dennis. "You want to carry out my—our—research proposal, searching for the mazeheart object? As if it were officially approved?" The human nodded, and Dennis asked, "What happens when we find it?"

"Let's leave something to the imagination."

"I see." Dennis seemed to be thinking fast, but he said, "Could we have some time to talk this over?"

"I must have your decision before you leave today. Surely I've made the alternatives simple enough for people of your educational background."

But he did leave them alone. She went to Dennis' chair and put her hands on his shoulders. They were trembling. "Dennis, did you tamper with the computer records?"

"I had a friend in the department do it for me. Shel, he swore up and down that nobody but an Interface could ever discover the overlay!"

Bleakly, she said, "There are other careers, other ways to make a living. Look at Khelin and Ley."

He jumped up and rounded the chair, taking her hands. "No, no! I'm a Lakely. And so are you, Shel! Lakelys aren't quitters, not ever. I'm going to go along with him! Remember back in Firestrip, when I called you to see the news segment that launched us into this line of research?"

"Yes," she said, realizing that he knew that the office had to be live with recorders. "I said I couldn't do it, so you found a different way to apply my talent."

"Right, and I think you've led us right to what we were originally hoping to find!"

Balachandran is 'Ossminid'? But he'd admitted that he was working for somebody else. Or was that merely a blind? Her glands ached with sudden excitement. "What if I have?"

"When we've got all the data, nothing else will matter."

She thought about it. True, if they found the object and exposed 'Ossminid,' the falsified records would pale to insignificance. They'd have both the reward for trapping 'Ossminid' and the fame Dennis craved for finding the City. They'd never have to work again.

When Balachandran returned, they agreed to work for him on his terms. During the next days, they continued to attend all the best parties. Balachandran was at their side constantly. Khelin and Ley began to drift out of their orbit, although she was sure that Dennis hadn't said a word to them about Balachandran. She saw them at one Nipshelanti party with another human, a young male who seemed vaguely familiar, but they only paused at a distance. There was an ache of regret over that. She'd begun to feel stirrings for Khelin. Meanwhile, the Search Bill extension was defeated.

And then, very rapidly, the outfitting of the expedition ships was finished. Balachandran saw them off, assuring her bhirhir, "The Interface will be joining you at the site as soon as you have something to report."

The only highlight of the trip was her discovery of a new Lantern novel titled *Maze Builder.* As it was by her three favorite authors, she grabbed a copy. But every time she sat down with it, the words went through her mind, refusing to link together into images, ideas, and story. She put it down to anxiety. Dennis planned to locate the City and then contrive to get a message through to LEAHPs exposing Balachandran as 'Ossminid.' But it was a dangerous game they were playing.

Dennis' attitude disturbed her ever more deeply as the days went by. She couldn't forget the falsified records yet he acted as if it were a trivial thing he didn't need to discuss with her. She didn't know this man.

But soon after they finally made orbit over the target world, she got to work with her bead string. She had the computer room print out for her the planet maps as they currently had them. Since the drones were constantly reporting new data, her requests interrupted work there but were filled quickly.

Working over the flat projections, she discarded the splash shaped continent. Moving north, she was hoping that the find wouldn't be under one of the glaciers. Passing over a large desert plateau, her hanging beads gravitated toward one spot.

When she told Dennis, he groaned. "Desert! Three of my top dating experts are Ciitheen!"

"No matter what the climate," she pointed out, "somebody is going to be inconvenienced or eliminated!"

He sat down right then to compose one of his daily messages to Balachandran. "He's got to get us either a human or a Theaten Interface if it's going to be desert work. A Brenilak would wilt and a Jernal would always be complaining about the grit in its fluff. Oh, Shel, what a mess!"

The next day, he had all three ships train instruments on the desert. Recent tectonic activity had shoved one of the strata up on end, and the diverted winds had scoured clean some highly regular remains. They had decided that there had been a city there contemporary with the Crystal Crown plus or minus thirty thousand years.

"That's as close as we can come," the Ciitheen informed him, "without an Interface."

Dennis fired off more message torpedoes to Balachandran and struggled to cope as the pressure mounted. Arshel outside the main current of events, was able to watch him as she never had before. She decided that the more harried he became, the more he enjoyed himself, because he could show his subordinates how tremendously difficult his job was and, consequently, how well he was doing it.

It wasn't long after the discovery of the site that the news capsule brought word of the death of another Guild Interface, a Brenilak. Dennis shut their viewer off in the middle of the funeral. "At least he wasn't of one of the species I need."

Arshel didn't bother to rebuke him. She knew that he'd no longer understand her objection to his attitude. She stretched gingerly and left him at his desk. He didn't notice her leave the room. He hadn't even become aware of her molt symptoms yet.

She soaked herself alone and made shift to spread venom over her stiffening hide. But she could no longer reach some of the areas that itched the worst. *He'll notice soon.* But she wasn't sure which would be worse: his inattention or his reluctant attention. It worried her that she shrank from her own bhirhir, but no amount of concentrated meditation eased the feeling.

Meanwhile, Dennis had the biosphere studies completed, and the medical department very efficiently immunized each member of the ground staff and supplied them with skin emollients and sun protection.

"Well," said the human doctor, "there isn't much I can do for that hide of yours, Arshel, is there?" He handed her a supply of the antibiotic tablets used in molt, advising her not to go down to the planet until her new skin had been seasoned.

The rest of the day she agonized over having to tell Dennis and she finally made up her mind to wait until he noticed of his own accord. Maybe she couldn't molt alone, but she'd go as far as she could.

When Dennis came in late that night, he hit the door lock behind him with a balled fist and turned to where she was sitting and watching the star viewer. "Of all the rotten times for a molt! And I have to learn of it from the surgeon in the middle of the mess hall while I'm appointing the first shuttle crew, and somebody asks how come you're not there, so the surgeon says you're in molt and can't go down, just after I announce your name! How was I supposed to explain that I didn't *know?*"

She could feel his embarrassment as if it were her own. Her venom glands ached with it.

"Do you know what the Jernal who runs the mineral lab said to me after the meeting? He said he hoped you weren't in a dangerous condition because he'd seen you wandering around by yourself. I could tell his opinion of me had plummeted."

The itchy streak in the middle of her back was torturing her now that her meditation was broken. Venom oozed throbbingly into her sack. "Dennis, I didn't mean to cause trouble."

"Oh, you've caused trouble, all right!" He paced to the bedroom door and turned to face her, fists on his hips. "And just to teach you a lesson, you can take care of yourself until tomorrow morning!"

He stalked into the other room and presently, through her shock, she heard the shower stall activated. By the time she went in, he was asleep and snoring.

Arshel was sure that she hadn't slept, but at one point she turned and found Dennis' bed empty and light coming from the sitting room. When she joined him there, she found that a message had come from Balachandran, saying that he was bringing them a human Interface and asking them to delay setting foot on the planet until he got there.

"Shel! We're saved! We couldn't go down today if we had to! You'll be through molt by the time he gets here. Come on, let's tend that hide of yours."

He was rough and perfunctory, all skill and none of the sympathy he'd once had. Whereas she had felt comfortable and secure under his hands before, she now endured the process with all her Mautri training, wondering whether this was anything like what the white priests endured at the hands of strangers during molt.

As days passed, she found that she'd been keyed up to get down to the ruins and try to read them. Frustration turned to irritability and restlessness over and above the miseries of molt. She fretted until two consecutive nights passed without sleep, and then she approached Dennis one morning.

"Couldn't we just send the lander down and look over the site? I need to *do* something!"

"We have to wait. Balachandran is due any day now. But we're finished with the main conference room. Why don't you use the big screen in there to work on? I'll have the bridge pipe you the newest stuff from the drones. I'll even have them send another live drone right down over it so you can see it directly. But I can't land anything, Arshel."

She accepted that as the best she could get from him. She, too, dreaded Balachandran's arrival, not just because he was bringing an Interface, but because he frightened her.

Settling herself in a chair at the end of the conference table nearest the big screen, she tried to put them all out of her mind. The blank screen filled with a soaring desert view.

The entire area that was now a desert wasteland had once been urbanized. The drone and satellite photos, instrument readings, and probe results had been spliced together now, but without the help of an Interface. The result was a very informative hodgepodge that gave her a headache.

She dissected out of it several interesting stills of the ruins showing a circle and a blurred rectangle that seemed interesting. *Perhaps the Emperor's Crown and the Maze.* Her eyes steadily on that, she drew out her bead string and set herself the question, *What does that ruin mean to me?* She had to pull her mind back to the question several times as if trying to control a skittish draft animal. But that inner resistance only made her more determined to learn the answer to her question.

While she was still struggling, Dennis interrupted, and she unlocked the door for him. He presented her with a large, amber glass laboratory box. "Here, I figured if I couldn't take you to the site, I'd bring the site to you." He put it on the table and, exerting some strength, slid the top aside.

Taking out a piece of gray-gold rock, he said, "One of the drones picked this up on the outskirts of the urbanized area near some markings that might have been a large public building. I thought you might find it helpful. The live drone won't be ready to go for a couple of hours yet."

When she settled down again, she held the chunk of rock between her hands, her bead string draped over them, and once more addressed her problem: *What does that ruin mean to me?*

Her eyes closed, but the circle and blur pattern on the screen had burned into her retinas. Superimposed over it came the image of one of the stalwart, feathered bipeds she'd seen building the Crystal Crown. Only this one had Dennis' human face and a dark green crest.

She recoiled from the grotesque image, and it cleared. But no other image would come until at last she summoned again the strange being with Dennis' face. This time, however, it had a face to match its body. She knew that it *was* Dennis.

I was here in the past, and I knew Dennis here. This is where it all began for us! For a moment, she remembered Khelin swimming beside her, offering the only advice he could: Find the beginning of the problem.

Deliberately, she conjured her memories of the golden sphere. She had worn feathers, too, when she made it. Dennis' feathered green crest and hard, immobile features began to look even more like him. She began to construct in her mind what the streets and buildings had looked like in the city below.

An image flashed into being: arched porticos jutting from a towered structure and colored lights panning across the building walls where inlaid jewels etched the sigil of the Empire of Stars. It was the Emperor's palace at the end of the street before her.

It was night, with stars shining ferociously overhead, breezes scurrying in that inviting way that made feathered creatures ache for the freedom of the upper air, whether they had wings or not. She was hurrying, the claws of her feet clicking loudly on the paving where they overreached the ends of her shoes. She couldn't afford to be late, for tonight the Emperor's Crown Council would vote on the proposal to build a Persuader's Maze next to the Emperor's Crown and to sanction the Persuader's Corps as an official arm of government.

She'd worked a lifetime opposing this move, and she knew that she was going to win tonight.

Out of nowhere, a figure landed in front of her. The dark green crest identified him. *Dennis!*

"What are you doing here?" she asked, her anger not bringing the slightest twinge of venom but genuine nonetheless. "You should be with the Council, making sure your colleagues all vote our way!"

He just looked at her, barring her way with a strange insolence. She had bought his way into the Crown Council using money she held in trust for two young heirs of her former patron. She didn't consider it stolen money, as she had Dennis' promise that when they were of age, he'd see the children inducted into the Crown Operators, which was the best career they could ask for. He was her ally against the Persuaders, as her patron had been.

"We've *lost*, Cheeal."

"That's not possible. You told me yesterday."

"I lied. Just to keep you happy. Now I don't need you anymore." He pulled a weapon from his cloak.

She backed away, disbelief warring with shock.

Arshel came to herself with a shattering crack echoing in her head. Dazed, she realized that she'd remembered one of her own deaths. It had been so real; her venom sack was throbbing with fear-venom.

She caught her breath, trying to make sense of what she could remember of the vision. Dennis had betrayed her in a past life. Now she was giving him the use of her resources again, and he was facing the test once more. Could he handle the responsibility of the temptation of great power? Suddenly, she liked even less the personality change she sensed in him.

"Shel! Let us in! Hey, are you still alive in there?"

Only then did she realize that she'd been hearing the door signal for some time. When she threw the lock, she found Balachandran and another she recognized with a peculiar dual consciousness. Image: two boys beside a fountain. Image: two boys in a car. Image: huge crystal monoliths arrowing down from space. The humans, unfeathered, pushed past her into the conference room, and Dennis closed the door behind them.

"Well" said Balachandran, "speak up! Is that the City of a Million Legends down there?"

"Yes," said Arshel. "At least it was the seat of the First Lifewave government." She had almost said "Empire of Stars government." "That is the crown and maze."

"Then," said Dennis, "we may not need him after all." He indicated the other human. "We'll be able to go right to the mazeheart object!"

"Dennis," Arshel objected. *What about our plan?*

Dennis said to Balachandran, "I have to tell her. She's a full partner in this."

Balachandran considered and then flipped some switches on a wall panel. "That secures the room. Go ahead."

The strange human, a wasted scarecrow figure with slumped shoulders and tired eyes, drifted to keep Dennis between them. But she smelled no fear from him, even as his eyes followed her hands where the skin showed the chalkiness of molt.

Dennis said, "Balachandran has some First Lifewave documents that change everything, Arshel. The mazeheart object was made like the Crystal Crown, and it, too, might have survived functional! Shel, that object *made* Persuaders! *We* can become Persuaders, too, just like Skanqwin!"

She could see the avidity in Balachandran striking a similar fire in Dennis. "I'm not convinced that bringing First Lifewave technology into our time is safe or even possible."

"It's not safe," said the strange human.

Balachandran stepped between Arshel and Dennis to get at the human. "Quiet! You belong to me now, not the Guild! You'll answer only when I ask you a question."

Now the man emitted a whiff of fear that was gone before she was sure it was there. *An Interface!* She recalled clearly where she'd seen him last: with Khelin and Ley at some party.

She was terribly curious, but Dennis was saying, "Maybe it's not safe, but you have to expect to take risks if you want to win anything worth having in life."

The Interface's eyes were fixed on the bracelet she still wore despite the irritation it caused her molting skin. To Dennis, she said, "Do you want to bring the Persuaders back, Dennis? Wouldn't you rather be a Crown Operator?"

He stepped between her and the Interface, taking her shoulders in his hands with cruel pressure on her skin. "We, Arshel, *we* can be both!"

Wincing, she said, "Do you know what you're saying?" Her half-loaded venom sack stretched painfully against the molting skin as her glands burned with a sullen fire, oozing thick venom into her sack.

He tightened his hold, oblivious of her painful skin, his eyes focused far away with a glassy stare. "Shel, nothing can stop it now. A new order is coming to the galaxy, and 'Ossminid' is going to rule it, with you and I at his side!" He brought his eyes to focus on her. "Forget everything else we planned. We were naive. Look at the Interface there. He's a living example of First Lifewave science combined with modern knowledge. And the Guild lost him to us. He's going to be our Wild Interface! There's nothing we can't do now, Shel."

She turned her head, despite the full sack threatening to split her skin open, and met the Interface's eyes. The human shook his head in a negative ever so slightly and then said rapidly, "They're holding my brothers MorZdersh'n hostage!"

Before Balachandran could react, she felt the throbbing trickle of venom turn to a wild flood. Her fangs came down. She knew the venom she raised now, strange as it was: hate-venom.

The pain at her throat etched a line of cold fire as her skin began to split, slowly, painfully, prematurely. But she barely felt it against the pulsing of her glands.

Her fangs bit deep into Dennis' left shoulder, pumping in sharp, satisfying contractions.

Hard human hands ripped her from her prey. The body fell with a dull thump, but her fangs found a new target—the large human muscle of a forearm—and the satisfying contractions went on.

CHAPTER FOURTEEN

Zref boarded the *Dancing Mayfly* wholly unsuspecting.

The hiring routine he'd just been through had been handled by Explorer Corps channels in the most routine way. He'd been ushered into the shuttle with all the usual deference his Guild medallion commanded, and he'd been assigned a spacious cabin for the trip.

The first surprise came with a hand delivered dinner invitation. He thanked the uniformed corpsman, closed the door, and read the card: "The Venerable Lower House Representative Lumar Balachandran requests the pleasure of your company for dinner at the seventh tone. Private dining lounge 18. Dress: ship's casual. Menu: Terran, all varieties. Atmosphere: ship's standard. Gravity: ship's standard. Sound: ship's moderate. Security: total."

He hadn't even known that the man was aboard. The *Dancing Mayfly* was a small Explorer Corps personnel transport designed for speed, not comfort. The dining room was the largest open area on the ship, and when Zref arrived, it was sparsely populated by a few dozen people. Around the edge of the room, doors opened into smaller rooms. Zref could see that some of them had been fitted out as offices whereas others were in use as dining rooms for species with variant habits. The door to number 18 was closed, and the light above it registered occupied.

He laid his palm on the signal plate, and the door slid aside, revealing an elegant dining room. Tables and chairs filled the center; luxuriant curtains hid the harsh ship's bulkheads; soft lights and faint sounds of surf overlaid with piano music completed the relaxing atmosphere. There were even some fresh cut flowers on the table that Zref identified as a variety of Terran carnation.

The table was set for two in full, formal Terran style. Along one wall, a buffet cabinet was plugged in. The faint smell of fresh baked bread and brewing coffee filled the room. As he stepped in, the door closed behind him but didn't lock.

Zref amused himself by toying with the access channels to project a beach scene onto the screen and then working to synchronize the waves to the background sound. When he got it right, he added a sunset with a slice of moon and timed it for Terran equatorial zone sunset pace. He was about to start playing with the star patterns of his creation, when the door behind him opened.

"I don't believe we've ever met formally," said Balachandran. "But it hasn't been for your lack of trying, Venerable MorZdersh'n."

Zref turned slowly. "I'm known as Zref, Guild of Interfaces."

"Yes, of course, but do please be seated. I'm hungry, and I've been assured that even Interfaces get hungry."

Zref took his seat opposite the tall, bearded man. Immediately, his host began serving the meal with impeccable precision, selecting liqueurs and asking his preferences. Over the salad, Balachandran discussed the cuisine of half a dozen worlds. With the soup, he blended his culinary knowledge with economic considerations and import-export laws. The entree ushered in another monologue on sociological structures as reflected in the dining habits of various species.

Zref ate politely and listened. He responded in monosyllables when asked questions, all the while battling the pressure of curiosity that the Low Rep's opening remark had aroused. After dessert, the final cup of coffee seemed to bring them at last to business.

"The best example of all this is, of course, the kren concept of family, so very different from that of other species, yet easily as strong a tie as any based on genetics. That's why I was so satisfied to get a human MorZdersh'n for my Interface on this project."

"I'm afraid the logic of all that escapes me." It would have been virtually impossible for even a Low Rep to trace the identity of Zref, Guild of Interfaces, back to Zref Ortenau MorZdersh'n. *How had he done it? And why?* Zref's curiosity was reaching unmanageable levels.

"I really must be leaving now," said Balachandran, rising. "Let us con-tinue the discussion over dinner tomorrow. Same time, but we'll sample

Camiat's cuisine."

Zref spent the next day making short excursions into the comnet, trying to pick up traces of Balachandran's researches. He dropped notes to various others who'd been helping him. Nobody had a clue about how Balachandran had traced Zref or about what he was up to now. There was a security lock on the course computer, and so even Zref's exact location was now a mystery. Pacing his cabin, Zref became ever more convinced that Balachandran was indeed 'Ossminid' replacing his lost ghost Interface. As he dressed for dinner, Zref found the old scratched trinket among the items in his pocket. It was totally blank now, but he remembered how he'd picked it up in distraction as he surveyed the wreckage of his parents' house. *It's finished now,* he thought, and crushed the thing over the disposal chute.

But his heart was no lighter. By the time the appointed dinner hour arrived, Zref had reached a state of frustration he had never felt before. He was determined to get some of his questions answered.

Deliberately, he arrived late, but Balachandran did not come in until five minutes later. Again the bearded man put on an urbane performance, carrying on a monologue when Zref refused to participate. Every time Zref asked a question, the answer diverged into the abstract levels of sociology or the outer reaches of interspecies economic theory.

Zref ate from the familiar foods of Camiat with less attention than he'd lavished on the Terran cuisine. But then Balachandran presented his entree plate from a different compartment of the buffet.

"I regret there is one culinary delight denied those not accepted into a kren family. So I shall eat my quite ordinary gheeling while you may feast on a true venom kill."

Zref stared at his plate; the ashen-gray gheeling was obviously a venom kill. Questions warred with his determination not to open. *Who had killed it? Why is this being presented to me?*

"Go ahead," urged Balachandran. "Eat, it's safe for you."

The aroma was definitely that of a venom kill. "Naturally," he said, "I'd like to know where you obtained such a luxury."

"I rather thought you might not have eaten venom-killed gheeling since Sudeen died. I was only being a thoughtful host." He chewed and swallowed while Zref considered. Then the bearded human said, "All the data on the origin and preparation of these dishes are in the ship's computer."

The aroma was very tempting.

"Go ahead," said Balachandran. "Check the computer for yourself. The gheeling has been properly prepared, and it would be such a shame to waste it."

Zref had to do something. He nodded and averted his gaze to open. He traced the carcass to where it had come into the kitchen, still warm and supple after being killed. The entry before that in the food processor's log had the animal swimming in a tank. *Who killed the venom-killed gheeling?*

There was no direct answer to his query. *Then where did the venom come from?* Zref couldn't imagine any kren donating venom for such a purpose. But kren did give venom to the common-immunity program that provided offworlders with at least as much general immunity to the kren as any member of the community would have. And they gave for the serum bank. Such venom could get on to the black market.

Zref found himself fully open to the comnet searching for traces of such a black market. Perhaps some kren stranded on Eiltherm might have sold venom in desperation, but not a MorZdersh'n! Why, Khelin and Ley were right—*Khelin?*

He sorted to the personnel locater files. Salary checks had been drawn on time, restaurant charges and other incidentals had been processed yesterday, and their mail had been picked up. They were still on Eiltherm.

There was no way they could have gotten Khelin to surrender a venom-killed gheeling, not for any amount of money, not any more than they could have gotten Sudeen to kill for a stranger.

The scream shattered the thought, claiming his whole mind in one searing sheet of pain. His last thought before he blacked out was: *He did this on purpose! He seduced me with curiosity!*

He woke disoriented, groping for memory.

There had been a dream, his private file told him. Through the barest crack of an opening that could not be closed short of disconnection, the memory of the dream leaked back to his conscious mind.

He had been a kren in molt. He'd felt every itching inch of himself crusted over with dead, cracking skin. The crawling misery of it centered in the base of his throat, where his glands poured forth molt-venom until his distended sack split the old skin open. The sudden release would have caused blue-voiding, but he knew how to control it. Kind hands held a venom bottle for him, working in deep sympathy with the rhythm of his pumping muscles as the venom squirted hot and thick from his fangs.

Other hands soothed the warm fluid over his crisp hide, and still different hands banked the warm sand over him so that the skin would dry as he rested. He was a white priest, and he knew that he was dying.

With a shudder, Zref found himself sitting up in bed, his head spinning and his stomach threatening to rebel. He dropped back onto the pillow with a groan as he recognized his cabin on the *Dancing Mayfly*. The dream had been particularly vivid, and he hadn't known that Interfaces could dream. But now he knew that he'd had that same dream every time he'd passed out from the scream.

Before Zref could think it through, Balachandran came in, followed by a Theaten wearing the clear yellow uniform of the ship's medical staff.

"It's such a pity," said Balachandran. "Your gheeling was wasted. But when you're well enough, I think I can replace it for you. If your curiosity can't be satisfied, at least your stomach should be."

The doctor silently produced an injector and flooded Zref's system with an analgesic that controlled the pounding in his head. "That's about all I can do for you, I'm afraid," said the Theaten. "But I understand your condition will improve with time and bed rest."

Balachandran dismissed the physician and, when they were alone, said, "You've no need to fear medical incompetence here. I know more about the modifications that have been done to you than the people who did them. After all, they stole them from me."

"Are you trying to tell me *you're* 'Ossminid'? I don't believe it. The real 'Ossminid' wouldn't admit it."

The big bearded man strolled about the room, idly examining the apparatus for care of the ill. "I've no time to play games. I have you here, cut off from contact with the Guild, and I have a job for you."

"I thought I was working for you before."

"No. You were here to spy on me. You were head of a Guild task force trying to locate and destroy 'Ossminid'."

"If that were true," said Zref, wondering how his hobby had rated him task force status, "I wouldn't be willing to work *for* 'Ossminid'."

"Oh, the pay is irresistible," said the pacing man with a nasty gleam in his eye. "You see, I know what the Guild did wrong with your surgery, and I can fix it for you." He planted himself at the end of Zref's bed and looked down at him. "Imagine your curiosity never thwarted by recurrent trauma!"

"Are you trying to prove you're 'Ossminid' by casually mentioning classified information?"

"Aren't you curious about what you'd have to do to merit such a reward?"

"I don't have to open to guess that. You want me to replace your second freelance Interface, the one who killed Zaviv and died doing it."

"Ah, so you admit I'm 'Ossminid'."

"No, but there's a good chance you work for him." He saw the angry tightening of muscles around the eye, and he pressed the advantage. "What's he really like? We've all considered him a formidable opponent."

Balachandran put his hands on the end of the bed and leaned toward Zref with a poisonous expression Zref associated with hate-venom. "Would you like to know where that gheeling was killed?"

The bearded man stared down at Zref, his eyes flicking in tiny arcs as he searched Zref's face. The watchdog function kept firm control on Zref's heartbeat and respiration; Zref seemed emotionless even while his mind gnawed at itself.

"I'll show you!" Balachandran heaved himself erect, the careless jouncing of the bed sending new waves of agony through Zref's nerves. Striding to the monitor screen, Balachandran muttered commands. Just before the screen cleared, he turned to Zref. "This job comes not only with a reward but also with a punishment!"

When the screen cleared, he saw Khelin in the bare room of a ship's brig. The chalkiness of impending molt was still faint over the kren's exposed skin, but there was no immersion pond in the brig. Khelin was pacing, and as the pickup moved to follow him, Zref could see that he was alone.

"Where's Ley?" he asked in cold defeat.

"Right next door," said Balachandran. The view shifted to show the corridor and then panned to show another door blocked by a translucent force field. Zref could identify Ley through the shimmer. "Now, if you cooperate, I'll have them put into the same cell. If you're aggressively helpful, I'll even provide them with immersion water. If you wax stubborn or deceitful, I'll torture them in ways meaningful only to a bhirhir."

"How do I know they're on this ship?"

Balachandran looked mildly surprised. "The fresh killed gheeling. You'd have recognized the taste, I'm sure. Would you like me to have him kill you another?"

The computer records from Eiltherm could have been false. He imagined what Khelin must have gone through when they got him to kill the first gheeling. "No, that's not necessary."

Balachandran left him to rest under the doctor's care for a few days. But when he was on his feet, the Low Rep sent for him. He was ushered into one of the cubicles off the dining hall, fixed up as an office. Balachandran was seated at the desk, a cartridge from a message torpedo protruding from the reading screen.

"The basic part of your job for me will be simple translation. I have here a full copy of the Vrashin tapes," he said, slapping a regular cassette into the reader. "And my own translations are worked up from the keys your parents so thoughtfully provided. Here," he added, laying a huge hand over another pile of cassettes, "are translations of inscriptions in other languages of the period. For security reasons, I don't have these entered into the permanent memory of our files, but you'll find appropriate programs for processing this data under the reference 'codedog.' I expect you to be proficient in the use of my system within two days."

"At the moment, I can't even open let alone do any data processing or translations."

"Don't fret. I'll have that cleared up for you shortly. But first I want to be sure you understand the situation. The effect of my treatment of you will be temporary. Please me, and I'll have it made permanent. Meanwhile, your brothers will experience a quality of life dependent on your behavior. But that's not all."

Zref waited.

"If anything happens to me, proof will come to light that you have been working for me all along, that you engineered the siphon of Lantern's money, that you killed Zaviv for me, and so forth. This will accomplish two things. The Guild will be out to execute you, and the public will learn that Guild Interfaces can go Wild. The Guild's stranglehold will be broken.

"You needn't bother hunting for my plants. They're hidden behind what you dubbed flypaper shields even better camouflaged than my Lantern siphon. My doctors will allow you only a limited amount of open time. If you trigger that trauma again, you probably won't survive it."

"You build very neat boxes," Zref commented, surprised at how calm his voice sounded while his mind yammered in panic.

"Very strong boxes," Balachandran agreed. "Don't go telling your colleagues about any of this. If you do, I'll know." Zref figured that he was probably bluffing. But it was a bluff he didn't dare call—not yet.

The doctors put him in a tilting chair and hung machinery all about him.

He wondered how much of it was only for show. But curiosity couldn't force his interface open.

They gave him injections. The cassettes from Balachandran's desk were all slotted in a console in one corner. The machinery was turned on, lights flashed softly about the room, and a low voice said, " 'Codedog' functions, open interface. Read file XW-11."

He heard his own voice begin to drone, reading off a glossary table, before he fully realized that he was open. The startlement wakened him from the drugged stupor, and the interface within slammed shut, choking off the flow of words.

The doctors, a Jernal and a Sirwini, looked at each other. The Sirwini opened an intercom and reported, "We got him to access the XW-11, but we've lost it for today." A pause, and then, "Right." He closed the intercom and turned to the Jernal. "We'll try again tomorrow."

The next day, Zref knew what to expect. He let the opening come, welcoming it from a depth he hadn't realized was still in him, and he grappled with the language files until he had the system conquered.

"All right, give me something to read, and I'll show you I can do it."

Skeptically, the doctors complied, and Zref took the outlandish First Lifewave text, a section his parents had pored over for months. By half opening to run simultaneous comparisons, he read it off as if it were in his native language. It was simply a description of the table of the elements, and so when fatigue made the opening tremble, he feigned total exhaustion.

"Very good," said the Sirwini. "You should be ready by the time the Venerable requires your service."

Before that, Balachandran spent two more sessions with Zref; the wall monitor screen now showed Khelin and Ley in a cell equipped with an immersion pond. He showed them being well fed. But he also showed Ley expressing Khelin and noted with that smile Zref did not like at all, "Wouldn't it be interesting if they knew they were being watched *all* the time? I don't know if a blue priest in molt could tolerate that. It would be nice to find out."

Zref didn't think so.

When they made orbit, Zref went over to the command vessel with Balachandran. He had not been able to duplicate on his own the miracle of opening that Balachandran's doctors had produced. He felt no nearer finding a way to stop Balachandran than he had been the day his family, was killed. His mind alternated between adamant determination to protect Khelin and Ley at all cost and reflexive guarding of the Guild's reputation. The short amounts of open time he had been allowed had not sufficed. He felt his sanity crumbling as if from sleep deprivation.

They didn't make him wear the Guild medallion. He didn't let them see his relief. He was a sorry excuse for an Interface now.

Dennis, the saltwater girl's bhirhir, met them as they climbed through the lock tube. Then they were in a private conference room, and Balachandran called Zref to demonstrate his talents to Dennis. "So you see, I have myself a new Interface. I can have any number of them when I want them. Now, wouldn't you rather join the winning side?"

Zref could not force himself to pay attention to the rest of the conversation. He realized that he'd been drugged again. Balachandran had a hand unit that he pointed at him when he wanted him to open. At other times, the world about Zref seemed unreal.

He pried desperately at the crack opening of his private file and at last gleaned some of the gist of the conversation he'd witnessed but not heard. While they were walking along gleaming corridors, he found that Balachandran had blackmailed Dennis in much the same way that he'd boxed Zref in. Only Dennis hadn't needed to be blackmailed. He wanted what Balachandran was offering, and he trusted the man.

They came to another shut port. Zref had no idea how long they clamored for admittance, but a feeling of impending horror stirred deep within him. Then they were facing a kren female, ashen with impending molt.

The association jarred him back to reality. *Khelin.*

"Well, speak up!" demanded Balachandran. "Is that the City of a Million Legends down there?"

"Yes," said the woman. "At least it was the seat of the First Lifewave government."

Zref remembered now that this woman was Dennis Lakely's archeovisualizer. She wore the green medallion, he noted, and on the conference table lay a bead string such as the Mautri used. She was in molt. Zref drifted into a position that put Dennis Lakely between himself and the woman. For reward, he saw her notice his courtesy and relax.

The drug was beginning to wear off, and Zref listened with fascination as Dennis enthusiastically sold the scheme to Arshel. She answered, "I'm not convinced that bringing First Lifewave technology into our time is safe or even possible."

"It's not safe," he said without thinking. Balachandran came at him then, raw rage flashing through his eyes. "Quiet! You belong to me now, not the Guild! You'll answer only when I ask you a question."

The girl's eyes searched his face and froze. *She recognizes me now!* He noted the MorZdersh'n bracelet on her arm and wondered whether Khelin had ever told her about his brother the Interface.

Arshel was saying, "...want to bring the Persuaders back, Dennis? Wouldn't you rather be a Crown Operator?"

Lakely seized her shoulders roughly. "We, Arshel, *we* can be both!"

Zref moved to where he saw her half-full sack surging with new venom, and he remembered Khelin's words: *She hates Interfaces with more passion than you'd ever want to know. There's something wrong between those two.* Dennis' touch was raising her venom, but it should have had the opposite effect.

"Look at the Interface there. He's a living example of First Lifewave science combined with modern knowledge. And the Guild lost him to us. There's nothing we can't do now, Shel."

She turned to lock eyes with him as if pleading. *She's not on their side.* He shook his head slightly. "They're holding my brothers MorZdersh'n hostage!"

Her move blurred into the lightning flick of a strike and her fangs buried themselves in Lakely's neck. Zref still drugged, had not been prepared for that. Balachandran moved to rip her away from her prey.

But he didn't know how to immobilize a kren in strike, and so in an uncontrollable reflex, she buried her fangs in his arm, venom still pumping from her sack. In seconds, the big man dropped to his knees, unable to hold the kren woman. From the speed of Balachandran's collapse and from the fact that her own bhirhir had not moved, Zref deduced that she'd struck with hate-venom.

The moment the big human released her, she fled to, the door. As she struggled with it, Zref could see the new split in her skin over the venom sack; her molt was beginning. But there was a line of dark, oozing blood trickling from that first split. *Premature; must hurt like hell.* She got the door open; Zref bent to check Lakely. He wasn't breathing, and no blood pumped from the twin punctures where the neck joined the shoulder. The surprise frozen on his features curdled Zref's blood.

Balachandran was bent double. Clutching his arm, his face white, he was struggling to get to his feet. Zref thought that the man might live since he was so large and had caught only the tag end of the strike. Zref took off after Arshel, her pain compelling him to help her, though he couldn't imagine how.

Behind him, Balachandran hollered after him, "Come back here and help me, you bastard!"

Lumbering, stumbling steps came out into the corridor. Ahead, Arshel turned a corner, and he paused to look at Balachandran. The man was lunging and staggering toward a corridor marked "Landers."

Down to the surface? thought Zref. He could be going to the maze that had been marked clearly on the conference room screen. If he lived through the poisoning, he could escape to become the first tyrant Persuader the Hundred Planets had known. Zref knew that he could stop the man. The drug had all but worn off, and Balachandran was nearly dead on his feet. But even so, a fight with him would take time. Meanwhile, Arshel was surely bent on swift suicide, or perhaps slow suicide by tearing her unready skin off. He turned and raced after the kren woman.

Miraculously, they met no one in the passenger section. She disappeared through a cabin door. When he came to it, he drew up, panting.

He tried the door signal, certain that she wouldn't answer. She didn't, and he thought of trying the door plate to see whether it was unlocked. But the idea of walking in on a kren in her condition, made him draw back.

From that distance, he saw the portal before him, and a searing flash of déjà vu wiped everything else from his mind. He'd gone through a door and found Tess and Sudeen dead. Through that tiny crack opening to his private file, a paralyzing dread seeped into Zref's consciousness.

But the kren woman was suffering, alone, probably for the first time in her life. He couldn't let her die alone.

The icy grip on his innards melted, and the world turned normal around him. There was no effort in lifting his hand to the door plate, no startlement when it flashed aside, revealing the compartment within.

She whirled to face the opening door, a long gutting knife in one hand, the other hand covered with blood. She had ripped unsuccessfully at her splitting skin. Dark purple-reddish blood dripped from her venom sack.

"I came to help you shed," he said, stepping slowly in so that the door could close behind him. He put out his hand and set the lock. "What happened out there, you could say I provoked you to it. Khelin told me you two had trouble."

"Khelin."

"My brother. You're wearing his bracelet. He's in molt, too, just about now. Because I played along with Balachandran, he let Ley get to Khelin for the molt."

"He's all right, then?"

"Yes. But he told me how much he was looking forward to mating with you, how disappointed he was when you left Eiltherm. He could hardly talk of anything else for days." That was an exaggeration. Khelin had mentioned it once, but Ley had told him privately of Khelin's agony.

Zref had circled away from the door, putting some furniture between them. In the adjacent room, he could make out an immersion pond with a force field dome to contain the water in free fall. She was staring at her green medallion.

"I once sat for admission to the Mautri Inner School," said Zref, his voice soothing. "I remember the first day I sat. It was the hottest day of the year, dry and dusty in the courtyard where they make you wait. Eight days I sat. I showed them I had the disciplines of stillness, fortitude, and persistence. Anyhow, they rejected me eight days running until my parents came and took me away, even though I fought with all my remaining strength. I was only five years old at the time."

"My white priest!"

The knife hand lowered, forgotten, as she turned to follow him with her eyes. He kept on talking now that he'd gotten her attention, even though the molt hormones had her babbling.

"My first big failure in life, and I was only five. The second came when I was in my teens—but I didn't know it until years later—when I let my own bhirhir, Sudeen, die instead of going to his rescue." He told her that story, all the while feeling the inward pulsating of the interface, a sort of mental flutter that usually presaged the reopening for him after being knocked out by the scream.

"I saw about that on the news," she said when he had finished. "And then you became an Interface. How can you have such feeling for these memories when they're only recordings in a computer on Hengrave?"

"I think that's part of what went wrong with me during the surgery."

He told her about the scream and what it did to him. As he talked, relating incident after incident, she listened avidly. At some point, she dropped the knife and folded herself gingerly onto the sand bed. He noted the venom bottle on the shelf over the bed and kept slowly easing toward the bottle as he talked.

When he'd run down again, she asked, "Would it change your attitude if I said I was the cause of Uslin's death?"

"He killed himself."

Then she told him a story. "I think he needed that mating much more than I could realize at the time. And if I kill you, too, what have I done to Camiat's chances with the Guild?"

"There may not be a Guild much longer," he said, and told her about the elaborate trap Balachandran had set.

"So that's the end," she said, dispirited. "I killed Balachandran, so I don't have to kill you. The Guild and the Hundred Planets are as good as dead."

"He might live. Last I saw, he was reeling toward the lander bay. I think he's planning to walk the maze."

"No!" She leaped to her feet and pushed Zref toward the door, her venom sack sloshing. "What are you doing here, then? Go. Stop him!"

He went with the push a step or two and then held. "No, we'll both go. Just as soon as you're finished with molt."

"Zref, you've got to hurry. Don't you remember—oh, of course not. An Interface can't recall past lives."

To calm her, he said, "Well, Iebe Arai Then did say, in a life-reading on me, that I was involved in building the maze and that I died in it. I'm not too anxious to go down there!"

"But you don't remember it?"

"No," he admitted. "But I think I believe it now, because he also said I'd been a white priest of Mautri, and I just discovered a dream I've been having about dying as a white."

"Then maybe you can believe this. Dennis and I were involved in opposing the building of the maze. He betrayed me then, as he betrayed me this time, only that time he killed me. I think I'm here to finish the battle I started then, to stop the building of a new maze. Will you help me stop Balachandran?"

"I don't know what help I can be. I can't open at all yet. I'm not an Interface, and I'm not a whole man, either."

"But you don't want to turn Persuaders loose on this galaxy, do you?"

"No."

Her venom sack was filling slowly but steadily, and the stretching caused new blood to seep down her chest. "Then I'll take you bhirhir."

"Oh, Arshel, I'd have liked that." He was surprised at how much he meant it. "But I belong to the Guild now."

She collapsed onto the sand bed, wincing at the pain of movement and shivering.

The decision came from deep inside, and he spoke before thinking it through. "I'm not free to pledge bhirhir for life, Arshel, but I will pledge to see you through at Mautri until you can live balbhirhir. If the Guild won't let me do that much, well, I say to hell with the Guild. If it's still around." He didn't know why this woman's life was so important to him, but nothing would make him turn away from her now.

She watched him taking down her venom bottle and did not object. "I thought Interfaces didn't have a conscience. But I guess I was wrong, at least in your case." Moving with exaggerated slowness, he knelt beside her.

"Zref, you'd better not come any closer. I could strike now." Her voice was choking off as her sack filled. She reached out for the venom bottle, but he withheld it.

"You're a green priest. You do have *some* strike control. Relax, breathe easy, and let's see if I can express you. Then we'll know if I can help you through this." Zref knew that he was not in the least immune to her venom, but he'd felt more fear with Sudeen on occasion. *Being an Interface does have advantages.*

She was making an effort to regulate her breathing. He had the venom bottle in his left hand, and the solid feel of the leather against his palm reminded him sharply of Sudeen's bottle. Anticipating the pleasure of working against her strike rhythm, he eased the wide lip of the bottle toward her as her fangs came down, already dripping the thick bluish molt-venom as she held her strike. Her control, he judged, was phenomenal.

He moved to bring his right arm about her shoulders. She flinched at his move, and he anticipated the strike, dropping the venom bottle to catch her forehead with his left hand and grasping her lower jaw with his right, muttering encouragements as calmly as he could while every muscle strained against her.

The strike that would have hit his arm was now voiding venom into midair, but it was venom she couldn't afford to lose. He caught her rhythm and, between contractions, grabbed the venom bottle. As her head came down again he slid the wide opening up around her fangs so that her weight was supported on her upper jaw, which was resting against the soft, smooth padding of the bottle lip.

On the next contraction, he shifted his right hand up to her forehead, and then for the remainder he worked with her to expel the venom, feeling the searing pain at her bloodied venom sack as if it were his own.

When it was over, she sat back on her heels, panting. "That was beautiful," she said, letting her eyes meet his again. "Sudeen was very lucky."

He had given relief, even pleasure, and something deep in his muscles, sinews, cells, and bones had enjoyed it more than he could say. He set the venom bottle down. "You'll let me help you?"

"Zref, now I do want to live." She handed him back the bottle, charging him with it as one would a bhirhir. "I'll try not to strike at you again."

He took the bottle back, and it was as if a new mantle of responsibilities had settled over his shoulders, comfortable and welcome. "You know, if I let you immunize me, Khelin will never forgive me because then he'd count you as family. And that's not what he wants with you."

"Not immunize—" She riveted him with her gaze, slowly accepting his terms. "I can't sow dissension in MorZdersh'n. I never told Khelin I was ready to try again. Do you suppose they'll come back to Firestrip when you take me to Mautri?"

"Sure. But first we have to get them out of that brig."

Her hand went to her blood soaked blouse front. "Then let's get this over with before I go screaming mad with itch."

He helped her get the crusted blouse off and then peel off the rest of her clothes. Her movements were badly hampered by the brittle and breaking skin.

"I think first a good warm bathing," he said. "And then dry warm sand. Have you been taking your antibiotics?"

"Yes. I'd never considered suicide until after I killed my bhirhir." Her sack throbbed, and the hysteria in her voice was barely controlled.

He got her into the saltwater pond and found medication put aside for premature molt. He skinned out of his clothes, which had already collected enough sand to be unlivable, and went into the water.

She had sunk herself totally under the surface, but at the entry of a nonfamily member into her waters, she rose with venom pumping.

"Easy! Easy," he called softly.

"You don't smell right," she complained, but she let him treat her venom sack.

He sprayed on an anesthetic bandage, wiping it carefully. He didn't want the bandage to glue the old skin to the new and cause another tear.

He had turned on the heat under her sand bed. When be took her back there, he buried her whole body under the warm, dry sand. This caused the old skin to dry in large bubbles.

Her molt-venom was coming in long surges. Her face had taken on that characteristic distance. The molt hormones would have their way with her now.

Before her sack had filled to the stretching point, he sat her up and brought the venom bottle into place, triggering the expression with a feather touch. When it was over, she lay back, helpless. But her eyes focused on him.

"Now I know why Jylyd wouldn't admit me to the blue trials. You can't go balbhirhir before you've been tended by your true bhirhir."

He felt a moment's resentment at Dennis and a moment's compassion for him, too. Then he wondered at himself. These were not echoes of emotions. They were there for him in the present, leaking in through the crack to his private file.

There was no time to puzzle over it, though. Now that he had the venom, he began laving it on gingerly. Feebly, the strike reflexes jerked her head up and down, and she made small protesting sounds about his odor. But as he worked, his touch becoming more sure, and firm, she became lost in the sensations he was causing her. The skin came loose in large patches all over her body, except the middle of her back, where it was sticking, dry and too brittle. *Neglect too?*

Handling her limp, helpless body brought back a bone deep tactile memory of Sudeen's molts. When he expressed her again, he found himself breathing in rhythm with her as he had so often with Sudeen. A place inside him that he hadn't known was empty was now filled again. *Pledge or no, immunity or no, leaving her is going to hurt just like leaving a bhirhir.*

She seemed to respond to that knowledge, which was communicated through his touch. All over, the bubbles of skin were cracking open, but neglected patches on her back and the soles of her feet were bonded to the new skin. When she began to writhe with the need to shed, he could do nothing but let her go. He'd never faced such a problem with Sudeen. *There has to be something I can do, but what?*

Curiosity swept through his mind, flinging open the inner barriers. *In the case of premature molt when partial adherence occur the best treatment is the application of ice packs to the affected areas. This should cause the shrinking of blood vessels connecting the two layers of tissue and thus allow removal of the outer skin without appreciable blood loss. Caution: This leaves the victim susceptible to infection and countermeasures should be taken.*

Before it was all unreeled in his mind, Zref was at the sink, ordering ice from the dispenser. He dumped the crushed ice into a hand towel. When he got back to the sand bed, she had thrashed about so that her head was pounding against the rim.

Carefully avoiding her fangs, he got her back into position and expressed the collected venom, laving it generously over the bad patches of skin. Then he applied the ice packs, and suddenly he didn't know what to do next. Then he realized that he was following instructions from the comnet.

He was back in the gardener's cottage in his parents' house, bent over Zaviv and pumping air into the Brenilak's lungs. Sounds of pounding feet, small arms fire, and, ripping through his consciousness, the scream.

He heard it clearly this time, words emerging from the inarticulate blur of a kren in high venom: "Help Zaviv! Zref, save Zaviv! Zref!"

And then the last mind-curdling scream: "Zrrrreeffff!"

But this time he found himself still wide open, more fully open than he'd been since the very first time. His whole mind was filled with one thought: *I didn't fail. I did what my bhirhir wanted done!*

Zref, is that you? Diebold. The message came through the drop.

Diebold? Zref.

I got something unsigned saying, 'I didn't fail.' Was that you? Diebold.

Yes I guess it was. I didn't know I was so open. Zref.

Something new? We all thought you must be dead. Diebold.

You may all wish me dead before this is over. Things are complicated here at the moment. Zref.

Don't stay open too long this time. We'll try not to die of curiosity. Diebold.

I think my problem with opening may be solved. I'll report soonest. Zref.

When Zref focused his eyes again, Arshel had squirmed free of the last crusted shreds of skin, even the bad patches, and lay on the sand, panting heavily and staring up at him.

"You were open! Did you lie to me?"

"No, Arshel, I don't think I'll ever be able to lie to you, any more than I could to Sudeen. Or don't you feel it?"

"We didn't pledge. You still don't smell right." Breathing more normally, she reconsidered. "But I didn't kill you, either. And you enjoyed it, didn't you? I didn't know a human *could* feel that way."

"Arshel, by serving you, I found out what was crippling my ability to open. That happened because you gave me what Sudeen had always given me. It's going to be very hard for me to keep my word and turn you over to Mautri."

He gathered up the last pieces of her shed skin, took them to the disposer opening in the bulkhead, and picked up the spray bandage on the way back. "Turn around slowly."

"You're not going to cover me with that stuff? My sack feels like ancient parchment now!"

"Just these difficult areas here," he said, spraying her back. "Now pick up your feet, one at a time." He sprayed the bottoms carefully. Then he fed her antibiotics while she was gingerly pulling clothing over her sensitive skin.

He shook the sand out of his clothes and climbed into them. "If you'll pardon me a moment, I'll see what the ship's computer can tell us about what's been going on."

They had found Dennis' body. The fleet captain had finally accepted the fact that Arshel had killed him. Accordingly, the fleet captain had her guards posted outside Arshel's door. Zref's absence had been noted, as had Balachandran's, but it wasn't known whether Zref had left in the lander with the Low Rep. Zref apprised Arshel of the situation.

"I don't think the captain is in this with Balachandran," she said.

Zref told the ship's computer to open a channel to the captain's desk. The woman was startled when her screen lit up by itself. She was an older woman, tall and thin, but human.

Zref said, "Zref, Guild of Interfaces, Captain Diesen."

"Where are you?"

"Arshel Lakely's quarters, being held prisoner by your guards."

Her gaze went beyond Zref, and he knew she was looking Arshel over. "Well, they told me the only way she'd survive was if someone pledged her bhirhir."

"Is there any reason we must remain prisoner now?" Zref asked.

She considered. "I'm not sure. I didn't know an Interface could take a bhirhir. You'll vouch for her? We could really use your help. We seem to have lost the Low Rep and a lander down on the planet. Would you raise the lander's computer?"

Zref averted his eyes just in time for the opening reflex. He was back to her in less than an eyeblink. "I have the lander's ID beacon. Arshel and I would like to be on the ship that goes down." The captain put out a hand to open the intercom and issue the appropriate orders and then turned back to Zref. "With Lakely dead and Balachandran missing, I don't know who's in charge of the civilian half of this expedition. Does the comnet have anything on that?"

"Full command of the expedition falls back on your shoulders, Captain," Zref answered almost without pause. "But if I were you, I wouldn't try to order Balachandran's own crew—" He flicked open to the *Fly's* computer and had to breathe twice before he could go on. "Apparently, he missed a routine check-in, and now there is open fighting on that vessel. I believe Balachandran was known to be 'Ossminid' by some of the crew but not by others. The followers of 'Ossminid' are trying to take over the ship and send another lander down."

" 'Ossminid'?" she said, incredulity marring her professional calm.

"Yes. He admitted it to me."

"I'll have to send over an armed boarding party, then." There was the sound of the door signal. Arshel went to answer it, while Zref said, "Captain, there are two prisoners aboard that vessel who must not be harmed. One is a kren blue priest named Khelin, and the other is his bhirhir, Ley. They were being kept in the brig."

"I'll see to it."

The two guards at the door now flanked two Jernal pilots. Zref and Arshel followed them to their lander, which was fully stocked for the archeological mission. The two pilots took their places at the rear of the cabin, while Zref and Arshel along with four Sirwini males, their sharpened horns gleaming, armed and ready for anything, occupied the six seats.

"Master Interface," said the Jernal pilot with the pink tones to its fluff. "The guidance computer is yours."

"Thank you." Zref went to stand behind the pilot, pointing to the screens as he said, "There's the blip from the lander. See it?"

"Yes, very near the center of the ruins where we were told not to land."

"The other lander has already plowed a trough of destruction there. We'll come in along the same mark and not do any additional damage." He coordinated the data from the downed lander with the orbital data they carried. "Balachandran was no pilot, and he made a mess of that landing. See?" He put the numbers on another display. "Now, if we can shave a bit off our landing speed . . . Yes! We can do it."

Two of the Jernal's spindly appendages flew delicately over the board, lighting up the computer circuits. The other pilot picked up communications with the fleet. Zref returned to his place beside Arshel.

"You could have done that from here," she said.

"Yes, I suppose."

"Why did you do it like that?"

He shrugged. "It made them feel secure." And, he admitted, it had felt utterly splendid to work the computers, better than ever before. Exhilarated, he said, "Arshel, we have some time until we land. With your permission, I'd like to file my report to the Guild." He told her about accidentally contacting another Interface. Interfaces must be dropping dead of curiosity all over the galaxy!"

His wry humor lightened her mood. "Oh, I certainly wouldn't want to be the cause of that! Go right ahead."

They settled back in their deep cushions as the pilot jammed the ship out of orbit. Zref filed his report and then added a plea: *I'm already bhirhir to Arshel in all but formal pledge. Now she's totally fixed on the Balachandran problem. But when that's over, she may become hysterical or despondent, and I won't be able to control her as a bhirhir must. I ask permission to pledge to her formally and then to take her to the Mautri at Firestrip and stay with her until she can survive balbhirhir. Zref.*

Your request will be considered. Rodeen.

When Zref came to awareness again, the cabin was shaking under the strain of reentry. He checked the computer, watching the grounded lander being used as guidance by the one in motion. It all ran as smoothly as any landing at a major shuttleport. And then, with a screeching crunch, they were down and bouncing to a halt just behind Balachandran's vessel.

Two of the Sirwini went first, arms ready, alert for predators of any kind. Then Arshel and Zref went down the steps and picked their way carefully through the rubble.

Zref put out a hand to stop her. "Wait while I record all this for the archeologists." He scanned the area, putting it all into his private file.

"Over there, Zref," said Arshel, pointing.

Two more of the Sirwini climbed out behind them, while the two pilots and two more guards stayed with the vessel. The first two guards had worked their way up to Balachandran's lander. As Zref moved forward and out, he could see where the first lander had sustained damage as it bumped to a halt on the rubble.

He turned his attention to the terrain. All around them, knee-high building blocks covered the ground. Between them, sand and smaller rocks made for an impossibly dangerous footing. From this angle, higher walls obscured the maze pattern, but he knew that they were on the edge of it. He didn't need to see it through the computers on the orbiting ships. *I built this.* The two guards were fanning out ahead of the downed ships, and the two who searched Balachandran's ship reported negative and fell in behind Arshel and Zref. The captain in orbit was very nervous about sending an Interface down.

About four ship's lengths ahead, they found the body. Prone, one knee flexed as if he were trying to crawl, his right hand extended in a last effort to reach for something, Balachandran lay amid the rubble of the maze. Carrion birds and smaller scavengers were already at the body.

"Zref!" Arshel had picked her way just beyond where Balachandran lay and was brushing dust off the face of one of the larger pieces of rock. "Can you read this? Or at least record it for us."

He saw the inscription, which resembled the writing found on the gold sphere. Even as his private file was recording the tracing, a sudden surge of curiosity activated the information tapes Balachandran had kept so carefully. On the *Dancing Mayfly,* translation routines were readied by the neglected machines. The translation unreeled before him with many gaps:

TO ALL WHO COME AFTER——BEWARE: DANGER: WARNING. SEE WHAT WE HAVE HAD TO DO TO THE GLORY THAT WAS OURS. WE HAVE DESTROYED IT. ——OBLITERATED UTTERLY. THE CAUSE WAS——. HEED THIS TALE.

IN THE HEIGHT OF OUR——THERE CAME ONE WHO——ALL THE——POWER. HE CALLED HIMSELF OSSMINID AND WALKED THE MAZE RIGHT HERE AHEAD OF WHERE YOU STAND NOW. HE EMERGED SUCCESS-FUL, ACQUIRING THE POWER TO PERSUADE ANY LIVING CREATURE TO HIS WILL.

BUT THIS WAS NOT ENOUGH FOR HIM. HE——THE CROWNS AS WELL. USING HIS POWER, HE BENT THE CROWN COUNCIL TO HIS WILL AND WAS GIVEN THE CROWN——AS WELL. HE IT WAS WHO SET OUT TO PROVE THERE WAS NO REAL NEED TO——CROWN AND MAZEMASTER.

FOR A TIME, THE GLORY OF OUR——INCREASED. OSSMINID RULED AS

MAZEMASTER AND LEFT THE CROWNS TO THE CROWN COUNCIL. BUT AS HE RULED, HE CHANGED.

——HE SOUGHT TO CHOOSE CANDIDATES TO WALK THE MAZE. FEW OF HIS CHOICES SUCCEEDED. FEWER AND FEWER PERSUADERS EMERGED TO DO THE WORK OF OUR——.

ONE DAY HE WRAPPED HIMSELF AS MAZEMASTER AND WALKED INTO THE EMPEROR'S CROWN, AS WAS HIS RIGHT. HE HAD NO PERSUADER TO SEND TO THE WARING PLANET, AND SO HE SENT HIS OWN THOUGHTS THROUGH THE EMPEROR'S CROWN.

THIS WAS NOT JUST A MESSAGE FROM THE EMPEROR OF CROWNS. THIS WAS A FORCE FELT OVER THE WHOLE PLANET. NONE COULD RESIST. THE POPULATION WAS——.

WE SOUGHT TO REPLACE OSSMINID. HE WOULD NOT LOOSE THE——HE HAD GATHERED. THERE WAS KILLING. HE WOULD NOT YIELD. ON THE DAY HE ENTERED THE CROWN FOR A SECOND TIME, HE——TO DESTROY US.

TO STOP HIM, WE DESTROYED OURSELVES, KNOWING THAT WITHOUT CROWN AND MAZE, OUR——WOULD DISINTEGRATE.

WARNING. WARNING. WARNING.

THE MAZEHEART THAT——US THE POWER TO PERSUADE COULD NOT BE DESTROYED. WE HAVE REMOVED IT AND CONCEALED IT.

WARNING. WARNING. WARNING.

THE——OF HOW THE MAZEHEART——DIES WITH US.

KNOW ONLY THAT WE DARED NOT——INTO A——FROM WHICH NOTH-ING EMERGES. ALL OUR——WOULD NOT LET US PREDICT WHAT WOULD HAPPEN.

IF THE MAZEHEART IS FOUND——DESTROY ITSELF.

THE LAST PERSUADER

He'd been reading aloud. He looked to Arshel, who still stood with one hand brushing the inscription. "That's what it says. Can you pick up any impressions?"

"I thought there was something wrong with *me* at first, but it's not that. Zref, these stones, this place—it's as dead, as shallow and bereft of a past as a newly manufactured shoe. Whatever they did to destroy this place, they destroyed not just the physical buildings but the very thought forms be-hind the buildings."

He could see the desolation himself. "So Balachandran staked everything on finding something that wasn't even there. Arshel, you told them the truth. This was the City of a Million Legends. But I don't think archeologists will ever find anything more informative here than this inscription."

"But they will continue to search for the mazeheart object. I don't want to be a part of that search, Zref. Right now, I think I'd be content to live out the rest of my life at Mautri."

"Yes," said Zref. He supposed that if the Hundred Planets went the way of the First Lifewave, Mautri would survive as a bastion of learning through the centuries of darkness to come. Distractedly, he watched the Sirwini, who had drifted away from them after the reading of the inscription; they were poking at the rubble and collecting specimens. "But there is a barrier to our plans: Balachandran."

At her puzzled look, he said, "When the evidence of my involvement with him and his plans for the fate of the Guild surface—Arshel, if I'm branded as a renegade Interface, they'll disconnect my interface and leave me a blubbering vegetable long before you can take the white."

She eased her jaw, letting her fangs come down and out to relieve tension, much as a human would sigh. She squatted down and smoothed some sand that lay on a wide rock.

"You shouldn't be touching things here!" he said.

"Deal with infection later. I have an idea. Your problem is that you must locate some information that Balachandran hid in the comnet. I'm a finder of information. Not things, Zref, information. Everything I've located has been an inscription of some kind. Draw me a map of the whole comnet web. Just the broad outlines, the major planetary nodes, and the clearance/storage centers."

He hesitated, but the representation of the comnet was really no different from any map. He sketched the major access points and primary linkages, producing a sprawling network of lines and dots in the sand.

"That's enough," she said. "Now be quiet a moment. Let's see if I can open in my own way."

She let her fingers drift over the diagram, her eyes half closed. He saw the telltale tremor in those fingers, the faint twitch of her eyelids. She was going on nothing but nerve, and he dreaded the moment when she finally relaxed. "There," she said. "Draw me a detail picture of this one." She was pointing to the Eiltherm node itself. As Zref smoothed the sand and sketched the internal structure of that node, she pounced on the dot that represented a temporary storage facility.

"There, that's the place. Something strange—like—opposite?"

At once, Zref knew. "He's got a permanent storage program running in a temporary storage bank. Just a moment."

He dropped to Rodeen: *I'm going to tackle one of those flypaper blinds the last one in existence, I think. Monitor me. Zref.*

Then he allowed the dire curiosity to claim all his attention. The information file was there, all right, along with a program set to insert evidential data into various primary files about the Hundred Planets, supporting the evidence in this file. Zref got that far because he knew what he was looking for. But then the ghostly shimmer of the flypaper shield closed in about him, and his questioning became a logical circle that could not be stopped.

He wasn't sure how long this went on, until he could gather enough vital determination to instruct: *I am not curious. I do not want to know.* The tightening circle of meaningless questioning loosened a little. He insisted: *The data will never be needed. Wipe this data bank and its program.* He repeated the order three more times in rapid succession.

Code challenge, came the machine's reply.

Zref knew that it could be anything at all, but during the trip out from Eiltherm, he'd studied Balachandran. He took a wild guess. *Code challenge answer: codedog.*

Instantly, the mists vanished, the compulsion to question evaporated, and he was aware of the rapid wipe of the entire evidence file.

A message dropped into his file: *It seems that Arshel has done for you what I and all my staff could not. And with your new health you've done for us what we couldn't do for ourselves. So despite arguments against your plea I vote to permit the establishment of the bhirhir and your assignment to Firestrip for the duration of Arshel's training. Nesfil.*

It is decided. Roylanta.

When his vision cleared, Zref saw Arshel squinting at him anxiously. "It's all right," he said, rising and helping her up. "The file is wiped clean, and the Guild is so delighted, they've authorized me to offer myself bhirhir to you."

The glow that lit her face made the entire adventure worthwhile for Zref. "Then let's get his body aboard and go back to the ships. How's the fighting for the *Fly* going?"

He let the question open him, reveling in this new freedom, and his own curiosity about Khelin and Ley brought him the news. "The fleet captain has the ship in hand, and Khelin and Ley have been removed to her flagship. Khelin keeps asking the computer about us, *you* really! Arshel, before I take your immunization, I think you have some unfinished business with Khelin."

She looked at him. "I think I'd welcome that, now. Tell him we're coming home with him."